Simone sat in silenc
and Reece sat at the
at his ex-wife. She l
of her cheek, the soft chestnut sheen of her
hair. If he hadn't known differently, he'd have thought the morning was no different from any of the others they'd shared during their marriage.

Except that somehow he'd crossed through the mirror, everything turned inside out as if he were Alice through the looking glass.

His head was insisting that what was done was done. That he needed to let it go and move on. But his heart wasn't having any of that. His heart wanted his wife back. Wanted the life they'd shared. And nothing—not even the pain of knowing that none of it had been real—could change that fact.

God, what a mess. And to top it off, in less than an hour they were heading into what was quite possibly a trap....

Critics hail Dee Davis as a master of romantic suspense!

EXPOSURE

"The searing conclusion to Davis' mesmerizing trilogy gives readers all the deft characterization, taut suspense and sizzling romance they have come to expect. Davis and romantic suspense are an unbeatable duo!"
—*Romantic Times BOOKclub*
(4½ stars, Top Pick)

"Another non-stop action romance from the fascinating imagination of author Dee Davis."
—*Huntress Reviews*

ENIGMA

"Tremendously gripping...truly riveting."
—*Romantic Times BOOKclub*
(4½ stars, Top Pick)

ENDGAME

"Dee Davis is at the top of her game in this clever and quick-paced ride over dangerous ground. With a hot love story and a coldhearted villain, *Endgame* is romantic intrigue at its best. Davis never disappoints."
–Mariah Stewart, bestselling author of *Dark Truth*

And stay tuned for Dee Davis's next romantic thriller

Coming from HQN in June 2007

DEE DAVIS

EYE OF THE STORM

ISBN 0-373-77163-0

EYE OF THE STORM

This edition published by arrangement with Harlequin Books S.A.

www.HQNBooks.com

Printed in U.S.A.

To my mother

EYE OF THE STORM

PROLOGUE

Missoula, Montana

BEATRIX BRASEL STOOD in the grocery line trying not to look behind her. It was ridiculous really, but she couldn't shake the feeling that someone was watching her. She reached down into her basket and pulled out five or six items, mentally counting again to make sure that her total didn't exceed ten.

No one else ever seemed to bother to count. But then they weren't as attuned to detail as she was. And anything that deviated from the norm was a sure ticket to being noticed. She readjusted a couple of soup cans to make room for Ben and Jerry, then shot another furtive glance behind her.

Four tired and probably cranky people were lined up waiting their turn. An old man with cookies and a six-pack. A working stiff with mud-caked boots and a bottle of Pepto-Bismol. A businessman with a newspaper and a quart of milk. And a mother with a placidly sleeping toddler. She rocked the baby as she pushed the cart forward with her knee.

Ten years away from it all and Bea still couldn't imagine anything more American pie than her sparsely furnished apartment and beat-up old Chevy. She'd tried to fit in. To find her place. But that had turned out to be an exercise in futility. Still, she'd done all right for herself, holding down the same nine-to-five for almost eight years. Granted, the only time she saw anyone outside of work was at the company picnic and the Christmas party. Or maybe when she stopped to exchange hellos with one of her ever-changing neighbors.

Not exactly the picture of domestic life. But Bea was nothing if not a realist, and from a very early age she'd learned that society was never going to welcome her with open arms. There was just something off about her. A stillness that had been present even in the cradle. She'd tried to hide it, and when that had failed, she'd used it to her benefit. Trouble had followed in her wake with magnetic certainty, until she'd found a way to channel it into something productive.

Bea sighed and added a loaf of bread to the conveyor belt. Maybe reality was overrated. Maybe she'd been better off before. God knows she'd been happier. But all good things came to an end. Sometimes explosively.

The point here was that her old life was over. Had been for almost a decade, which made her present situation all the more laughable. There'd been a time when her sixth sense would have been accurate, when someone very well could have been stalking her. But not anymore.

As if to argue the point, her skin pricked with sensation, and she shot another look behind her. Nothing but tired shoppers and a sale on frozen vegetables. A swarthy man in jeans and a flannel shirt gave her a moment's pause. His dark hair curled at his ears, a John Deere baseball cap hiding the upper half of his face.

She studied him for a moment, careful to keep her

interest concealed. The man reached over to grab a Hershey's bar from the candy rounder, adding it to his sparsely populated basket. Just a guy with a sweet tooth on his way home from work. She was obviously losing it big-time.

The woman in front of her finally made sense of her pile of coupons, presenting them to the clerk as if they were a trophy. Bea never bothered with coupons. The payoff just wasn't worth the hassle. Behind her the baby started to cry, the mother's tone gentle as she shushed her child. Bea felt a pang of envy, but quashed it. Everyone had their place in life. And there was no sense in trying to change the status quo.

What was the saying? "You could give a pig sheet music but you couldn't make him sing?" She laughed to herself and pulled out her wallet, watching as the clerk scanned the items with all the enthusiasm of an automaton. Not that she blamed the kid. As jobs went, clerking in a grocery store was pretty near the bottom of the food chain.

Like answering phones all day was any better. She shot what passed for a smile at the checkout boy and handed him two twenties. One habit she'd never outgrown was dealing solely in cash. Checks and credit cards were too damn easy to trace.

Like anyone was looking for her.

Unease slid down her backbone with pointed nails and she shivered. God, she was getting morose. Grabbing her two sacks of groceries, she headed for the doors, dodging people as she went, her speed dictated more by instinct than any kind of logic. Near the exit, she collided with a well-heeled woman in fur, her scent overpowering in that cloying way of women over a certain age.

Mumbling an apology, Bea tightened her fingers on the grocery bags and stepped out into the frigid night air. Spring in Montana could be a beautiful thing. A rebirth of sorts. But just at the moment, winter was having a last hurrah. Snowflakes fell like confetti stars, sticking to the sidewalk and mixing with melted muck to form lethal sheets of ice.

Treading carefully, she walked to the parking lot, her eyes lighting on the Chevy two rows away. Counter to her usual practice of parking away from the crowds, she'd chosen instead to park in the midst of the congestion, her need to avoid the drifting snow more imminent than her innate caution about keeping under the radar.

The streetlight above her row blinked ominously and then went black, the cars beneath immediately shifting into shadow. If she'd believed in signs, this would have been a doozy. But Bea was a pragmatist, and the row was, for the moment, devoid of activity, the other patrons evidently opting for the warmth of the store.

Keys in hand, she fumbled with the trunk lock, thinking that maybe she ought to consider a new car. At least then she'd be able to open it with the touch of a button. But the Chevy was a known quantity and Bea wasn't big on change. Dumping the groceries into the trunk, she slammed the door down in a flurry of snow and stomped over to the driver's side, trying to get the muck off her boots before she slid behind the wheel.

Automatically, she checked the area around her, the motion as natural to her as breathing. Nothing moved except the languidly falling snow, and with a sigh, she unlocked the door, yanked it open and got inside. The car was dark and quiet. Shivering, from the cold she assured herself, she turned the key in the ignition and smiled as the Chevy leapt to life. Old faithful wins the day.

The engine was soon joined by the sound of the windshield wipers as they swooshed through the falling snow. With a final look out the window, Bea hit the driver's side lock and threw the car into reverse.

Although she'd started her life in far warmer climes, she'd long ago mastered the art of driving on snow and ice, and so it was only moments before she turned out of the parking lot and onto the access road that led to the highway and home.

The green dial in her car indicated that it was later than she'd thought. Almost ten. Which meant she was too late for her television programs. In the old days, she wouldn't have even known what was on, much less cared if she missed it. But times had changed, and truth be told, the television was her only friend.

God, that sounded pathetic.

She steeled herself against self-pity, and steered onto the highway. Actually, "highway" was probably overstating things a bit. It was a county road, narrow and curving at times, particularly treacherous in bad weather. But she'd been driving it for years and so was familiar with every inch of it.

Bea was about a mile from Cloudburst Creek when she noticed the flashing light in her rearview mirror. Automatically she slowed, her eyes dropping to the speedometer. She'd only been a few miles over the limit.

She checked all the other gauges as well, inventorying the Chevy's condition with the precision of a mechanic. Nothing else was wrong. As if to challenge the thought, her gaze moved to the registration sticker, the month "October" standing in relief against the glow from the dashboard.

Damn it.

She hated making mistakes of any kind, but one that resulted in a paper trail was particularly galling. Especially when she was always so careful to drive within the limits. Blame it on her stupid ruminations about something being wrong.

Pulling the car onto the shoulder, she applied the brake and then reached for her wallet and license. The officer tapped on the window, and she rolled it down with a sigh, pasting on a smile to go with the plastic card in her hand.

It only took a moment to realize that it wasn't an officer at all. The man at the window wore a parka and a hat, his face obscured by the heavy knit. Her mind shifted into high gear, the gun in the glove compartment only a couple feet away, but her reflexes, once razor sharp, had dulled with age and disuse.

The man pulled the trigger almost before Bea had identified the silenced Beretta for what it was. And in the instant before the world went black, she had the irrational thought that at least she'd been right—someone *had* been following her.

Someone who wanted her dead.

CHAPTER ONE

Corpus Christi, Texas

"GOD, YOU SCARED the life out of me." Simone Cooper Sheridan skidded to a stop at the doorway of her kitchen, hand on chest, her heart pounding to beat the band.

Her brother-in-law, Martin, squinted myopically up at her from the kitchen table, looking almost as startled as she felt. A half-finished peanut-butter sandwich dangled from one hand, the other circling a glass of milk. "Well, the feeling's mutual. I thought you were gone."

"Which gave you the run of my kitchen?" she asked, anger replacing fear, the emotion centered more on herself than on Martin. She was getting soft.

"I'm sorry. I knocked."

"I was in the basement working out." She'd bugged Reece for almost a year to rig the doorbell so that she could hear it downstairs. Truth was she should have done it herself. And now—well, now she had no other choice.

"When no one answered, I let myself in." Martin set down the milk and picked up a key, his smile beguiling. "I didn't think you'd mind."

"I don't," Simone was quick to assure him. "I was just surprised, that's all. I thought you were in Florida." Martin was a senior at the University of Texas, majoring in information technology. But at the moment he was supposed to be in Panama Beach celebrating spring break.

"Randy's car broke down. No wheels, no trip." Martin shrugged. "I figured I'd crash here for the duration. Get some studying done."

"And laundry." Simone tipped her head toward two overflowing canvas bags parked by the door.

"Well, yeah." Martin laughed, the sound so much like his brother's Simone winced. "That, too." His expression turned serious as he studied her for a moment. "It's all right, isn't it? I mean, it's not me you're divorcing?"

He sounded a little lost, the sharp edge of loneliness coloring his voice. But then, Simone knew the feeling only too well. "Of course not. You're always welcome here. You know that."

Martin reached for a stack of papers lying on the table. "You haven't changed your mind, have you?"

Simone blew out a long breath, staring down at her divorce papers. It wouldn't matter if she did change her mind. Reece wouldn't. Once he made a decision it was final. And even if it wasn't, there was no going back. Too much water under the bridge.

"No. I haven't." She shook her head to underscore the words, not certain whom exactly she was trying to convince.

"But they're not signed."

"They just got here." A little white lie, actually; they'd been on the table for almost a week. "I just haven't had time." She turned her back on the papers, going instead to the refrigerator for some water.

"I'm sorry," Martin apologized. "It's none of my business, really."

"Of course it is." Simone turned back to him with a smile. "We're family." And she meant it. Before Reece and Martin, Simone had never had a real family. At least not in any normal sense of the word. "Just because Reece and I can't live together doesn't mean I have to cut you out of my life, too."

"I'm not sure you have to cut either of us. Reece is stubborn, I'll grant you that. But whatever happened between the two of you, it can't be totally irreparable."

Simone smiled, her thoughts bittersweet. Martin's optimism made anything seem possible. But she'd lived in the shadows far too long to believe in things like happily ever after. Her life with Reece had been impossible from the very beginning. She'd just been too in love to see the truth of it. "It's over, Martin. Believe me, there's no going back."

Martin sighed and reached for the sandwich. "Well, at least you still have me."

"Yeah. And you have someone to feed and clothe you." She tipped her head toward the laundry again, and he laughed.

"It's a tough job, I know." His words were garbled over the peanut butter.

"And who better to do it than me? How long you staying?"

"The whole week, if that's okay. I thought I'd spend some time on the island. The waves aren't as good as Florida, but they still rock."

Padre wasn't exactly a surfing capitol, but this time of year there was at least enough surf to make it worth taking a board out.

"Sounds good. It'll be nice to have the company."

Simone was surprised at how much she meant it. She loved her house, every rambling foot of it. But living here on her own was a far cry from living in it with Martin and Reece underfoot. "The carriage house is waiting."

"Carriage house" was a bit euphemistic, but the name had stuck. Sometime in the forties, the old barn on their property had been converted into a one-car garage. When Simone and Reece had bought the place, the dilapidated structure, like the rest of the house, had practically been falling down. But the lines were good, and so when they remodeled, she'd suggested turning the building into a two-car garage with an apartment for Martin above it. He'd been almost ready to head off to UT at the time, so it had seemed right for him to have a space of his own in their new house. A subtle nod to his need for independence.

"Great." Martin jumped out of the chair, brushing crumbs onto the floor. "I'll just settle in, and then maybe head for the beach." He stopped by the back door, turning a guilty look to the overflowing laundry bags. "Maybe I should get started on these first?"

"Go on." Simone shooed him out the door with a smile. "I'll start the wash."

"You're sure?" It was a question, but his grin signaled he already knew the answer.

"Positive. Go." She leaned against the doorjamb, watching as he walked down the back drive. Even his gait was reminiscent of Reece's. Separated by almost sixteen years, the two brothers had too much of a gap between them to have ever been joined at the hip. In fact, growing up, Martin had hardly seen his older brother. But when their parents were killed in a traffic accident, Reece had been there, ready to take responsibility for his eight-year-old brother.

He'd given up a promising career in the military and instead come home to south Texas to put himself through law school, all the while serving as a surrogate parent for Martin. It had been tough for them both. But a real relationship had developed.

When Simone had met Reece, Martin had simply been part of the package. And in all honesty, she'd fallen in love with them both. After Reece had asked her to marry him, Martin had followed up with a proposal of his own. And from that moment on, they'd been a family.

The three of them against the world.

It was everything she'd ever wanted. An instant connection. Two people on whom she could lavish all the love she'd been hoarding over the years. It had seemed a perfect existence. Unfortunately, it hadn't held up over time. What had started as mutual attraction had devolved into mutual distrust, Reece's constant questioning turning into an inquisition that ultimately had forced Simone to retreat behind the facade she'd depended on for so many years.

And now there was simply no crossing the gulf that had grown between them, but that didn't mean that Martin couldn't remain a part of her life. She'd held his hand through first dates and football injuries, flunked tests and college entrance exams. He was part of her family. And nothing was going to change that.

She knew better than most how fleeting human connection could be. And she wasn't about to lose Martin just because she hadn't been able to make a life with his brother.

She stood for a moment more, fighting against the empty feeling gnawing at her gut, then drew in a deep breath, letting the sound of the ocean soothe her. The bay was calmer than open water, but there was still a peaceful ebb and flow as the water lapped gently against the shore.

She'd loved this house almost from the minute they'd found it. It had needed a lot of TLC, but the work had been almost as important to her as the house itself. It had filled her days. In the beginning of her marriage, she'd been content with the role of wife and surrogate sister to Martin. But with Martin heading off to college, she'd found her days empty. So the restoration had been a godsend.

Reece had had opinions, of course, but the day-to-day elements, the planning and creation, that had been hers alone. Every detail took on special meaning, her personality reflected in the house's grace and beauty in a way she couldn't possibly have imagined.

And now it was all hers. Reece had removed it from the settlement, instead agreeing to sign it over to her completely. The cynical part of her brain insisted his generosity had stemmed from guilt, but the part of her that had fallen for him knew it was more than that. Reece had understood her attachment to the house, even without knowing the reasons behind it.

A seagull's plaintive cry echoed above, and she shielded her eyes with a cupped hand to look out over the water. The sky was a crystalline blue with only the faint wisp of a cloud here and there, the sea glistening like sequins in the dancing light. In the distance, she could see a freighter making its way between buoys as it moved toward the great arched bridge and the port beyond.

If left to her own devices, she'd probably never have

chosen to come to Texas, let alone Corpus. She'd have probably found a job that let her travel. Avoid roots altogether. But Maurice had had other ideas, placing her in a temporary job with a Houston oil company. Unfortunately, it hadn't been a good fit. Actually, Houston hadn't been a good fit. So she'd jumped at the chance to transfer to Corpus, hoping for something better.

And then she'd met Reece.

And, in truth, even if she'd known how her marriage would turn out, she'd still have made the commitment. Without him, she wouldn't have Martin, or her house, or at least for one brief moment the feeling that she belonged.

With a smile, she reached down to pull a weed from the potted bougainvillea on the back porch. The day was still young. And she was free to do with it as she wished. She reached down to grab the laundry bags, thinking that she'd start the washer and then maybe go for a run.

One of the things she'd never lost sight of was the need to stay in shape. Her body was her best ally and she wasn't about to lose that edge. It had become a family joke actually that if Simone missed a workout it was obviously the end of the world. When she and Reece had remodeled the house, they'd turned half of the basement into a gym, and Simone still found solace in the mind-numbing routine of weights and aerobics.

But even with all the high-tech gadgetry they'd installed, nothing could beat the rush of running. Maybe it was being outdoors, or feeling her body work as a unit. Or maybe it reminded her of different times. Hard to say, but she still loved it.

Heading down the hall, she stopped at the basement stairs, and then with a shrug dumped the bags. Laundry could wait. It was a beautiful day, and Martin could live a few more hours without clean clothes. She opened the front door and headed down the steps, stopping at a honk from the curb. Laura, the post woman, waved as she pulled her cart up in front of the mailbox. Simone returned the gesture, already heading for the box.

"Got big plans for the weekend?" Laura asked, handing her the mail.

Laura had been delivering their mail since they'd moved into the house three years ago. And since then, she and Simone had formed a friendship of sorts. At least as far as front-yard conversations allowed.

"Well, the plan was to veg on the sofa. But Martin is here."

"So the two of you have plans?"

"Martin and I? No. Other than a date with his laundry, I'm on my own."

"You all right?" There wasn't much Laura didn't know about Simone's situation. She'd been through much the same herself.

"I'm fine. Just taking it day by day." It had been almost four months since Reece had moved out. But in some ways he'd been gone much longer than that. Besides, she was used to surviving on her own. "And today is a day for doing nothing. I'm going for a run, and then I figure I'll order a pizza, open a good bottle of wine and watch the new Johnny Depp movie."

"I'd kill for a weekend of vegging." Laura grinned. A single mother, she didn't get a lot of "me" time. "The last time I had the bathroom to myself, it was still the twentieth century."

"Trust me, it's not as exciting as Calgon commercials

would have you believe." Simone had meant to be funny, but somehow the words came out on an almost wistful note. "Not that I'm complaining."

"It's hard, I know." Laura nodded, her tone commiserating. "I remember when Jack left. I wasn't sure I'd make it through the day. But I had the kids, and well, time does heal all wounds."

"And mine aren't that severe." Simone forced a smile. "We parted amicably." The minute the words were out she knew how stupid they sounded. "Amicable divorce" was an oxymoron.

"I know." Laura's eyes were wise. "But that doesn't mean they don't smart a bit."

"True enough." Simone nodded, then changed the subject. "How're the kids?"

"Fine. Ethan informed me yesterday that he didn't need me to take him to school anymore. He wants to ride the bus." Laura's oldest, Sally, was in fifth grade, and Ethan, the youngest, was in first.

"Are you going to let him?"

"Yeah, I guess so. Although I might follow behind the bus the first couple of times just to be sure he's okay."

"I think you're brave to even consider it," Simone said, meaning every word.

"What about you?" Laura asked. "Have you given any more thought to what you want to do? Now that you're on your own, I mean?"

It was an ongoing conversation. "No. And I know I should," she said, heading her friend off at the pass. "I just haven't been able to really focus on what it is I want to do next. It's all a little overwhelming, you know?"

"I do," Laura said. "But it's important that you figure

out what you want. Besides, even if it's only temporary, it beats hanging out at the mailbox waiting for Netflix."

"Although when we're talking Johnny Depp…" Simone shrugged.

"'Nuff said," Laura said, shifting the cart back into gear. "Same time tomorrow?"

"Absolutely." Simone smiled. "As you so eloquently pointed out, I haven't got all that much on my agenda."

"Guess I know where I rank."

"Hey, just commenting on *my* very dull life."

"Be careful what you pray for," Laura quipped, laughing as she pulled away from the curb, heading for the next house on the cul-de-sac. Simone waved goodbye and then turned back toward the house, thumbing through the mail. Predictably it consisted of bills and junk mail, the junk only slightly outweighing the bills.

She quickly sorted things into two groups, bills on top, everything else on the bottom. As she moved the final catalog to the back of the pile, a card fell out, drifting in the breeze to land at the foot of a pot of moss roses.

She bent to retrieve it, surprised to find a postcard rather than the advertisement she'd expected. The photograph on the front showed an overforested mountain, the thick undergrowth making it look hot and oppressive. Simone shivered, memory flashing with intense clarity.

It was just a postcard.

She drew in a shaky breath and turned it over, her heart stutter-stepping as she read the message.

Trip is fine, but storm is coming. Must seek cover.

—M

The card fluttered from her fingers as she struggled to breathe. Then with a force of sheer will, she cleared her head, banishing her roiling emotions, and leaned over to once more retrieve the postcard, tucking it into the pocket of her jeans.

Once inside the house, she threw the mail on the credenza in the hallway and walked into the kitchen, her movements rote as she opened the pantry and began removing cans of green beans and peas.

Three minutes later the shelf was empty, and Simone carefully peeled back a Velcroed square of wallpaper. Despite the fact that her stomach was churning, her fingers were steady as she reached for a knife and levered it between two planks of the shiplap wall. There was a click, and then the bottom plank swung free, revealing a dark cavity.

Simone reached inside and pulled out a plastic-wrapped package. Pushing the wood back into place, she replaced the wallpaper, and then the cans. Certain that everything had been returned to normal, she crossed to the table and opened the package.

The gun was in pieces, but it took only a few seconds to put it together, the magazine sliding into place with a gratifying click. She slid it into the waistband of her jeans, the metal cold against the small of her back, then reached for the passport, flipping to the photograph, satisfied that it was a good enough likeness to serve her purpose.

Next she grabbed a black leather wallet, checking the contents briefly. Driver's license, social security, even a library card. The pictures were all of her, the name matching the one on the passport. She closed the wallet and picked up a manila envelope. Inside, she thumbed through four stacks of bills. A hundred thousand should take care of her needs. At least until she'd sorted things out.

The only remaining item in the package was a cell phone. She took it and shoved it into her purse, along with the wallet, envelope and folded square of plastic.

Then with a shuddering sigh, she removed her old wallet, cell phone and key ring, placing them on the table. Her current life summed up in paper, plastic and leather.

She turned slowly, her eyes falling on the divorce decree. All it needed was a signature. A line of ink, and her marriage would be nothing more than a memory. The thought broke her heart. But then sometimes life made decisions for you.

She grabbed a pen and scribbled her name.

What was it Laura had said?

Be careful what you pray for.

CHAPTER TWO

"SO IT'S YOUR TESTIMONY, Mr. Zabara, that you had never met the victim?" Reece Sheridan stepped forward slightly, shifting so that he could see both the defendant and the jury. Juror number nine was fidgeting with his jacket zipper and juror number six was rubbing her temples, her headache a result, no doubt, of the long and admittedly convoluted testimony.

"I don't know how many different ways I can say it. I don't know the woman." Zabara's tone bordered on arrogance. He'd been unshakable so far, Reece's cross-examination yielding exactly nothing.

But that was about to change.

"But you had seen her at the bar where you worked?" Reece stepped back, slumping his shoulders a bit in a staged effort to build Zabara's confidence.

"Yeah, I seen her. Although I wouldn't have known it until the cops showed me her picture." He shot a befuddled look at the jury and juror number two smiled.

"So it would be fair to say that before seeing the police photo, you wouldn't have been able to pick her out of a lineup."

"No way." Zabara shook his head, waving his hands to underscore the point.

"Then tell us, Mr. Zabara, how is it that you knew she had a tattoo?"

Juror number nine's hand stilled, six's head shot up, and two frowned at the question.

"I'm sorry. I don't know what you're talking about."

Reece heard the rustle of paper behind him as the defense attorney tried to make sense of his line of questioning.

"The tattoo you mentioned earlier."

"I didn't mention a tattoo."

"Not specifically, no. What you said—" Reece reached for his notes, pretending to consult them, giving the jury a moment to process "—was that 'a woman wearing the rose and blade wasn't no innocent—'"

"Objection." The defense attorney actually rose to his feet, a sure sign Reece had hit pay dirt.

Reece held up a hand. "If you'd prefer to have the court reporter read it back verbatim..."

"I assume you have the record marked?" the judge asked.

"I have it right here." He held up a sticky-noted piece of paper.

"You may approach." The judge motioned him forward, reviewed the sheet and then handed it back, her attention focusing on the other attorney. "I'm overruling the objection. Your client opened the door, so Mr. Sheridan has every right to go through it."

The defense attorney sat down, running a hand through his hair. Zabara shifted uneasily, darting glances at the now rapt jury.

"So you knew she had a tattoo?"

"I must've seen it in the police picture."

"Is this the picture?" Reece held up the photo.

"Yeah."

"It's a head shot, Mr. Zabara. The tattoo was just below her left breast. There was no way you could have seen it in this photograph." He handed the picture to the court officer, who in turn handed it to the jury foreman to pass among the jurors.

"In fact, Mr. Zabara, wouldn't it be fair to say that the only way you could have seen the tattoo was if Ms. Olivera was naked?"

"I told you I didn't know the woman. So no way did I see her naked."

"Unless you raped her."

"Objection." The defense attorney's voice rang through the silent court.

"Withdrawn." Reece moved closer to Zabara, closing the noose with every step. "So tell us, Mr. Zabara, if you've never seen the victim naked, and the tattoo wasn't in the photograph, how did you know about the rose and blade?"

"I must've read about it in the paper, or heard it on the news."

Reece shook his head with a grim smile. "Wasn't in the papers. The police held it back. You saw the tattoo when you raped her, didn't you, Mr. Zabara?"

"I didn't know her." He stressed the words, his composure clearly crumbling.

"You didn't have to. All you had to do was follow her home from the bar, wait for the right opportunity and then break in." Reece moved to within a few inches of the box, careful to avoid blocking the jury's view. "Was it something she did, or was she an easy mark?"

"The bitch had it coming," Zabara spat out, his face contorting with anger. "She thought she was better than me. Better than everyone from across the bay. But she was nothing. A slut who forgot where she came from."

"And so you showed her?" It was a statement, not a question. But Reece raised his voice at the end, just to cover his bases.

The defense attorney stood up, but not before Zabara sneered his answer. "Yeah. And then I slit her throat."

"No further questions." Reece held on to his smile, turning to walk back to the prosecutor's table.

"Redirect?" the judge asked.

But the defense attorney shook his head, cutting his losses. There'd be a last-minute plea. And then no doubt some attempts at appeal. But for all practical purposes, it was over.

Slam dunk. Zabara would be lucky to avoid the needle.

"Nice play," Tim Whitman whispered as Reece sat down. Tim had started with the D.A.'s office about the same time as Reece, the two of them working together for more years than Reece liked to admit.

Truth was, he was getting old. At least for this job. At thirty-eight, he either needed to run for D.A. or start his own practice. The former appealed, but wanting it wasn't the same as winning the coveted position.

But the reality was that he preferred prosecuting to defending. Finding a weak spot and then going for the jugular suited his style far more than a plush corner office with a harbor view. Maybe it sounded coldhearted, but every time he maneuvered some scum bag into admitting his guilt, the man was off the streets for good—or at least a couple of decades.

He'd felt the same way during his stint with the

Rangers, but those kinds of missions weren't conducive to raising a kid. Martin had deserved more. And so Reece had reinvented himself and landed here. Not all that much of a transformation, really. He'd just traded intel for deposition, both the key to the interrogative.

"The bastard set himself up," Reece responded. "All I had to do was connect the dots."

"It was more than that, and you know it. A lot of prosecutors would have missed the reference."

"They wouldn't have lasted in this business if they had." He shrugged, focusing on the judge, who had called a recess for the day and instructed the jury to be in court bright and early Monday morning.

The long weekend would give them a lot of time to think. But he didn't have any doubt as to where they'd end up. The man had admitted his guilt. Reece started to pack up his paperwork, his thoughts already moving on to his next trial. Tim could bring this one home on his own.

"You thought any more about my proposal?" Tim had decided to take on the rigors of private practice, and was in the planning phase of starting his own firm. For the past couple of months, he'd been trying to convince Reece to come along for the ride.

"I just don't know if I'm ready."

"Ready? Hell, you're past ready." Tim laughed, reaching into his briefcase. "You know as well as I do that it's time for a change. Look, I even had business cards made up." Tim held out the embossed card for Reece to see.

Sheridan and Whitman. Attorneys-at-Law.

"You're not playing fair." Reece held out the card. "Putting my name first."

"Hey," Tim laughed, waving for him to keep the card. "Whatever it takes. You up for a drink? We can talk about it some more."

"Let me check my messages first." Reece stuck the card in his wallet and then reached for his cell phone, clicking it on. Not that he anticipated much there. His cases were pretty much all in order, and he hadn't a social life to speak of. Not since the separation.

He pushed the thought away, banishing the image of Simone as well. His ex-wife was just that—ex. Although until she signed the papers, it wouldn't be final. The cell phone vibrated in his hand, and he glanced down to check the text message.

Martin. From Simone's.

A shiver of anticipation worked its way up his spine, and Reece frowned as if one gesture could negate the other.

"Bad news?" Tim's voice broke through his ruminations.

"No." Reece shook his head. "Just my brother. He's in town for spring break. Staying at Simone's."

Tim's eyebrows shot up in question. "Alone?"

"Jesus, Tim, get your mind out of the gutter. He's my brother. Besides, he's just a kid."

"He's twenty-two." His friend frowned in speculation. "Look at Demi Moore."

"Oh, come off it. Simone wouldn't do something like that." Nor would Martin.

"Probably not." Tim shrugged. "Forget I said anything. We still on for that drink?"

"One. And then I need to head over to Simone's." Tim opened his mouth, but Reece lifted a hand to hold him off. "To see Martin. That's what the message is about."

"Right."

Tim ducked his head to avoid eye contact, but not before Reece saw the twinkle in his eye. "What?" He grabbed his briefcase and headed for the courtroom doors.

"Nothing." Tim paused, then sighed. "It's just that for a divorced guy, you still seem to spend an awful lot of time with your ex. Weren't you just there last week?"

"We're not divorced. At least not yet. And there was a problem with the plumbing. I volunteered to help. Hell, it's only been four months. Old patterns are hard to break. Besides, I told you I'm going to see Martin. Not Simone."

"And maybe get her to sign the papers?" Tim prodded.

The idea made his stomach ache, but then he'd always hated change. Even hated moving a chair or a photograph. Everything in its place and all that. It had driven Simone nuts. "Yeah. That's a good idea. And then maybe I can finally put this all behind me."

Tim wisely stayed quiet, but his expression remained skeptical. "Well, I think you need a drink first for fortification."

Reece nodded, wondering how it was that he could undermine some of the best criminal minds in Nueces County and still not be able to understand his wife.

Ex-wife.

Whatever.

SIMONE STOOD in the driveway, trying to make up her mind. She was wasting valuable minutes, but beyond the postcard, she'd seen no real signs of danger. Her quandary was pedestrian at best, but in some obscurely intangible way important. She needed transportation, but she hated the idea of taking anything that didn't clearly belong to her.

The car was still registered in both of their names. And though Reece had given it to her in the settlement, the ink on the papers wasn't yet dry and she preferred the idea of traveling without baggage.

On the other hand, if she called a taxi, she'd leave trace, at least to the point where she got out. In truth, neither option appealed, and she cursed herself for her indecision. She had grown soft. A fact that only irritated her into further inertia.

She ran a hand through her hair and opted for the car. It seemed the lesser of two evils. Eventually Reece would get the car back, but by then she'd be long gone. Her disappearance would cause questions, but with Maurice's help, they'd never find her.

Her past wasn't something she'd wish on anyone. Especially not Reece. Which meant that getting away clean was imperative.

She moved toward the car, noting automatically the music drifting from the open window above. Martin was still upstairs.

Forcing her face into a mask of banality, she slowed her stride. Just a quick jaunt to the market. Home in a flash. The words echoed inside her head as she edged nearer to the Honda parked in front of the open bay.

She reached the car with no sign of her brother-in-law and breathed a sigh of relief. She fumbled through her purse for a moment before remembering that the keys were on the ring she'd left inside on the table.

Swallowing a muttered oath at her stupidity, she walked to the back door and into the kitchen. She picked up the key ring, and separated the Honda key from the others, working to inch it off of the split metal ring.

The key popped free, and she closed her fingers around it, dropping the key ring back on the table. With a last look around the kitchen, she turned back to the door, already reaching for the screen.

Just before pushing it open, she froze, inner alarm bells sounding with ferocity. All five senses went on immediate alert as she tried to locate the source of danger. But before she could fully mobilize, the soft hiss of a bullet ripped through the dirt in the garden just outside the door, embedding with a hollow thunk in the wood at the base of the house.

Hitting the floor, she rolled into a crouch, pulling the Sig Sauer from the small of her back. It had been a hell of a long time since she'd handled a gun, but instinct overrode everything else and she swiveled, sighting the gun as she sought out the bullet's source.

The wind blew lazily through the palm trees out back, the tall elephant grass bending almost double. She could smell salt and sand, and just a hint of sulfur. But there were no other shots. Except for the breeze, the backyard was quiet.

The silence was unnerving, something about it ringing false. And then she remembered Martin's radio. It had been blaring out the window.

She inched the screen open, and peered toward the garage. The window was still open, but the music had definitely gone quiet.

Oh God, if Martin was hurt.

Anger, hot and heavy, filled her chest, making it difficult to breathe. But she forced it aside, knowing there was no time for sentimentality. She had to draw the killer into the open. Then she could make certain that Martin was all right.

Glancing back at the kitchen, she reached for a mop. Not exactly the most innovative of ideas, but it just might work. Staying low, she positioned herself under the open window by the table, and then carefully raised the mop.

On a good day her hair probably didn't look as good, but hopefully the silhouette would do the trick. She counted one one hundred, two one hundred, and flinched as the mop splintered above her. Popping up before the shooter had time to regroup, she narrowed down possible trajectories, and then ducked back to the screen door.

The practical thing would be to head out the front door and never look back. But there was no way in hell she was leaving Martin. Swinging the door wide, she kept low, her eyes sweeping the area for signs of life.

A shadow detached itself from the garage wall, the pot of bougainvillea at her feet knocked over as a bullet whizzed past. She jumped back into the kitchen, running to the front door and then around the left side of the house. The covered patio would provide protection until the killer figured out where she was and changed positions.

What she needed to do was draw him out, away from the garage and Martin, then double back and hopefully gain access. She had one advantage in that she knew every inch of the property. And even if the assailant had studied the plat he wouldn't be as familiar with it as she was.

There was no question in her mind that he was gunning for her. Which meant that if she gave him the opening, he'd take it. All she had to do was be ready to move when he did.

She rounded the corner on a crouch and inched forward until she was situated just below the stone wall that lined the left side of the patio. The pool glistened turquoise in the dappled sunlight, the soothing sound of the waterfall totally at odds with the reality of the situation.

Taking a deep breath, Simone tightened her grip on the Sig and swung around the end of the patio firing. Three shots, all aimed away from the garage, and she rolled back around the corner as a spit of bullets stirred the dirt in the garden fronting the patio.

Bingo.

She held her position, waiting. If life were good, then the man would show himself. But she knew it was unlikely. If someone was after her after all these years, he had to know what he was doing. If nothing else, there was the fact that he'd found her.

She steeled herself for one last check of his position, and inched around the corner, this time staying low to the ground. Her instincts were in full force now, and she heard the hiss of the bullet, diving for cover while marking the trajectory, satisfied that she'd accomplished her objective.

Running full out now, she whipped back around the house, and down the right side, staying as close to the wall as her rosebushes allowed. Reaching the corner, she pivoted left, gun ready, and dashed across the open space toward the garage. A hail of bullets followed her footsteps, the sound of metal against concrete keeping her moving.

Inside the bay, she sprinted for the stairs, and was up them into the apartment in only seconds.

But she was too late.

Martin lay slumped in the corner.

Dear God, what had she done?

CHAPTER THREE

RACING ACROSS THE ROOM, Simone kept her gun aimed at the window as she knelt beside Martin, searching for a pulse.

"Martin? Can you hear me?"

There was silence for a moment, but a definite heartbeat, and then his eyes fluttered open, his expression a mixture of confusion and terror. "What's happening?" he whispered.

"You've been shot." She ran her hand over his shoulder and pectoral muscle until she located the wound.

"Is he still out there?" he mumbled, working to sit up, his pupils dilated with fear.

"I think so. But we can't go anywhere until I get you bandaged. So hold still." She pushed him back down and then grabbed a T-shirt off a chair, ripping several strips off the bottom. Quickly she tied it around his shoulder, effectively adding pressure to the wound. Not the best field dressing, but it would have to suffice. "Can you walk?"

"Dunno," he said, but tried to rise anyway, the result complete failure.

"Come on, Martin. I know this is scary but I can't get you out on my own. You've got to try and support some of your weight. All right?"

He nodded, shifted, and managed to stand, only leaning slightly against her. "Is he—is he still out there?" His words were slurred, which meant shock was imminent. She had to get him out of here now.

"Yes." She moved toward the door and the stairs, careful to keep her arm around him. "But he won't have made it back to the garage."

She wasn't entirely certain, but she was banking on the fact that their assailant would assume she'd stay by the window, effectively cutting him off from crossing the yard to the garage. Eventually, he'd figure out how to make his way to the back of the building, but hopefully by then they'd be out the back door and onto Reece's boat.

The house was situated at the end of an inlet of water, allowing for a boathouse and dock. Reece's pride and joy was his ocean-rigged sports cruiser. Rechristened *Antigua* in honor of the island where they'd spent their honeymoon, it was the one thing he'd insisted on keeping in the divorce settlement. The only reason it was still here was that he'd been unable to find the right berth elsewhere.

Nothing was good enough for his baby.

Well, he could have it—as soon as she and Martin managed to get it out to sea and away from whoever the hell was trying to gun them down.

Martin's head jerked and he slumped against her shoulder. "Martin?" She slapped his cheeks and was rewarded with a groan. "You've got to stay with me. We're going to try and get to the boat."

He sucked in a ragged breath and righted himself. "I can make it." He swayed slightly but held his ground; she tightened her arm around him, careful to keep her right arm free. Martin's eyes widened as he noticed the gun for the first time. "You know how to use that?"

"Yeah. I do." Something in her tone either placated him or frightened him into complete silence. Either way she hadn't time for further explanation. "Come on. Let's go."

They headed for the stairs, moving slower than she would have liked, but finally reaching the landing. Struggling to keep her balance, she supported him as they moved sideways down the stairs.

The bottom landing was their most vulnerable spot. At that point, they'd be visible from practically the entire backyard.

She stopped on the next to last step. "I need you to concentrate." She spoke slowly, waiting until she was certain he'd heard and understood. "We're going to need to run past the doorway and into the other bay." The garage's second door was closed, and if they could make it there, that should provide the cover they needed to duck out the back and into the boathouse.

"I'll give it my best." Martin's voice was weak, but there was determination reflected in his eyes.

"All right. I'll count three and we'll go."

Martin nodded, his gaze trained on the shadowy back wall and the boathouse door.

"One…two…*three…*" They shot off the step and headed for the safety of the opposite side of the garage. The report from the assailant's gun echoed through the building, signaling that he was too close for comfort. Simone pushed Martin forward and pivoted to get off a shot, turning then to sprint after her brother-in-law.

They moved together again, her arm around him as they headed across the remaining distance to the boat house door. Yanking it open, she shoved Martin through, turned to fire again and then ducked after him, slamming the door to the sound of bullets spattering against metal.

Score one for fireproof doors.

After hitting the switch to open the boathouse doors, she helped Martin on board the gently rocking cruiser, and then climbed the ladder to the pilot's chair and turned the key in the ignition. Thank God Reece always left it engaged. They'd fought over it numerous times, but if she ever saw him again, she swore she'd retract all the nagging.

She turned to check on Martin, surprised that he'd followed her. "Shouldn't be alone," he said, then collapsed on a bench next to the pilot's chair. She wasn't sure what he thought he was going to do, but she admired his gumption, especially considering he got motion sick just looking in the bathtub.

Still, she wished he'd gone below, out of range. But it was too late to argue. She pushed the throttle, sending the boat out into the channel. Steering the boat by touch, she turned to look behind her, scanning the shoreline for signs of movement.

An answering bullet lodged in one of the aft armchairs, sending it slamming across the deck.

"Get down, Martin," she barked, relieved when he obeyed by sliding off the bench onto the deck floor. "Keep watch behind us."

She turned her attention back to the canal in front of them, increasing speed slightly. The farther she got from the shore, the more likely it was that they would be out of range of the intruder's gun. In less than fifty yards they'd reach the main channel, and from there she'd head for the open water of Laguna Madre.

Reece's family had a cottage in Port Aransas, about half an hour's drive from Corpus. It was closer by water, and she figured if she could make it there, she'd be able to get Martin some help and regroup before heading for the rendezvous.

But first she had to clear the canal.

It was narrow and shallow on the edges, which meant she had to make her way cautiously. Grounding out now would mean certain death, so she focused on the buoys, keeping the cruiser to the middle of the channel.

A noise behind her sent a shard of alarm piercing through her, and she twisted to look over her shoulder, her worst fears confirmed as a smaller boat rounded the bend, closing the distance.

"He's coming in fast," Martin said, his eyes glued to the boat on their tail.

Built for speed in open water, the cruiser was more unwieldy in confined areas like the canal. However, the jet boat behind was giving her little choice. She had to make a run for it.

Pushing the throttle forward, she felt the cruiser lurch as it picked up speed. It cut cleanly through the water, keeping the smaller boat from getting any closer. She'd be able to maintain the speed until the very end, when she'd have to slow to make the turn into the bay. If she was lucky, she'd catch him off guard, unprepared for the banking curve, and ground him.

If not, she'd at least have the chance to reach the shipping channel and from there, open water. Then she could open the engines and the cruiser should be able to outdistance the jet boat.

Concentrating on timing the turn, she tightened her

hand on the throttle, the sound of the jet boat's engines taunting her from behind. They'd come too far to lose now. She shot another look behind her, trying to make out the driver's face, but he was too far away, and there was nothing distinguishing about the man except the green baseball cap on his head.

A pro—no doubt about it.

But she wasn't exactly a lightweight herself, and she'd be damned if she'd let the bastard catch her.

As the bend loomed in front of them at almost a right angle, Simone held her breath, waiting for the last second to decelerate. She felt the boat fishtail as she slowed to make the turn, the shimmy sending things flying across the deck.

"Grab on to something," she yelled at Martin. "It's going to be choppy."

She pulled the wheel to the left, holding it with all her strength, the boat keeling to the port side, righting as she straightened it out. She waited a beat, then opened the throttle, feeling the surge of the engine beneath her.

Risking a look behind her, she saw Martin hanging on to the railing, his face white, his eyes still glued to the jet boat as it too rounded the curve, the rear of the vessel skidding up onto the bank. Just for a moment she thought she'd beaten him, but the momentum of the boat's forward motion pulled it back into the water, right behind her.

She'd managed to make the open channel leading to the bay, but she still had an escort.

"He's closing in again," Martin yelled above the engine noise.

She glanced at the radio but dismissed the idea of calling for help. Even with the dire nature of the situation, she was better equipped to handle it herself. And quite frankly, until she understood exactly what was going on, she didn't dare risk exposing herself to the authorities.

Best to head for the island and lose this son of a bitch somewhere along the way.

She headed toward the shipping lane, well aware that under normal circumstances leisure craft were restricted from using it. Nothing about this situation was normal, however, and any advantage she could gain was all for the better. The deeper channel might give her an edge as her boat was designed for the ocean.

The jet boat was not.

Even better, she could see a barge off in the distance making its way across the bay toward the port. If she could close the gap between them, then there was a chance she could use the slow-moving ship to her advantage.

Moving closer to the barge, Simone swerved across the channel, whipping around two buoys in the process. The boat behind her, unprepared for her motion, slowed visibly as the driver reacted to the sudden change in direction and the buoys in the way.

The maneuver gave her an idea as she sped toward the barge, now no more than a hundred yards away. If she could time it right, she could cut in front of the barge just before it crossed the channel, blocking the jet boat and allowing her the precious seconds she needed to secure her escape.

Timing was everything and she concentrated on the rhythm of the cruiser and the slow, steady progress of the barge. The barge signaled its approach, and then gave a second bellow in warning as she tore forward, close enough now to see the red rust streaks staining the black metal hull.

"What the hell?" Martin's voice was ripped away in the wind, but she could see the question in his eyes.

"It's our only chance."

The barge signaled again, a crewman waving frantically from the bridge. Ignoring his apparent panic, she gripped the wheel and swerved left, gunning the cruiser's engine to full capacity.

The boat surged past the barge, so close she could have reached out to touch the prow. Urging the cruiser onward, she let out a sigh as she slipped past, the enormous ship filling the horizon behind her.

She'd escaped on a whistle and a prayer.

The thought made her smile, the archaic saying bubbling up from somewhere in her past. A foster parent maybe. Hard to say. But just at the moment it fit her mood perfectly.

Resisting the urge to let out a whoop, she glanced over at her brother-in-law, who was still staring openmouthed at the ship behind them.

"Oh my God," Martin mouthed, his face ashen but his eyes triumphant.

Simone headed into the sun-kissed waves of the bay, the barge behind her growing smaller and smaller as it meandered across the channel.

She'd won this round.

But she had no doubt at all that there'd be another.

Whoever had found her would be back. It was only a matter of time.

"YOU HAVE FOUND HER?" Isabella Ramirez whispered into the phone, warily eyeing the door. If Manuel caught her, there would be hell to pay. And here in Managua, even the walls had eyes.

"For only a moment, and then I lost her," Carlos said.

"Can you do nothing right? I risked everything to get you a name, and now," she spat the last word, "now you have nothing?"

"I am doing the best that I can," her brother said. "It is not my fault that the woman got away from me."

"She was our best chance at discovering the truth." Isabella blew out a breath, fighting her fury.

"I know. But I will find another lead."

"And how will you obtain this lead?"

"I have my sources." Her brother, as always, was enigmatic, choosing only to share with her what he wanted. "I have not lived in America all this time and gained nothing."

"But it was I who gave you the information you needed."

"*Sí*, you gave me a start. But my contacts, they are giving me the additional help I need. It was regrettable that there were complications before."

"What kind of complications?" Isabella worked to contain her impatience.

"It doesn't matter. What is important is that I have not failed. Only been delayed. You must have a little faith."

"That's not as easy as you make it sound. If this falls apart, if word ever reaches Manuel that I have betrayed him with the Americans, then my life is worth nothing."

"You are not the only one taking a risk, little sister." Carlos's reminder only made her angrier. Angry that she was a woman and could not handle such things herself. Angry that her brother had failed at something so painfully simple.

"I am the one living a lie in the house of our enemy.

He cannot know that I am helping you...." She trailed off again, staring at the closed door, assuring herself that she was still alone.

Manuel Ortega was the president of Nicaragua, and as such he was privy to information that was invaluable to her family's organization. So when he had shown an interest in her, it had made sense to capitalize on his infatuation. Let him believe he had tamed Hector Ramirez's daughter. She knew that he had not.

"It is a thin wire I am walking, Carlos. You know that."

"But it is more than worth it if it helps us to gain vengeance. And I tell you I will find the truth."

Isabella closed her eyes, reliving the horror of Sangre de Cristo. She'd only just turned ten, her childhood smashed in an instant of violence and blood, the man she loved most in the world brought down like an animal for slaughter.

Even though it had been almost ten years, the memory shriveled her heart, leaving her empty except for the bitter desire for vengeance. Her father's killer lived in her brain, taunting her with the act. Her father's blood flowed across her mind's eye, leaving her drowning in her pain.

Hector Ramirez had been betrayed, his legacy destroyed. And now, Isabella was left to hold his banner, to keep his dream alive. She was head of her family now. And as such, she must curtail her bloodlust. Allow her brother to pursue those who had dared to harm their family. Over the years, she'd found ways to make the others pay, but always the one who mattered most—her father's killer—eluded their grasp.

But now they were so close.

"I have given up much for you, Carlos. And for the

family." She shuddered at the thought of Manuel's thick lips against her skin. "But it will all be worthwhile if you find the ones we seek and make certain that they pay."

As the oldest, Carlos should have been the head of the family. Should have been the one to continue the fight for her father's cause. But the murder of her father and mother had changed her brother forever, his hatred robbing him of any chance at leading his people.

So the job had fallen to her.

And she had risen to the challenge.

She alone protected her father's ideals. He had believed in his country, in his people. He had worked singlehandedly to overthrow the despots who tried to profit from their power, never seeing the people they destroyed in their quest.

Her father's methods had not always been the most pure, but he did what had to be done to protect the rights of all Nicaraguans. It took money to mount resistance, and the fact that the money came from questionable sources was simply part of the cost of freedom.

She didn't have to justify it. Surely some evil was necessary in the fight for something so right?

The sound of the door opening had her swiveling to hide the phone, her fingers fumbling to disconnect.

Her heart stilled as she recognized Ramón Diego. The older man glanced behind him, satisfying himself that they were alone, and then stepped into the room. He was a swarthy man. Handsome in his youth, but thanks to a penchant for good wine, he had slid into the lassitude of age along with its accompanying paunch.

Ramón had been with her since her father's death. He had protected her and taught her, and ultimately helped her win her place at the head of her father's organization.

Both politically and physically, Ramón was her right-hand man. He'd even gone so far as to secure a job at the palace directing the household staff so that he'd be in a position to protect her.

"Who were you talking to?" he asked, eyes narrowed.

"No one," she lied. Even her second in command could not be told everything. Some things were better if they happened in a vacuum. "I was trying to reach Carlos, but I had no luck." She shrugged.

"Interesting that you should mention your brother. I just had a very disturbing conversation with Fermin Cortez."

Fermin was a flunky of Manuel's. A man who desired more than he would ever achieve. "What did he have to say?"

Ramón's expression darkened. "They know about your meeting with the American."

"That is impossible. I covered my trail well."

Ramón shrugged. "I am only telling you what Fermin told me. That Manuel was not happy to hear that you had been cavorting with the American CIA. Combining that with the fact that your brother is known to be in the States, the president cannot help but be worried."

"It was only a meeting, Ramón." She fisted her hands, wondering who it was that had turned traitor.

"You and I know that is not the truth. And if you are not careful, this house of cards you have built will come tumbling down."

"I know what I am doing."

"You are allowing your passion for revenge to color every decision you make. Your position here is important to the family, but it is tenuous at best. Manuel is a dangerous man, and you're playing with fire, *carita*.

You know that." Ramón's frown was fierce, but she was not afraid.

"It was not planned to see this man. I simply took the opportunity when it arose." Another lie, but again the less Ramón knew, the better.

"And did you find out what you wanted to know?" It was a trick question. Ramón wanted her to admit that she was working with Carlos.

"No. The old man kept quiet. Even with my best efforts, there was nothing there to discover." The last of course was not the truth, either. There had been much to learn if she read between the lines. But she had promised Carlos she'd tell no one about what she had managed to put together.

"You cannot keep taking these kinds of chances, Isabella. It's too dangerous," Ramón scolded.

"Stop treating me like a child. I've lived with danger all of my life."

The old man's expression softened. "Yes, but to court it freely—to invite it willingly into your life—that is a different thing. Your father would not wish you to put everything he worked for into jeopardy just to avenge his murder."

"My father would want exactly that." She squared her shoulders, holding Ramón's gaze until he looked away.

"I want only what is best for this family. And I worry that you are walking a fine line with Ortega. I tell you he is suspicious. And if he believes even for a minute that you have done something to threaten his power, he will not hesitate to kill you."

"But he knows nothing. Only rumor. And I can handle that." She smiled at Ramón, praying in the name of all that was holy that she was right.

CHAPTER FOUR

REECE PULLED into the driveway and killed the motor, resisting the urge to park in the garage at the back of the house. No matter how much it felt like it, this was no longer home. Home was his new condo on Ocean Boulevard. Sterile and practical, it was the perfect environment for the beginning of his new life, an untested canvas ready for whatever came next.

What a load of bullshit.

Reece opened the door and slid out of the Jag. Since he'd been a small boy he'd felt the need for speed. It had started virtually with video games and Nintendo, and then moved into the real world when he'd discovered go-carts. From there he'd survived a motorcycle phase in high school, a Porsche 911S in college and the ultimate defeat of an inner ear problem that kept him out of jet training. But old habits died hard, and he still had a penchant for all things built for speed.

Including his cruiser.

He shot a look in the direction of the boathouse, knowing his baby was berthed safely inside.

He smiled at the pun and headed for the front door. Maybe he'd talk Martin into going out in the boat later. His brother had missed the speed gene, motion sickness threatening almost every endeavor. But a little Dramamine went a long way, and with the patch, Martin could actually last a couple of hours. Not that he really enjoyed it.

Reece sighed, thinking of Simone. Whatever else lay between them, the woman loved fast rides. He could see her in his mind's eye, head thrown back, laughing as the wind whipped through her hair.

God, he was a sap.

Those days were long gone. He couldn't remember the last time he'd seen her smile, let alone laugh. Maybe he'd just imagined her happiness, adding fantasy to fact to justify what just might turn out to be the biggest mistake he'd ever made.

Pocketing his keys, he strode to the front door, bracing himself for an encounter with Simone. Next time Martin came to town, he was staying with Reece. No more crossing enemy lines.

He flinched at his use of the word *enemy,* wondering how it had all come down to this. He cleared his face, settling into the neutral expression he used when cross-examining a witness, and rang the doorbell. Seconds ticked by. He rang again. Nothing.

They'd probably gone out for dinner.

He started to leave, then changed his mind. Technically, it was still his house. At least until she signed the papers. No reason he couldn't go inside. Maybe have a drink. Wait for Martin.

He pulled the key ring out of his pocket and slid it into the lock, feeling an odd mix of elation and guilt. If marriage tethered a man, divorce cuckolded him. And in Reece's mind the latter was far worse than the former.

The door opened on a silent house. He stepped inside,

letting the familiar smells of home surround him. They'd worked so hard to turn what had been an eyesore into a retreat. And despite the change in circumstances, there was no denying the remnants of their life.

Memory could be dangerous though, and so he pulled in a cleansing breath and forced away the sentiment. Maybe he'd skip the drink and just head out on his boat. Next week, he'd finalize the papers for a slip at the T-Heads. Only a few blocks from his condo, the new berth would be ideal. The yacht club wasn't particularly his cup of tea, but it was a better alternative than housing the *Antigua* with Simone.

He stopped in the foyer, automatically reaching for the pile of mail on the credenza. There was nothing but bills and catalogs, most of them in Simone's name. He tossed them back on the table, wondering why she'd left the bills. Simone was a stickler for paying things on time. She practically wrote a check the minute the bill came out of the envelope.

When they'd first married she'd insisted on paying for everything with cash. A nightmare when it came time to present receipts to their accountant, Fred. But she'd explained that she hadn't had a lot of money growing up and that her grandmother had insisted they always use cash. He'd finally managed to convince her that banks weren't the enemy, but she'd never truly relaxed into the concept, preferring instead to micromanage their accounting to the point that he'd finally had to fire Fred, despite the fact that the man had been his accountant for almost seven years.

Maybe she'd just been excited to see Martin.

The thought reminded him of Tim's comments about Martin and Simone, and he scowled as he made his way toward the kitchen. There was no fucking way. And he was a traitor to them both for even entertaining the notion.

At the door to the basement he almost tripped over Martin's laundry. One bag tipped over, spilling out onto the parquet floor. Again he frowned, unease niggling at the back of his brain. Surely Simone hadn't done a complete reversal in his absence and turned into a slob?

He bent and straightened the bag, stuffing the odd pair of underwear back inside, his attention now focused on the details of the house. Everything was quiet, and except for the laundry and the mail, seemingly normal.

But something felt off. Some indefinable thing that teased at his senses. Years as a prosecutor had hardened an already keen ability to cut through the facade to the heart of a situation, seeing it for what it was and not what it appeared to be.

"Simone?" he called out. "Martin? Anybody home?"

There was no answer except the methodic ticking of the grandfather clock in the den. He walked into the kitchen.

The room smelled of lemon and verbena, the open window by the table filling it with the scents of the garden. The dishes were neatly stacked in the sink. A broken old mop lay drunkenly against the yellow step stool. A plate on the table held the remnants of a peanut-butter sandwich. Testament to Martin's presence. Simone had always spoiled him. The baby brother she'd never had.

Or so she said.

She certainly hadn't grown up in Wilmont, Ohio. He remembered the night she'd volunteered the information like it was yesterday. He could see the restaurant. See Helen and Tim as they'd all enjoyed a much-needed evening out.

It had started innocently enough. Helen telling a story

about her mother taking on a plumber in the East Texas town she came from. The conversation had turned into "top that story" as was so often the case, with Tim and then Reece trotting out their own parental foibles. When Tim had turned to Simone, Reece had joined his friend's cajoling. And after a baited pause, she'd told them about growing up in Wilmont. He could still hear her telling her animated tale about the tiny town. Bringing the residents to life as if they'd sprung fresh from the pages of a book—or a magazine.

He'd thought it a breakthrough, the first time she'd ever opened up about her past. But later, when he'd come across the article about rural Ohio, he'd recognized the details.

Maybe if he'd gone to her then it would have ended differently, but he'd been hurt, and suspicious. So following his instincts, he'd dug deeper on his own. And when he had proof it was all a lie, then he'd confronted her, his actions widening the already cavernous gulf between them.

Maybe he'd pushed too hard, but damn it, surely he, of all people, had a right to know the truth.

Whatever it was.

Some things are better left buried.

The words echoed through his brain, a lame line from an old movie he'd seen recently. But perhaps the warning was an apt one. His curiosity had cost him everything that mattered most to him.

He shook his head, dispelling his melancholy thoughts. It was the house. It was drawing him in, bringing back things better left forgotten. It had been a mistake to come here. He started to turn back for the door. To hell with his boat, better to just go home and forget he'd been here.

But as he turned, the papers on the table grabbed his attention.

The divorce decree.

With a morbid sense of curiosity, he crossed over to look at them, flipping to the last page, his stomach twisting at the sight of her spidery signature.

It was over.

Finito.

Kaput.

Damn it all to hell.

He fingered the papers, tracing the signature line with his thumb. It was tempting to take them. To…

God, he didn't know what he wanted to do with them exactly. Emotion roiled in him, churning his gut. He just wanted it over. Wanted it behind him. Like cutting out a tumor or something. He wanted to be healthy again—whole again.

With a sigh, he tossed the papers back on the table, for the first time seeing Simone's wallet and phone. The niggling feeling was back, but this time it was full-blown worry. She never went anywhere without her phone. Not even the bathroom.

He picked it up and, in doing so, revealed her keys. They'd slid under the wallet, only the silver heart visible. He'd given her that heart for her birthday one year. From Tiffany's. So many little things that made up a marriage—and destroyed it.

He dropped the phone and headed for the back door. Maybe she was out there with Martin. That wouldn't completely explain the wallet and keys, but it would go a long way.

He crossed the driveway, stopping to right a pot of bougainvillea, and then headed into the garage. "Simone?" Again he called her name, trying not to give in to his rising sense of urgency. "Martin?" There was no answer, and he took the stairs two at a time.

The apartment was empty. The window curtain swayed lazily in the evening breeze and except for his growing sense of unease, everything looked placidly normal.

He turned in a circle, trying to find something—anything—that looked out of place. There was a T-shirt wadded up in the corner by the wing chair, and Martin's boom box on the table by the window.

And no sign of either Martin or Simone.

He moved to the window, scanning the yard for signs of life. The Honda sat in the driveway and Martin's beat-up old Volkswagen was parked in the garage. He'd seen them both on his way up the stairs.

So where the hell were they?

Suddenly a light went off. The boat.

They'd taken his boat.

It didn't make a bit of sense, but it was the only option remaining. The only one he was willing to consider. He dashed down the stairs again, this time turning to the boathouse door. Yanking it open, he ran inside, then skidded to a stop.

The boat was gone.

He pivoted back toward the door, anger threatening to consume him. It was his boat. And his brother. How dare she take them both without so much as a by-your-leave? He knew his thinking was irrational, but he'd been so worried. Afraid that something had happened to them. And the discovery they were merely out cruising the bay left him with adrenaline to spare.

He stopped by the door, pulling in cleansing breaths. No need to lose it over something as stupid as a boat ride. Simone would be careful. She knew how much the *Antigua* meant to him. And it wasn't as if she hadn't taken the boat out before.

He leaned a hand on the door, then pulled it away with a frown. The garage side was pockmarked. The paint marred in a couple of places as if it'd been struck by hailstones. Which was, of course, impossible. He rubbed one of the indentations with his index finger, wondering what the hell had happened.

The door wasn't new. But as far as he could remember it had been unblemished. And based on the rough edges of the paint, he'd say whatever had caused the marks had happened recently.

He lifted his finger to his nose, the smell of metal and paint mixing with something tantalizingly familiar.

He bent to retrieve a piece of cotton caught on the hinge, and as his eyes took in the brownish stain on the material, he knew what it was he'd smelled.

Sulfur.

He stared at the indentations on the door, his heart constricting. Simone hadn't taken the boat for pleasure.

She'd been trying to escape.

SIMONE STOOD in the shaded alleyway beside the clinic. Port Aransas was overflowing with people, spring break in full swing. All the better to blend in. And fortunately, the clinic was already closed for the day, the parking lot empty, the traffic on Alister fairly light.

She'd already cased the clinic and there were no signs of occupation. There'd probably be a cleaning crew later on, but for the moment she seemed to have the place to herself, which was exactly what she needed.

She'd have preferred taking Martin to the hospital in Aransas Pass instead of the cottage, but just at the moment, she couldn't risk the questions and attention his arrival at the medical center would generate. Fortunately, the wound seemed to have stabilized.

She needed to remove the bullet, but to do that she needed the proper supplies.

The clinic should have everything she required.

Checking once more for last-minute returnees, she skirted the left side of the building, moving around to the back. The lock took only a few seconds to pick, and with a last furtive look behind her, she was in.

It didn't take much longer to secure the items she needed. Suturing thread, disposable scalpel, tweezers, needle, antibiotics, pain pills and bandages. She'd have Martin as good as new in no time, and hopefully on his way back to Reece. She shuddered to think what her ex's reaction to all of this would be. But hopefully, she'd be long gone before there was hell to pay.

Not that she was a chicken exactly. In fact, truth be told, she was probably just the opposite. Or had been anyway. But assassinations were nothing compared with facing Reece. She'd rather brave the Nicaraguan jungle any day of the week if the alternative was squaring off with her soon-to-be ex-husband.

So much for people skills.

Simone slipped out the back door, stopping to make certain that there were no prying eyes. Walking with practiced nonchalance, she fronted the highway and was across as soon as the traffic allowed.

Half a block more, and she was safely on Sheridan property. Rose Cottage, named after one of Reece's mother's favorite books, had endured fifty-odd years of sand and salt. Faded seagull-gray, its weathered planks were bowed and warped but still standing strong.

Reece and Martin's parents had bought the cottage for their retirement, but of course had never made it, leaving the boys with an inheritance that was short on cash but long on love. They'd occasionally come up here for the weekend, more for the memories than anything else, but neither of them ever really loved the place the way their parents had.

Just at the moment, however, it was a godsend, and Simone was grateful that Reece had decided not to rent it out for the season.

She let herself on to the screened-in porch, and allowed a moment to survey the situation. Though the neighborhood was residential, the cottage sat back from the road at an angle, its back bordered by the sand dunes fronting the beach. Not exactly isolation, but good enough for what she needed. Approach was limited to the front of the house, as the only access from the back was a narrow boardwalk with a locked gate. The dunes themselves were full of goat heads, the stickers enough to slow down even the most determined of assailants.

Satisfied that nothing looked out of place, she opened the front door and headed for the master bedroom. "Master" was probably a bit enthusiastic, as the room wasn't particularly big, and with its beat-up maple bedstead, definitely not commanding.

Martin lay in the middle of the mattress, his eyes closed, the even breathing signaling that he was asleep.

Simone dumped her supplies on the nightstand and reached out to wake him. Her brother-in-law sighed and then opened his eyes, pain shadowing his gaze.

"How long have I been out?" He squinted, reaching up to touch the bandage.

"About an hour, maybe a little less." Simone sat beside him on the bed, holding out a glass of water and a pain pill. "I've got to get that bullet out."

"What about the hospital. Wouldn't I be better off there?"

She felt her face tighten with regret. What the hell had she gotten him into? "Too risky, I'm afraid. Since it's a gunshot, it'd have to be reported to the police."

"And I take it that's not a good thing." It was more of a statement than a question, and Simone suppressed a smile. Martin was still young enough to take life in stride. Age changed all that. Age and responsibility.

"No." She shook her head to emphasize her point, then began removing the strips of cotton.

"Shit." The whispered word was probably an understatement, and certainly there was worse to come, but Simone still felt a lurch in her stomach.

"I'm sorry. It's stuck where the blood has dried." She bit her lower lip and ripped off the last bit. "That's all of it."

"Maybe the bandage, but I've got a feeling there's a lot more pain to come." He wrinkled his nose, the gesture almost comical. Almost. "I'm assuming you've done this before?"

She nodded, concentrating on the wound. It had stopped bleeding for the most part, the slight ooze the result of the bandage being removed. It was a clean entry, the edges slightly blackened from impact.

Gently, she lifted him up, verifying again that there was no exit wound.

"Still in there, huh?"

Simone recognized Martin's need to talk. Anything to distract himself from the reality at hand. Hell, she'd been there herself more times than she cared to count.

"Yeah, but it ought to be a clean removal. It's not lodged against the shoulder, and I'm guessing it passed through the muscle without causing too much damage."

"But I was knocked out?" Martin frowned.

"Probably hit your head on something when you fell." As gently as possible, she ran her fingers over the back of his skull, stopping when she hit a small hematoma. "Right here."

Martin felt the bump gingerly. "Leave it to me to do the bulk of the damage after the fact."

"Your falling probably saved your life. This is going to sting." She soaked some cotton in alcohol and washed off the wound.

"So what happened back there?" he asked, his voice tight as he fought the pain. "Who the hell was shooting at us?"

Simone finished cleaning the injury, considering how much to tell him. In all honesty, the less he knew, the better. "I'm not sure, Martin." It was the truth, at least as much as she was willing to share.

"Are you in some kind of trouble?"

"You mean beyond someone gunning for me?" It was a flip remark, but she needed time to think, to figure out the best course of action.

"Simone, you're scaring me." Martin waited, but Simone shook her head.

"Look, I'm sorry." She squeezed his hand. "I understand that this is frightening. And I'm going to do everything in my power to get you out of it. But until I do, the fewer questions you ask the better. All right?" She picked up the scalpel.

"Or what? You'll hurt me?" He'd meant to be funny, but she could see his fear.

"Don't be ridiculous. I'm just going to get this bullet out." She turned her attention to the entry wound. "I'm going to cut now. You ready?"

"Shouldn't I be biting on a bullet or swigging whiskey or something?"

Simone frowned, halting just short of cutting. "You've already had a Vicodin. It's better than whiskey. Do you want something else?"

"No. I was just kidding. I can take it. Just get it done." He closed his eyes, the muscles in his cheek tightening as he prepared for the pain.

She made a quick cross cut, and replaced scalpel with tweezers. Fortunately, the bullet hadn't gone far, the back edge in plain sight. In just a few seconds she had it out. "You okay?"

"Working on it." His voice shook, belying his words.

"You're doing great. All I need to do now is suture it closed."

"Oh God, I've seen your sewing."

She'd tried to make curtains for his apartment, the result more dime-store rummage sale than Martha Stewart. "I'm better at this. I promise." She quickly took three stitches and tied it off.

Martin was frowning again. "You *have* done this before."

"Let's just say I was a Girl Scout."

His eyes met hers, the expression in them full of doubt. She hated the fact that she'd put it there. But there simply wasn't a choice. "Almost done," she said with a forced smile. "All that's left is to clean it and fix you up with a new bandage. Got a pressure one right here."

"Where did you get all the props?" He nodded at the tray holding the bullet and the full array of surgical prep.

"Let's just say I borrowed them."

"Resourceful..." His voice trailed off as he fell asleep, the Vicodin finally kicking in.

There'd be more questions later. But with any luck, by then the cavalry would have arrived, and she'd be long gone.

CHAPTER FIVE

"I GOTTA BE HONEST with you, Reece, I'm just not seeing anything that looks like foul play." Detective Mike Iago shook his head, his expression apologetic. Iago had testified in around a dozen cases Reece had prosecuted, and over the years the two men had struck up a friendship of sorts.

Currently they were standing on the driveway, Mike's partner Rico still inside the garage. A pair of uniforms had responded to the call, as well, one of them in the house, the other in Martin's apartment. "Are you certain she didn't just head out for a ride in the bay?"

"Without her cell phone or her keys?" Frustration crested, but Reece pushed it aside. He needed to keep a clear head.

"I can see that. I mean, why would she need them on the boat? Or maybe Martin has his phone."

In Reece's panic, the idea hadn't occurred to him. "Hang on." He pulled out his cell and called his brother. There was a moment's silence, and then ringing, the sound in stereo as it echoed through the phone's receiver and out the open window above the garage.

"I still say they could just be out for a ride." Mike's expression remained neutral.

"But what about the marks on the door? Or the fact that I smelled sulfur."

"There weren't any casings, Reece. We looked."

"Then maybe someone cleaned them up. Mike, something isn't right here. I may not be able to prove it, but that doesn't mean I'm wrong."

Mike stared down at his shoes for a minute, shifting his weight uncomfortably. "Have you considered that maybe they ran off together?"

"What?" It was the second time today someone had suggested the idea, and Reece still found it ludicrous. "There's no way."

Mike shrugged. "I've seen it before. Deserted wife, young lover."

"I didn't desert Simone. The divorce was mutual."

"And she signed the papers. I'm just saying maybe she's starting a new life."

"With my boat?" The minute the words were out, he regretted them. He didn't give a damn about the boat. Not when his wife and brother were missing. It was just that the idea of Simone running off with the cruiser was insane.

"Maybe she's trying to hurt you."

"Or maybe something happened to her." He forced himself to breathe evenly. "At least put out an APB. If I'm wrong then there's no harm, right?"

"You know better than that." Mike shook his head as Rico Morales joined them. "Got to wait at least forty-eight hours. And besides, if you're wrong the department takes all the heat."

"So blame it on me." He sounded desperate and he knew it. "Damn it, Mike, you know me. Hell, you know Simone. Surely you can do something more."

"You find anything?" Mike shot a sideways glance at his partner.

"Nah. No casings, no blood, no sign of a struggle..." Rico trailed off with a shrug.

"What about the flowerpot?" Reece pointed to the bougainvillea. "It was upended when I got here. I straightened it without thinking." As if to make mockery of his line of thought, the wind picked up, toppling the plant, bits of potting spoil tumbling across the driveway.

Mike and Rico exchanged glances, and Reece felt his blood pressure rising.

"I'm telling you something's wrong. I don't know what, but there's no way my wife and my brother ran off together." If he'd been prosecuting himself, he'd have gone for the jugular right about now, correctly surmising that he was at the end of his rope and therefore vulnerable to attack.

But he wasn't prosecuting anyone, and he was positive that Simone and Martin were in trouble, the lack of concrete evidence not withstanding.

He mentally ran through a list of people he could call on for help, including the mayor, but quickly dismissed the idea. If Mike didn't believe him, then what chance did he have with an official he only knew in passing?

And the truth was, if someone brought him the same story, he'd probably have jumped to the same conclusion. Ex-wife, newly divorced, brother-in-law on the premises. What the hell was there to stop them?

Except that they were talking about Simone and Martin.

One of the officers walked out the back door, his expression carefully neutral. Not a good sign.

"What'd you find?" Mike had clearly recognized the expression, too.

The uniform shot a look at Reece, eyebrows raised in question.

"It's okay. We're all friends here." Mike's tone indicated something more, but Reece wasn't up to considering the implications.

"Looks like there's some clothes missing from the lady's closet. Stuff thrown around the room like maybe she was packing."

"She could have been doing laundry. Or heading for the dry cleaners. Anything." Actually Simone was neat to a fault, everything in its proper place. It was one thing they totally agreed on. But he'd shared enough. It was clear the officers had already drawn their conclusions, and short of producing a body, nothing was going to change their minds.

"Maybe." The officer shrugged. "She have a set of luggage?"

"Yeah." Reece glared at the man, daring him to take it further. "Leather. Three matched pieces." They'd gotten them in Italy while on vacation. Simone had loved them on sight, but thought they were too expensive. So he'd bought them as a surprise and had them delivered to the hotel. Her laughter rang through his head, and he shook it to clear his thoughts.

"Well, there's only one left. A little carry-on." The guy stared at his feet, clearly unwilling to face Reece.

"I'm sorry, man." Mike reached over to touch his shoulder, but Reece shook it off.

"This isn't right. They wouldn't do this to me." It sounded so damn selfish, the way he'd said it. But hell, it was the truth. There was still a bond between him and Simone. And even if there wasn't, Martin was his brother, for God's sake.

"It happens." Rico shrugged, his expression sympathetic.

Reece clenched his fist in his pocket, a conscious effort to find control.

"Got no sign of clothes at all up there." The second officer joined them, tilting his head toward the apartment. "Just this." He held out the crumpled T-shirt.

"Let me see?" Reece took it before the officer had the time to protest. It was ragged, the bottom torn off, but the Coldplay album cover was still in tact.

"You recognize it?" Mike asked, liberating the shirt from Reece's grasp.

"Not specifically, no." Reece shook his head. "But Martin loves Coldplay."

"And Simone?" It was an innocent question on the surface, but there was more. Innuendo if nothing else.

"She likes all kinds of music." He shrugged, pushing aside the thought that she'd never shared his love for country music. Preferring instead the driving beat of newer bands like 3 Doors Down and Train. "It could be hers. I can't say for sure."

"Nothing here to tell us anything, anyway." Mike handed it back. "I wish I could do more for you, Reece. You know that. But there's nothing here to indicate anything's wrong."

Nothing except the voices screaming in his head.

"Why don't you just wait it out. And if they don't show up, give me a call. I'll put out that APB."

Reece wanted to scream at the man. To tell him that by then it might be too late. But there wasn't any point. It wouldn't change the situation. If he was going to find his wife and brother, he'd have to do it on his own. And the sooner he got rid of Mike and his associates, the better.

"Fine. I'll call you." He reached out to shake his friend's hand. "Thanks for coming."

"Anytime," Mike said, his expression full of regret. "I just wish I could have helped."

"It's all right. You did what you could."

"I really am sorry. You and Simone made a good couple. But I guess everything has to end." Like all cops, Mike tended to see the glass half-empty. Hell, most of the time Reece saw the same; it was part and parcel of dealing with bottom feeders day in and day out. But this time he knew Mike was wrong.

Simone and Martin hadn't taken a pleasure cruise, and they hadn't run off together. Something else was going on. And he intended to find out what.

SIMONE PACED back and forth across the cottage's front room, trying to figure out what to do. The way she saw it, there were three options. One, she could leave Martin on his own, knowing that once he was feeling better he'd contact Reece and be all right. Two, she could take him to a hospital and leave him there. And three, she could call Reece and alert him to the fact that Martin was here.

All three options had risks.

Martin might take a turn for the worse, and leaving him alone could complicate the fact. At any kind of hospital or clinic she risked someone seeing her. In and of itself not a major problem, but certainly something that could impede her progress. And calling Reece meant explanations that she just wasn't ready to give.

She hated the idea of lying to him—again. It had become too much of a habit. But some things he was better off not knowing. In the beginning he'd been so caught up in the idea of her and of falling in love that he hadn't asked for anything more than what little she had told him.

She'd known that it wouldn't last, but she'd convinced herself that when he started to question her, she'd be able to handle it. And at first she'd managed to do exactly that. Handing him vague answers that meant nothing and were impossible to trace.

But all that had changed the night she'd fabricated an entire past. In truth she'd had one too many glasses of wine, and everyone was having so much fun. At the time it had seemed like a good idea. In retrospect, of course, she recognized just how stupid she'd been.

It hadn't taken him long to work out that she'd lied. And after the initial confrontation, she'd managed damage control. But the blow to her marriage had been irreparable.

And whose fault was that, a little voice nagged.

Maybe it had been her fault.

But surely he was to blame, too. He'd accepted her "as is" and then changed the game— wanting more. The truth was, it was just too damn hard to sort it all out. And there wasn't any point anyway. The marriage had broken, and there was no way to put it back together again.

She sighed, running a hand through her hair, looking out at the dark night.

Stars twinkled overhead, the soft murmur of the surf giving a false sense of serenity.

Somewhere out there in the dark was a hunter. Coming for her. Rising like a shadow from her past, reaching out with deadly intent. And if she didn't get the hell out of here soon, Martin was going to be the one to suffer.

In the old days there would have been no indecision. Standard operating procedure would have dictated all. But then in the old days there hadn't been anyone to worry about. The people in her life had been as capable as she of taking care of themselves.

Self-sufficient to the core. But at least part of her had moved past that. Learned that it was possible to let someone else into her life.

She'd let Reece in. And in doing so she'd let Martin in, as well. He was her brother as surely as if there were common blood, and she wasn't about to just leave him here on his own.

She'd have to call Reece.

And she'd just have to find the right words. Explanations had never come easily for her. But she didn't have to tell him anything except that Martin needed him. She'd be sure that he was coming. And then she'd hot-wire a car and hit the road. By the time he arrived, she'd be halfway to Austin.

It wasn't the perfect plan, but it was the best she could do on the spur of the moment.

She walked over to the table and pulled the new cell phone from her purse. It was a satellite phone. Secure and untraceable. She remembered taking it from Maurice, certain that she'd never have cause to use it, her pain over all that had transpired tempered by the fact that for the first time in her life she was going to be free.

Freedom. It was one hell of a seductive word. And at least in her case, it was an illusion. A cruel joke whose punch line had always been to destroy any semblance of happiness she'd managed to acquire.

She pushed aside her thoughts, forcing herself to concentrate. The sooner she got Martin out of this mess the better. He needed his brother. And they were both better off without her.

Simple truth.

But God, it hurt.

She dialed and was about to hit Connect when a sound outside the door had her hitting the floor on a roll. The gun was just above her on the table, and in one quick motion she reached up and grabbed it, crouching again beneath the table, already sighting the door.

The handle turned once slowly and then again with more force. Whoever was out there wasn't afraid of being seen or heard. Imperceptibly Simone relaxed, but she still kept the gun trained on the door.

There was a muffled curse and then a key slid home, the lock disengaging and the door swinging open.

Reece.

Damn it, while she'd wasted valuable time trying to decide what to do, the decision had been made for her. Beginner's mistake.

Only she wasn't a beginner.

She fought a wave of frustration. She'd been out of the game too damn long. If she was going to survive she had to hone her instincts. React first, think later. Her training would do the thinking for her.

Suddenly she felt old.

Reece stepped into the room, his expression a mixture of fury and relief as his gaze met hers. "What the hell is going on here?"

CHAPTER SIX

"I ASKED YOU what was going on. Why are you under the table?" Tightly controlled anger glittered in Reece's eyes.

Simone slid the gun into the waistband of her jeans, grateful for the shadows that hid her movements. Waiting another beat, she stood up, searching for an explanation he could believe.

"I dropped something."

They stood for a moment facing each other, the crackling electricity between them the product of anger and other emotions she wasn't about to try and identify. The bond they shared had been severed. The final cut—the papers lying on the kitchen table.

They were divorced, her life officially no longer a part of his.

"Like hell." Reece said, closing the gap between them. "You were hiding. From who?" He blanched as a thought occurred to him. "From me?"

"No." She was quick to shake her head, reaching out to touch his arm in reassurance. The contact had been a mistake, and she jerked her hand back. "I just wasn't sure who was at the door. That's all."

"Right, an odd knock at the door always sends you scrambling for cover." He took her by the shoulders, his eyes dark with emotion. "Not to repeat myself, but what the hell is going on?"

"Someone was trying to kill us. Earlier at the house."

"That's what I tried to tell Mike Iago." She could see the wheels turning in his head as he assimilated the information. "I saw signs, but then he couldn't find any casings or blood or proof that someone had been there."

"Sanitized." She spoke more to herself than anyone.

"What are you talking about?" He broke contact, stepping back to study her as if he'd never seen her before tonight. Which in an odd sort of way was completely true.

"The killer obviously cleaned the place. He must have gone back after I lost him. Removed trace. It wouldn't be perfect, but it would be enough to stall the police. He had to have known he'd shot Martin." The words came out as an afterthought, and she immediately regretted her insensitivity. She hadn't meant to break it to him like that.

"Where's my brother?" He moved to shove past her, his eyes flashing fire. "Is he all right?"

"He's fine. " She held up her hands, as if physically trying to stop him. "The bullet didn't do any major damage. I removed it and cleaned the wound. He's asleep in the bedroom. I was about to call you." She nodded toward the cell phone on the table.

"Why didn't you take him to a hospital?" Reece looked as if he'd fallen down the rabbit hole.

"I thought it would be better if I handled it."

"Better for whom?" There was an edge now, a tone she recognized as suspicion. Her ex wasn't a fool.

"At the moment, all of us." She kept her voice low, not wanting to wake Martin. Dealing with one Sheridan at a time was about all she could handle right now.

"What the hell does that mean?" His explosion was contained to a whisper, but he might as well have screamed the words.

"It means she knows what she's doing." Martin leaned against the doorjamb connecting the living room with the bedroom. He was still pale, but he seemed steady on his feet. "You've never been able to see that."

Simone marveled at Martin's insight. The eyes of the innocent, or some such nonsense.

Reece had always been a ride-to-the-rescue kind of man, never stopping to consider that maybe the rescuees could have handled things just fine on their own—given the chance. She'd loved the trait in the beginning. It had made her feel safe. And God alone knew she'd needed that. But later, it had only proved to be suffocating. And with the pattern of their lives already in motion, she hadn't known how to break free.

But she was chasing water down a drain. It was too late to fix the past. Better instead to concentrate on the here and now.

"I hardly think we're talking about the same thing." Reece frowned, the action giving his expression a sardonic twist. "Someone shot you, for God's sake. How is anyone supposed to deal with that?"

"Simone saved my life," Martin said, glancing down at his bandaged shoulder, suppressing a shudder. "It's as simple as that. If she hadn't been there, I'd be dead."

If she hadn't been there, none of this would have happened. But there was no way to turn back the clock.

"Maybe so. But my guess is the gunman wouldn't have been there at all if not for Simone. Which sort of evens the score." His expression was hard, almost condemning. "So what the hell have you gotten us involved with?"

"I'm not sure. There hasn't exactly been a lot of down time for me to think about it." She walked over to Martin and lent him her shoulder, helping him to the sofa so that he could sit down. "I've been kind of busy dodging bullets."

"So you don't have any idea where this is coming from?" His laugh was harsh. "Kind of like the fact that you don't know where exactly you were born?"

"Oh, I know where I was born. It just wasn't Ohio. And if you'd bothered to ask me outright, instead of delving into my past without my permission, maybe I'd have told you the truth."

"Like hell." It was a whisper, but she heard it anyway. God, they always seemed to fight the same battles.

"Look. I don't know who it was." The list of possibilities was pretty damn long. "But I do know it was a pro."

Reece's eyes narrowed. "And you know that because..."

"Trajectory. Weapon choice. His method of approach. The guy knew what he was doing." And what he was hunting.

"Apparently so do you." Reece sank down onto a chair.

"I've had some experience." She paused, tightening her hand on the edge of the breakfast bar. "A long time ago."

"So, what, you're wanted for robbery? Drug trafficking? Murder?" Reece wasn't a prosecutor for nothing.

She flinched but tried to keep her face impassive. "How about all of them? Might as well go for the gusto."

It was his turn to blanch. "I don't know what to believe."

"Hey, it fits the scenario. No police, no hospitals." She opened her hands and shrugged. "Look, I told you I was about to call you. That's the best I have to offer."

"And if I want to call the authorities?" He was baiting her. And doing a damn good job of it.

"I'd have to ask you not to." The words were low,

almost a whisper, but Reece heard her, the muscles in his jaw tightening in response.

"Then I'd say you owe me an explanation."

"I probably do." She leaned back against the breakfast bar, the butt of her gun digging into her back. The feeling familiar and yet foreign.

"But you're not going to give me one." His face tightened with anger.

She opened her mouth, then closed it again. There really wasn't anything to say.

"Just like always. You're shutting me out."

His words hurt, but she swallowed the pain. She'd made her choices long ago, accepted the risk, the danger. But Martin and Reece were only involved by association, and the quicker she ended that the better. Let him think what he wanted.

She steeled herself. "I'm doing what's best for all of us. It's as simple as that." She reached for the cell, and then her shoulder bag, dropping the phone inside. "I'm going to leave now. And you're going to take Martin home."

"And how am I supposed to explain your disappearance? I told you, I've already talked to the police."

"You tell them whatever you have to. That I've run off with the gardener." She checked her words at his wince. "Look, just do whatever it takes to distance yourself from me. You'll think of something."

"But when will we see you again?" Martin's face was full of confusion now. Vicodin and adrenaline wearing off at the same time.

"You won't." Just saying the words ripped at her heart. They'd been her whole world—Reece and Martin. But nothing lasted forever.

She squared her shoulders and lifted her chin, her gaze locking with Reece's. "I want you to stay here tonight, and then go back to Corpus. Tell the police that I signed the divorce papers and walked out. That Martin took the boat, and you found him here in Port A. Keep it simple. You know the drill."

"I'm not going to let you walk out that door." He took a step toward her, and she reached for her gun. His surprise was almost comical, except that her heart was being torn to shreds.

"You can't stop me."

"Simone…"

Tears pressed against the back of her eyelids but she held them off, wanting only to get the hell out of there before she lost her nerve.

"Move, Reece. This is for the best. Believe me."

There was a moment of indecision, and then he stepped aside, his face a mirror of her pain. She pulled open the door, the fog-drenched night enveloping her as she stepped onto the porch. Her instinct was to turn around. To go back inside where it was safe and she was loved.

But the idea was a fallacy.

Just like her life with Reece.

The screen slammed behind her as she sprinted up the driveway, the finality of the sound underscoring her decision.

It was past time to go.

"YOU LET HER GO?" Martin stared at the doorway, as if waiting for her to come back.

"She had a gun. What the hell was I supposed to do?" Reece glared at his brother, still trying to make sense of the situation.

"I don't know." He shook his head, his bewilderment giving way to dismay. "I just can't believe she left."

"Well, she did. And we'd best get used to it." Reece wasn't sure who he was talking to, his brother or himself.

"You didn't really believe what you said…about her being a murderer?" In that moment, Martin looked a hell of a lot younger than his twenty-two years, and Reece was reminded of the somber boy he'd come home to after his parents' car wreck.

Martin had taken the news of their deaths with a stoicism that had belied his tender age. And it had been almost a year before Reece had seen his brother smile again. Theirs had been that rare kind of family where everything worked, their mother and father more in love on the day they died than on the day they'd met. And the boys had simply basked in the glow.

It had been a *Happy Days* existence that had allowed Reece a carefree independence. But the accident had taken his center—his rudder—and until he'd met Simone, he'd thought that perhaps he'd never feel whole again.

"No, Martin. I don't believe Simone is a murderer." At least he didn't think so. God, none of this made any sense.

Reece walked over to the window, moving the blind aside, almost expecting to see her on the porch. They'd fought so often in the past few months of their marriage that the movements had become routine. They'd argue, yell, throw insults, until Simone couldn't stand any more. Then she'd slam out the door, damning him to hell. Only she never went anywhere. She'd just sit on the front porch and wait for him to come and find her.

But this time she hadn't waited.

"Do you see her?" Martin asked, pulling Reece from his memories.

"No." He let the blind fall and turned back to face his brother. Sometimes the end came with a bang. Sometimes with a whimper. He'd never understood that poem before, but suddenly, heartbreakingly, he did.

"So what do we do?"

"We do what she said. We wait here until tomorrow. And then we go home."

"And make up a sto—" Martin's words were drowned out by the sound of shattering glass.

"Get down." Reece dove for his brother, the two of them skidding across the floor as a second volley shattered more glass.

Reece rolled to a crouch and grabbed a poker as the door crashed open.

"Don't think that's going to do a hell of a lot of good." Simone motioned them toward the door with the gun in her hand. "Better to fight fire with fire, eh?" Her smile was weak, but just at the moment he'd never been happier to see anyone. "Come on. I'll cover you guys while you make a run for the car."

"I'm not leaving you."

"Believe me, I'll be right behind you."

He searched her face to be certain she was telling the truth and then nodded, his gaze falling on his brother. "Can you make it?"

"I think so," Martin said.

"We've got to go now, before he has time to reposition himself." Simone motioned.

As if to underscore the thought, a third volley of

bullets ricocheted through the room, the trajectory the same as before.

Simone crawled to the window, crouching just beneath the sill. "On my go," she said, as they moved into place near the door.

"You're coming." It was a statement, not a question, but Reece looked to her for confirmation.

"I promise. Now go."

He nodded and, looping an arm around his brother for support, headed out the door. Behind him he heard shots, and knew that Simone had engaged their hunter.

It seemed to take forever to reach the Jag, but in fact it had only taken seconds. He fumbled with the key and then slid it home, Martin settled into the back. Without flipping on the lights, he hit the gas, traversing the gravel drive until the passenger side faced the front door.

A flash of gunfire erupted from the palm trees to the left of the house. Their stalker had obviously heard the engine and shifted position. Simone appeared at the door, firing into the trees. The assailant answered with his own volley, effectively pinning her in the house.

Cursing under his breath, Reece gunned the car, gravel spitting beneath the wheels as he spun the car up onto the porch, the Jag acting as a momentary barrier. The rear left window blew out with a hail of glass as Simone threw herself into the car. Reece pressed the pedal to the floor, and the big car lunged off the porch and up the drive, plumes of dust following in its wake.

"You okay?" He risked a quick look at his ex.

"I'm fine." Simone rolled down the window and stuck her head out to see if the shooter was following. "I can't see a damn thing in this fog." As if in answer to her frustration, they heard the sound of an engine pushing its limits as headlights appeared behind them in the mirror.

"Looks like we've got company," Martin said, his voice tight with pain.

Reece glanced again in the rearview mirror, this time at his brother. Fresh blood stained his shirt. "You're bleeding again."

Simone pivoted around so that she could see Martin. "When did it start?"

"When we ran for the car. I think maybe I tore the stitches." He shrugged. "There's really not a lot we can do about it now."

"You can get down." Simone's tone was surprisingly gentle. "And keep pressure on it. All right?"

Martin nodded as the lights behind them grew brighter.

"He's gaining on us." Simone's eyes were back on the car behind them.

Reece agreed but hesitated to push the needle higher. There was no doubt the Jag was capable of more speed, but the fog made it hard to maneuver.

"You don't have a choice." As usual, Simone had read his mind.

He pressed the Jag forward.

Except for the glow of the headlights behind them, the highway was quiet, the island completely blanketed by the mist. The moisture invaded the car with salty fingers, the oppressive feel of it giving added urgency to their flight.

The car lights behind them stayed steady, neither gaining nor losing ground. For the moment at least they were safe. But Reece wasn't certain how long he could hold the advantage. A light rain had begun to fall, the asphalt slick with it, traction receding with every passing minute.

And time was running out. Mustang Island ended with the causeway, the well-lit bridge both a blessing and a curse. While it would be easier to drive, the added light would also illuminate the Jag, making them more easily targeted.

"We could try the beach," Martin said, his voice weak from exertion.

"Too wet," Reece responded. "We'd just bog down in the sand. I think the causeway is our best bet."

"There's bound to be more traffic," Simone agreed. "And if we're lucky that'll hold him off and give us time to figure out our next move."

The lights behind them suddenly grew larger as their hunter, obviously following the same line of thought, made a play to reach them. The fog parted for a second, the black Lexus behind them momentarily visible.

Reece pushed the pedal to the floor, giving the Jag its head, the car responding by surging forward into the night.

A green highway sign flashed by, indicating that the causeway was coming. Ahead of them they could see the line of light streaking out into the bay as it headed across the water to the mainland.

"Maybe I can throw him off." Reece gunned the car again, the rear end fishtailing a little as it picked up even more speed. "I won't get off until the last possible moment."

Simone turned to look behind her. "He's closing in again."

A sharp crack echoed through the car as something hit the back window, a spiderweb appearing in the left-hand corner where the bullet had hit.

"Everyone okay?" Simone's voice was filled with worry as she turned to check on Martin.

"All in one piece. Although I can't say as much for the Jag." Martin motioned to the windshield behind him, as usual using humor to hide his fear.

The car lights had moved back again, as if waiting to see what their next move would be. Another green sign flashed by out of the mist, this time overhead. "The exit's just up ahead. I'll wait until the very last minute and then veer right. With a little luck, it'll be too late for the shooter to follow."

Simone nodded her approval, then hung out the window, taking a shot at the car behind them. The lights receded a little in response.

"At least he knows we're still armed," Simone said as she settled back into the seat.

The causeway exit loomed to the right, and Reece pushed the accelerator as he kept the wheel straight, for all intents and purposes appearing to be passing the exit.

"Brace yourselves," he said, shooting a sideways glance at Simone, "this isn't going to be pretty."

Yanking the wheel hard to the right, he felt the Jag skid across the wet pavement. For a moment he thought he'd lost control, but the tires found purchase and the car swerved onto the exit ramp, then straightened to merge onto the causeway.

There was a moment of blessed black behind them in the rearview mirror and then the flash of headlights as the Lexus hit the pavement of the causeway, sparks flying behind it.

"Damn it," Reece mumbled under his breath, but Simone reached over to touch his knee.

"You're doing great."

"Son of a bitch just keeps coming."

The lights along the edge of the causeway caused an eerie reflection in the water on either side of them. Traffic was a little heavier here. Although most of it was coming from the other direction.

The Lexus closed the distance a bit, but not enough to put it within shooting range. All Reece had to do was keep up the pace and he'd make the mainland with them all in one piece. Then they'd be able to lose their stalker. He knew the back roads like the back of his hand, having traveled them most of his life. Surely an advantage over whoever the hell was behind them.

"He's getting closer." Martin had popped up again and was turned to look out the back window.

"Get down," Reece barked, shooting a quick look at his brother over his shoulder.

"Reece, watch out," Simone's tone was sharp as he turned back to focus on the road.

A tractor-trailer rig loomed out of the mist, seemingly heading right for them. A trick of the light, and despite his instinct to slow down and veer away, Reece forced himself to hold his course. The truck whizzed past them, spraying rain from the puddles on the road as it moved by.

For an instant Reece's view was obscured by the cascading water, and the car hydroplaned in the backwash. He fought for control, but the car skidded to the right, fishtailing back and forth as he struggled for traction.

One minute he could feel the tires spinning against the pavement, and then there was nothing—a moment of complete and utter stillness followed by the impact of the Jag smashing into the storm-tossed waves of the bay.

CHAPTER SEVEN

ICY WATER RUSHED through the open window as the car crested on a wave and then began to sink. "Everyone okay?" Simone yelled as she fumbled with the wet buckle of her seat belt. The car was going down fast, whatever buoyancy remaining countered by the open and shattered windows.

Martin groaned from the back, and Simone twisted so that she could see him. The car had slammed through a restraining barrier before hitting the water, the brunt of the impact on the back right quadrant of the car. As a result, Martin's door was jammed inward, pinning his right shoulder and arm to the seat.

"Martin?" This from Reece, whose face was covered with blood. Fortunately, he seemed to be moving all right, and had managed to free himself from his seat belt. "Can you hear me?"

Martin groaned again in response, his eyes fluttering open and then closed once more.

"He's in shock." Simone yanked herself free of the belt. The water was already at chin level and rising fast. They only had a few more minutes. "We've got to get him out of here."

"Martin, wake up." Reece's voice held a note of

command, and Martin opened his eyes. "I need you to stay conscious, bro. And when I tell you, I want you to hold your breath. All right?"

Martin nodded, but his eyes weren't focused.

"Martin," Reece barked again, starting to climb over the headrest. Martin blew out a breath and then sucked in another. He was with them.

"Let me do it," Simone said, already moving between the seats. "You go through the window and see if you can kick out the back panel. It'll be easier to get him out that way."

Reece opened his mouth to argue, but Simone shook her head. "There's no room for us both back there. And you're stronger. It's our best chance." Their eyes met for a moment, and then he pushed past her over the headrest and through the shattered passenger window.

Simone followed, gulping air before ducking beneath the surface of the frigid water to free Martin from restraint. The buckle yielded on her first try, but Martin was still pinned.

Surfacing for air, Simone met Martin's eyes, his expression surprisingly calm. "Breathe," she whispered, and then ducked under the water again. Working from bottom to top, she felt along the line where the door had buckled against Martin. From waist to underarm the door had only clamped onto his shirt. At the shoulder however, the metal pushed against muscle, pinning him to the seat.

She surfaced again, noting that there was only a fraction of air left available, the car now totally submerged. As she drew in another breath, she saw Reece outside the rear window, working to break the already splintered glass.

If they could wait until the pressure inside had equalized with that outside, they'd be able to open the door. But in all honesty she wasn't certain Martin could hold on that long. He'd tipped back his head, his nose protruding into the last bit of open space. It wouldn't last much longer. But at least she had another minute or so.

Working off of pure adrenaline, she grabbed a last breath, knowing there wouldn't be another until they were out of the car, then ripped the T-shirt from neckline to shoulder. Free of the shirt, Martin was now held only at the shoulder.

With her pulse beating out a frantic rhythm, she worked to free him. She simply wasn't strong enough to move the door. So she pushed on the seat instead, relieved when the leather moved inward, compressing its padding. If she could give it enough force, she might be able to create enough space between the leather and the door for Martin to slide free.

Bracing her feet against the front seat, she pushed backward with all her strength, the leather indenting, but not enough to free Martin. Her air was running out. And when hers was gone, so was Martin's, the only difference being that she could head for the surface.

Martin could not.

Fighting against a thread of panic, she pushed harder, but the upholstery held firm. She just didn't have the necessary force. Her lungs tightened to bursting point, instinct demanding that she take a breath. She fought the urge as she scrambled to try and figure out an alternative to moving the seat.

Suddenly beneath her fingers the leather moved. Reece appeared through the murky gloom on the other side of

Martin, adding his weight to her attempt. At first the leather refused to compress any further, but then, as if finally giving in, it mashed inward, and Reece jerked his brother free.

Swimming through the cleared rear window, he turned to grab Martin, and together they slid him through the window. Certain that she was going to explode, Simone focused on Reece and Martin, swimming through the window and following them as they headed for the surface.

In seconds, she'd broken through the surf and was bobbing in the waves, gulping blessed oxygen. A couple of yards away, Reece treaded water, still holding Martin, both of them swallowing air as if it were liquid chocolate.

As soon as her head cleared, Simone searched the bridge for signs of the shooter, but was met instead by the bright lights of a couple of cars. The fact that there was more than one seemed to indicate that the shooter had fled, but there was no way to know for certain.

Better to swim the other way.

Glancing over her shoulder, she spied a spit of land that had served as an older road. If memory was correct, it would take them back to the mainland but keep them out of sight. She swam over to Reece and after motioning silence, pointed to the old road bed.

He glanced at the bridge, then nodded his understanding. Martin was conscious but not capable of swimming on his own. Simone offered to take him, but Reece shook his head, already striking out away from the bridge.

Simone paused for a moment, still treading water, and glanced first at the darkened shore of the island and then toward the bridge. She'd won this round. Managed to evade the killer, twice in fact.

Of course, the third time was the charm.

The question being—for whom?

THE ENTERPRISE RENTAL office in Flour Bluff was thankfully both warm and open. They'd met no one on their trek along the old road, and wet people in a seaside city hardly raised eyebrows. Even when one of them was injured.

A quick stop at the Wal-Mart, and from there a gas-station bathroom, and even those problems were solved, Martin freshly bandaged and everyone kitted out in dry clothing. Simone had even managed to restitch the wound. If the situation hadn't been so ludicrous, Reece would probably have admired his ex-wife's handling of the situation.

The fact that his new Jag was currently sitting at the bottom of the bay notwithstanding, everything seemed to be going fine. There'd been no sign of the shooter. And thanks to Simone's fake credentials, no need to deal with reality.

It was as if he'd fallen into one of the suspense novels he loved to read. Normality giving way to the frighteningly absurd as the plot progressed. All they had to do now was retrieve their rental car and ride off into the sunset.

Obviously shock was taking its toll.

Martin, despite his close brush with death, seemed to be all right. Fresh air had done wonders for his color, and thanks to Simone, his wound was again on the mend.

Simone stood at the car-rental desk, talking with the uniformed clerk, her hands waving to underscore her words. Some things never changed. The walk along the old road had been a quiet one, most of the conversation centering on Martin's welfare and checking to be certain they weren't followed.

How easily he'd allowed himself to be sucked into her world.

By necessity, his inner voice argued, but he knew it was more than that.

He still hadn't a clue what this was all about. But he was sure of one thing. No matter what the hell kind of trouble she was in, whatever she'd done, or been involved with, it was clear she'd had training of some kind.

There was a stillness about her that he had only seen in soldiers. And not just regular army. The elite units. Marines, Delta Force, Rangers.

Fresh out of college, the military had seemed an obvious choice given Reece's predilection for adrenaline rushes. And after he'd failed to qualify as a pilot, he'd needed to prove himself. To find something bigger and better. So he'd become a Ranger.

And somewhere along the way, he'd developed a knack for ferreting out information with the tenacity of a tunnel rat. His expertise with intel had shot him from the frying pan into the fire, coordinating a series of top-secret assignments during Desert Storm. As a part of those missions, he'd worked closely with some of the cagiest men alive. Men who lived so deeply inside themselves that they were almost shadows.

Simone had that stillness now. The deep focus that meant she was always alert, always on guard. In point of fact, she'd always had it—when she'd insisted on using cash, or obsessed about working out, or when she'd successfully eluded his more pointed efforts to get her to open up. He simply hadn't recognized the trait out of context. He'd written it off as charming eccentricity.

Whatever she was involved in, it was serious shit.

There was no doubt in his mind.

Military training didn't preclude any of the things he'd accused her of. But at least until he'd given her another chance to explain, he wasn't going to turn her in.

The pertinent question, of course, being whether or not she'd open up enough to tell him.

Probably not.

At least willingly.

He smiled, the gesture tight, mocking. He was barking at the moon if he thought he'd get anything out of her. He had tried forcing his way in once before, the result being divorce. Whatever the hell was going on, she was determined to handle it on her own.

If Martin hadn't been caught in the middle of things, Reece had no doubt Simone would be long gone by now. The keys and phone on the table at home had been testament to the fact. But she hadn't abandoned either of them. And it would have been easy enough to do so on more than one occasion. Hell, she'd probably saved Martin's life—twice.

"Do you think he'll ask what happened?" Martin asked. He was sipping a cup of tepid coffee they'd bought at the gas station. It was amazing what waterlogged money would buy.

"No. As long as she has money, they don't give a damn."

Martin nodded, concentrating on his coffee.

"We're all set." Simone walked over to them, keys in hand.

"What did you tell him?" He asked as they headed out the door.

"That we'd had a breakdown. He offered to get someone

to tow the car, but I said we'd already called the auto club." She shrugged, exhaustion only serving to ratchet the tension stretching between them. "It seemed the easiest way to deal with things. I'm sorry about your car."

Reece almost laughed. "The car is the last thing on my mind right now."

"Well, sooner or later someone is going to find it. So you'd better have answers ready."

"The implication being that I should avoid the truth."

"Damn it, Reece, I'm too tired to argue. Tell them any damn thing you want." She stopped in front of a blue Ford and unlocked the door.

"Just keep *you* out of it." He met her eyes across the top of the car.

"Obviously it would be better if you did."

So they were back where they started. Full circle. Stop.

"So what next?" Martin asked, eyeing them both as if they were contaminated explosives. Probably not far from the truth.

"We hole up for the night." Reece looked to Simone, waiting for her to protest. To try and walk out again. "We need to put a little distance between us and what happened out there." He tilted his head toward the pounding surf outside the Enterprise office.

"Fine." Her agreement came surprisingly easily. "But I think we need to get out of the area."

Reece nodded, opening the door for Martin. "Maybe San Antonio?"

"Too far and too high profile. We need somewhere big enough to get lost in but small enough to seem improbable." Again he was aware of the fact that she'd clearly been in this position before, and was trained to deal with it.

"So maybe Victoria?" The little town was halfway between Corpus and San Antonio, well off the beaten track.

"There's a Holiday Inn Express there," Martin volunteered, sliding into the back seat.

"It might work." Simone said, her expression hard to read. "It's far enough away to be certain that we're not being followed, and close enough to be overlooked."

"So we head for Victoria." Reece slid into the front passenger seat. He'd had enough driving for one day.

Simone put the key into the ignition. "Thanks for not forcing me to go to the police."

"Didn't see that it would help anything." He shrugged. "At least not right now. The best thing we can do is get Martin somewhere safe and warm. Then maybe you can explain what the hell is going on."

She nodded, but her face hardened, and Reece wondered if he'd ever really known her at all. They sat for a moment, the silence stretching between them.

"You think he's still out there?" Martin asked, staring out the window at the cars driving down the interstate.

"Yeah." She didn't pretend to misunderstand, just answered the question, backing the car out of the parking lot. "And he'll be back. He'll stick with it until he gets what he wants."

"And what would that be, Simone?" Reece waited a beat, not certain that she'd answer.

"Me." Her lip curled at the corner, a cynic's smile. "He wants me."

CHAPTER EIGHT

"YOU GOT MY BROTHER SHOT, you drew a gun on me, and you sank my Jag. I think at the very least you owe me some kind of explanation," Reece demanded, using his best prosecutor's voice. There were times she loathed that voice. And this was one of them.

They were holed up in two adjoining rooms at the Holiday Inn. Martin was spread out on one of the beds, and Reece was pacing in front of the heavily draped window. Simone had made certain they had rooms facing the front of the hotel on the fourth floor, but despite those precautions, she'd still drawn the drapery.

No one had followed them here. She'd ensured that, using side roads and evasive tactics the entire journey. But one could never be too cautious. And until she had them safely out of this, she was determined to watch Reece and Martin's backs.

"I didn't exactly sink the Jag. That one's really on you."

He stopped pacing to glare at her, his anger palpable. So much for taunting the lion.

"I'm sorry. That wasn't funny."

"No, it wasn't." He started moving again, back and forth in front of the drapes. She'd learned a long time ago that it helped him to process information, but she still found the habit unsettling. "And it's not going to stop me from asking again for some semblance of truth. We are caught in the middle of a nightmare here. And I want to know why."

"I don't know for certain." The possibilities were unfortunately endless. And until she talked to Maurice, there was no way of figuring out who was pulling the strings.

"But you said the killer wanted you." Reece stopped and turned to face her, his stillness almost more alarming than his agitation. "If you know that, then you must have an idea who it is that's doing the hunting. Or at least who is behind it."

"I wish it were that simple." Simone sighed and sat down on the end of the other bed, trying to find the easiest way to explain things. "But it's not. The truth is there are any number of people who could be after me. And most I probably wouldn't know if I ran into them on the street."

"And why is that?" It was a deceptively simple question.

But Simone chose to misunderstand. Putting off the moment when she had to reveal the part of herself she'd hoped was dead and buried. "Why wouldn't I know them?"

"No. Why is there a long list?" Reece still stood in front of the window, so still she could see him breathing. For a moment it was just the two of them and the secret that had torn them apart.

But Martin was there. And the shades of her past. In all its horrible incarnations. The secret she had to share was far less intense than the ones that had preceded it. Yet she still couldn't seem to find the words. She blew out a breath. "Because I used to work for the CIA. Division 9."

"I've never heard of it."

"The CIA?" Martin asked from his spot on the bed, incredulity coloring his voice.

"Obviously I've heard of the CIA." Reece leaned back against the table under the window, his relaxed stance in no way lessening the tension permeating the room. "Just not Division 9."

"You wouldn't have heard of it. It's an off-the-record black ops group used to do the CIA's dirty work."

"What kind of dirty work?" Martin asked, his youthful exuberance making her wish she could lie. But the time for that was past.

"Arms deals, extractions, assassinations—anything they needed done that they didn't want the U.S. getting credit for. We were so far undercover most of the agency didn't even know we existed."

"*Existed?*" Reece asked, his expression still inscrutable.

"Yeah. Things went south about ten years ago and we were put on ice, and then relocated."

"To Corpus." He said it like it was a curse. But then considering everything that had happened, maybe it was.

"Actually, they put me in Houston." She offered a weak smile. "But I hated it. I wanted somewhere smaller, I guess. Somewhere I could find peace. The first time I saw the bay, I knew I was home."

Reece opened his mouth to argue, but shut it again, his face tight with emotion. "Why didn't you tell me?"

"I couldn't. We were instructed to keep it all secret. To pretend it never existed. Any mention of CIA involvement was out of the question. They made it clear that there would be repercussions if any of it ever leaked out."

"And so you pretended to be someone you weren't."

His words were harsh, but understandable under the circumstances.

"It's not like she had a choice," Martin interjected. He was trying to protect her, and while she appreciated the loyalty, she could also understand Reece's anger.

"Just because I couldn't share my past, that doesn't mean I wasn't honest about other things. A relationship is based on a hell of a lot more than where a person was born or what things they have or haven't done with their life. So yes, I lied to you. About things that didn't matter anyway. The stuff that did matter, like who I really am, and what I want from life—the things that really define a person—those things I never lied about." She'd said more than she meant to. But then, Reece knew how to push her buttons.

"But the things you did tell me—they were all fictional, right?"

"You already know the answer to that." Her lie about her past had cost her her marriage. Which was ironic, because she'd only told it to please Reece. To give substance to the part of him that wanted her to be the girl next door. His parents had been the perfect couple, with him and Martin coming along to create the perfect family.

When his parents died, Reece had filled the void, raising Martin and making a new life for the both of them. By the time she'd come along, the two of them were a package deal. And in many ways Reece had seen her as the icing on the cake. A way to replicate the family he'd lost.

And she'd played to the fantasy. Surprised when he never called her on it. It was only when she'd pushed it too far and forced a confrontation that he'd demanded the truth. But she couldn't tell him. It was as simple as that.

From there, the gulf between them had just kept growing. And she'd watched helplessly as the foundation they'd built crumbled around her like a house of sand. But then the whole thing had been fantasy anyway. Believing, even for a minute, that it had been something genuine and enduring—now there was the real lie.

They stared at each other, Reece's anger at her betrayal arcing between them like a living thing. She'd reached for her own happiness and in the process destroyed his. There was nothing left to say.

"So what happened?" Martin interrupted, forcing them both to break with the past and face the present. "Why did they shut down Division 9?"

Simone tipped back her head, rubbing the back of her neck, her agitated pulse beating against her fingers. "We were betrayed." She started to stop there, to edit the story, and then abandoned the idea. What difference did it make now? "We were in Nicaragua. On a mission to extract a local. He was working with us as an informant, providing crucial information about the drug cartels in the area. He was well connected and the information was invaluable. But he was also an insurgent. Head of a junta opposed to the government of the day. They were planning a coup. But the government got wind of the fact, and sent troops to dissuade them. Our mission was to get our man out before the troops arrived.

"We were already in the country, so it wasn't difficult to access the village. Unfortunately, someone who knew the plan leaked the information."

"Someone on the team?" Reece asked, clearly interested despite himself.

"No way. We'd worked together for years. None of us

would ever have put the others at risk. I think it must have been someone attached to Ramirez."

"The guy you were supposed to rescue?" Martin asked, sitting cross-legged on the bed now.

"Not Hector Ramirez?" Reece's eyes narrowed. "You were in Sangre de Cristo?"

"Yes." Simone's gaze met Reece's as understanding dawned.

"There were rumors of CIA involvement."

"What the hell are you talking about?" Martin interrupted impatiently. "San what?"

"Sangre de Cristo." Reece said. "There was a massacre there ten years ago. An entire village slaughtered when government troops opened fire on what they believed was a revolutionary stronghold. Women and children were killed right along with the men. And afterward, there was never any real proof that there were dissidents in the village. And there was strong rumor among the international community that the CIA was behind it all." His hooded gaze met hers, his lawyer's face again neutral.

Martin let out a long, low whistle. "And you were there?"

"In Sangre de Cristo, yes. But we weren't behind any of what happened. We were only there to retrieve Ramirez."

"But you failed. Ramirez was killed along with the rest of them, wasn't he?"

"Yes. By the time I found him, he was dead. And we were surrounded. Cut off from escape. And since officially we didn't exist, there was no help coming."

"So what did you do?" Martin asked.

"We fought our way out." Simone shrugged, a futile

effort to try and shut out the memories, the cries of the wounded and dying echoing through her head as if she'd heard them only yesterday. "People were dying everywhere. I remember a kid standing by a fountain in a plaza, crying. I grabbed her just before a mortar blew the fountain to bits.

"There were eight of us working the operation. Six at the drop zone. Two in the jungle to facilitate retrieval. When we got to the city we split into two groups of three. Code-named 'blue' and 'red'. It made it easier to blend in with the locals. Once it all went south, we worked toward the rendezvous. Blue team never made it. They were slaughtered along with everyone else."

"The engineers from Altech."

"You know a lot about Sangre de Cristo."

"It was an international incident." It was Reece's turn to shrug. "And I've always had an interest in human-rights law." It seemed she wasn't the only one who hadn't exercised full disclosure. But she shouldn't have been surprised. Reece had always been about doing what was right. Good versus evil and all that. Everything in black-and-white. It was part of why she'd fallen in love with him.

Too bad the world was all about shades of gray.

"But you made it." Martin urged her back to the story.

"Yeah. We did. Almost lost Bea along the way, but eventually we got out. It took about a month to work our way out of the mountains, and another month after that to make it back to the States."

"And then you were disbanded."

"Quarantined at first, actually. Tempers were running pretty hot, and the CIA was under pretty heavy scrutiny. As I said, we were responsible for handling the Company's dirty work. And after Sangre de Cristo, no one wanted our endeavors coming to light. After things died down, they relocated us."

"And now someone from your past is back." Reece had crossed his arms over his chest, looking every bit the inquisitioner.

"Yes." Simone reached into the inside pocket of her purse and produced the postcard. "When we were relocated, we were given a password—a set of coordinates actually, to initiate a locator program—and the instructions that if anything happened to threaten the sanctity of D-9, we'd be sent a warning. A call to bring us all together again. I got this in the mail today." She handed the postcard to Reece, and Martin got off the bed to stand behind his brother.

"'The storm is coming'?"

"That was the message we were told to expect. The *M* is for Maurice Baxter. He was our handler. The official unofficial head of D-9. He's the only one left who even knows we existed."

"Have you seen him?"

"No. Not since we were relocated. I haven't seen any of the team. The powers that be thought it better if we were separated permanently."

"Weren't you tempted to try and find them?" Martin asked, tipping his head to one side, observing her as if she were a specimen in a lab.

"I'll admit sometimes I think about how nice it would be to talk to someone who understands my past. A kindred spirit, so to speak. But no, I've never tried to find anyone. Nor has anyone contacted me. It was made pretty clear that if we did try, there'd be serious consequences."

"So this message, what exactly does it mean?" Reece waved the card as he spoke.

"'The storm is coming' means that D-9 has been compromised. Conceivably by an enemy. 'Take cover' is code indicating we're to head for the rendezvous."

"And the rendezvous would be the coordinates you spoke of?" Reece as usual had cut to the heart of the matter.

"Yes. The first coordinates will lead to the second and so on until a precise latitude and longitude emerges as the final meeting place."

"But for all you know the rendezvous has been compromised as well. I mean, clearly someone has found you."

"They haven't found it. The beginning of the message is 'trip is fine.' That's meant to signal that the rendezvous is safe. We had alternate messages to cover other possibilities."

"It's just like James Bond." Martin's enthusiasm would have been humorous, except that this wasn't the movies and the game was deadly.

"In the movies the good guys live," Reece said. "I'm not thinking that's the plan here." Even though he was talking to his brother his gaze never left Simone's.

"Apparently not. Anyway, I was about to leave for the rendezvous when the shooter found me. And now, more or less, you know as much as I do."

"There's nothing here to give you any idea where the threat is coming from?" Reece frowned, studying the postcard again.

"No. But there wouldn't be. There was a huge risk in just saying as much as Maurice did. There are still a lot of bureaucrats and politicians who'd like to hang D-9 out to dry, along with any of its supporters. The U.S. took a lot of heat over Sangre de Cristo. And D-9 unveiled would make a perfect scapegoat. That's why we were disbanded in the first place."

"So just the fact that Baxter risked sending this means there's real danger." Reece was back to leaning against the table.

"Yes," Simone said. "That's why I cleared out as soon as I got it. Or I would have if Martin hadn't been shot."

"Sorry." He cringed, looking suddenly more like a kid than a man.

"You've got nothing to be sorry for." Reece's anger laced his words, making them sound more sharp than intended.

"It's my fault, Martin." Simone wished she could turn back the clock and change things. If she'd never met Reece. Never allowed him past her defenses, then neither of them would be sitting here right now.

"You couldn't have known the guy was coming. It's been over ten years, right?" There was something deeply moving about Martin's faith in her. It was one thing to put lip service to the idea of their being family and quite another to sec that it was in fact the truth.

She nodded, struggling for words. "I don't even know who *he* is. But I need to get to the rendezvous to find out. Which means first thing in the morning I've got to leave."

"What do you expect us to do?" Reese asked, his ferocity daring her to answer.

But she wasn't afraid, because there wasn't a choice. "Go home. Nothing has changed."

"So what? We're just supposed to pretend this never happened? Wipe you out of our lives? It's not that simple, Simone."

"Look, coming with me would just mean more danger. For both of you." She shot a significant look toward Martin, knowing Reece would never purposely place his brother in danger.

"I just need a little lead time." She hated the note of pleading in her voice, but anything else would only lead to more angry words.

"To disappear."

"To head for the rendezvous and figure out what the hell it is I'm facing. And yes, to disappear. At least as Simone Sheridan." She used Reece's name without even thinking. The link was the last thing she had that made her real. Without it she'd become a shadow again.

Reece clenched and unclenched his fist, the little muscle in his jaw working overtime. She held her breath, waiting for him to comment. To tell her how angry he was, to blame her for everything that happened. But he didn't say anything at all. Just turned on his heel and strode from the room, his broad back signaling the end of all of her dreams.

CHAPTER NINE

"YOU HAVEN'T SAID a word in almost an hour." Martin said over the voices of the ten-o'clock news team. "Even for you that's a record."

"I don't know what to say. Shit, I don't know what to think. Part of me wants to throttle her, and part of me wants to well, hell…throttle her. God, she makes me so damn angry."

"That's because you care."

"It's because she lied."

"Well then, come sunup we'll just ride away and forget all about this."

"Like hell we will."

"So we're staying?" Martin's expression held equal parts triumph and trepidation.

"I am." Reece was quick to throw a blanket on any ideas Martin might have about coming along. On that fact, he and Simone were in total agreement.

"What about me?"

"You're going home. Or at least somewhere out of the line of fire."

"What if she won't let you come, either?" Martin asked, wisely avoiding an argument about his own situation.

"It's not like she really has any choice. Either I can

go with her, or I'll just follow her." He hadn't realized he'd made up his mind until he heard himself say it out loud.

"She's CIA." The sentence spoke for itself, but Reece wasn't in the mood for common sense.

"And I used to be a Ranger."

"A million years ago." And he didn't even mean it as an insult.

"That doesn't mean I'm not up to the task. I'm not exactly an old geezer."

"I'm sorry, I didn't mean it like that. It just wasn't yesterday. But then Simone's been out of the game a while, too. And look at how well you did with the car chase."

"I drove my car into the ocean."

"Well, it wasn't like there weren't extenuating circumstances. Anyway, the point is you're not just some green-assed pansy lawyer."

"Thanks, I think. But maybe you're right. I'd only be a liability." The idea of helping her faded almost as quickly as it had come.

"No, that's not true. I should have just kept my mouth shut." Martin shook his head to emphasize his point. "You were right. It's really simple. Simone is in trouble and you should help her. She's your wife."

"We're divorced."

"Semantics." Martin waved his hand through the air. "Besides, I don't think she's signed the papers."

"No. I saw her signature. It's over. Believe me." He blew out a breath, his mind spinning. "Anyway, I hear what you're saying. But whether I go or not, you're not coming. That much I'm certain of."

"You are one stubborn dude." Martin cranked the

volume on the television, the talking head rambling on about a charity regatta on Saturday.

Reece tried to keep his attention on the screen and off the connecting door. What he really wanted to do was go in there and confront her. To try and make sense of everything she'd told him. To make decisions together.

But that ship had sailed. Hell, as of today, they weren't even married anymore.

Which under the circumstances ought to be a good thing, considering what she'd put them through, at least indirectly, in the past twenty-four hours. The fact was, the Simone he'd fallen in love with didn't exist. It ought to make him feel self-righteous. But instead it just made him ache. For what he'd lost. For what he'd thought he had.

Damn it all to hell, she might as well have just shot him. It would have been less painful than having his guts scraped out and dumped on the floor.

He closed his eyes, trying to shut it all out. Part of him wanted to walk out the door. But another part of him simply couldn't leave her on her own. Competent or otherwise, she needed someone to watch her back.

Rule number one in the military.

And despite all the hostility between them, he simply couldn't countenance the idea of it being anyone but him.

"Hey, Reece," Martin's voice interrupted his internal tirade, "get a load of this." His brother nodded toward the TV and Reece focused on the droning voice. "They're saying you may have had a hand in our disappearance."

"What?" Simone's picture flashed on the screen, followed by Martin's. And then the anchors were off to a story about food poisoning at a local Mexican joint.

"According to the report, the police are investigating

you in regard to our disappearance. Something about a lover's triangle." Martin was still frowning at the television.

Reece winced. "It can't be based on anything. I told you I had the police out to the house. They didn't find anything. And even if they had, why the hell would I have called them if I was guilty?"

He grabbed the remote and changed to another station, but they had already moved on to sports. Fox and CBS were the same. He flipped the TV off, sinking down on the bed. "So what are they claiming?"

"According to the report, they found blood and spent casings hidden in a trash can. The theory is you cleaned things up and then tried to cover it all with a call to the locals."

"That's insane."

"Well, considering no one has been abducted, I tend to agree." Martin held his hands up in defense. "What do you say you try not to kill me after the fact?"

"Did you see the news?" Simone pushed through the connecting door, eyes flashing. "That son of a bitch set us up."

"The bullets and blood?" Reece asked, running the facts back through his head.

"Yeah. You said the cops didn't find anything when you called them, right?"

"Right. In fact, they even went as far as to suggest that you'd run off with Martin."

"No shit?" Martin managed to sound proud and pissed all at the same time.

"I told them they had it wrong. That you'd never do something like that." He shot his brother a warning look, and smug was replaced by contrite.

"If you guys would holster the testosterone for a minute, we've got bigger problems than whether your brother has the cajones to take me on."

"But it's all bullshit," Martin said, frowning. "Everyone's fine."

"We know that. But taking the information to the cops is going to cause more than a few questions."

Reece ran his hand through his hair, feeling a hell of a lot like he'd fallen onto the White Queen's checkerboard. "So you're saying that clearing my name is going to put you in danger."

"I'm saying it's playing right into his hands."

"The killer."

She shrugged. "Someone put that stuff in the trash. And someone put your fingerprints on it."

"Fingerprints?" Reece frowned.

"According to the news report, the casings had your prints on them."

"So you were right, the shooter doubled back for the setup?"

"Either that or he was there when Mike Iago was spouting his nonsense about Martin and me and decided to put it to good use."

"But what's his angle? I'm not sure I see the value of framing me for something that I can prove I didn't do."

"Well, that remains to be seen, actually. If he'd succeeded in taking us out at the cottage, then you'd have taken the fall for him."

"But we got out alive..." Martin began.

"Yes, we did. And I was all set to go to ground. If this guy knows anything about me, he's more than aware that if I choose to stay lost, I can do it."

"But he's found you twice. So it makes sense he'd believe he could find you again."

"Not necessarily. I wasn't on the run in Corpus, didn't even know I was being hunted. And if he had any idea of our history, then eventually he was going to find the cottage. It was just the best I could do under extreme circumstances."

"So you're saying he's worried that if you go to ground now, he'll lose the trail." Reece studied Simone, impressed with her logic, realizing he'd seen it before in countless ways. Like when she'd helped him sort through the minutiae of difficult cases, or dealt with the ups and downs of Martin's adolescence, or managed the ins and out of remodeling their house—daily problems solved in a way that Reece had never truly appreciated.

"Right," she agreed, pulling him out of his ruminations. "So he manipulates the situation to his advantage. Not a slam dunk, mind you. But an odds-on shot. There's a weird sense of logic here." She sat down on the bed, chewing the side of her lip, the gesture familiar and foreign all at the same time. "I mean, if the killer jams you up for my disappearance, he knows one of two things will happen. Either I'll come forward to clear your name, and I'm back in his sights again."

"Or," Reece continued, following her train of thought, "you'll be forced to travel with us. At least until you can figure out what's what. And three people traveling together are easier to track than one."

"Exactly."

"So we need to split up." After all his internal debating, it seemed the decision had been made for him.

"Unfortunately, I'm not sure that's an option anymore."

"What the hell are you talking about? Not more than an hour ago you were dead set on exactly that."

"Things have changed." She'd lowered her voice, her attention shooting to Martin, who had fallen asleep despite their arguing.

Reece followed her into the adjoining room. "So now you're saying we shouldn't split up?" He'd lost all perspective on the argument. Which was how it always was with Simone, her mercurial changes of position sometimes leaving him dizzy with the effort to keep up.

"I'm saying that you're going to be a target wherever you are. If the killer gets to you, he gets to me. It's as simple as that."

"But we're divorced." They were standing nose to nose now, their voices contained, but nonetheless fierce.

"Like that matters." She waved off his words with her hand. "I was married to you for almost six years. I don't think that I can wipe all that out just because we can't get along anymore. We may be officially kaput. But the guy after me is well aware of the fact that I don't just erase relationships. Hell, I'm loyal to a fault. That little character trait almost kept me out of D-9. If I hadn't been so damn good at other things, it probably would have."

She'd just told him more about herself in two seconds than she'd told him in the whole of their marriage. Maybe there was something to this divorce stuff after all.

"Look, I don't need a fucking babysitter." He was doing it again, arguing against the very thing he'd thought he wanted in the first place. How the hell did she manage it?

"Normally I'd agree. But you have no idea the kind of people I deal with."

"Dealt with," he corrected, his anger blending with

something else, something that he wasn't about to try and put a name to.

"Considering your brother is in there recovering from a bullet wound, I'd hardly say past tense."

"So where the hell do we go from here?" The minute the words were out, he wished them back, knowing that he was no longer referring to the killer and his manipulations.

"I don't know," she said, dropping down on the end of the bed. It wasn't an answer, but the words were genuine.

"Look, Simone." He sat down next to her on the bed, relieved when she didn't immediately move away. "I know you didn't mean for this to happen."

"That doesn't change the fact that it did. Or the fact that I don't know who is behind it or why."

"Isn't there someone from your D-9 days that jumps out at you?"

She shook her head. "Our missions weren't sunshine and light, you know? The list of possibles is pretty damn long. But Maurice will know. That's why I've got to get to the rendezvous." She looked up, her eyes dark with worry. "If the killer could find me, he's capable of finding the others, too. Maybe he already has."

"He can't be everywhere at once."

"Yes. But he could have help. Or maybe the guy here is only a hired gun. I don't know. That's the point. I need to find out."

"So what do you want to do?" He resisted the urge to reach out and take her hands. They weren't married anymore.

"According to my GPS—" she reached over and picked up her cell phone "—the rendezvous point is in southwestern Colorado. Somewhere in the San Juan Mountains. I figure the sooner I get there, the sooner I'll have a handle on what's happening."

"And you want me to come along."

"I think it's for the best. Martin, too." Reece opened his mouth to argue, but she waved him quiet. "I know what you're thinking. And in theory I agree. But honestly, I don't know that there's anywhere we can stash Martin that the killer can't find him. Martin isn't exactly adept at this kind of thing. Better for you both to come with me to the rendezvous. Maurice will know what to do. He'll find a way to set things right for you. And make you safe."

"You put a lot of store in this guy."

"That's because I trust him. " She laughed, the sound pleasant after all the anger.

"Sounds like D-9 was more than just a blacks-ops division." He kept his voice gentle, as if he were leading a witness.

"We were really young," she offered by way of explanation, her mind on images of the past. "I was just sixteen."

Reece resisted the urge to comment. Sixteen was too damn young for black ops, no matter how talented she might have been.

"The others weren't much older. At least physically. Emotionally we'd all grown up hard and fast. So there was commonality from the very beginning. We were a ragtag family of sorts. And Maurice did everything he could to make certain we stayed that way."

Something in the way she said it made him think of subversive groups, regiments that depended on brainwashing to keep their recruits loyal to the cause. He started to push for more, but she cut him off with the wave of a hand.

"Look, it doesn't matter how it happened." She was

back with him now, the past firmly shut away again. "What's important is that I trust these people with my life. And with yours."

He reached over to lift her chin with his finger, the feel of her skin against his sending sensory memory dancing along his already jangled nerves. Her dark hair played against the back of his hand, soft and silky. A part of him wanted nothing more than to bury his face in it. To turn back the clock to a time when there were no shadows between them. But that was a fool's dream. A moment of intimacy couldn't erase all that stood between them.

He pulled away, ignoring the flash of hurt in her eyes. "All right then. It's decided. We'll come with you as far as the rendezvous."

She nodded, accepting the decision. "We'll leave at first light. Martin needs to sleep. I hate that he can't just hole up somewhere and recuperate."

"Maybe we can have the best of both worlds." Reece moved to the couch, increasing the distance between them. "I have a friend—a defense attorney—who has a cabin outside of Creede. You remember Peter Welmer?"

She frowned, shaking her head.

"Big guy. Drank too much at the Bar Association picnic?"

Less than a year ago, they'd sat in the corner laughing at the antics of his intoxicated colleagues. So much had changed since then.

"I remember him. Big voice, red nose?"

"Yeah, you called him Rudolph."

"If I remember correctly, Shelia Becker was calling him stud."

They laughed, the sound comforting, but the silence that followed was awkward.

"Anyway," he said, cutting into the stillness, "depending on where in the mountains your rendezvous point is, maybe we can use the cabin as a base."

"I don't think it's a good idea to contact anyone. Even a friend."

"That's the beauty of it. I don't have to call. He's been on me to use it for years. Even told me where the key is. So all we have to do is head that way and we should be good to go."

"What if he's there?"

"He won't be. He's got a big case right now. The Mendoba murder. It'll be at least another month before he comes up for air."

"All right. It might work. You and Martin can hole up there until I figure out what's what."

"Look." He leaned forward. "I know you're perfectly capable of taking care of yourself. You wouldn't have lasted this long if you weren't, but I can't just let you go out there on your own. Chalk it up as being a part of who I am."

She opened her mouth to argue but he didn't give her the chance.

"I'm not backing down, Simone. This bastard was shooting at me, too. I might not be ex-CIA, but I've faced my share of combat. It may have been a hell of a long time ago, but some things you never forget. And taking down the enemy is one of them."

"WHY WAS I NOT INFORMED of this visit of yours?" Manuel Ortega paced in front of his ornate desk, his hands moving with his displeasure.

Isabella squared her shoulders, carefully keeping all emotion from her face. Thank God, Ramón had given her warning. Despite Manuel's wrath, she was ready for him. "I wasn't aware that I had to inform you of every move I make." Her voice held just the right amount of disinterest. It was her icy facade that kept Manuel's attention. That and the fire she brought to his bed.

"Maintaining my position is a matter of delicate balance. You know this. And yet you continue this vendetta of yours, despite my objections."

Isabella bit into her bottom lip, swallowing the heat of her anger. "It is not a vendetta. I simply want to find out who killed my father. Surely you can understand that?" It was a stupid question. Manuel only cared about the things that affected him or his party. As far as he was concerned, her father's death was of no consequence.

Unless her actions interfered with his plans.

"You are not listening to me, *carita*." The endearment was deceptively soft. Manuel was many things, but he was not stupid. "I am telling you that it is only a matter of time before your connection with this man comes to light. And since it was your affiliation with me that allowed for your journey in the first place, your meeting can only harm what I have been working so hard to build."

"Accord with the Americans?" she spat, unable to keep the scorn from her voice. "It is impossible."

"You are a fool." Manuel's face contorted with anger, his palm connecting with her cheek. "And now you have laid the stones to make a fool of me as well."

Isabella raised a shaking hand to her face, fighting for control. "I merely spoke with a man in the American CIA. I fail to see how a simple conversation has caused you or your precious party any harm."

"We are in the middle of delicate trade negotiations with

the Americans, and your questions evoke memories best left buried. What happened in your village was an atrocity. But it is also ancient history. The world has moved on."

Again she swallowed fury. Perhaps some people had moved on. Some had probably never even engaged in the first place. But she would never forget, and someday she would find a way to get retribution.

Until then she must appease Manuel.

"I'm sorry I did not make you aware of my plans. I honestly believed they were of no matter."

Manuel's eyes narrowed as he searched her face. "You truly do not know, do you?"

Isabella frowned up at him, still rubbing her jaw. "Know what?"

"The man you went to see—he's dead."

Isabella kept her features frozen, but her heart lurched nevertheless. "Are you certain of this?"

"My sources are accurate." Manuel's gaze was still assessing.

"I didn't do it."

"I wasn't saying that you did. But there will be conjecture. And there is always your brother. Have you spoken with him?"

"You know that he does not talk to me." Manuel still believed that Carlos was a crazed man living on the edge, with no connection to the remnants of her father's junta. A notion she'd encouraged as it suited her purposes. It would never occur to him that she had stepped in for her brother. "But I do not believe he is even in America. Antonio told me that he was seen recently in the brothels of San Salvador."

"Are you telling me the truth?" Manuel's eyes were narrowed, and she flinched, her cheek still stinging.

"I always tell you the truth."

"Like your trip to America?" He slammed his palm on the table, and she forced herself to hold his gaze. There was no pride in being cowed.

"I didn't lie except perhaps by omission." She released a hint of her anger in order to camouflage her fear. "And as I said, I had no idea it would matter in the least. You know that I wish to find out what really happened in Sangre de Cristo. I have never made a secret of the fact."

"But you have never before reached out to the Americans. And now this man is dead."

"When I left him, he was very much alive."

"And did he give you the information you seek?"

Baxter had told her nothing, the old man holding tight to his honor even at the end. But she had still gained information, a piece of the puzzle that when added to the others had yielded a name.

"No. He gave me nothing." Isabella wondered when she had become so adept at lying. First to Ramón and now to Manuel. It was a dangerous path, but in the end the reward would be well worth the risk.

"Well..." Manuel waved his hand, his signet ring catching the light. "If Carlos does try to contact you, I will expect you to alert me immediately. And I hope for your sake that he is in San Salvador." It was clear from his tone that he had not believed her.

"The Americans have not yet discovered your meeting. But when they do—" the words came out on a whisper, his expression ugly "—and believe me they will—I want you completely distanced from the affair. If not, then I will have to take other measures."

He paused, the silence between them almost palpable.

"Am I making myself clear?"

"Perfectly." She nodded, feigning acquiescence.

He watched her for another moment beneath hooded lids, and then nodded, seemingly satisfied with what he saw.

She dug her nails into her palms, wishing she had a weapon. What she wouldn't give to wipe the self-satisfied smirk from his lips.

Arrogant bastard.

"In deference to our relationship, I will try to make this go away. But until I do, you will remain here, where my men can keep an eye on you. Am I making myself clear?"

Again her stomach churned with unspoken words. How dare he sequester her like some sort of concubine? The little voice in her head reminded her that she was exactly that. But she dismissed the idea. She did what she did for a greater cause. And no cost was too high.

The most pressing question now was who had killed the American. It was not part of the plan, but Carlos was not a patient man. She could not rule out the possibility that her brother had pressed the man for more information, and, unhappy with his responses, had killed him.

It was not what she would have chosen, but if it had happened, she must find a way to protect her brother and still maintain distance. Otherwise all that she had worked to achieve would be destroyed.

She sighed, wondering if it was possible to become trapped in one's own web. In the beginning it had all seemed so simple. But over time, the threads had become tangled and she was finding it more and more difficult to maintain the facade.

One thing, however, she was certain of: if Manuel learned of her deception, she would pay with her life.

CHAPTER TEN

RATON, NEW MEXICO SAT in the hollow of the mountains that separated New Mexico and Colorado. It was a squat town, faded by time and a floundering economy. They'd stopped out of necessity, bladders and stomachs needing the break. But now, as Simone emerged from the dingy restroom of the Mexican diner, she realized it wasn't just her body that needed the respite. Her mind needed a diversion, as well.

They'd been up before dawn, returning the rental car and purchasing a used one from a guy with a corner lot and a trailer. He hadn't asked questions. Just taken their money and waved them away. Funny how cash facilitated that sort of thing.

From there they'd hit the road, crossing Texas and the upper corner of New Mexico in record time, despite the fact that they'd changed course several times just in case they were being followed.

The trip itself had been uneventful, Simone and Reece taking turns driving while Martin napped in the back. The silence had been smothering, Reece's comments limited to one word questions like, "here?" or "gas?" Not that she was surprised by it. There wasn't, after all, a hell of a lot left to say.

Still, she couldn't help but compare it to earlier trips, when the two of them had been happy, and the conversation had flowed like wine. They'd spent two weeks in Tuscany a year or so after they'd gotten married, and it had been like a dream come true, the magic of Italy combining with their joy in each other to create the perfect trip.

They'd spent every minute talking and laughing. Exploring ancient ruins and palaces, eating pasta, drinking wine—just being together. In her mind's eye she could hear their laughter, see Reece sitting beneath the olive trees, a picnic spread on a brightly colored blanket.

And Italy hadn't been unique. Whether they were traveling or working on the house, or just lying together on the couch watching TV, there had always been a connection. And now—she sighed—now, thanks to her duplicity, it was gone.

"You get a fix?" She asked as she slid into the booth next to Martin, careful to keep her knees from brushing against Reece, who was sitting across from her. Martin held the satellite phone, the tracking system turned on.

"I'm not getting anything to change." He held out the phone, and she looked at the colored screen and its bleeping dot.

The program had been created by the CIA's IT department as a way for operatives to find each other in emergency situations. It was designed to give a general location, then as an operative approached the target, additional coordinates were fed into the program and the map became more detailed. If any of the coordinates along the way were wrong, the program terminated. And if they were entered before reaching the next stage, they failed to elicit the proper response.

It was an ingenious program, and at the moment it, and

the series of numbers that Simone had memorized all those years ago, were the only things leading them to the rendezvous.

All the more frustrating since according to the map, it was time for the next set of coordinates. Only they weren't getting the expected response.

"Well, at least we know my numbers are right," Simone said with a sigh.

"How do we know that?" Reece asked, his expression guarded.

"Because the thing would terminate if I entered the wrong coordinates, and it's not."

"If you ask me we're on a fucking wild-goose chase. Even if this thing did work once, it's been ten years." Reece waved at the machine, dismissing it, frustration cresting in his eyes.

"Nah, we're just getting something wrong," Martin said, ignoring the tension radiating between Simone and Reece. "The last set of coordinates worked. If the program was outdated or malfunctioning it wouldn't have taken those. We're just missing something. The instructions were to use new coordinates at the base of the mountains, right? Well, we're at the foot of the mountains. So it ought to work."

The waitress arrived with steaming platters of enchiladas, the requisite beans and rice filling the plates to overflowing. The smell started Simone's mouth watering. They hadn't had anything to eat since morning and it was well past seven now.

"So if the damn thing isn't broken, what's the problem?" Reece's control was absolute, but she'd known him long enough to recognize that he was running on empty. Too much had happened too fast, and although on the surface he was dealing with it, a deeper part of him was having trouble processing it all. Not that he'd ever admit it.

"I don't know. Maybe we're not in the right place?" Martin looked as tired as Simone felt, his color still a bit off. His wound was healing nicely though, the second set of stitches holding strong.

"We're at the foot of the mountains," Simone said, forking a bit of enchilada into her mouth, the melting cheese and green chilies a heavenly combination.

"Or maybe not." Martin frowned again at the display, then hit another button. The screen zoomed out to a less detailed map of the area. "The mountains run between here and Trinidad, right?"

"Yeah," Simone said, speaking over the rice in her mouth. "They're connected by a pass just north of here."

"So basically they're only separated by vertical mass."

"What?" Reece frowned at his brother.

"Mileagewise they're not that far apart. The major separation is vertical. The mountains."

Reece swallowed a mouthful of beans. "So you're thinking that the base of the mountains could be on either side of the pass."

"Exactly." Martin nodded.

"And if it's not working on this side," Simone continued, "then it's probably in Trinidad."

"So we head over the mountain." Martin finished off the last of his beans.

"It's better than sitting here waiting for something to happen." Reece pushed his plate away, too.

As if his words had evoked their enemy, Simone shot a look over her shoulder at the rest of the restaurant. It was packed. Locals crowded around the tiny bar, alternately cheering and booing as a college basketball team ran back and forth across a grainy television screen.

A family of five sat in the booth immediately behind them, two toddlers taking turns terrorizing the waitress by jumping off the back of the seats. It all seemed perfectly normal, but Simone couldn't shake the feeling that something was off.

"You seeing something?" Reece surveyed the bar and its patrons.

"No. Just suddenly have a bad feeling. You know, the kind that makes you jumpy?"

"Well, considering the stakes, I say we trust your intuition." He reached for his wallet and threw two twenties on the table. "Ready to roll?"

Martin started to stand up, but Simone shook her head. "Give it a minute. I'm going to go to the bathroom. As soon as I disappear from view, give it another minute and then you guys head for the door. I'll use the back door and come around from the side. If someone's out there, he'll react to your leaving, and hopefully I can catch him by surprise when I double back."

"And if no one is out there?" This from Martin.

Simone shrugged. "No harm, no foul."

"All right. Let's do it." Reece as usual cut right to the chase.

Simone grabbed her purse and headed for the bathroom. A loud cheer erupted from the bar as the New Mexico team scored a basket. No one else moved. She rounded the corner and passed the pay phone. Then cracked the door in the men and women's bathrooms, ascertaining that both were empty.

Hopefully she was only responding to her own exhaustion. But she still couldn't shake the feeling that something was wrong.

She waited about thirty more seconds to make certain that no one was following her, then slipped out the back door and around the corner of the building. The front door was illuminated by blinking blue neon, two pole lamps casting washed-out circles of light at each end of the parking lot. The rest of it was cast in shadows. Simone waited for Reece and Martin to appear.

Martin came first, ambling across the parking lot as if he hadn't a care in the world. It was a good act, but the line of his shoulders gave him away. Reece was about a minute behind. Unlike his brother he made no effort to hide his suspicion, his dark gaze moving around the parking lot, searching for anything out of place.

She followed his lead, letting her eyes sweep the lot. Martin was rounding a line of cars, heading across the last row toward their beige Buick. He was about halfway there when headlights flashed on, the light almost blinding after the near dark of the parking lot.

The engine raced, and the dark sedan sped straight for Martin. Simone sprinted forward, gun drawn, already recognizing that she was going to be too late. Reece, however, had seen the car as well, and was already diving for his brother. He hit Martin just before the car would have, the two of them rolling to the side of the row, almost underneath the Buick.

The sedan sped out of the parking lot, its tinted windows and the shadows keeping her from seeing anything about the driver. She covered the rest of the ground in seconds, and was kneeling beside Reece and Martin. "Everyone okay?"

"Yeah." Reece rolled off his brother, leaning back against a tire. "You get a look at the guy?"

"No. Tinted windows. But the plates were New Mexico."

"Doesn't tell us a lot. You get a number?"

"CRRO63. But I don't know what good it's going to do. We don't have access to a computer and we sure as hell aren't taking it to the police."

"I doubt they're looking for me in New Mexico, but I understand your hesitation."

"It could have just been a drunk local." Martin was sitting up, too.

"I don't think so." Reece shook his head, still staring at the highway in front of the restaurant. "Considering the circumstances, it's too coincidental."

"Something's bothering you." Simone met Reece's gaze, already knowing she was right.

"Well, we've assumed based on your past that this was all about you."

"And the fact that Maurice sent a warning."

"Right. I'm not saying I don't buy it. But if it is about you, then why target Martin?"

"Because I care about him?" She frowned. Reece was right; it didn't make sense.

"I've heard of loving someone to death, but this gives new meaning to the idea." Martin rubbed his head gingerly, his cheek already purpling slightly where it had come into contact with asphalt.

"Maybe. But before the killer opened fire at the house, he'd already shot Martin. And more importantly, he'd done it with a silencer, or you'd have heard it, right?"

She should have thought of it herself. "I didn't hear

anything, but it could have happened when I was out front talking to Laura."

"Laura was there?" It was Reece's turn to frown.

"Every day, like clockwork." She hadn't meant to sound snippy, but she was tired, her emotions stretched to the limit.

"Do you remember hearing anything, Martin?" Reece turned his attention to his brother.

"No. But then it all went kind of fast."

"Well, this sure as hell isn't about Martin." The idea was ludicrous.

"I'm not saying it is," Reece said, pushing to his feet. "But we can't ignore the fact that at least twice the guy has targeted Martin, and it doesn't make sense to me that someone from your past would pick him over me or you. Even if the ultimate goal is to get to you, there's got to be something more."

"Well, it's not like I saw the guy," Martin said.

"But maybe he thinks you did." Simone stood up and then offered Martin a hand. "Which would mean he's worried that you can identify him."

"Great," Martin said, sliding into the back seat. "Nothing like having a target painted on your back."

THE RAIN HAD COME from nowhere, socking them with an intensity that made it hard to maneuver the water-slick road. The road was four-lane most of the time, but with the steep grade and sharp turns it might as well have had a single lane.

Fortunately traffic was minimal.

Reece checked the rearview mirror for about the thousandth time, searching the stormy night for signs of the dark sedan.

"Whoever it was, he doesn't seem to be following us." Simone had also been checking the rearview.

"Maybe it really was just a drunk?" Martin asked, his tone wishing it so.

"It's possible." Simone gave an almost imperceptible shake of her head, negating the words.

"I'm not blind, Simone," Martin said, and despite the gravity of the situation, Reece smiled. In some really perverse way life felt normal for the first time since he and Simone had split four months ago.

"Sorry." She turned back with a grimace. "I just hate the fact that either of you are involved in this. And so I guess I just wanted it to be true."

"Well, join the club," Reece said. "At least we seem to have lost him for the moment. How much longer?"

Simone looked down at the display screen on the satellite phone. "We're almost to the pass, so I'd say we've got twenty more minutes until we get to Trinidad."

"After we check the GPS, maybe we should stop for the night?" Reece shot a sideways glance at Simone. "Martin could use the rest."

"Hey, I'm the one who's been sleeping the last twelve hours," Martin protested from the back. "You all are the ones who could use the sleep."

"If someone's on our tail, I'm not sure stopping is a wise idea." Simone tipped back her head, rubbing her neck. "We can stop when we're nearer the rendezvous. Assuming the coordinates work this time."

"They will." Reece reached over to cover her hand with his, the gesture as automatic as breathing. For a moment they held the contact, synapses firing, and then the road straightened, the pullout on their left indicating they'd reached the pass.

Behind him in the mirror, Reece saw two headlights breaking through the gloom. They'd passed several vehicles, but this was the first one to come from behind. "There's someone behind us."

Simone twisted in her seat. "It's too far away to see anything."

"It looks dark. Maybe black or blue. What color was the car in the parking lot?" Martin asked.

"I'd say black, but I wouldn't swear by it. Simone?"

"Definitely dark. Black or maybe dark green. Not blue though. And definitely not a Lexus like before. This one was domestic. I'd say a Cadillac or maybe a Lincoln."

"Lincoln," Martin said, frowning. "I remember seeing the crosshairs."

"Crosshairs?" Simone swiveled to look at him.

"Their symbol. It was on the front of the car. Kinda hard to miss from my angle, only I didn't think about it until you mentioned it."

"So he's changed cars." Reece frowned as the headlights drew closer.

"Or we're looking at two separate people." Martin sat back against the faded upholstery. The Buick had been around the block more than a couple of times.

"No. More likely he switched. It would keep us off guard and keep anyone else from tracing him. It's what I'd do."

"What you did do, actually." Reece tipped his head toward the dashboard. "We're on our third vehicle."

She shot him a look, clearly trying to ascertain if he'd meant the comment as a dig. And he wondered how they'd come to a place where every word had to be analyzed.

When they'd first met, they couldn't stop talking, holding hands under the stars on the beach like a couple of teenagers.

They'd stayed up all night on their first date, just trading thoughts, ideas. As stupid as it sounded now, they'd shared hopes and dreams. He'd never met anyone like her. She seemed so free and uncluttered. As if nothing had ever touched her.

In retrospect, he supposed it should have been a warning. What had appeared to be a free spirit was in fact a mechanism she used to hide her past. And he of all people should have seen it. But instead he'd buried his head in the sand. Some deeper part of him sensing that there was more to her—something darker that he simply hadn't been willing to face.

"I only meant you're good at what you do." He'd meant to be reassuring, but somehow it came out sounding condescending and he wished he'd just kept his mouth shut.

"I know," Simone said without really meaning it, her focus on the side-view mirror. There was a moment of awkward silence and then she leaned forward. "He's getting closer."

Reece increased his speed. The downhill stretch was more dangerous than the climb to the pass—the grade steep and the curves tightly banked. He couldn't risk accelerating too much. On these roads it would be easy to spin out of control. "Maybe we should just pull off. See if he passes us. There's a pullout ahead." The state of Colorado was proud of its topography and correspondingly had rest stops or scenic overlooks every few miles on most of its mountain roads.

"It's not a bad idea," Simone said, opening the glove

compartment. She produced a gun. A Glock by the looks of it. "You remember how to use this, right?" It was an honest question, but Reece felt a surge of inadequacy nevertheless. His wife was black ops. Past tense or present tense, she was a force to be reckoned with.

"The Rangers are nothing to sneeze at." Even after their separation, she was still able to read his mind. Especially when he didn't want it read.

"I know that. And I can handle the gun." He frowned as he took a hand off the wheel to take it from her. "Where'd you get it?"

"I bought it in Victoria. While you and Martin were checking out."

"There's a three-day wait in Texas."

She laughed, the first genuine one he'd heard in a while. "You just don't know where to shop."

"You get a gun for me?" Martin asked, almost hopefully.

"No." Reece and Simone said almost in unison. At least there were some things they could agree on.

"Sorry, Martin. Not a good idea," Simone added. "You don't have any experience."

"Just remember I'm the guy with the big red target." He slumped back in the seat, crossing his arms in dejection.

"When we get to the cabin, I'll try and show you a few things, okay?" As pacifiers went it wasn't the best, but it seemed to satisfy Martin, who sat up again and turned to survey the car behind them.

"I think he's closer. How far to the pullout?"

"Should be any minute." Reece peered ahead into the gloom, the sparkle of headlights against a road sign signaling he was right. "We're almost there. Everyone hold on. I'm going to do this at the last minute."

The overlook was on the left side of the highway, which meant crossing over oncoming lanes of traffic. Fortunately, the road ahead appeared to be empty.

Simone lowered the window halfway and lifted the gun. "Ready."

Reece adjusted the Glock so that it was braced against his thigh, ready to grab when and if it was needed. He sped up just enough to lose the other car as he rounded a bend and spotted the exit. "Okay, this is it."

He pulled the wheel to the left without slowing and the car skidded into the turn, the back wheels sliding, then catching the road. The car jerked forward across both lanes of oncoming traffic and into the overlook.

A horseshoe-shaped road curved toward the edge of the mountain and then back to the road again. Reece took the Buick to the center, hit the brakes, killed the lights and grabbed the Glock.

Holding his breath, he stared out the window, silently counting off the seconds until the other car appeared. Definitely not a Lincoln or a Lexus. More likely a Toyota or Honda. It was impossible to tell in this light. The car clearly slowed as it neared the exit, but after hesitating a fraction of a second, it sped up again, its taillights disappearing around the next bend.

"We did it!" Martin said on a whoop.

"We don't even know for certain that he was following us." Reece released the breath and the gun at the same time.

"Either way, we do seem to have managed to evade him. Good driving." Simone was still watching out the window.

"So what now?" Martin asked, a note of worry creeping back in his voice, his elation only momentary.

"We wait. See if he comes back." There was an edge to her voice Reece had never heard before—authority and control.

Simone was in her element in a way he'd never before witnessed. It was almost as if she were a stranger. But then again, that wasn't quite right, either. It was more like she was revealing parts of herself he'd never been privy to in the past. The idea should have made him feel better, but it didn't. It only made him feel more alone.

"And if he does come back?" Martin's eyes widened in anticipation of her answer, and Reece pulled his thoughts back to the situation at hand.

"Then we'll be ready." She checked the Sig, and shot a significant look toward the Glock.

"In the meantime, why don't I run the coordinates through the program again. We're clearly on the other side of the pass." Reece shoved the gun between his back and his jeans, the feel of the barrel against his skin oddly comforting. Ignoring the sensation, he reached for the GPS and typed in the coordinates.

The machine made a chirping sound and then the map changed, this one more precise than its predecessors. "We're in."

Simone leaned closer, her hair brushing against her cheek, and he fought the urge to push it behind her ear. Martin leaned forward, looking over Reece's shoulder at the screen he held in his hand.

"We're in luck. The rendezvous is just outside of Creede. Maybe ten, twelve miles."

"Which means we've still got a pretty good drive ahead of us." Simone sighed, rubbing her temples.

"You okay?" he asked, fighting to keep his tone neutral.

She might not be his wife anymore, but damn it, that didn't mean he didn't care.

"I'm fine. Just a little tired." She turned back toward the window. "Why don't we wait here a half hour or so and then head for your friend's cabin. The sooner we reach the rendezvous, the sooner we'll find out what this is all about."

If there was anyone alive to tell them.

According to Simone, five members of D-9 had been relocated. Add in Baxter and that made six. Not exactly an army. And if the killer could find Simone, there was no reason to believe he wouldn't have been able to find the others.

And if he'd gotten to the other operatives first—there was every possibility that the three of them were on their own.

CHAPTER ELEVEN

THE CABIN WAS basically three rooms on the side of a mountain. A remodeled miner's shack that had seen better days. But at the moment it was warm and dry and represented at least a hint of security.

Not that it meant anything to have such thoughts. Her old life was gone. All that remained was the fact that she'd inadvertently dragged Martin and Reece along for the ride. But that was about to end, too. Once she'd met up with the team, they'd figure out a way to get her family out of the line of fire. Get them back to Corpus and the sanity of their normal lives. All of this would just be a nightmare.

One she hoped they'd soon forget.

She swallowed the bitterness rising inside her, and walked into the living room and over to the window. Moonlight streamed through it, spilling onto the faded carpet. Martin and Reece were sleeping in the loft. She'd given the other bedroom her best shot, but tossing and turning wasn't accomplishing anything. So she'd given up, deciding her time was better spent going over the events of the past few days. Maybe there was something she'd missed, something that would help her figure out who was behind the attacks.

She hadn't lied when she'd said the list was long. There'd been secrecy to their missions, and there certainly weren't any records of their activities, but that didn't mean D-9 had gone unnoticed. There were always leaks. And though ancillary staff had been need-to-know only, there'd been times when others had had access to various details of their operations.

D-9 hadn't been an observation-only kind of organization. By the time they were called in, there was usually a mess, their job to make it go away. There hadn't been room for squeamishness. And the trail of bodies was long and in some cases memorable.

Hector Ramirez being a case in point.

It hadn't been their intention for him to be a casualty. But that didn't change the fact that he was dead. And his organization had been a big one. Assuming somehow they'd gotten access to D-9's operatives' identities, it could mean a long list of enemies.

She fingered the postcard in her pocket. Someone had obviously managed the feat. Whether it was Ramirez's people or someone else, the danger was real. It was tempting to leave this minute, to head for the rendezvous and end the suspense, but she doubted anyone was there. The instructions all those years ago had been to wait—three days—to give everyone time to get there.

Tomorrow was the day. Best to wait for it. Nothing was ever gained acting in haste. She thought of her marriage. It was the only impulsive thing she'd ever done. At least since D-9 had plucked her quite literally from the gutter.

And reinvented her.

She'd been three people in her life. The first not worth remembering. The second a trained killer, someone with nothing to lose and everything to gain. And the third—the most important of the three. Wife and lover. *Reece's* wife and lover. She'd loved him so damn much. Given everything she was capable of giving. Unfortunately, that hadn't been enough.

She pulled her thoughts away from the maudlin, scanning the area outside the window for signs of intruders. This was the here and now, and she'd do well to stay focused. It was the only way they were going to stay alive.

"Why didn't you tell me, Simone?" Reece's voice reached out of the darkness behind her, rasping down her spine. She spun around, searching the shadows for his face. He was sitting on the sofa, his feet propped up on the table. If she hadn't known him so well, she might have mistaken his posture for relaxed. But Reece never really relaxed, and his intensity was reflected in his stillness.

"I couldn't."

"Don't give me that. I loved you. You could have told me anything."

She flinched at his use of the past tense, and then lifted her chin, defiance her only armor. "That's not true. It might seem like that now. But you weren't in love with *me*. You were in love with the *idea* of me. The reality would have been more than you could handle, believe me."

"So what? You just made the decision for me?"

"You have no idea what I've done in my life. The kinds of things I've been party to." Hell, compared to her childhood, D-9 seemed tame. At least with the division somebody always had her back.

"I think maybe I have some idea. Considering we've spent the last couple of days running for our lives."

"This is nothing. Believe me." She leaned against the

windowsill, crossing her arms over her chest, feeling suddenly cold.

"You want my sweater?" Reece moved to take it off, but she shook her head.

"I'm fine."

They were silent for a moment, and she worked to sort through her cascading emotions. "Look, in part I didn't tell you because it was better for you not to know."

He opened his mouth to respond, but she waved him quiet. "But I also didn't say anything because I was afraid. I wanted what we had. And I thought that if you knew the truth you wouldn't want me anymore. Everything happened so fast between us. I mean, one minute you weren't in my life at all and the next you *were* my life. Those first months we were together were incendiary. You were part of me and I was part of you to the degree that I sometimes lost track of who was who. And then once it had all burned down to something more stable, it was too late. I couldn't just tell you that I wasn't the woman you'd fallen in love with."

"You didn't trust me." There was accusation in his voice, and unless she was completely misreading him, a note of disappointment, as well.

"That's not true. I trusted you more than anyone I've ever known. I just couldn't trust you with this."

"But *this* is everything, Simone."

"Maybe. I don't know. I only know that what started as a sin of omission took wings and began to take over my life. I couldn't be who I was. And I couldn't be who I was pretending to be. I was alone. And I was afraid."

"But you weren't alone. That's the part that I can't understand. I was there with you every step of the way. All you had to do was tell me."

"You make it sound so easy. But it's not that simple. When I found myself out of D-9 with the chance for something new, something untouched by my past, I grabbed it with both hands. It's not that I didn't trust you, Reece. It's just that I honestly believed the past was better left buried. It was over."

"If you really believed it was over, why the money and IDs hidden in the house? Why the secret postcard and GPS coordinates? Come on, Simone, give me a break. You didn't believe it was over."

"The money and IDs were part of the package we got when we were relocated. A contingency along with the GPS coordinates in case things went south."

"But you kept them all this time."

"Old habit. I don't know, maybe part of me always knew this would happen. But that doesn't change the fact that I truly *wanted* to believe it was over. You were offering me the chance at a real life. And I wanted that. I wanted you. So I wasn't about to do anything that would have endangered my chances. Surely you can see that?"

"What I see is a woman I thought I knew—a woman I pledged my life to—standing here trying to justify why she couldn't tell me the truth. How the hell could we have built anything worthwhile if it was all based on lies?"

"But it wasn't all lies. I was more myself with you than I have ever been in my whole life. You have to believe that. You gave me something I'd never had before. You gave me security. You gave me a family. For the first time ever, I belonged somewhere. Not because I was nimble-fingered or could handle a gun or infiltrate a junta, but just because I was me."

"Now who's in love with the idea more than the

reality?" He stood up, closing the distance between them, and reflexively Simone pressed back against the window.

They stood for a moment—silence reigning—the emotion pulled taut between them like an aerial wire. "You gave me a way out. A chance at normalcy. I took it. I won't apologize for that."

"I'm not asking you to. I'm asking how it was that you could say you loved me in one breath and lie to me in the next?"

She shrugged, the gesture meant to be casual but somehow taking on deeper significance. "Maybe because I don't know any other way."

"That's not good enough." He leaned forward, his dark eyes locking with hers.

"Then maybe it's because you made it difficult for me to do anything else." She pushed off the windowsill, the gap between them now only inches. She might be a lot of things, but she was not a coward, and she would not bear the responsibility for their failed marriage all on her own.

"You wanted someone to fill the void your parents left. You wanted a perfect marriage like theirs. So I gave you what you wanted. No messy past, no imperfections. Just a loving wife who never demanded that you take the time to get to know her. The truth is, Reece, you didn't want to know who I really was. And while that doesn't excuse my not telling you, it sure as hell played into the equation."

He studied her for a second, his eyes narrowed as he digested her words. "If I didn't probe, it was because I didn't think there was any reason to. For God's sake, I believed in you."

"That's why you hired the detective?"

There was a flicker of guilt. "Blame it on *my* occupation.

I look for inconsistencies. It's a force of habit. And when I found out your story about small-town Ohio was straight from the pages of a magazine, I wanted to know why. You wouldn't explain it so I arranged to find out on my own."

"Except you didn't find anything."

"Nothing conclusive. I couldn't prove that you lived there, and I couldn't prove that you hadn't. I can see now this Baxter fellow was probably manipulating things. At the time I was just more confused. And I felt shut out of my own marriage."

"But my past had nothing whatsoever to do with our present."

"It had everything to do with it, Simone. It's part and parcel of who you are. You were right—I was in love with a fantasy. But one of your making, not mine." He reached out to cup her chin with his hand, his touch deceptively gentle. "And for the record—I would have understood. I loved you. And that would have been enough."

Silence stretched between them, and she leaned forward, wanting nothing more than the feel of his lips against hers. The remembered comfort of his embrace, the slow heat that built until she couldn't breathe. Her marriage had been the only time in her life she'd been part of something real. Something that transcended the ugliness of life. And even though she knew it couldn't be real, she longed to go back there again, if even for a moment.

He leaned closer, his breath hot against her cheek, his gaze locked with hers, and then suddenly he let her go, turning away and walking from the room. She clutched her chest as if physically trying to stop the pain. It radiated through her, white-hot, spreading from her heart to her belly, leaving her fighting for breath, unable to move.

Tears spilled onto her cheeks and she brushed them angrily away. She was not going to cry. She'd done what she had to do. To protect herself, to protect her husband.

And if she had it to do over again, she'd do everything exactly the same. Which meant that in part Reece was right. She hadn't trusted him. Not completely.

And now she was paying the price.

BREAKFAST CONSISTED of powdered-sugar doughnuts and frosted flakes. Not exactly the breakfast of champions, but Martin had been in charge of shopping. Simone sat in silence at one end of the table and Reece sat at the other, trying not to stare at his ex-wife. She looked the same. The curve of her cheek, the soft chestnut sheen of her hair. If he hadn't known differently, he'd have thought the morning was no different from any of the others they'd shared during their marriage.

Except that somehow he'd crossed through the mirror, everything turned inside out as if he were Alice through the looking glass.

Martin was still in the loft, his injuries or perhaps his youthful resilience allowing him unfettered sleep. Reece, on the other hand, hadn't been as lucky. He'd managed to sleep maybe an hour, and that only in twenty minute spurts, alternately checking the perimeter for signs of their stalker and pacing the living room trying to make sense of the heated words exchanged in the middle of the night.

He was more than aware of the fact that it took two to make a marriage and two to kill it. He'd never meant to imply that it was all her fault. But damn it to hell, she'd stacked the deck against him.

His head was insisting that what was done was done.

That he needed to let it go and move on. But his heart wasn't having any of that. His heart wanted his wife back. Wanted the life they'd shared.

He could still remember the first time he'd met her. A blind date. A friend of a friend of a friend had set them up. His thought at the time had been that he was too old for that kind of thing. But then she'd stood there at the marina, dressed in white, with a crooked smile and a crazy hat. And he'd known right then, without even exchanging words, that she was the one.

He'd taken her out on his boat, his pride and joy even then. And she'd loved every moment of it, her laughter ringing out as he'd opened the throttle and pushed the cruiser to its limit. She'd captivated him then. And she captivated him now. It was as simple as that. And nothing—not even the pain of knowing that none of it had been real—could change that fact.

God, what a mess. And to top it off, in less than an hour, they were heading into what was quite possibly a trap.

He finished the last of his doughnut, wiped his hands on a napkin and leaned back in his chair, his gaze settling on Simone. "Tell me about the team."

Her head jerked up, her thoughts scattering at the sound of his voice. "What do you want to know?"

"The players, their motivations, anything you can think of that will help us prepare for what's to come." He kept his voice even, the district attorney deposing a witness. If nothing else, he was a master at hiding emotion.

Simone nodded, pushing away her half-eaten bowl of cereal. If it weren't for the topic of discussion and the Sig Sauer on the table, they could have been any normal couple having breakfast on vacation. "There were five of us that survived Sangre de Cristo. Me. Tate Montgomery, Bea Brasel, Mather Wilson, and Ed Hammond."

"Tell me about each of them."

She chewed the side of her lip, thinking. "In some ways we were a lot alike. We all came from nowhere. D-9 recruited off the streets for the most part. Desperate people with nothing to lose." She ran a hand through her hair, shivering from some forgotten memory. Obviously, she was still hiding something.

She'd had a life before D-9, but whatever that had entailed she clearly had no intention of sharing it with him. It was an old battle. He'd ask and she'd duck the question. Maybe things would have been different if he'd pushed early on. But he'd been so afraid that he'd lose her. And he'd told himself that her past didn't matter.

Hell, in a way, he was as much a liar as she was. The past did matter. He just hadn't wanted to face the elephant in the room until it was standing on his foot.

"You've never said what you were doing when they recruited you into D-9," he ventured, mentally steeling himself for her response.

"Nothing relevant." She shrugged, as usual deflecting the question. "In a lot of ways I suppose you could say my life began with D-9. Which is why it's important that you understand who the players are."

He contained a sigh. He'd interrogated enough witnesses to know when he'd hit a dead end. "So why don't you start with Mather," he said, picking a name.

"Mather was maybe four or five years older than me," she said, giving no sign that she was aware she'd won the skirmish. "She was a whiz with all things mechanical. Hell, she could fix anything. Build a space ship from a junk pile. And she had a knack for language. We were all trained to speak several languages, but Mather always nailed them. Spoke like a native."

"Do you have any idea where she might be now?" His mind shifted toward the situation at hand, trying to get a handle on the people Simone had called "family."

"Besides on the way to the rendezvous? No," she said, shaking her head. "Maurice didn't want us to know. Too tempting to contact each other. But I'd lay odds we were separated geographically as much as possible. So probably no one else in the Southwest."

"Narrows it down." Reece laughed, but there wasn't any humor in it. "Were you close with her?"

"Not as close as with Bea. But yeah, we shared pretty much everything. D-9 was a pretty rarified environment. When we were on a mission we depended on each other for survival. When we were home we depended on each other for camaraderie."

"What do you mean? Didn't you have other friends?"

"No." She shook her head, toying with her cereal. "We had our own compound. It kept our exposure limited."

"Sounds like a prison."

"Actually," she said, her expression darkening, "it was the alternative."

He wanted to ask her more, to probe into her past, but now clearly wasn't the time. "What about the others? You said you and Bea were close," he prompted, leading her away from painful memories.

"We were. As much of a sister as I've ever had. We had similar pasts, and shared the same insecurities. We even had some of the same dreams. I guess that gave us a bond. Anyway," she said, shaking her head to clear her thoughts,

"Bea was trained in ordnance. She can pretty much make a bomb out of anything. Disable one, too, if necessary. She handles explosives of all kinds. From hand grenades to chemical weapons. Whatever an operation called for, she could come up with something."

"She's the same age as Mather?"

"More or less. All the others were about the same, give or take a year or so."

"So three women and two men. Not what you'd expect."

"You sound like a chauvinist." Her mouth curved upward, the first sign of a smile that he'd seen since they'd talked last night.

"Nah, just basing my knowledge of subversive operations on fiction."

"James Bond."

"Well, I was leaning toward Jason Bourne. But you get the idea."

"We were actually split four and four. Joseph Clem, Natalie Oh, and Brian Hobart made up the rest of the team. They never made it out of Sangre de Cristo."

"Blue team."

She nodded, the little lines at the corners of her mouth and eyes deepening with the memory.

"So tell me about Tate and Ed."

She nodded, absently playing with the dry cereal in her bowl. "Tate's a little bit older. Was a mercenary before joining D-9. I always got the feeling he'd had a lot more experience than he let on. Definitely an opportunist."

"He have a specialty?"

"Long-range shooter. A sniper really. Dead-on shot. The kind of guy who always has your back. I depended on him for a lot of things."

A surge of something Reece wasn't quite ready to acknowledge surfaced and died. But he made a mental note to check out Tate Montgomery. "What about Ed Hammond?"

"Great guy. Has a really dry sense of humor. Kinda like Martin in that the more nervous he is, the more flip he gets. And like Martin, he's a whiz with computers. Also communication. Handled everything logistical. He usually stayed behind the scenes, making sure we got in and out in one piece."

"So he wasn't in Sangre de Cristo?"

"No. He and Mather stayed behind in the jungle. Tate, Bea and I comprised Red team."

"And it was a bloodbath."

"I've never seen anything like it. And I've seen a lot." She crossed her arms over her chest, containing a shudder. "The region was volatile. We knew that. Expected bloodshed even, but this was beyond anything we could have anticipated. Up until the massacre, the Nicaraguan army had been disorganized, fighting what was left of the resistance without much enthusiasm, instead, allowing the guerrillas to retreat to the mountains. It was a combination of incompetence and arrogance. Everything seemed to be status quo."

"And then Santiago took power."

"Exactly. And he saw Ramirez and his organization as a real threat. Made it a priority to stop the man."

"Probably not a bad decision, all things considered."

"Well, I'd have to agree that Ramirez had the ear of the people. He was a very charismatic man. And he had U.S. arms thanks to his agreement with the CIA to turn evidence on the drug cartels, but I'm not certain that it was enough for him to really have been able to take power. I think

Sangre de Cristo was more about the Nicaraguan government wanting to show its muscle. To send a signal to all revolutionaries that their interference would not be tolerated."

"With Ramirez as the sacrificial lamb."

"Yeah. And the people of Sangre de Cristo thrown in for good measure."

"But the U.S. wanted Ramirez alive."

She nodded. "Not that it did any good. Ramirez's men betrayed him. Santiago won the day, but nothing was accomplished. The junta survived even with the loss of their leader. Drug trade continued to flourish. And Santiago was brought down by the very men who put him in power in the first place. It was such a waste. All those people killed for nothing."

"Along with your friends."

"It's not the same." Her gaze met his across the table. "We knew the risks. Accepted them when we went in. Those children didn't sign on for what they got. No matter who their parents were. Reece, it was awful. Worse than any war zone I've ever seen. Dead bodies littered the street, sometimes piled two and three deep. Mothers clutching their children. Men forming human barricades around their families. There was so much carnage, the water in the gutters ran red with blood." She released a long, shuddering breath, the effort shaking her body. "I thought that only happened in movies."

"I remember the footage on television." He nodded. "Even third-hand it was frightening."

They sat for a moment, the silence of the mountains soothing.

"So what happened after that?" he continued, wanting to pull her away from the horror of her memories. "You mentioned quarantine."

"It was only supposed to be a debriefing. A couple of weeks of down time until the furor died down. At first we were glad of the break. Getting out of Nicaragua had been difficult. And we'd left behind some of our closest friends. It's like a platoon in the army. You know? These are the people you live with day in and day out.

"They fill every void in your life. They're your teachers, your friends, your students, your confidants, sometimes even your confessors. You love them, you hate them, you laugh with them, you cry. But above all else you know that they'd die for you. Give their life in an instant without thought if it meant that you went on breathing. That's not something you easily forget. And so losing Joe, Nat, and Brian was like having limbs amputated without benefit of anesthesia." She paused, wiping angrily at her tears.

"Which is why decompression was a good thing. For a while. But the powers that be had seriously underestimated the world's reaction to the atrocities at Sangre de Cristo. And instead of cooling down, D-9 stayed too hot to handle. Everyone was looking for scapegoats and our existence as a unit became a liability to the Company."

"Seems pretty cold."

"It's not a hearts-and-roses kind of occupation. We knew it was a possibility every time we went out. A compromised unit isn't worth anything to anyone."

"So they relocated you."

"There was talk of integrating us into other divisions, but we were all pretty burned-out, Ed in particular. He and Natalie were together. Strictly off-the-record, you understand, but the commitment was there. He took her death pretty hard. Anyway, bottom line, we'd lost our value. And believe me, we were always expendable. The only reason they went to such lengths to relocate us was the danger of our involvement in Sangre de Cristo coming to light. Otherwise I suspect we'd have been on our own."

"Not exactly severance and a pension plan." He wanted to ask more. To know why she'd chosen the life in the first place, but Martin stood at the foot of the stairs, his hair standing every which way, the dictionary definition of bed-head.

"So what? You all were just going to let me sleep through all the fun?"

"You needed your sleep." Simone's tone was soft, almost motherly. "And besides, you're not coming with us."

Martin pulled a face but presented no argument, just walked over to the table and, after grabbing the box of doughnuts, sat down. "When are you planning to leave?"

"The sooner the better," Reece said, more than ready to get on with it.

"I want to check the weapons, and go over the map one last time. Make sure we've correctly identified all possible access points. I don't want to walk into an ambush."

She already sounded different. Her old life reaching out to envelop her. The Simone he'd known evaporating like water on hot pavement. "I thought you weren't worried."

"I'm not, really. But I can't discount the fact that someone has been chasing us all the way from Texas. And while we seem to have lost him for the time being, it could be that he's just waiting for the right moment."

"The rendezvous being the perfect hot spot."

She glanced up from the map. "I just want to cover all the possibilities."

He picked up the Glock and checked the magazine.

After holstering the gun, he walked over to stand beside her at the map she'd spread out on the table.

It seemed Simone wasn't the only one being drawn into her old life.

CHAPTER TWELVE

THE VALLEY NARROWED toward the pass until the two sides almost touched, the river a line of quicksilver cutting between them. The undergrowth was thick, mosquitoes buzzing incessantly. The smell of pine permeated the air, the warmth of the sun barely penetrating their canopy.

If they hadn't known there was a trail here, they'd never have found it. When Simone's colleagues picked a rendezvous, they made damn certain not just anyone could stumble upon it. Reece dodged a low-slung branch, trying to make as little noise as possible. It was amazing how quickly it all came back to him—his days in Desert Storm, as well as his training stateside. Once a soldier, always a soldier. Although in all honesty he could have gone the rest of his life without revisiting the skill set.

He swatted at a mosquito and moved closer to Simone. "How much farther?" They'd had to leave the car behind, a move that concerned him should they need to make a speedy exit. However, there didn't seem to be much choice.

"We're almost there," Simone whispered, stopping to hold out the GPS with its blinking red dot. The readout indicated they were only yards from their goal, but the thickness of the trees obscured any kind of view.

"I don't like all the trees." He scanned the surrounding vegetation, trying to get a bead on whether they were alone.

"There's got to be a clearing." Simone set out again, following the GPS signal. He walked behind her, listening for anything out of the ordinary. Everything seemed heightened out here. The hush of the canopy of trees making even the slightest sound seem amplified.

They'd been following a stream, crisscrossing it as they made their way up the arm of the valley. The river was still somewhere ahead of him, but he thought he could hear the rush of the water.

Without warning, the trees dissipated, giving way to a clearing covered with grass and wildflowers, the river tracing its way across the far border. The rains in Colorado had been extreme, the Rio Grande swollen beyond its banks, its waters muddy and churning. At least it meant no access from the east.

And no escape.

Stopping near Simone in the shelter of a huge blue spruce, Reece drew his gun. Better to be prepared. Simone nodded her agreement, pulling out the Sig.

"What now?" Reece whispered, moving deeper into the shadow. Anchored by the river, the meadow was bordered by the stream on their left and more trees to the right. Nothing moved except for the lazy swaying of wild iris and Indian paintbrush, the cacophony of color worthy of Monet or van Gogh.

"Whistle." Her eyes sparkled with amusement, and Reece realized that she was actually enjoying the situation. Or at least the moment.

Simone's whistle was so precise Reece almost expected a flock of birds to arrive. Instead, after three very silent minutes an answering whistle emanated from the opposite side of the clearing near the river.

"Ed."

"How do you know?"

"We've each got a different call. Sometimes it's the blinding glimpse of the obvious. You know?"

A figure emerged from the edge of the trees, moving fast toward their position, keeping low and in the shadows. Whatever fun Simone might be having with the situation, it was definitely not a game.

The clearing remained silent, and after waiting a few seconds more, Simone stepped out into the sunlight. Ed Hammond was close enough for them to see his features now. Hardened in the way only seasoned military personnel can be, he was tall and deceptively lean. His hair was thinning, but that was the only sign that he'd given even a passing nod to aging. Like Simone, he carried a handgun. Reece found himself wondering if an Uzi might not have been a better choice of weapon.

Simone reached Ed and the two of them embraced briefly, then began to talk, Simone's hands flying as she no doubt explained their adventures getting here. Catch-up finished, the two of them turned together, heading for Reece.

He held his position, resisting the urge to go into the clearing and meet them. Better to remain an unknown entity. If Simone was right and Baxter had summoned the remaining team, there were still three people unaccounted for. As well as the big man himself.

Despite Simone's seeming confidence in her comrades, Reece wasn't as convinced, and as such kept his gun trained on Hammond. They were about fifteen yards out when all hell broke loose, a volley of shots ripping through the clearing with a speed that could only mean a machine gun.

Feeling as if he'd manifested the damn thing himself, Reece tried to place the shooter, and settled instead for firing in the general direction of the gunshots, knowing damn well that he was out of range. Tamping down all emotion, he stopped firing, concentrating instead on Simone and Ed, now running for the comparative safety of the woods.

Simone had an arm around Ed, who was stumbling forward but clearly not capable of independent locomotion. Swearing under his breath, Reece ran out from his cover, wrapping an arm around Ed from the other side. Ed's eyes narrowed for a moment, his body tensing in defense.

"My husband," Simone said as they moved forward, Reece's added support speeding the process up considerably. "We can do full introductions later."

Ed nodded, and grimaced as another bullet found home. This one sent a spray of blood as it exited just below his collarbone. Ed dropped to one knee, his weight almost toppling them over.

His eyes closed, his face ashen, the contrast to the rapidly spreading bloodstain making it seem even more pale. Reece had seen mortal wounds before, and he recognized this one for what it was.

So did Ed Hammond.

His eyes opened for a moment, his lips moving soundlessly. Simone shook her head, obviously following his train of thought. "We're not leaving you here."

"Have to," was the mumbled reply, but Reece had seen that look in Simone's eyes before. She wasn't about to give in.

The shooter had stopped, probably to reload, or maybe to reposition himself. Either way, Reece knew they only had seconds. "Let go."

Simone opened her mouth to argue, saw the determination in his eyes and instead released Ed. She scooped up his gun, pocketed it, then pivoted to open fire with the Sig in the direction of the killer. Moving as quickly as he could, Reece grabbed Ed and threw the man over his shoulder, praying that adrenaline would give him the strength he needed.

Ed's weight made progress slower than Reece would have liked, but he kept putting one foot in front of the other, knowing that if he stopped they were all dead. In what seemed like hours, but was probably only minutes they reached the shelter of the trees, the graceful arms of the spruce dipping down to obscure them from view.

With Simone's help they slid Ed to the ground, and Reece felt his neck for a pulse. "I've got it, but I think we're losing him."

Simone bit her lip, her gaze traveling back to the now-quiet clearing, the shooter no doubt reassessing his position. "We've got to get him out of here."

"What about the others?"

"There's no time."

Ed's eyes flickered open and he reached up for her wrist. "You need to find them. Danger. Too late for me." Their gazes held for a moment. And then Ed was gone.

Reece had seen people die before. But it didn't change the horror of watching a life slip away.

"No." The single word hung in the air, Simone's face contorting in the wake of her grief.

A bullet embedded itself in the trunk of the spruce

about two feet from the top of their heads. The shooter had obviously found them again.

"Come on." Reece stood up, grabbing her by the elbow. "We've got to get out of here."

Simone resisted for a second, her eyes still locked on Ed, and then she was up and running, the two of them making their way back toward the Buick and escape.

The woods shook with the sound of a rifle report off to their left, followed immediately by another volley of machine-gun fire.

"Someone else is out there." Simone switched directions, twisting toward the sound of the rifle fire without breaking stride. Reece followed on her heels, cursing D-9 and the CIA in general, but no way in hell was he leaving her on her own.

Sill following the sound, Simone wove her way between branches and undergrowth, ducking low to keep out of the line of fire. Reece followed suit, marveling at the fact that she so effortlessly had resumed the habits of her old way of life. Of course, being a moving target was extra incentive.

The ground at his feet spit rocks and dust as the machine gunner found them again, the only thing keeping the shooter from a sure hit the maze of spidery-armed pine trees that surrounded them. A branch a few inches above Reece's head splintered with impact, underscoring the thought. He dropped to the ground, crawling forward on his elbows until he pulled up beside Simone, who had found temporary shelter behind a lichen-covered boulder.

"You think there are two of them?" He whispered, his eyes searching the forest ahead of him for any sign of their assailant.

"No. I think he's just fast."

"What about the rifle fire?"

"Got to be someone from D-9. Unless I'm mistaken, the rifle fire was meant to draw the shooter away from us."

"So your man knows we're out here?"

She nodded. "Probably saw us in the clearing."

"All right. So what next?"

Simone frowned. "We try to find the rifleman. If I'm right, he's pinned now that he's made himself known. We need to figure out a way to give him the chance to withdraw."

"But that puts the bastard right back on our trail again."

"He's already there," Simone said with a shrug, throwing a branch in the air to demonstrate.

Pine needles rained down on them as the branch exploded above them.

"With damn good aim."

"I think we'll be better off if we split up."

"No fucking way."

"Reece, this isn't the time for emotion to get in the way."

"I'm not leaving you."

"If we want to get out of here it's our best option. Just hear me out."

He nodded, swallowing back his anger. She was right. They needed to stay clearheaded if they were going to get out of this in one piece. And that meant no me-man-you-woman bullshit. Especially considering said woman's time in black ops.

"Okay. Here's what I'm suggesting. I'll head east, toward whoever it is with the rifle. You'll cover me until I'm at least out of immediate range. I figure the shooter will follow me. So you give it a few more minutes and then head back for the car."

"What the hell good is that going to do?" He clenched a fist. "And don't tell me to go for help." This role-reversal shit was hell on a guy's ego.

To her credit, she smiled. "I wasn't going to say that. What I want you to do is bring the car to me. You can follow the stream. The trees are less dense there, and though it won't be good for the Buick, it's a tank, so it ought to make it. I'll grab whoever it is out there, and we'll start heading your way. With a little luck you'll get to us before the shooter does."

He nodded his acceptance but grabbed her hand before she could go. She turned to look at him, her eyebrows raised in question, but he shook his head. "Just be careful out there, okay?"

They stayed for a moment, neither of them willing to break the contact, the bond between them overriding superficial things like separation and divorce. Then with a muffled groan, he pulled her into his arms, his mouth crushing against hers, their kiss part combustion and part goodbye.

She pressed against him, her hands tangling in his hair, her need as desperate as his own. For a moment there was only the two of them, bound by the touch of their lips, and then she pulled free and sprinted into the woods.

Reece popped up and fired a couple of rounds into the trees. The shooter returned fire as Simone disappeared into the undergrowth. Reece fired again, then dropped back behind the rock, waiting. There was an answering volley, and then silence. Nothing moved.

Counting slowly to ten, he waited another two beats and then ran out from behind the rock, heading back the way they'd come. The gunman had obviously followed

Simone, just as predicted, the silence assuring Reece that he hadn't found her.

Yet.

Spurred on by that thought, he raced through the undergrowth, mindless of the tree branches cutting and scratching as he ran. The Buick was just where they'd left it, and he slid behind the wheel, jamming the keys into the ignition. The engine roared to life as he shifted into gear, gunning the car as he headed for the stream.

It was small but rocky, tumbling through a series of basins until it reached the Rio Grande. Choosing the bank over the rockier bottom, he kept the car right at the edge of the water, swerving to avoid bigger trees and smashing through saplings.

The bottom of the car scraped against the rocky bank, but Reece ignored it, keeping his mind focused on the fact that Simone needed him. Nothing else mattered.

Not the fact that she had a secret past. Not the fact that she wasn't the woman he'd married. And certainly not the fact that they weren't married anymore.

Right now all that mattered was keeping her alive.

SIMONE KNELT in the coniferous mulch at the foot of a pine tree and listened to the silence of the forest. Somewhere out there was an ally. And, probably just as close, an enemy. The trick was going to be to decipher one from the other.

It was a risk to signal. She didn't for a minute believe the assailant was part of D-9, but it was more than clear that whoever it was knew who they were. And if he did, he might know their calls.

But the only alternative was to wait until the shooting started again, or until Reece arrived, and by then it might be too late. Waiting another couple of minutes to make certain nothing moved, she whistled, the sound abnormally loud in the deep quiet of the forest.

She listened intently, the blood pounding in her temples threatening to drown out any reply. And then she heard it. A quick whistle followed by a longer one.

Tate.

She smiled for a moment, then swallowed the pleasure, the second whistle's meaning driving itself through the haze in her brain.

Caution.

Tate was telling her to be careful.

Her gaze moved slowly across the arc of forest in front of her. Tate's signal had come from the left, and based on the last burst of gunfire, she guessed the assailant was somewhere off to her right, probably working his way toward Tate's position.

Thanks to her whistle it was likely the man was aware of her presence, making it all the more important to keep moving. Staying low and using pine trunks for cover, she slowly moved in the general direction of the whistle, knowing that Tate, too, would be keeping mobile. The forest was still again, the only movement in the tops of the trees.

She strained for the sound of Reece and the car, but there was nothing. Either he was having trouble getting the Buick through the undergrowth or something had happened. Since she wasn't about to consider the latter, she settled on the former.

The valley here was thick with new growth, impeding progress, but the sound of shots dead ahead spurred her on. Pine saplings whipped against her arms and face, brambles grabbing the denim of her jeans. Close enough now to see the fire of the machine-gun bursts, Simone skidded to a halt and crouched behind a fallen log.

The shooter was about a hundred yards straight ahead, Tate's answering fire putting him about thirty yards away, still off to her left. Moving at a dead run now, she headed for his position, the spit of machine-gun fire filling the air with pine needles as the spray clipped trees and dug into the forest floor.

Out of the gloom a pile of boulders thrust its way up from the ground, providing natural cover. For just an instant, Simone saw the gleam of the rifle's barrel as Tate returned fire, buying her precious seconds to reach safety.

She dove for the rocks, landing behind them on a roll. She pulled upright immediately to crouch beside Tate, the Sig in her hand at the ready.

"What took you so long?" Tate grinned at her, and then raised himself enough to get off another shot at the machine gunner.

"Did a little sight-seeing on the way."

"You alone?"

"No." She shook her head. "My husband is with me. And Ed Hammond." She swallowed the bitter taste of defeat. "He's dead."

"Ed or your husband?"

"Ed."

"Goddamn it." He slammed his fist into the side of a tree, the resulting impact sending needles fluttering around them. "I never even saw him."

"It wasn't your fault. The guy had us cornered."

"But I should have been there. For both of you." Silence fell heavy between them, their loss punctuated by the still forest.

"Why the hell did you bring an outsider?" No reference to the fact that said outsider was in fact family. But then, that was Tate. And besides, he was obviously facing reality better than Simone was. Reece wasn't her husband any longer. At least not according to the state of Texas.

"I didn't have a choice. My brother-in-law is here as well."

Tate swiveled so that he could look at her, his eyes narrowed as he frowned. "Two noncoms? You're lucky you got here at all."

Tate Montgomery hadn't changed a bit. He'd never countenanced outsiders, preferring to leave his trust with only the core of D-9. Tate had been a mercenary before joining forces with the CIA. Simone had never really understood why a loner like Tate would agree to anything involving teamwork. Probably like her, Maurice Baxter had had something on Tate. Something to assure his cooperation.

But she'd never asked.

None of her damn business.

"The guy out there's hunting them, too. We've been dodging him through three states now."

"So you're the one I have to thank."

"Good to see you, too." She smiled, reaching out to squeeze Tate's hand. "You seen Maurice or any of the others?"

Tate's face clouded. "Maurice is dead."

"What?" Somehow Simone had always figured Maurice was invincible. One of those men who just never allowed fate to gain the upper hand. "Here?"

"No. In D.C. He was murdered."

It was Simone's turn to frown. "You're sure? I mean, I just got the postcard."

"Positive. I went there first. Thought I'd cut through the James Bond crap and go to the source. Someone beat me to it. I got there in time to see the body bag being loaded into the ambulance."

"Any idea who did it?"

"No. But I'm betting our boy out there had something to do with it."

"Have you gotten a look at him?"

"Not clearly. But enough to know he has a dark complexion. Latin, maybe Arab… I couldn't say for sure."

"So what do we do now?" A wave of hopelessness crested inside her, surprising in its intensity. She hadn't always liked Maurice, but in her own way she had loved him, and was more than aware of the fact that had he not pulled her off the streets, she most likely wouldn't be alive today.

"First we ditch Mr. Machine Gun and then we need to figure out what the hell is happening."

"Can we take him out?" She nodded toward the stand of trees obscuring the killer from view.

"Don't think so. He's got us outgunned." Tate indicated the rifle in his hand. "I'm almost out of ammo, and not to knock Sig Sauer but that thing's hardly a match for a machine gun."

"I sent Reece for the car."

"Reinforcements would have been a better choice." Tate scanned the area beyond the rocks. The stream bordered them to the right, the clearing to the left. The shooter-held post straight ahead with the Rio Grande directly behind them. "I take it Reece is the husband."

"Ex-husband, actually."

Tate tilted his head, his mouth twitching at the corners. "Sure you don't want to leave him behind?"

"It was amicable. And no, I don't want him hurt."

Tate shrugged, his expression still hinting at wicked. "It was just an idea."

"So what do you propose?" She risked a quick look over the rocks. "The clearing's obviously out. We'd be sitting ducks."

"The river, too. It's just too high for us to manage on foot. Where's this knight of yours coming from?"

"He's not my knight," she snapped, realizing too late that he'd been baiting her. "I told him to follow the stream. I figured it's the only chance he has to get the car through the woods."

"Unless it's got a backhoe attached, I'm doubting there's much chance of that." He nodded toward the thick growth of aspen and spruce.

Simone shook her head. "Buick." The word said it all.

"Right then, so we'll head upstream. It'll take us toward the car and away from the gunner. Our best hope right now is to lose him in the undergrowth."

"We've managed against worse odds." There was comfort in the thought.

"We'll move on my signal." Tate had always liked to take charge. A fact that hadn't always sat well with the rest of D-9, but only because they all wanted to do the same. There hadn't been a wallflower in the lot, all of them loners by habit or circumstance.

And now two more of the team were dead. Ed and Maurice. She shook her head, clearing her thoughts. If she didn't want to join them, she had to stay focused. There'd be time for mourning later.

Much later.

Tate popped up and fired two rounds in the direction

of their assailant. Then motioned her forward with a pointed finger.

Simone ran toward the stream, keeping as low to the ground as was physically possible.

Tate fired again, and followed behind her, the two of them holing up behind a large spruce that fronted the water rushing along the creek bed. "Let's keep moving. He can't shoot while he's trying to follow."

"There's an optimistic thought," she said, following Tate as he started along the creek bank. Ammo rounds slammed into the tree trunk behind her. "Flawed, obviously, but still optimistic."

The gunfire continued as they darted in and out of the trees lining the edge of the stream. Unless Simone missed her guess, he wasn't just keeping up with them, he was closing the distance.

The streambed narrowed as the terrain steepened, the bank strewn now with watermelon-sized boulders. It slowed their progress and gave their opponent a momentary advantage. Simone turned to assess the situation, pushing an aspen sapling out of the way. Before she had time to focus, Tate jerked her off her feet, the sapling snapping back into place and then splintering from the force of a spray of bullets.

"Shit."

"My sentiments, exactly," Tate said, rolling off her into a crouching position.

"Thanks." Simone knelt beside him, peering into the shadows, trying to find something to indicate the gunner's location.

Tate shrugged, the rifle pointed toward the forest. "You'd have done it for me. Besides, can't risk losing you when I've only just found you again." Despite the gravity of the situation, there was innuendo in his words. Hints of things long past.

Simone chose to ignore it. "If we try to climb the rocks, we'll be putting ourselves directly in his crosshairs."

"Yeah, I figure we've got one of two choices. Either we try to cross the stream and head deeper into the woods, or we move west, try to skirt the rocks and then head back for the stream." As if commenting on the strategy, the gunman opened fire again, the bullets just shy of their position.

Tate started to answer fire, but Simone shook her head. "We're too far away. Better to conserve the ammo."

He lowered the rifle.

"Judging from his range, I'd say skirting the rock fall is out. Which leaves us with the stream. If Reece is coming, he'll have the same problem with the rocks. Which means he'll be over there anyway." She pointed toward the far bank and its flatter terrain.

"All right. You go first, and I'll cover you with the last of the ammo. Once you're there, take cover behind that embankment and you can cover me."

She nodded, already pushing off. The water was icy, the sensation momentarily stopping forward momentum. But movement was her only asset, and ignoring the biting cold, she continued forward, working cross current to avoid being swept off her feet.

She could hear Tate firing behind her. Seconds ticked by and then she was on the other side and behind an embankment created by a fallen tree embedded with needles and dirt. Propping her gun arm on the top of the log, she waited until Tate appeared at the edge of the stream, then shot at the opposite bank while he maneuvered through the whirling water.

The magazine emptied, and she grabbed Ed's gun, firing again in the direction of the gunner.

Tate moved into position beside her, his gaze falling on her discarded gun.

"It ain't over until the fat lady sings," Simone said, keeping her voice light. But they both knew that with only Ed's gun left and its chambers almost empty, they were in serious trouble.

As if to emphasize the fact, a hail of bullets pushed them down behind the log.

"Son of a bitch," Tate said, his somber gaze finding hers. "Here comes the aria."

CHAPTER THIRTEEN

REECE CRASHED through the undergrowth, the bottom of the car screeching in protest as it scraped against rocks and debris along the way. Despite the sounds from the car, he could discern the popping of gunfire ahead, the noise signaling that hopefully he wasn't too late.

He'd traversed the stream several times trying to avoid the worst of the undergrowth and rocky outcrops, and was now moving along the east side at a fairly good clip. The stand of aspen directly in front of him precluded any view of the upcoming bend in the stream, but at this point he was driving on adrenaline anyway. Better just to barrel ahead and hope for the best. At least twenty minutes had passed since he'd left Simone in the woods. And in that amount of time anything could have happened.

He plowed through three saplings, narrowly avoided their fully grown cousin, and took the bend in the stream on two wheels. The length of rushing water straightened out for a short distance, and he could actually see the forest on both sides.

Slowing slightly, he listened for the sound of continued gunfire. At first there was nothing but the noise of the engine. And then off to his right about twenty yards from the stream he heard the echoing report of the machine gun.

Frantically, he searched for signs of Simone.

Nothing moved or seemed out of place, and he'd almost given up hope when a flash of color showed momentarily against a pile of rotting timber next to the bank. If he was right, they were only a few yards in front of him.

He slowed further, trying to gauge the distance between the embankment and the shooter. The bushes quivered again as the gunman fired another round, this time with answering shots from the fallen log.

Someone was there. And he or she was alive.

Reece struggled to remember if Simone had been wearing red, then shrugged off the effort. Whoever was there firing back at the machine gun was on their side. And no matter the situation, Simone would expect him to offer help.

Slamming the pedal to the floor and hitting the horn, Reece blazed a trail through the undergrowth, literally exploding into the tiny clearing that surrounded the fallen log. Simone, crouched behind the rotting pine, fired into the trees. Then, grabbing the arm of the man next to her, she signaled for him to make for the car.

He opened his mouth to argue, but Reece cut him off with an impatient hand on the horn. It was time for retreat. The guy stumbled to his feet and began to run, Simone still firing at the assailant in the trees.

Reece slowed the car as the stranger yanked open the door, both of them yelling for Simone to come. Swiveling, she started to run, then stopped, clamping a hand to her shoulder.

"Come on," Reece screamed, his heart threatening to break right through his chest. "Move it."

Whether it was his words, or simple instinct, she started to move again. The man slid into the passenger seat, slamming the door, and then twisting to lean over the seat and open the door behind him.

Simone slid into the back seat of the Buick as bullets literally pelted the side.

Reece floored the gas pedal, not even waiting for her to close the door, and the car fishtailed across rocks and pine needles as it lurched forward. Sighting an almost invisible pathway, Reece maneuvered the car between towering pines, knowing that despite the advantage of wheels, they still weren't moving fast enough.

"He's gaining on us," Simone said as the back window shattered.

"Can't you move any faster?" the man next to him barked, his eyes like Simone's on the forest behind them.

"Not without smashing into the trees." Reece tightened his hands on the wheel, anger flashing.

"You're doing fine," Simone said, her eyes meeting his in the rearview mirror.

The Buick burst through the trees into a rock-strewn meadow that fronted the river, and Reece spun the wheel to the left, keeping the riverbank tight on his right. The open terrain meant that he had the advantage of speed.

"We should be clear of this bastard in no time." Reece shot the words over his shoulder.

"No dice." This from muscleman.

"What the hell do you mean?" Reece asked, but the answer had already appeared in the rearview mirror. A Jeep barreled along behind them, the smaller vehicle built for the terrain in a way the Buick was not.

"He's closing on us," Simone said to no one in particular.

Reece pushed the Buick harder, a little burst of speed moving them forward. The river beside him ran swiftly, the muddied waters probably a good three feet above normal levels, the current giving added buoyancy to the usual assortment of flotsam and jetsam.

The Jeep was closing fast, which meant they were running out of time, but Reece figured they weren't down for the count yet. Jerking the wheel to the right, he forced the Buick into the river.

"What the hell are you doing?" Simone's companion thundered. "We'll stall out."

"Won't matter," Reece said, keeping his focus on the now wildly rocking car. "The current should carry us downriver. It's the quickest way I know to put some distance between us and the Jeep."

Water flowed through the cracks in the doors, flooding across the floorboard. The engine sputtered once but then held, the car cutting across the river. A quarter of the way in, the wheels caught on the rocks beneath and held, the Buick spurting forward on its own steam.

Behind him, the Jeep had pulled into the water, but the driver had slowed, clearly hesitant to move any farther into the river.

The Buick swept off the high ground and back into the current, moving downstream, the tires occasionally skidding against river rocks and other debris. The Jeep was growing smaller in the distance, the driver apparently having decided to abandon his quarry.

"He's not following us." Simone's voice was full of admiration. "Not a bad move."

"Except that now we're stuck in the middle of the fucking river."

"Come on, Tate," Simone chided. "You're just pissed you didn't think of it first."

The big man laughed, the sound easing the tension that had been building in the car. "Damn straight. So tell me, hotshot," Tate said, his attention back on Reece, "you got a plan to get us out of here?"

"More or less." Reece turned the steering wheel, and the car listed toward the far bank. Based on the trip up, there was a bend in the river coming up within the next hundred yards or so. If he could move the car far enough to the right, he'd be against the shallower far side of the bend, on the same side as the highway.

Seemed possible in theory, but now of course he had to execute the plan.

Everything depended on the tires finding purchase against the shallower rocks.

The bend rushed toward them, the car now sporting about eight inches of water on the floor. The engine still sputtered with life, but it wouldn't be much longer until it was as waterlogged as the rest of the Buick.

The front of the car swerved with the current, pointing it right at the far bank. Reece gunned the engine, the wheels spinning for his effort. More water surged into the car as it began to move back toward the center of the river.

Again he pressed the pedal, and this time was rewarded with the grinding of the tires as they hit rock. The engine coughed and seemed for a moment to have died all together, but then suddenly it roared back to life, the wheels pushing it forward as they finally connected with the riverbed beneath the now decidedly shallower water.

In minutes they were out of the river, the water receding almost as quickly as it had come. The Buick wheezed but held firm, carrying them up and over a small rise to the highway, which was blessedly empty in both directions.

"I don't know how the hell you pulled that off." Tate's voice held a note of honest admiration. "But I for one am pretty fucking delighted that you did."

Reece grinned over at the man. "Not too shabby if I do say so myself."

"Well, before we go into testosterone overload," Simone said, her tone colder than the water at their feet, "I suggest we get the hell out of here. We'll hold the high fives until we're sure the bastard's gone."

"SO TELL US what you know." Reece leaned back against the windowsill, arms crossed, his gaze locked on Tate's.

Once they'd made the cabin and ascertained that no one was behind them, Simone had performed introductions, ignoring the tension that flowed between Reece and Tate. Strong men never responded well to one another, the threat to their alpha male status taking precedence over anything else.

Even common sense.

She'd seen it before, so wasn't surprised. Just mildly annoyed. Far more important that they figure out what was going on. Martin at least seemed oblivious to the undercurrents. Or maybe he was just ignoring them.

Smart man.

Tate waited a beat, then shrugged. "Not much more than you do. I got the postcard the same time as Simone. But I've been living close to D.C., so I figured I'd catch up with Maurice there."

"Maurice Baxter," Martin said to no one in particular. "He was the head of D-9, right?"

"Yeah," Simone and Tate answered together. Once upon a time they'd practically been of single accord, working in tandem almost without the need for words.

"Anyway, as I told Simone, when I got there, Maurice was already dead. Someone shot him."

"Seems to be the modus operandi of the day." Reece pushed off the sill, pacing in front of the window. "So we've got two team members dead. And two others MIA. Is it possible that one of them could be behind all of this?"

"Doesn't track." Tate shook his head. "I mean, what reason would they have for pulling us out of the cold after all this time?"

"Maybe something Baxter said or did?"

"Anything's possible," Simone said, trying to sort through what they knew. "But I agree with Tate. This doesn't feel like D-9."

"Well, even if he didn't mean for it to turn into a setup, Baxter's summoning you all has done precisely that."

"You mean by pulling us all together again," Simone said.

"At least three of you."

"Did you see anything out there that would indicate Bea or Mather were in the forest?" Simone searched Tate's face, already knowing the answer.

"I didn't even see Ed." Tate shook his head, his eyes filled with pain. "Did he say anything before he died?"

Simone sighed. "Just that there was danger."

"All right, so no help from that corner." Tate dropped down into a tattered armchair, his frustration mirroring her own.

"How's the arm?" Reece had moved to her side, his fingers probing the wound on her shoulder.

"Fine. It wasn't much more than a scratch." She pulled

away from his touch, not liking the way her nerve endings reacted to the feel of his skin.

"What we need is to find Mather and Bea," Tate said, pulling them back to the situation at hand.

"Is there any way to figure out where Baxter sent them?" Reece asked.

Simone shook her head. "None that I know of. Tate?"

"I don't know any more than you do. Unless…" The man frowned, then reached into his pocket, producing a postcard identical to Simone's. "Let me see yours."

Simone reached into her pocket. "It's a little soggy."

Tate suppressed a smile and studied them both for a moment. "Well, it may not mean a thing, but I was right. Mine's different from yours. There are some numbers here. In the margin."

Simone took the card, Reece and Martin looking over her shoulder. They were apparently random, ringing the message on the card. There were ten of them. Three at the top and bottom, two on either side.

"What the hell is this supposed to mean?" Reece asked. "I take it your card didn't have numbers?"

"No. Just the message." Simone frowned down at the postcard, then looked up at Tate. "You have a theory as to what they mean?"

Tate shook his head. "I was hoping you'd know. Or that you had something similar on your card."

Simone blew out a breath, handing the card to Martin. "We're just going in circles. Meanwhile our assailant is out there regrouping. And unless I miss my guess, it won't be long before he finds us again."

"So we're on borrowed time." Tate shrugged. "Won't be the first time."

"Well, my bet is that these are coordinates. Look at this." Martin laid the card on the table, and they all gathered round it. "There are ten numbers and five of you, right?"

Simone nodded.

"So if you figure two numbers for each coordinate, that would mean this is a template for finding all of you. A fallback position in case something goes wrong."

Reece studied the card. "I'll bite. But how do we know which numbers go together?"

"We don't for certain. But the only way to connect all the numbers is to go through a center point. And Maurice, to hear you tell it, was the heart of D-9."

"The center," Simone said, shooting a look at Tate, who shrugged.

"It's possible."

Martin grabbed a pencil and made a dot in the center. "See, if you connect on angles through this point you get a star of sorts. And each ray has a pair of numbers associated with it. One at each end."

"All right." Reece said, producing Simone's GPS. "If you're right, then one of the coordinate sets should be for Corpus."

Martin studied the numbers. "There. It should be this one." He traced a ray that ran from upper right corner to the lower left.

"How did you figure it out so fast?" Simone asked with a smile. As usual, Martin's prowess with numbers was impressive.

"Nautical charts. We used them a lot on the *Starlight.*" Martin had spent the summer between his junior and senior year working on a shrimper. Reece had thought the hard physicality would be good for his brother. But Martin had reveled in the mathematical probabilities, like mapping possible places to drag for shrimp. "These coordinates are close to the ones we used. So I figure they have to be Corpus." Even Tate looked impressed.

Reece entered the numbers into the little tracking device. It hummed for a moment, and then presented them with a map of Texas, the south coast town flashing red. "I'll be damned."

"Where were you, Tate?" Simone asked. "You said it was somewhere close to D.C."

"Virginia. Richmond, actually. But I wasn't there very much."

"This looks right." Martin said, tracing another ray.

Tate took the GPS and entered the coordinates. Richmond flashed red.

"All right. So we've got three left." Simone leaned against the back of a chair. "And one of them was Ed's. How do we use the information to find Bea and Mather?"

"Any idea what names they're using?" Reece asked as Tate typed the coordinates into the GPS.

"Probably their own. We used code names when we were part of D-9. So changing our identities wasn't all that necessary. Remember, our relocation was only a precaution. At that point there was no one on our trails, and presumably no one interested. The only risk came from someone discovering a) that the division existed, and b) that we were present in Sangre de Cristo."

"I've got a location in southwestern Montana. And another in Pennsylvania. In the north. Looks like maybe the Poconos."

"What about the third one?" Reece asked.

"Silicon Valley in California." Tate frowned. "That's got to be Ed. He was a whiz with computers."

"Or maybe that's too obvious," Simone said. "But at least we've got three places to check out."

"And you think they're using their real names?" Martin was still staring at the postcard.

"It's a possibility. Or if not, then maybe a variation." Simone studied her brother-in-law. "You think you can find them?"

"Maybe," he said, looking up from the postcard. "It's almost impossible these days not to leave some trace on the Internet. Even if you're laying low, there's usually something. A credit or utility account."

"But we don't have a computer," Reece said.

"Actually, we do." Martin's smile was smug. He was obviously feeling more comfortable now that he was out of the line of fire. "While you all were out providing target practice for our shooter, I was exploring our abode."

"Don't tell me this place yielded a computer." Tate shot a doubting look around the sparse accommodations.

"Not at first glance. But I'm an inquiring kind of guy." Martin pointed toward the kitchen. "There's a cellar here. And in the cellar a closet. Apparently our host isn't so trusting of uninvited guests."

"Turns out his concerns were warranted." This from Reece, who was trying not to laugh.

"Anyway," Martin said, refusing to allow his brother to ruin the moment, "I managed to unlock said closet. And among other things…" He walked over behind the sofa, producing a laptop. "Voilà."

"Does it work?" Tate asked.

"Don't know. It booted up. You all came back from

your river adventure before I had the chance to find out anything more. But there's an Ethernet cable. So I'm figuring that means there's a broadband connection somewhere around here."

"So much for escaping it all." Reece laughed. "Should have known Welmer wouldn't be able to leave civilization behind."

"Hey, stop complaining," Martin said, already starting the hunt for the cable outlet. "If there really is Internet access, I bet you anything I can find your missing team members. Or at least where they were living until Baxter's little bombshell dropped out of their mailboxes."

"It's as good a place to start as anywhere." Tate said, loading the hunting rifle he'd pulled from over the fireplace. "While you do that, I think I'll check around outside. Make sure we haven't been discovered."

"Why don't you let me do that," Reece said, reaching for the weapon. "You and Simone need to come up with a list of people with a motive to come after D-9."

"There's no way to name them all," Tate said, not surrendering the gun.

"Well, we're going to have to try," Simone said, looking first at Reece and then at Tate. "Reece's right. The quicker we figure out who's behind this, the quicker we'll be able to figure out a way to put a stop to it. And despite the fact that we made a lot of enemies along the way, there are probably only a handful that would carry the grudge after all this time."

"All right." He nodded, handing over the rifle. "Guess you've got a point."

Reece took the gun, wondering if he'd imagined the other man's reluctance to part with it. Even if he hadn't, he told himself it didn't mean anything. Just a natural desire to maintain some semblance of control.

And he, of all people, certainly understood that.

SIMONE STOOD on the front porch, letting the stillness of the mountains surround her. Sunset in the mountains was quick, the moment between light and dark divided by a second when the sun hung motionless against the tops of the mountains. There and then gone, taking with it the world's light. There would be stars soon, but for the moment there was only the deep cloak of darkness.

Light from the cabin spilled out across the porch and onto the cropped grasses that passed for a lawn. Simone stepped off the wooden planking and made her way toward the split-rail fence that surrounded the house.

Reece was standing near a corner at the driveway. He was barely discernible in the half-light, but Simone figured she'd be able to find him even in the dark. "Thought maybe you could use some company." She stopped, looking out over the fence at the trees beyond. "You see anything?"

"If there's someone out there, he's keeping to himself."

"We're way off the beaten path, and assuming we lost him when we were in the river, it won't be easy for him to pick up our trail."

"But eventually he'll find us." Reece turned toward her, his face still hidden in shadow.

"Yeah. I think we can count on that. Unless we find him first."

"You guys come up with any ideas about who it might be?"

"As I said before, the list is long. But we both agree that

one of Ramirez's followers is a good bet. Tate caught a glimpse of the guy in the woods and said he could have been Latino."

"But I thought no one knew you were in Sangre de Cristo?"

"They weren't supposed to. But the speculation was there. And the truth is that Martin was right. If a person wants to find someone badly enough they'll find a trail. Internet or otherwise."

"You think Maurice cracked?"

"The Maurice I knew would have taken it to the grave. But he was getting older. And things change. Priorities shift." She shrugged. "Doesn't really matter who gave us up. What's important is to identify the hunter."

"So what about relatives, or henchmen or something. Your original intel say anything about Ramirez's family or friends?"

"There was a wife, of course. And three children, if I'm remembering right. At least two of them were in Sangre de Cristo." She thought again about the children who had died in the village, the memory making her shudder.

Reece noticed, his brows drawing together in worry.

But she shook her head, waving a hand. "It's just so hard to forget."

"Is that what the nightmares were about?" The question was cautious, as if he wasn't certain she would answer. But she owed him that much. At least this part of it. Her nightmares weren't always about the massacre. Sometimes it was her mother or sometimes others from her past. But it really didn't matter; they all revolved around the same theme.

"Yes," she said, looking down at her hands, searching for the right words. "They were worse when we first met. That's why I wouldn't stay the night for so long. I didn't want you to know. But eventually, I just took the chance."

"You said you never remembered what you were dreaming about." He stared into the dark, clearly trying to control his emotions. "I thought maybe it was something to do with me. Especially when we started to fight so much."

"Oh God, no." She reached out to touch his hand, but stopped herself mid-action, letting it fall to her side instead. "It was never about you."

"But it seemed like they came more frequently toward the end of our marriage."

"Reece, I've always had the nightmares. Maybe you were just more aware of them at the end."

He frowned, started to say something more, and then dropped it, clearly not wanting to start something that couldn't be finished. At least not here. "Do you still have them?"

She nodded. "I doubt they'll ever go away. Some things just can't be processed completely. And that's what a nightmare is, isn't it? Our subconscious trying to deal with the incomprehensible?"

"Something like that." He turned to look at her. "You know, for a kick-ass CIA agent, you're pretty damn philosophical."

She smiled in the dark. "Don't tell anyone. I wouldn't want the word to get out." She put her foot up on the railing, staring out at the mountains. "Do you ever think about the beginning, when we were first in love and it seemed that nothing could stop us?"

"Sure. I think about it a lot. I wonder what the hell happened."

"I don't mean that. I'm just asking if you remember the good times. I'd like to think that no matter what happens between us, those memories can't be corrupted."

"Preserving the fantasy?"

She turned to look at him, thinking he was making fun of her, but he only looked sad. "I suppose you could call it that. But sometimes when I'm looking out at the sunset I remember those nights on the beach in Antigua."

"Our honeymoon."

She nodded. "It was magical. Like the whole world belonged to us. And every little thing was meant for our pleasure or amusement."

"It must have been really different from what you were used to."

"It was like waking up on a different planet." She tipped her head to look up at the stars. "But it was the same one. See." She pointed at the sky. "There's Orion. And Cassiopeia, and Ursa Major." She sketched the Big Dipper with her index finger. "Wherever you are, they're always there. Stupid, I know, but I find it comforting."

"No. I understand what you're saying—it's nice to have constants. Something that you can hold on to. Like a memory."

"Yeah."

They stood in companionable silence, the first she could remember in over a year. How sad that they'd lost the ability to be comfortable just being alone together. It had been such a beautiful gift.

"Martin have any luck with the computer?" he asked, forcing her thoughts to the here and now.

"Yeah." She blew out a breath, running a hand through her hair. "He's holed up in the loft trying to get a bead on Mather and Bea. We were right about the Silicon Valley coordinates. Martin found an article in a computer journal citing an Edward Hammond. There was even a picture. Seems he capitalized on the government's training." An image of Ed bleeding in the forest presented itself front and center. "Not that it did him a damn bit of good."

"I'm sorry about your friend." Reece reached over to touch her shoulder and she jumped at the contact. "Did I hurt you?" There was real concern in his voice, and so she answered honestly.

"No. I'm fine. It's just that I…" She trailed off, wishing she'd lied. That she'd told him it was the torn skin from the bullet graze.

"What?"

"Nothing. I guess I'm just not sure of how we're supposed to interact. Now that we're…"

"Divorced?"

She nodded, feeling really stupid. She'd thought she'd had it all sorted out. But now she just felt raw—and confused. So much had passed between them in the last forty-eight hours, feelings she'd thought dead rekindling. But still nothing tangible had changed.

"I know what you mean." Somehow he'd managed to close the distance between them, his breath warm against her face. She knew every inch of him. Every mole, every scar. In many ways she knew him better than she knew herself. And the idea that he was no longer a part of her was as inconceivable as it was unavoidable.

"Do you really think we could have made it if I'd told

you the truth?" She tipped her head up to meet his gaze, trying to find some hint of what he was feeling.

"My instinct is to say yes. To blame your lies for all our problems." He reached out to cup her face. "But that wouldn't be fair. It takes two people to make a marriage, and I suppose in my own way I was as disengaged as you. The truth is we both have issues. But the simple fact remains that, whatever the reasons, we couldn't make it work."

It was a pronouncement of ultimate failure, and though she'd had the same thought herself, it hurt to hear it out loud, the words hanging between them with the finality of a death knell.

"Hey guys, anything happening out there? Tate was worried when you were gone so long." Martin stood on the drive, his frown indication that despite his mention of Tate, *he* was the one who was really worried.

Simone took a step away from Reece, the distance more than just physical. "We're fine. Just trying to make sense of everything that's been happening."

"You find anything more?" Reece asked, turning toward his brother.

"Nothing yet on Mather. Tate says she wasn't exactly a spill-her-guts kind of gal. Makes finding traces of her that much harder."

"She was a linguist. But her passion was mechanics. She could take apart and put together anything. Especially cars. I remember once in Rwanda, Tate and I were pinned down in the bush. The rest of the team was about a mile away, but there were a couple hundred pissed-off guerillas in between. The truck we'd commandeered broke down. And nothing short of a miracle was going to get it going again. Honest to God, I thought we were done.

"Night closed in and we could hear gunfire everywhere. Then all of sudden, Mather comes tearing out of the bush, gun blazing like the sheriff in a spaghetti western. She had the truck running in three minutes flat. And we got the hell out of Dodge. If it hadn't been for her..."

"I'm sure you returned the favor."

Simone shrugged. "She said that, too, but some things you can't repay. Anyway, you don't want to hear old stories. The point is that if I had to call it, I'd say that Mather would have found a job that at least let her tinker with something mechanical."

"Not a bad idea." Martin turned to go, already following the new line of thought.

"What about Bea?" Simone asked, knowing full well that in all likelihood her friends were dead. Otherwise they'd have been at the rendezvous.

Already almost halfway to the cabin, Martin stopped and spun around. "Sorry. I guess I fixated on finding Mather." He shrugged. "I did find a reference to a Brasel. It was on an Internal page at the Missoula library Web site. The page is an index of computer use. Could be for employees, could be a roster of public users. No way to know for sure. And since I've only got the last name, I can't even say that it's her. But the coordinates seem to back it up. And the time is right."

"So we're heading for Missoula." It was a statement, not a question, and for the first time since their ordeal had begun Simone felt like they'd moved from defense to offense. Of course it all depended on Martin's information being correct, and then them finding Bea alive.

But hell, hope sprang eternal.

CHAPTER FOURTEEN

MISSOULA, MONTANA BEGAN life in 1860 as a town called Hellgate. Reece wasn't sure where the moniker had originated, but the little town located at the base of Mount Sentinel was anything but hellish. Nestled in the heart of the northern Rockies, Missoula was a thriving university town that also served as county seat. The valley was home to three rivers and a couple of national forests. Definitely not a bad place to settle after a life spent working for the underbelly of the CIA.

Of course they didn't have any actual proof that Bea Brasel had relocated here. At least not yet. It had taken the better part of two days to make their way from Colorado to Montana. After securing another car, they'd avoided the main highways, choosing instead a circuitous route that provided at least some degree of certainty that they weren't being followed.

After checking into a motel, they'd split up, Martin heading for a cyber café and a more powerful Internet connection, Tate checking in with some old contacts to try and get a bead on Ramirez's organization, leaving Reece and Simone to check out the library and its possible connection to Bea.

The building was located in the heart of downtown

and, like all libraries everywhere, was permeated with the smell of good books.

"Penny for your thoughts." Simone's words broke into his reverie.

"Just letting the smell take me back."

"The smell?" Simone asked, curiosity coloring her voice.

"Yeah. Leather and paper combining with ink and a twist of the imagination. When I was a kid we spent a lot of time in the library. My mom brought us every week. It was like having my own private portal to the world."

"Now who's sounding philosophical?" Simone asked, fighting a smile.

"Hey. There's still nothing in the world I can think of that tops the satisfaction of turning that first page, knowing that adventure awaits."

"Ludlum. I remember." She laid a hand on his arm, and just for a moment he forgot the gravity of the situation and the fact that they were not a couple anymore. "But we're not here to find a book."

Her words brought reality home again, and he sighed, pulling away to walk over to a row of carrels, each containing a PC. The carrels were all occupied, the various tenants running the gamut from middle-school-aged to retirement. The gentleman on the end was obviously new at the computer game, judging from the colorful language emanating from his carrel. "Looks like Martin was right about public access to computers."

"Which actually might make it more difficult to get information," Simone said, her brows drawing together in a frown.

"It's a small town." Reece shrugged. "If we're lucky maybe someone here will remember her being here."

"Can I help you?" A middle-aged woman in a sweater and chinos tilted her head with the question, the patient smile of a librarian lighting her face.

Simone's hand tightened on his arm. "I hope so. We're looking for someone…"

"A friend." Reece finished for her. "My wife and I are vacationing in Yellowstone, and thought it might be fun to look Bea up."

"Does she work here?" The lady's smile faded ever so slightly, perplexity taking over.

"No. At least not that we're aware of. But she's mentioned using the library computers on several occasions, so when we didn't find her at home, we thought she might be here."

The librarian nodded as if it all made perfect sense. "What's your friend's name? I know most of the regulars."

"Bea Brasel," Reece said.

"Don't recognize the name. What does she look like?"

"About my height," Simone said, smoothly picking up the conversation. "Maybe a little taller. Brownish hair, probably cropped short. A few years older than me."

The woman shook her head. "I'm sorry. Doesn't sound like anyone I know." She frowned. "Might be that Janece would know."

"Janece?" Reece prompted.

"She's the head librarian. She's here most days. I'm only part-time," the woman said by way of explanation.

"Is she here now?" Reece tried to keep the impatience from his voice. Wouldn't do to antagonize the woman.

"Yes. Over at the circulation desk." She pointed to a young woman handing a stack of books to a kid in faded blue jeans. "I hope you find your friend." Her smile now was a little forced. She'd obviously decided they were a couple of oddballs, looking for their friend in the library.

They walked over to the circulation desk and waited their turn as Janece checked out books to a line of patrons. Finally at the front of the line, Reece smiled down at her. She looked to be all of about twenty, making her role as head librarian seem a stretch. "We're trying to track down a friend of ours," he said by way of introduction. "And your associate over there thought you might know if she'd been in today. Her name is Bea Brasel."

The sunny disposition disappeared into distress, and Reece ran back over his words to try and figure out what he'd said to offend.

"We're old friends from college," Simone offered. "Up here on vacation. Thought it would be a lark to see Bea, and so here we are. She told me she came to the library quite a bit. Have we got the wrong one?"

"No. Not at all. Bea came here all the time. She loved to use the computer. Said she'd never be able to get the hang of one on her own, but with me to help, she enjoyed surfing the Web." The woman was on the verge of tears, and Reece shivered in anticipation. "I don't know how to tell you this." The woman's face filled with concern. "Bea is dead."

"Oh, my God." Simone's reaction was as genuine as they came. "When?"

"Almost a week ago. I still can't believe it." She shook her head, clearly upset. "She ran her car off the side of the road up near Cloudburst Creek. We've been trying to get better lighting along that stretch of highway for years. The curves are deadly, especially when there's snow. I'm so sorry to be the one to tell you." She stood up, her hands fluttering uselessly.

"Was there an inquest?" Reece tried to keep his voice casual. A stricken friend. But the authority of the attorney snuck in just the same.

Janece blinked twice, seemingly considering the question. "Don't think so. The car was badly burned. Not much left of—" She paused, wringing her hands now. "What I mean is that I don't think there was anything much left to examine. If you've got questions, I'm sure they'd be able to answer them over at the police station."

Simone touched his arm, and Reece realized that the patrons in line behind them were hanging on every word. "Thank you," he said. "You've been very helpful. I'm sorry to have dredged it all up again. It's just that she's special to us, too."

The woman nodded, clearly wishing she could drop into a hole in the floor.

"Is she buried near here?" Simone asked, her voice quivering with emotion.

"Yes, out in the cemetery near the fountain."

Simone nodded her thanks and the two of them made their way out the door. They stood in the sunlight in silence, the sound of street traffic providing a gentle blanket of normalcy.

"She seemed convinced that it was an accident," Reece said, putting voice to both of their thoughts.

"But it sounds like there was no way to be sure."

"Excuse me." The cursing man at the computer station had followed them outside. "I didn't mean to listen in on your conversation, but you were asking about Bea Brasel."

"You knew her?"

"I did. Worked with her out at the plant."

"Plant?"

"Plum Creek Timber. She's been the receptionist there for the past eight years. You were friends of hers?"

Simone nodded. "Long time ago."

"Bea never talked much about her life before Missoula. Hell, who am I kidding, she never talked much at all. Real quiet one, our Bea. But I liked her. And I don't believe for a minute she drove off the road."

"What do you mean?" Reece asked.

"I mean that woman could drive a car like nobody's business. There ain't no way she drove off that embankment. And even if she did, car shouldn't have caught on fire like that."

"So why wasn't there an investigation?"

"There was a cursory one, but no one was pushing for answers and it was just easier to call it an accident. Anyway—" he shot a nervous glance over his shoulder "—isn't any of my business, but I thought you all deserved to know."

"Thank you." Simone reached over and gave the man's hand a squeeze. "I'm sure Bea was really lucky to have you for a friend."

The man smiled, the sun lines on his face crinkling with the gesture. "I best be getting back." He turned and took the library steps two at a time, his vigor belying his age.

"So what the hell do you make of that?" Reece turned to ask Simone.

She shook her head, brushing away tears. "Burning a car is the easiest way I know of to cover up evidence of foul play. And if no one was seriously investigating, there's no reason it would be questioned."

"He seemed pretty convinced that this one had help."

"Yeah. But I'm not sure what we can do about it. It's not

like I can walk into the police station and ask for the investigation report. We've already been too high profile as it is."

"I hardly think news from Corpus has traveled all the way to Missoula, Montana."

"It's possible. But even if they haven't heard about our disappearance, there'd still be questions. Why we were here in the first place. And how the hell we knew to go to the library. I think the best thing now is to head back to the motel and regroup. Maybe Martin or Tate have come up with something else."

"My guess is there's no way we'll ever know for sure."

"Probably not." The regret in her voice mirrored his own. "But given everything we know, my gut tells me that the killer found Bea before he found us."

"THERE'S NOTHING in the paper. At least in the online archives. But then maybe it wouldn't be. I mean, if they listed every traffic fatality there'd be no room for anything else." Martin closed the laptop with a sigh.

"Short of demanding an autopsy, I don't know what else we can do," Tate said, his voice tight with anger. "We may not be able to prove it wasn't an accident, but I tend to agree with you, Simone. There are too many coincidences. Maurice calls us in. Maurice gets killed. Bea gets killed. And then someone chases you halfway across the country with obvious deadly intent."

"So we're left with Mather," Reece said. He was perched on the windowsill, fiddling with the blinds. Simone resisted the urge to reach over and still his fingers.

The motel they'd chosen was on the outskirts of Missoula. One of those throwbacks to the fifties with little cottages for guests. A bubbling stream ran behind it, the mountains in the distance, giving the place a scenic backdrop. Of course if one looked out the front window, the whizzing cars on Interstate 90 removed all illusion.

Still, it was functional. And for the moment that's all they needed.

"You find anything at the cyber café?" Tate asked.

"I'm afraid she's even more of an enigma than Bea. But I did find a Wilson Mather listed as working for a tool and dye in Stroudsburg."

Simone considered the possibility of Mather switching her name. "It's not inconceivable. Did you follow up on it?"

"Yeah. And the news isn't good. Wilson...or Mather did indeed work for the tool and dye. She served in an engineering capacity, working with their manufacturing equipment."

"So this Wilson was female?" This from Tate, who was sitting in a chair with his feet propped up, his casual pose at odds with the intensity of his gaze.

Martin nodded.

"You said the news was bad," Simone prompted, her stomach twisting. Mather had always seemed so alive. She'd been a tiny thing. No more than a hundred pounds soaking wet, but she'd been larger than life, taking on things even the guys in D-9 had hesitated over. Simone had always admired her fearlessness.

"According to the guy on the phone, Mather was killed when her house burned down. Investigators said it was the electrical wiring."

"No fucking way," Tate said, shooting out of his chair. "Mather would have checked and double-checked any wiring within a fifty yard radius. She wasn't the type to ignore shit like that."

"Things happen, Tate." Reece's tone was probably meant to be soothing, but it had the opposite effect on Tate.

"Maybe to some people, but not to Mather. Not like that."

"We don't even know for certain that it's her," Simone said, knowing damn well that it was. Mather had walked into the line of fire so many times and escaped unscathed—it just seemed so unbelievable that it all could have ended like this.

"I've got a picture. From the obit." Martin held out a faxed photograph and Simone took it, waiting a beat before looking at it, not wanting confirmation of what she already knew.

"Is it her?" Tate's voice was deceptively quiet.

Simone fought against tears. Damn it all to hell. These people had been her friends. The only family she'd had before Reece and Martin. "Yeah," she said, holding out the photograph. "It's her."

Reece took her hand, his touch comforting and alarming at the same time. Caring about people caused pain. If she'd learned one thing in this life it was that.

"So we've got three dead," Martin said, trying to pull them back to the issues at hand.

"Four. If you count Maurice. And if it hadn't been for your brother, he'd have probably gotten Tate and me, too." Simone pulled away from Reece and squared her shoulders. "So what did you find out about Ramirez's organization?"

"Plenty," Tate said, dropping the photograph on the table. "As we suspected, the organization is going strong. Still opposing the government and, best I can tell, still financing operations through drug trafficking. The Company has had them on a watch list since Sangre de Cristo, but they've never been able to make inroads into the inside or build a case against them." He opened a file folder. "There is some disagreement about who is running the organization these days. But the key candidates seem to be Ramirez's right-hand man Ramón Diego, his daughter Isabella and his son Carlos."

"So the children survived." Simone wasn't sure why she was pleased, but she was.

"Two did," Tate said, consulting his notes. "According to intel, Amon, the youngest, was killed at Sangre de Cristo. Isabella was also there but she survived. Carlos was actually in America at school when it happened."

"How old are they now?" Martin asked, tapping something into the laptop.

"Isabella is twenty and Carlos is twenty five."

"Seems kind of young to be heading an organization like Ramirez's." Reece frowned. "How old is Diego?"

"Somewhere in his fifties." Tate looked up from the file to answer the question. "But you have to remember that this sort of thing is often treated almost as a monarchy. When one family member dies another ascends to the throne, so to speak."

"More like Mafia, if you ask me," Martin muttered.

"You're not too far wrong." Simone smiled at him. "There is a certain similarity. Especially on the drug-running side of the equation. But there is much more at stake here. These people are fighting for more than financial success. They're fighting for ideals. And whether we agree with them or not, the scope is bigger than what we think of as organized crime."

"Still sounds pretty Godfatherish to me." Martin shrugged.

"So do we know where these key players are? Is the operation still based out of Sangre de Cristo?"

"This is where the intel gets really murky," Tate said. "Understandably after the massacre, the junta went underground. Deep underground. Partially to regroup and nurse their wounds and partially to avoid detection. My contacts believe that they're still centered in Nicaragua, a compound near the Honduras border the locals call *El Ojo de la Tormenta*."

"The eye of the storm. Interesting connotation." Reece sat down on the tweed monstrosity that passed for a couch. "So are the key players living there?"

"No. And that's what makes it so hard to determine exactly who is in charge. Isabella is living in Managua. According to the intel I got, she's the mistress of the current president there, Manuel Ortega. Ramón Diego is working there as well. It's unclear whether his association is with Ortega or Isabella."

"She could be a plant. Her father's organization would never support a man like Ortega." Simone frowned.

"Either way, she's an asset for Ortega. The daughter of his government's enemy on his arm has got to carry a lot weight." Reece leaned back against the sofa, arms crossed, as he analyzed the situation.

"What about the son? He's the eldest. It would seem logical that he'd succeed his father."

"That's where it really gets interesting." Tate grinned. Simone concealed her own smile. Despite the gravity of the situation, he was enjoying himself. Of all the D-9 members, Tate was the least likely to have found peace in civilian life. The man was a born soldier, no matter whom he chose to fight for. "Carlos seems to have disappeared. The latest scuttle has him in the U.S. But no confirmation as to where."

"So he could have been the man you saw in the woods," Simone said.

"What's the time frame?" Reece asked. "Does it coincide with Maurice's death?"

"Nothing definitive. But word on the street is that he was destroyed by his father's death, and that the only thing that keeps him breathing is the thought of revenge."

"So he's got a motive to come after us. But there's no way in hell Maurice would have willingly met with him. And it's even less likely that he'd have given him information."

"There are all kinds of ways to get information. Maurice was the only one who knew how to connect the dots that separated us. But there were others with pieces of the puzzle. Maybe Carlos got the information that way and put it together."

"Maybe, but we don't have anything solid. Just a lot of conjecture based on circumstantial evidence. Carlos may be in the country. He may have been in D.C. He may even have been in the woods today. All of it interesting, but none of it absolute." Simone ran a hand through her hair, feeling again like a sitting duck. A position she did not relish at all.

"So we need more information." Reece as usual injected a note of rationality. "And the best place I can think of to get it is from Maurice."

"But he's dead," Martin said, stating the obvious.

"Yes, but there's still his office. There could be clues there. Hell, I make my living finding the truth after the fact. I assume the two of you can figure out a way to get us in?"

"It's doable." Tate nodded, his gaze locking with

Simone's. "What do you think? We still have friends out there. I think we could call in a few favors."

"It might work. But we're running out of time. Driving cross-country is only likely to make us more of a target."

"I can get us transport. No problem." Tate's enthusiasm was catching. "I'll make the arrangements. We'll plan for the morning. I'll be back in a couple of hours. In the meantime, Martin, see if you can dig up anything else on Carlos and Isabella Ramirez. Despite Simone's doubts, I think they're behind this. And the sooner we understand what we're up against, the better."

CHAPTER FIFTEEN

"HAS IT OCCURRED to you that Tate seems to be a little more connected than he should be for an operative who is supposed to have been out of the business for ten years?" Reece asked, coming to sit beside Simone on the picnic table in front of the cottage.

The wind had come up, giving the air a chilly edge, but Simone relished the feeling. She'd needed to clear her head, the mountain air as always working its magic. A little stand of pine trees off to one side of the cabins rustled in the breeze. "You're never really out of the business, Reece. I'm proof of that."

"But could you call on resources to get us a plane, or the latest intel on the Ramirez organization?" His frown underscored his distrust of Tate.

"Yeah, I think I could. There's sort of an unwritten code. Operatives help their own. Just because we've been out of the game doesn't mean that we haven't got people we can call on. People we've worked with in the past."

"But ten years is a long time."

Simone shrugged. "Folks in espionage have long memories. And even though we were black ops, we still had contacts we worked with on a regular basis. Anyway, I assure you if I put my mind to it, I could secure pretty much anything I want."

"But how can you be sure that the people you're contacting aren't going to put you in greater jeopardy?"

"They just aren't. Look, it's like a big family. We don't always agree on things. And sometimes the right and left hand are not working in tandem, but push comes to shove, we're going to back each other up."

"So you trust him?"

"Tate?" She tried to keep the surprise out of her voice. "Of course. I told you, he's had my back more times than I can possibly count. In fact, if it hadn't been for him, I wouldn't have made it out of Sangre de Cristo. Yeah, I trust him. With my life."

"I see." He stared out at the line of mountains ringing the valley, his expression carefully neutral.

"Look, I know this is hard for you." She turned to face him. "It's all coming at you so fast. But D-9 was good people. The division did something for us that nothing else could have. It gave us a reason to get up in the morning. Something we could count on. And over time we grew to trust each other. Depend on each other.

"It was a unique world we lived in, I'll grant you that. And some of the things we did maybe weren't acceptable in polite society. But we made the world a better place. That much I'm sure of." She knew she sounded defensive. And hated herself for it.

"I'm not questioning D-9, Simone. I'm just trying to assess our current situation, and it seems to me that Tate is being remarkably forthcoming with information."

"So is Martin." She smiled at him, recognizing that there was a hint of jealousy present. Maybe not a me-Tarzan-you-Jane kind of thing. But a little bit of the green-eyed monster nevertheless. If it hadn't been Reece she'd have been flattered. But she suspected the jealousy was as much over the fact that Tate had been able to provide things Reece couldn't as it was about the fact that Tate and Simone had once been close.

Really close.

Liaisons within the division were not uncommon. Like most occupations where access to others was limited, there was an inbred motivation to hook up with one another, Ed and Natalie a case in point.

But though Simone and Tate had been an item for a while, there'd never been any potential for something long lasting. The chemistry wasn't right. But she wasn't about to share the fact with her ex.

"I didn't mean to start an argument. I just thought it was worth bringing up."

"I understand." They sat for a moment in uncomfortable silence, and Simone mourned again the fact that they'd lost the ability to communicate without talking. Once upon a time she'd wanted nothing more than to sit with him like this, surrounded by beauty, full of love.

God, she was getting maudlin.

"Hey, you guys, come in here," Martin called. "I think you'd better see this."

Simone pushed off the table, feeling as if there was still something left unsaid, something more they needed to settle between them. But now wasn't the time. "We're coming."

She followed Reece into the cottage, and settled down onto the sofa in front of the TV.

"They're talking about us."

The newscaster's head was replaced by footage of an ambulance and stretcher.

"That's our house," Reece said, as usual forgetting that technically it was no longer his.

The picture cut to an on the scene reporter. "The investigation of the disappearance of Simone Sheridan took a turn for the dark side this morning with the discovery of postal worker Laura Dominguez unconscious in the woods near Sheridan's home. Dominguez, shot twice in the chest, was taken to Corpus Christi Medical Center, but doctors are saying there is little hope for recovery. Currently comatose, Dominguez was reported missing four days ago. Police are not saying whether the two incidents are related, but questions continue to center on Sheridan's ex-husband, Assistant District Attorney Reece Sheridan…"

The voice continued, but Simone couldn't focus, an image of Laura laughing at the mailbox filling her mind. "Oh, my God, her kids…" The words came out of their own volition, somewhere between a whisper and a sigh.

Reece was beside her in an instant, his arms warm around her. "It's not your fault."

She broke free, tears welling. "The hell it's not. If it weren't for me, for my past, none of this would be happening. Martin would be at home on spring break, and you wouldn't be under investigation, and Laura…Laura wouldn't be lying in a hospital bed at death's door."

"No matter what you did in the past, Simone, it doesn't warrant someone hunting you down. You're as much a victim here as anyone."

"Except that I shouldn't have let any of it happen."

"There was no way you could have known someone would pop up like this. And even if you did know, you couldn't have predicted when. Laura was caught in the wrong place at the wrong time. It's horrible, I agree." He was holding her with both hands now, looking down into her eyes, his expression protective. "But it's not your fault."

"She was my friend." It was a ridiculous statement considering the friendship consisted of shared conversations at the mailbox, but Simone had treasured every moment.

"I know that, sweetheart. And I know you're hurting. But we've got to stay focused. It's the only way we're going to put an end to it."

"We'll get this guy, Simone." Martin stood beside Reece, his eyes filled with concern. God, what had she ever done to deserve this kind of loyalty?

Pushing aside her pain, she squared her shoulders, scrubbing at her eyes. She needed to find answers and find them fast. Only then could she clear her husband's name and maybe, just maybe, bring Laura a little peace.

"I'm all right." She met Reece's gaze, her own steady. "It was just such a shock."

"I know. I hate being manipulated. But it's obvious that this guy, whoever he is, is intent on keeping us in the game. If I couldn't go home before, I sure as hell can't now. I could have produced you and Martin as living proof of no harm done, but unfortunately, I can't do the same with Laura."

Simone shoved her emotions deep. Grief was only a detriment to what had to be done. Long years of training stood her in good stead, and she pulled away from Reece and Martin, her mind turning to the business at hand. "We've got to change how we look. There'll be pictures of us everywhere."

"God, I can't believe we're doing this." Martin's tone, as usual, was a mixture of trepidation and excitement. "It's just like a movie."

"This isn't a lark, Martin," Reece said. "This guy means business. He's killed at least two people that we know of. And potentially three more if our suspicions are right about Bea, Mather and Maurice. We've got to think through every move or we're going to be next."

"Exactly why we need to get to D.C. as quickly as possible." Tate stood in the doorway, his expression impassive. But it was clear he'd been there long enough to assess the situation. "The arrangements are all made. We leave at dawn. And since I'm the only one whose face isn't plastered all over the media, I'll go and see if I can round up disguises."

SIMONE SAT on the picnic table, running a hand through her newly shorn red hair. The shorter length brought out the natural curl, and the hair dye had done the rest. She'd been transformed. A pair of color contact lenses and a change of posture, and the new look would be complete.

She wasn't the only one with a new image. Martin now sported a spiky multicolored haircut that was more fitting a punker than a college senior. A pierced ear and a couple of henna tattoos completed his ensemble. Tate had left no detail to chance.

But it was Reece who was most changed. His dark hair was cropped close to his head, making his features seem harsher. Chiseled from stone. It was as if he'd stepped out of the body of the lawyer into the body of an outlaw, the battered Stetson only adding to the perception.

His weathered jeans hugged every curve, the muscles in his arms accentuated by the tight black T-shirt. She'd never seen him as anything but the buttoned-up-suit type. Had fallen in love with him because of that, in fact. How the hell had she missed this side of him?

She struggled to breathe, her mind playing out fantasies that she'd given up when she'd signed on the dotted line. Damn it all to hell. She still wanted him. It was as simple as that. And nothing, it seemed, not even the chasm between them, could stop the chemistry.

"Thinking about your friend?" Tate's voice broke into her reverie, and she felt ashamed. Laura was lying in the hospital, dying—or worse still, already dead—and she was daydreaming about jumping her ex-husband.

"All of it, really."

He dropped down onto the picnic table next to her. "You miss the old life?"

It was a complex question, and demanded a complex answer. But she wasn't sure she was up to the task. "Sometimes. The people more than the situations."

"Oh, come on, you've got to miss the adrenaline rush. You were more of a testosterone junkie than any man I ever knew."

She smiled at the image he'd conjured. "Surely I wasn't that gung ho."

"Well, maybe I'm oversimplifying. But I always figured you were more like me than most of the others."

"In what way? Besides the rush?"

"I don't know. It's hard to put something like that into words. The Spanish have a word, I think—simpatico? Like we're in sync. I'm not expressing myself very well."

"I think the phrase you're looking for is 'kindred spirit.' But I don't know that I ever thought of you like that. You were so damn intense."

"And you were butterflies and roses?"

She laughed again, feeling at ease in a way she hadn't

in a very long time. "I guess I had a few issues. But that was all a long time ago. Things change. People change."

"Is that what happened with your marriage? You changed?"

She turned to look at him, thinking that maybe he was teasing her, but his eyes were serious, as if he really wanted to know. "No. I lied. That's what happened to my marriage."

"About what? Another guy?"

Leave it to Tate to take things to a baser level.

"No. About my past. I lied about everything, Tate."

"You didn't tell him any of it?"

She shook her head. "I just exaggerated the past Maurice invented for me."

"Well, some of that's understandable, I guess. They made it pretty damn clear we weren't supposed to ever admit any knowledge of D-9 or its operations." He rested his hands on his knees, mulling it over. "But you should have told him about your life before division."

Tate was one of the few people who knew about the years before D-9. Every warped little detail. Maurice knew some of it, of course. And she'd confided in Bea. But outside the three of them, no one else knew anything at all about her childhood. Not L.A. or Chicago.

Especially not Reece.

"But you said you understood."

"I said I got the bit about D-9. But the rest is who you are, Simone. You can't run away from that."

"I can try."

"Yeah, and look where it got you." He waved a hand at the night-darkened woods.

"Look, my childhood was fucked-up. There's no

question about that. But that's not what got me here, Tate. D-9 got me here. D-9 and all the sons of bitches out there who'd still like to see us dead."

"Don't be so quick to dismiss your childhood, Simone. It's *that* mess that landed you in D-9. Besides, life isn't about what happens to you. It's about what you make happen."

"God, everyone's turned into a philosopher."

Tate shrugged with a grin. "Not me, sister. I'm just seeing a side of you I didn't know existed. And from my vantage point soft and pliable doesn't suit you. The way I see it, you're more of a take charge kind of woman. So all I'm saying is you need to decide what it is you want and go get it."

"But I can't. That's the problem. Every time I reach out to grab it, something gets in the way. It's like every time I get up, someone just knocks me down again. So after a while you wonder if you'd just be better off staying low, you know?"

"Or you come up swinging."

She sighed, tipping her head back, wondering when Tate had gotten so smart. "So do *you* miss it?"

"What? The old life? No. I learned a long time ago to never look back."

"But you just told me I should be honest about my past."

"No. I said you should be true to it. There's a difference. We are who we are. Situations may change, but we don't, at least not fundamentally."

"So have you made a new life? Found someone?"

"No." He shook his head. "Relationships, in my opinion, are highly overrated. In the end, the only person you can really trust is yourself."

"From philosopher to cynic in under five minutes—not bad, Tate."

She expected him to laugh, but instead he sighed. "You used to agree with me."

And for the first time she considered that maybe Tate was wrong. Maybe people could change. Or be changed. Maybe loving Reece had made her less cautious. Less cynical. Or maybe it had just turned her into a fool.

"Maybe I did. I don't know. I'm not seeing anything clearly right now. Everything's been turned inside out, my life with D-9 and my life with Reece colliding into some kind of unrecognizable conglomeration."

"I thought your life with Reece was over."

"So did I…."

"Well, you know what Maurice would say." He slid his arm around her shoulder, the feeling comfortable in the way of a favorite sweatshirt or blanket. In some weird way, Tate felt like home.

She leaned against his shoulder, memory taking her back. "He'd tell me to stop with the emotional bullshit and keep my eye on the ball." She could feel the rumble of Tate's laughter as he, too, was transported back.

"And what would you tell him?" He reached up to stroke her hair, as if somehow their physical connection could bring the old man back.

"I'd tell him to go to hell." She whispered the last, tears filling her eyes. So many people lost.

"I hate to interrupt. But I thought maybe we ought to go over the plans for tomorrow." If ice could metamorphose into a voice, Reece had accomplished the feat.

Simone jerked away, color flooding her face. She opened her mouth to explain, but Tate beat her to it.

"We were just catching up on old times. Remembering Maurice." Tate's tone was neutral, friendly even, but based on the muscle ticking in Reece's jaw, he wasn't taking it that way. "So, what's up?"

At first she thought Reece wasn't going to answer, but then he shrugged, the gesture at odds with the anger simmering in his eyes. "I just thought it'd be a good idea if we talk through the details."

"It's pretty straightforward," Tate said, still sitting next to her on the picnic table. "I arranged for a private plane to pick us up at a corporate airstrip just outside of town. Seemed better to avoid the airport. It's pretty small, but there's bound to be security."

"So how the hell is it that you managed to arrange a plane?"

"Friend of a friend who owed me a favor. I kept up with as many contacts as was feasible. A guy never knows when that sort of thing will come in handy. You know?"

"So did you have contact with any of the others after the relocation?" Reece's eyes were narrowed in speculation.

"Not unless you count Maurice."

"You saw Maurice?" Simone almost choked on the words.

"Once or twice," Tate shrugged. "He had a couple of things that needed to be taken care of and I'm really good at that sort of thing."

"When was the last time you saw him?" Reece asked.

"About a month before all this started."

"Why the hell didn't you tell us before?" Simone tried, but couldn't contain her exasperation.

"I would have, but the opportunity didn't present itself.

And nothing happened that sheds any light on any of this. Believe me, I've been over it again and again."

"Well, humor us, and go over it one more time." Reece straddled the end of the bench, looking almost dangerous in the light spilling from the cottage windows.

"All right." Tate tipped back his head and released a long breath, gathering his thoughts. "Maurice called and said he needed to meet. We set up a place and time. I told you I was in Richmond, so I wasn't far away. Anyway, once we were together he told me that he had to take a meeting with someone that could be a threat to D-9, or what was left of it."

"What did he want you to do?"

"He wanted me to be prepared to handle it, if the meeting didn't turn out the way Maurice wanted it to."

"Did he say who the meeting was with?"

"No. But I got the idea that it was someone from our past. Which is why I thought of the Ramirez connection. Especially in light of the fact that Carlos is purported to be in the U.S."

"So what happened?"

"I don't know. We left it that he'd call me. Only he never did. And about the time I was starting to get worried, I got the postcard. You know the rest."

"You should have told us." There was censure in Reece's voice.

"I meant to. We've just been going at it nonstop and as I told you, I didn't think it mattered."

"Everything matters. And you know it." Simone stood up, clenching her fists. "I agree with Reece. You should have told us you'd seen him."

"Look. First off, for all I knew you were on the wrong

side of this thing. And second, I've been working my ass off to keep your family safe. So I didn't mention the fact that I'd seen Maurice. I'm sorry. But honest to God, it's not worth getting this worked up over."

Simone's anger evaporated as quickly as it had come. Tate was right. It didn't matter. "I'm sorry, too. I overreacted. It was just a shock to hear that you were still involved with the Company." A small part of her was actually jealous.

"Only a couple times, I swear. And then only working for Maurice. I guess maybe part of the reason I didn't say anything was that I was afraid you'd blame me. I should have sensed something was off. But I didn't. Until it was too damn late."

"All right." Reece still wore the look he had when he disbelieved someone's testimony, but at least his jaw had stopped twitching. "I can accept that. But I still have another question."

"Shoot." Tate frowned, waiting.

"How is it exactly that you're still alive?"

There was a moment of complete silence, even the insects seeming to go quiet.

Then Tate's eyes narrowed in anger, his muscles bunching in reaction. "I beg your pardon?"

Simone opened her mouth to try and intercede but nothing came out. So she looked over at Reece, trying to understand where he was going, but coming up empty.

"Everyone in D-9 has had a killer on their trail. Mather, Bea, Maurice, Ed, even Simone. Everyone but you. How do you figure that?"

"Obviously you've forgotten the Buick ride from hell."

"I haven't forgotten anything. It's just seems odd to me that you're here unharmed when everyone else is dead."

"I'm alive. Are you questioning my survival, too?" Simone asked, her loyalties pulled between her friend and her ex-husband.

"You know I'm not. Hell, I'm not even sure I'm questioning Tate's. I just think the inquiry is relevant."

"I agree," Tate said, surprising them all. "In fact, I've thought about it myself. And the only explanation I can come up with is that I've been on the move. I told you I'd met with Maurice from time to time, and took on the odd job here and there."

"Yeah, as recently as last month." Reece's tone was dry, but his distrust seemed to have evaporated a little.

"The point is," Tate said, "that my activities keep me on the go. So it wouldn't be easy to track me down." Simone opened her mouth to argue, but he waved her off. "At least not as easy as it was to find the rest of you. Look, as far as I know no one tried to get to me until I got to the rendezvous. Same as Ed. Only I was luckier." He shot Simone a look of gratitude, and she turned to Reece.

"It makes sense. The killer can only be one place at a time. And we've got a solid timeline with Maurice, Mather, Bea and then me. Maybe Ed and Tate were just farther down the list."

"Only Maurice inadvertently upped the ante when he called for the rendezvous," Tate added.

"I just had to ask the question." If Reece's words were meant as an apology, his tone didn't mirror the sentiment.

"I understand." Tate's voice held a note of respect. "If the situation had been reversed, I'd have done the same."

"So now that we're all on the same page," Simone said, trying to cut through the radiating tension, "why don't we talk about tomorrow?"

Reece nodded. "I assume you have a plan for when we get to D.C.? We can hardly drive out to Langley and announce ourselves."

"I admit I haven't had time to think that far ahead." Tate shrugged. "But we'll work out something."

"We can call Marguerite," Simone said, the idea growing in appeal once it was spoken out loud.

"Who's that?" Reece asked, turning to her with a frown.

"An old friend. She was a deep cover operative for years, and then she retired. But like all of us—" she shot a look at Tate "—she couldn't stay out of it, so she signed on as a consultant for D-9. Helped us with logistics, and sources, really with everything. If anyone can get us into Langley, it's Marguerite."

"Yeah, but it's been ten years. How the hell do we find her?" Tate asked.

Simone ducked her head. "You're not the only one who had contact with someone still on the inside. Marguerite has been my lifeline. She was all that kept me sane at times. Especially in the beginning."

"You've seen this woman?" The muscle was ticking again.

"No." Simone shook her head. "There was too much risk in that. For both of us. But we write. Lately by e-mail."

Tate opened his mouth, but she waved it shut. "We used secure connections and alias routers. There's no way anyone could have traced it."

"Still, you were taking a chance." For once Tate and Reece seemed to be of one accord.

"No more so than your doing odd jobs for Maurice. Anyway, the point is I know where she is, and I know she'll help us."

"Are you sure we can trust her?" Reece asked, ever the skeptic.

"Yes," she and Tate answered together, and somehow the tension of the moment eased.

"All right. So we'll contact her when we get to D.C., agreed?" Tate looked from Reece to Simone and then back again.

"It'll be good to have an ally," Reece capitulated.

"All right, then. I suggest we get some sleep," Tate said, pushing off the table. "You coming, Simone?" There was nothing untoward in his voice, but she could see Reece stiffen.

"No. I think I'll sit out here a while longer."

Tate nodded and, after a sideways glance at Reece, headed for the cottage, the sound of the screen door slamming indicating he'd gone inside.

"Walk with me," Reece said. It wasn't a request, and she was too tired to argue.

They walked across the parking lot toward the pine trees that bordered the little steam. The water gurgled along, the sound soothing, a sharp contrast to the tension that filled the air. They moved in tandem, finding a rhythm even in their discord. Soon the trees surrounded them, the moonlight barely penetrating the pinecone-laden branches.

Reece stopped to pick up a pebble and tossed it into the stream. It skipped three times, skimming over the water as if it hadn't a care in the world. Simone wished life were as easy.

"Were you lovers?" He turned to face her, his dark eyes clouded with emotion she couldn't or wouldn't put a name to.

"I'm not sure I'd choose that word, exactly. But yes, we were together. A long time ago."

"Was it serious?"

"Tate and I? No. I mean, we were friends. Are still friends. But the rest was just a way to connect with someone. To belong somewhere if even for just a moment. We were isolated from the rest of the world. There was no one to depend on but each other. And sometimes the only way to prove we were alive was..."

"Physically." He finished for her.

"Yeah."

"And now?" He was talking about the little interlude on the picnic table.

"Now I know that there can be something more. Something based on a hell of a lot more than need." She caught his gaze and held it, desire arcing white-hot between them.

"Really?" he asked, the corner of his mouth turning up almost imperceptibly.

"Yeah." She was repeating herself, but it was becoming difficult to think clearly.

He closed the distance between them, his hands tangling in her hair as he pulled her to him. There was an urgency between them that had never been there before. The need to come together overriding common sense.

His mouth slanted over hers, their tongues meeting in a well-rehearsed dance. They hadn't been together in a long time, but nothing had been forgotten in the interim. The feel of his skin against hers, the rasp of his five-o'clock shadow, the smell of his cologne, the soft rhythm of his breathing, all the things that added together, made a man—this man.

Simone closed her eyes, giving herself over to sensation, letting go of reality in favor of dreams. This was what she wanted. This feeling, this moment. Now.

The kiss deepened as he ran his hands over her shoulders and back, settling for a moment to cup her rear and then sliding upward again so that his fingers encircled her breasts, his thumbs creating a heat that went beyond normal physics, morphing instead into something that straddled the physical and spiritual.

New lovers might have the joy of discovery, the pure sensation of chemical combustion. But lovers who knew every inch of each other had something more—a connection that couldn't easily be severed. Not by angry words, perhaps not even by lies and deception. But as she had the thought, it faded in the wake of the pleasure rising inside her.

Pleasure—and desire.

She knew what lay ahead of her, and wanted gratification now. As if reading her mind, Reece pulled her T-shirt over her head, baring her breasts. It had always been a joke between them that she had never worn a bra. She'd sworn that it was because she really didn't need one. He'd sworn that it had been her way of letting him know how very much she wanted him.

He'd been right.

His thumb found the taut bud of her nipple, the circling friction ratcheting the tightening wire of desire that coursed through her. She reached for the hem of his shirt, wanting nothing more than to feel his skin against hers. For a moment, they broke apart, his eyes asking questions that both of them were afraid to voice, but she shook her head.

This was not the time for words.

Slowly, teasing him with the fire in her eyes, she

slipped the black T-shirt up and over his head, the cool breeze brushing against the hair on his chest. For one beat more they stared into each other's eyes, and then he was kissing her again, their bodies pressed together, moving against each other, teasing, probing, exploring, the momentum driving them backward until she felt the callused bark of an aspen digging into her back, the pricking pain a counterpoint to the ecstasy of his touch.

There was a fury to his lovemaking, almost as if he was afraid she would disappear, that the connection between them would shatter in the cold of the night. Her hands found the zipper of his pants, wanting to hold him, to feel the pulse of his penis in her hand.

As if with a life of its own, it sprang free of its denim confines and she circled its strength with her fingers, kneading and stroking as he moved again to kiss her lips. The taste of him was as heady as wine and she drank him in, wishing there were a way to capture this moment forever, knowing in her heart how fleeting this kind of joy could be.

As if he understood her sense of urgency, he deepened his kiss, taking possession of more than just her lips. Their tongues moved in rhythm, building to a crescendo that fanned the flames building inside her. With a moan, she pressed against him, her hand moving up and down the long hard length of him, signaling with her touch all that she wanted to do to him.

With a groan, he swung her into his arms, and then laid her on a bank of pine needles, using their discarded shirts as a blanket. For one moment she was alone in her pine-scented bed and then he was there, his weight comfortable upon her. A remembered pleasure.

With moans of need and frustration, they managed to remove the rest of their clothing, both of them wanting nothing between them, as if with one physical act, they could remove all that happened. All the lies, half lies and omissions.

Kissing her again, his hand slid across the soft skin of her belly and reflexively she breathed in, moving her legs to open for him. His fingers slid between the moisture-slick lips of her labia, stroking the tiny bit of skin that seemed at the moment to be the center of her soul. Flicking back and forth in a motion designed for both pleasure and pain, she writhed beneath him. Wanting more, needing more.

Wanting him.

His mouth moved from her lips to her neck, trailing tiny kisses along her collarbone, the act sending gooseflesh dancing along her already sensitized nerves. He grazed in the hollow between her breasts, kissing first one and then the other, slowly circling each nipple with his tongue as if savoring the flavor.

Her body cried out for more, and she pushed him downward, seeking release.

It had been so damn long.

He paused at her belly, sinking his tongue into the indentation there, stroking, laving, hinting at things to come. Then finally, finally, he slid lower, his tongue teasing as he traced lines along her inner thigh. She opened her knees as if welcoming him home, and his mouth found her pulsing flesh, sucking deeply as her body lurched off the pine needles, sensation robbing her of all control.

His fingers slid inside her, moving in and out, following the rhythm of his tongue. Faster and faster, until she couldn't feel anything except the exquisitely building tension, the urge for release taking her beyond all rational thought.

And then in an instant she slid over the edge—free-falling through slivers of light, her eyelids shuddering in time with the contractions that racked through her. He waited then, sliding forward to cover her body, letting her fly free for minutes, hours, seconds—and then just before she landed, he was inside her, taking her up again, each thrust pumping new life, new blood through her veins.

Higher and higher they flew, his body becoming part of hers. Their movement together as essential as breathing—each stroke giving life.

His hands tightened on her shoulders, and the familiar planes of his face came into focus, his dark eyes connecting with hers, completing the circle, and together they crashed through velvet and starlight into the sun.

Then softly, slowly, they sank back to earth. The heady smell of their lovemaking mixed with the scent of the pines and, for the first time in a long time, Simone felt at peace. She knew in her heart it couldn't last, that the peace, like everything else about their relationship, was a figment of her imagination. But just for the moment, she desperately wanted to believe in forever.

CHAPTER SIXTEEN

REECE AWOKE to the prickle of pine needles against his back and something sharp poking into his hip. The air had turned cold, the copse of trees providing little shelter against the damp of the night. Simone shivered in her sleep, still nestled into his side, one leg thrown across his hips in the possessive manner that had always provoked equal amounts of pleasure and amusement.

Of course he'd always thought of himself as the protector, and her attempt to dominate in sleep had always made him laugh. Now, in light of all that he had learned about her past, the gesture took on a slightly different perspective. One he wasn't sure he was ready to embrace. There had simply been too much information to process so quickly, everything he thought he knew about his wife suddenly called into question.

It was as if he'd awoken to find himself living someone else's life. And he wasn't at all sure that he was pleased at the prospect.

Their lovemaking had been, if anything, better than ever, and yet he knew that no amount of physical contact could erase the barriers they'd built between them. The honest truth was that he didn't know the woman he'd just made love to.

The thought was both frightening and infuriating. Along with about a hundred other emotions he couldn't put a name to.

The problem was that he'd built his entire life on quantifying things. He'd made his career on an ability to read people. To see the truths they were hiding, and to cut through all the bullshit. And yet, in the single most important area of his life, he'd failed completely. He'd looked into Simone's eyes and seen nothing but what she wanted him to see.

What *he'd* wanted to see.

God, he'd failed when it mattered most, overlooked what he now realized were glaring signs in favor of the sweet smell of her hair, and the whisper-soft silk of her skin. Like all men, he'd succumbed to his baser side, despite a lifetime of depending on internal radar.

And yet, that was oversimplifying as well. Simone was, in part, the very things he'd fallen in love with. She was funny and intelligent and whimsical and endearingly devoted. She laughed at his jokes, understood his fears and even knew when he needed to find solace in the comfort of her arms.

The truth was, he'd never really done that for her. She'd never seemed to need him like that. Maybe it was the fact that she hadn't wanted to reveal herself. Or maybe she hadn't thought he'd want to listen. He'd been so caught up in the idea of their perfect family—he and Simone and Martin.

When he'd come back to take care of Martin, he'd worked so hard to make a life for his brother, to somehow fill the void that had been left in the wake of his parents' deaths. But even with all his efforts, there had always been something missing. And when he'd met Simone, he'd seen more than just a soul mate: he'd seen completion for him and for Martin.

Maybe it had been unfair to thrust all of that on her.

But she'd been so damn good at it. Loving him and Martin with a ferocity that had made them both feel whole again. But somewhere along the way, he'd forgotten about Simone's needs.

She'd given him so much, and what the hell had he ever given her except a roof over her head and a cocoon against the outside world? A part of him recognized that maybe that was all she'd wanted. But another part knew she deserved a hell of a lot more.

He'd seen her there with Tate. Open and sharing. Maybe not in a sexual way. But in a more important, all-trusting kind of way.

He wanted that kind of intimacy. Wanted it with Simone, damn it. But she hadn't been able to be honest with him, instead hiding behind a facade. There was a part of her that she'd locked away and kept from him at all costs.

If a client had done something like that, he'd have dropped them. If a defendant had pulled that kind of routine, he'd have buried them. So how the hell was he supposed to just forgive and forget? He blew out a sigh, and stroked the soft curls of her hair. Even in the pale moonlight he could see the wash of red.

The color suited her somehow, the new cut making her seem at once softer and yet more defined. With the disguise, everything about her had changed externally. But she was still the same. Red hair or brown, she was the woman he'd married. And maybe that was the lesson to be learned.

Maybe everyone had secrets—some never discovered, others brought to light at the most inopportune times. The point being that most people wore masks. It was an accepted methodology for wending one's way through the intricacies of social interaction. Husband, son, brother, attorney. They were all roles. Each of them highlighting different facets of a person's psyche.

Simone's deception had in some ways been no different from anyone else's. Except that she'd deceived *him.*

He tightened his hold on her, pulling her even closer beside him. In the end it was always personal, wasn't it? A perceived slight painful whether it was intended or not. And yet in that moment, wasn't he at fault, too? Hadn't he, perhaps, expected too much?

It was too damn much to consider in the cold Montana night.

What he needed now was to quit analyzing and accept what he had.

All he'd wanted since they'd separated was to find a way for them to come back together. A way to undo the hurt, to erase the angry words. To go back to before the time when everything had started to unravel. Maybe he'd been looking at it wrong, trying to fix what couldn't be repaired. Maybe instead he needed to find a way to start again. To build on a new reality.

Easily said. Not so easily done. Once a chasm had opened, it was not a simple matter to close it again. Nor was it easy to bridge the gap. If for no other reason than because it was so damned difficult to let someone else in.

He shook his head at the esoteric nature of his thoughts. Maybe it took someone trying to kill him to make him let go of his selfish nature long enough to see the two of them as a couple, and not just Simone as an extension of himself.

All he knew for certain was that he'd be willing to die

if it kept her safe, and now that they'd found each other again, even if only for a moment, he wasn't ready to let her go.

SUNLIGHT FILTERED through the trees and Reece pulled his blanket closer, trying to remember why exactly he'd chosen to camp without benefit of sleeping bag or tent. Smothering a yawn, he opened his eyes, reality returning with a rush.

Last night.

Simone.

He rolled over only to find her place empty, his clothes neatly folded where she had been sleeping. There was sentiment in the fact that she'd brought him a blanket, but also a message in the fact that she was gone.

He wasn't sure at the moment that he was up to reading something into either act. Better to just move forward. What was it his mother had always said? Baby steps?

He'd never really thought there was merit in the idea. But then he'd never walked through such an emotional minefield before. Maybe his mother had been right.

Pushing aside the blanket, he stood and stretched, then quickly donned his clothes. From the slant of the sun through the trees, he guessed it was still early. Maybe just after sunrise. He grabbed the blanket and threw it over his shoulder, serape style. Unless he missed his guess, everyone would already be up and preparing for the flight to D.C.

Tate had arranged things so that they would be able to move quickly and hopefully avoid whoever was tracking them. So far there hadn't been any sign of him in Missoula. But things weren't always as they appeared, and Reece had learned a long time ago not to take anything for granted.

He walked out of the trees and into the parking lot of the roadside inn, the activity around their newest car evidence that he was right about it being time to move. Tate looked up from the trunk of the car as Reece approached, his expression carefully neutral.

"You see anything out there?" Either Tate wasn't aware he'd spent the night in the woods, or he was simply avoiding discussing it.

"No." Reece shook his head, rubbing a hand over what was left of his hair. "It's quiet. Only sound besides the brook is the occasional rumble of a truck moving down the highway."

"I checked a couple times last night, too, and didn't see anything but the local wildlife." This time there was definitely a hint of innuendo, but Reece wasn't about to rise to the bait.

"So we about ready here?" He nodded toward their ragtag assortment of Wal-Mart purchases—the sum total of their luggage.

"Yeah." Tate slammed down the trunk. "Simone is trying to reach Marguerite. Give her a heads-up that we're coming. And the kid's still working on the computer."

Reece hadn't thought of Martin as a kid in about four years, so the word seemed almost funny. Especially in light of the fact that Martin was the one who'd provided most of the intel they'd managed to accumulate so far.

"What about the transport? We still good to go there?" Reece studied the other man, trying to figure out what it was that felt wrong about him. Probably just his connection with Simone and the fact that he knew her in a way that Reece couldn't. The idea was galling, but hardly a reason for distrust.

"Everything's fine." Tate looked down at his wrist-watch. "Pilot should be there waiting for us now."

"All right, why don't I round up Simone, and you get Martin." He could see his ex standing near the front office, gesturing into her cell phone.

Tate paused for a moment, looking like he wanted to argue, and then shrugged instead, heading for the screen door of the cottage.

Reece strode across the parking lot, trying to find the right words. He hadn't spoken to her since last night. And based on her absence this morning, he wasn't exactly sure what his reception was going to be.

Sunlight streamed through a towering blue spruce that shaded the cottage serving as the motor court's office. A tiny brook trickled past the entrance, down the hill toward the line of cabins making up the rest of the motel. There was a dilapidated kitsch to the place that reminded Reece of a family trip to Colorado. Martin, in fact, had fallen into a stream very similar to this one.

He crossed the little bridge and headed off to the right toward the bright orange of the poppy bed where Simone was still talking. She waved her arm, then nodded once and snapped the cell phone closed, turned and almost collided with Reece as he stopped in front of her.

"Sorry," she said, stepping back a pace, the distance intentional. "I didn't see you coming."

Considering it was a wide-open space with only the spruce to break it up, Reece had his doubts, but having been married to the woman for almost six years he was more than aware of when it was wise to hold his tongue. "I didn't mean to sneak up on you. I just wanted to let you know that we're ready to go."

"I was talking to Marguerite," she said, the sentence only adding to the building awkwardness between them.

"She going to help us?" he asked, wishing he could turn the clock back to last night.

"Yeah. She's going to work on arranging a way for us to get into Langley and Maurice's office. If anyone can do it, she can."

They turned to walk toward the car, where Tate and Martin were loading the last bits of their gear. "About last night…" It wasn't the best of openings, but the longer they went without talking about it, the harder it was going to be to broach the subject. He stopped, putting a hand on Simone's arm to impede her progress.

She swung around to face him, releasing a breath. "There's nothing to talk about. You were angry. I was angry. Tension is unbelievable right now." She shrugged off his hand.

"Simone, I'm not Tate. And what we had last night wasn't about comfort."

"No." She shook her head, her new red curls dancing with the motion. "It wasn't. But it wasn't real, either. Nothing has changed, Reece. At least nothing important." There was the barest trace of regret in her voice, or maybe he just wanted to hear it.

"Well maybe *I* want it to change." The words came out of their own volition, but surprisingly, he didn't regret them.

"You're forgetting that I lied to you. That our whole marriage was based on a fabrication."

"You said yourself that not all of it was lies."

"Yes, but as you were so quick to point out, the part that counts was. Look, Tate made me realize last night that I've got to take charge of my life and quit apologizing for what I can't change. I am who I am. And face it, Reece, you don't know me."

"Maybe I don't know everything. But I do know the part of you that matters most. Last night was proof of that. We are connected, Simone. Whether you like it or not. Hell, whether I like it or not. And until we accept that fact, we're never going to be able to move forward. Together or apart." The minute the words were out he recognized the truth of them.

"Listen, I really don't think now is a good time to sit down and delve into our feelings." She started to walk away, but he easily kept pace with her.

"I'm not proposing anything of the sort. I'm not exactly a touchy-feely kind of guy, you know? But I am cognizant enough to recognize that a door has been reopened, and I'm not about to just slam it shut again. We have unfinished business between us, Simone. And you might want to ignore it. But I'm not going to let that happen. Not this time."

"This time?" She slid to a stop, her eyes flashing. "What's that supposed to mean?"

"It means I let you back off last time. Disengage when it got too uncomfortable. But I'm not going to do it again. There aren't any secrets anymore, Simone. Nothing you can hide behind. It's just us, sweetheart, the good and the bad. And this time we're going to ride it through and see where the hell it takes us." He could almost feel the blood pumping through his veins, his anger rising to match hers.

"It's not just about what you want, Reece. I'm in this, too, remember?" The minute the words were out she realized what she'd said, fisting her hands in instant regret. But it was too late.

Reece smiled, the gesture tight across his face. "My point exactly. We're in this together. You accused me of thinking of our marriage as an extension of myself. Well, maybe you were right. But that's not the case anymore. My eyes are wide open now, believe me. And if you think I'm just going to stand by while you walk away, you've got another thing coming. Our past may be fucked-up. Hell, maybe if I'd known the truth I wouldn't have given myself the chance to fall in love with you. But it didn't happen that way. I did fall in love with you. And I'm pretty damn sure you were in love with me, too."

"I never said I wasn't. I only said you don't know me. D-9 is just one piece of my past, Reece. And facing the fact that I'm a trained operative isn't enough. It gets uglier. And I for one don't know that I want to go down that road again with anyone. Which means that—"

He waved a hand to cut her off. "Love is a funny thing, Simone. It's tenacious as hell. I don't know if we can find our way back together. But I do know that last night I remembered why it might be worth the effort to find out."

She stared up at him, her eyes narrowed as she considered what he'd said. Then with a sigh, she spun on her heel and headed for the car.

But not before Reece saw the flash of hope in her eyes.

THE AIRSTRIP WAS really just a cleared parcel of land, a wind sock, and a long length of packed dirt. Simone wasn't certain what its original purpose had been, but clearly the place hadn't been used in a while. Weeds of almost every variety encroached on the so-called runway, giving the place a deserted, lonely feel.

But under the circumstances it was exactly what they

needed. Bordered on three sides by mountains, its limited access gave them the added advantage of being able to easily watch for intruders. And more importantly, the switchback road leading to the airstrip was the kind that required someone knowing of its existence in order to find it.

If Tate hadn't been with them, she wasn't certain she would have realized the road was even there. So things were falling nicely into place. At least with regard to their attempt to get to D.C.

Her personal life, on the other hand, was about as muddled as it could possibly get. Last night with Reece had been amazing. There was simply no denying it. But in the cold, hard light of day, it was impossible not to face the fact that one night of hot sex couldn't possibly solve all their problems.

And even though he'd made it more than clear he wasn't going to let her go without some kind of a fight, she wasn't convinced that either of them was willing to go the distance it would take to repair the damage that had been done.

Damn it, she really had started letting emotions get in her way. Definitely not D-9 standard operating procedure. In fact, that sort of thinking was the kind that got a person killed.

She shook her head and got out of the car. Reece and Tate had already headed for the weathered Beechcraft at the end of the makeshift runway. Martin was gathering up his pilfered computer equipment. He'd spent the ride up reading over several documents he'd pulled off the Web, still trying to find something to tie Isabella or Carlos to members of D-9, most particularly Maurice.

"You ready?" she asked Martin as he slammed the door and slung his computer case over his shoulder.

"As I'll ever be." His response was colored by the skepticism in his voice as he eyed the plane in front of them. "You think that's big enough to get us all the way to D.C.?"

Simone shot a look in the direction of the six-seater with a laugh. "I've flown a lot farther in aircraft a lot smaller. Compared to them, this is the Ritz."

"If you say so," he said, obviously still not convinced.

She marveled at the fact that this was the first time he'd shown hesitation about anything. "Considering all that we've been through, a battered plane is the least of our worries, believe me. Besides, Tate knows what he's doing. If he arranged for this plane, then you can be certain it'll get the job done."

"All right, then." Martin grimaced. "Let's do it."

They started down the edge of the runway toward the plane. In the distance, Simone could see Tate and Reece loading their scant possessions onto the plane. The pilot had the engines started, the resulting hum saturating the air around them.

The rest of the meadow was still except for the occasional ripple of the tall grasses in the breeze. Simone followed the line of the foothills leading to the mountains, but like the meadow, everything seemed still. A stand of aspen off to the left rustled in the wind, the sound soothing in its own way.

She inhaled deeply, as if just by breathing she could clean away all the accumulated grit of urban life. Maybe someday, when this was over, she'd follow in Bea's footsteps and find a home out here. Begin again.

Even as she had the thought, she dismissed it. There was no such thing as a new beginning. If she'd learned nothing else from the lies that had brought down her marriage, it was that. Reece was right; if she was going to move forward, she first had to make peace with her past.

They were close enough now that she could see the pilot sitting in the cockpit, headphones protecting his ears from the roar of the engine. Tate had disappeared inside the plane, but Reece was still standing beside the ladder leading into the cabin. His hand shaded his eyes as he scanned the hills behind them.

She wasn't sure what alerted her first, a familiar tingling of her nerve endings or the sudden change in Reece's posture. Either way, she didn't stop to analyze, instead reaching for the Sig tucked into the waistband of her jeans.

"Run," she shouted, reaching out to give Martin a shove. He broke into a sprint, just as the ground at his feet exploded into dust, bullets cutting into the hard-packed clay of the runway.

In an attempt to draw fire away from her brother-in-law, Simone dropped to a crouch and moved away from the plane, all the while trying to find the source of the gunfire. There was a brief pause and then the shooter took the guesswork away, firing at her from the protection of the aspens.

"Simone." Reece was yelling. She could hear him even as her brain tried to sort through the best options. A couple of rusted oil drums lay about five feet to her left. Spinning again, she dove behind them, bullets slamming into the metal sending a cloud of rust into the air.

Martin had reached the plane and was clambering up

the ladder, the shooter following his progress with another volley of gunfire. Reece had disappeared from view, hopefully already on board the plane.

Which meant that she was the only one left at risk.

The best possible solution was to make a run for the plane, but that meant crossing directly into the shooter's line of fire. And while the confusion of them splitting up had bought Martin the time to reach the Beechcraft safely, she wouldn't have the same advantage.

Nevertheless, she prepared for the dash, but before she could begin, the plane started to move, picking up speed as it made its way down the improvised runway. She followed its course with her eyes, working on the trajectory of distance to intersection.

Clearly, Tate had instructed the pilot to take off. The idea being that she make a run for it when the distance between her and the plane was the shortest, ideally, keeping the oil drums between her and the shooter.

The trick, of course, was going to be to board the moving plane. But she'd done it before.

A lifetime ago.

Still, there wasn't really an alternative, and so she tensed, watching the moving plane, allowing her senses to find the rhythm. Success would depend on her instincts and not her brain, so it was crucial that she release herself into the moment.

Seconds passed, and suddenly the plane was only feet from her decided trajectory. Moving into a crouch, she holstered her gun and then pushed off, running toward the plane with all the speed she could muster.

The roar of the engine covered any sound of gunfire, but she could see the tiny clouds of dust caused when a bullet sliced into the ground. Despite her brain screaming at her to run straight for the plane, she kept her pathway jagged, cutting to the right and left to keep the shooter from being able to target her. Her muscles protested the movement, but she pressed forward, knowing there wouldn't be a second chance to board.

The plane was moving fast now, the front tires already in the air. Two more seconds and it would be airborne.

She pulled parallel with the wing of the plane just as it took off. She could see Reece and Tate in the open hatch. Reece was lying on his stomach, his arms extended outside of the fuselage, something dangling from his hands. "Come on." He mouthed, his words carried away in the wash of engine noise.

She sprinted within inches of the bottom of the plane, the hatch now several yards above her head. She glanced up at Reece as he worked to release the object he held, her beleaguered mind telegraphing the image of a ladder—a rope ladder.

The fuselage ruptured in several places as bullets grazed the metal, a sure sign the killer was closing the distance. It was time. Pushing herself to the limit, she gained ground until she was parallel to the hatch, then just as the plane curved responsively away from the shooter, she dove for the trailing end of the ladder, her hands closing around the nylon rung.

Her feet cleared the ground as the plane rose. Holding tight with her left hand, she swung her right up until she grasped the next highest rung, continuing the process, alternating arms, until she actually had a foot on the bottom rung.

The plane lurched, and for a moment she thought she'd

lose her precarious perch, the nylon jerking from her right hand. The rope ladder whipped back and forth, slamming her into the fuselage as she struggled to regain her hold.

In a shift of momentum, the ladder swung back out, her body weight snapping the rope, her left foot sliding off the rung, swinging free. The ground was falling away at an alarming rate, assuring her that if she fell now, she wouldn't be able to walk away from it. Which left only one alternative. Sucking in a breath, she concentrated on the rung above her, and through sheer force of will, threw her right arm upward.

There was no resulting contact with the ladder, but just as she started to swing out again, she felt fingers closing around her wrist.

Reece.

Seconds later, he had her left wrist as well, and inch by inch he began to pull her upward. Abandoning the ladder, she used her feet against the body of the plane to help him, the wind still threatening to jerk her away.

She looked up, her eyes locking with his, concentrating on each movement. One foot and then another, and then she was there, halfway into the plane. With one last jerk, he pulled her all the way inside, their bodies tangling together as they fell against the floor of the plane.

"Didn't think you were going to get away that easily, did you?" Reece's breath was warm against her temple.

"Just at the moment, getting away wasn't exactly what I had in mind." She waited a beat, then rolled off him, feigning indifference, knowing full well that in all probability she'd just tossed a bloody steak to a starving tiger.

CHAPTER SEVENTEEN

THE NIGHT SEEMED abnormally still. As if it were waiting for something. Isabella stood on the balcony of her room, looking out at the empty street below. Even the usually steady stream of traffic had abated. Nothing moved, not even the languid air. She shivered and fingered the crucifix at her throat.

She had learned long ago not to ignore her premonitions. Something would happen. Something tonight.

She walked into her room, turning back to grasp the shutters and pull them toward her, effectively sealing her room. It was an old habit, born of a lesson learned too late. But the presence of the heavy wood always made her feel safer somehow.

Her nightgown was made of the finest cotton. More threads than an Egyptian could count. And yet inside she was still the daughter of a peasant. A man of the people. A man who had been murdered for daring to dream.

She picked up a Baccarat bottle from her dressing table, pulling the cork, inhaling the soothing smell of perfume. It was her favorite. An expensive blend of vanilla and honeysuckle. Available only from a small perfumery in Paris. Her father had given it to her on her ninth birthday. Her mother had said it was too sophisticated a gift for a girl her age. But Isabella had loved it. Loved the way it made her feel. And she had never again worn anything else.

Her hand tightened on the bottle as thoughts of her father flooded through her. Memories of his face, his voice, his laughter. Isolated moments that, added together, created the man he had been. The man she would never forget.

Anger, hot and heavy, flooded through her, and she threw the bottle against the wall, the delicate crystal shattering on impact. The smell of honeysuckle filled the air as she knelt to try and reclaim the pieces, to make them whole again. But like her father, the bottle was gone, the scent already evaporating in the still night air.

She swallowed her pain and sat on the edge of her bed, reaching for the phone, her thoughts turning to her brother. She stared at the receiver, willing him to call, but the machine was silent, mocking her.

Manuel had been watching her day and night, his suspicions growing with every passing hour. She knew his men would be looking for Carlos, too, and that if they found him, they would kill him.

She sent a silent prayer heavenward, praying for her brother's safety, praying for a way out. Vengeance was within their grasp; surely fate would not be so cruel as to take it away. She dropped the phone on the bed, standing instead to pace back and forth across the room, her agitation built on a combination of fear and worry.

Ramón had been right. The house of cards she had so delicately constructed would not bear the weight should proof of Carlos's guilt be found. She bent to retrieve a sliver of the broken decanter, the edge sharp against her finger, wishing her father were here to advise her.

A soft knock at the door sent her pulse pounding, her ruminations igniting her fear.

"Who is it?" The question came out more sharply than intended, but at this hour it was not normal for someone to knock. The door opened, and she cursed the fact that she hadn't thought to bolt it.

Antonio Montoya entered, a finger to his lips. "Say nothing more." His whisper sent shivers running along her spine. Like Ramón, Antonio had worked for her father. His loyalty to the family absolute. Now he served as a palace guard, his connection to Isabella kept secret. "There are ears everywhere."

She moved to the portable player that served as her stereo. Pressing a button, the mellow sound of Frank Sinatra filled the air. Her father's favorite.

Antonio nodded his approval and moved closer, his gaze darting around the room, searching for anything out of place.

"Where is Ramón?" It was unlike him to have sent Antonio in his stead. "Is he all right?"

"He's fine. He has gone ahead to make arrangements."

"Arrangements?" Her fear blossomed to dread. "Is Carlos all right?"

"You misunderstand, it is not your brother who is in danger. It is you."

"Manuel." In one word she personified all of her fears.

Antonio nodded. "He has decided your presence here is a liability. Things have not gone well with the Americans."

"They know about my visit with Baxter?"

"They have not admitted as much, but they are nosing about. Asking questions that Ortega cannot answer. The trade negotiations have broken down. Ostensibly because the Americans do not trust him."

"A wise decision."

"Yes. But now he must find a way to turn the distrust elsewhere."

"To me." She saw the truth of it there in Antonio's eyes.

"*Sí*. You are the one who will take the blame. He has told his advisors of your meeting, playing it as a betrayal of him and of the country."

"And they believe this?" There were many in the government who still followed her father in their hearts.

"It doesn't matter what they believe. They value their lives and their welfare more. You are nothing to them, *carita*. Especially if you threaten their well-padded lives."

"So they'll just stand by and let him kill me?" The silence hung heavy between them, her words taking on a life of their own.

"If it solves their problems."

She swallowed, squaring her shoulders. This sort of thing had always been a risk, but now that she was facing it, she found the prospect more daunting. "I take it there isn't much time."

Antonio shook his head. "We must get you out of here tonight. Ramón has made arrangements for you to be transported to *El Ojo de la Tormenta*. You will be safe there."

"And if Manuel follows me? We cannot risk another war." Shades of Sangre de Cristo filled her mind, sending shivers racing down her spine. She would not subject her people to such torture again. Not even to save her own life.

"We'll see that he doesn't. We are working now to create misinformation that will lead the Americans away from you and your brother once it goes public. Then when the pressure is off and the interest in Baxter's death dies down, I believe you will no longer be a target. But it is important, Isabella, that you tell me where Carlos is."

"I don't know." In actuality she had no idea. At least not for certain. And even if she did know, she would never give Carlos away. Not even to Antonio.

"Sometimes it is most difficult to do what is right." Antonio took her hands, his dark eyes knowing.

"I don't know where he has gone. I swear it."

He searched her face. "And the American? Did your brother kill him?"

"I don't know." She didn't, not definitively.

"Very well." Antonio dropped her hands, a shadow crossing his face. "But if you think of something. Anything he said that would lead us to him. Or if you talk to him again…"

"If he calls me, I promise I will let you know."

Someone rapped again on the door, this time with force, no question of secrecy.

"Come. We must go," Antonio whispered, drawing his gun.

He pushed her toward the window. The knock sounded again as he opened the shutters and shoved her out on the balcony, pulling them closed again as he followed her.

Peering through a crack, he watched whoever it was entering the room, tension radiating from his shoulders. Isabella looked at the ground below her, trying to figure out how she was going to manage the drop in her nightgown.

"It's all right." Antonio said, his breath coming on a sigh. "It's only Ortiz."

Ortiz had been with her family for almost as many

years as Antonio and Ramón. It seemed she was surrounded by old men. "He is alone?"

"*Sí.*" Antonio pushed the shutters open and stepped into the room.

"They are just behind me," the other man said. "We must move quickly."

"Is there time to change?" Isabella asked, glancing down at her nightgown.

In answer Ortiz shook his head and drew his gun. "It may already be too late. Use the balcony. I'll cover you as long as I can."

There was a finality in his words that had nothing to do with her and everything to do with her father.

"Someday you will command that kind of loyalty," Antonio whispered, reading her thoughts. "But to do that you must stay alive." He grabbed her arm and pushed her in front of him out to the balcony again. "There is a boat waiting. At the private jetty. Ramón will be there. But you heard Ortiz, we have to hurry."

She nodded, reaching down to pull the back of her gown through her legs, tucking the hem into the elastic of her panties. "I'm ready."

Antonio indicated a rose-filled trellis, snaking up the wall beside the balcony. "It won't hold your weight forever, but it will give you a chance to get closer to the ground."

"You are not coming?"

"I'll be right behind you." He flashed her a smile, and then helped her over the railing.

The trellis groaned under her weight, and she worried that it would not hold Antonio at all. But then there was no time for worry as shots rang out above her. Mindless of the thorns, she slid down the trellis, taking large chunks of the roses with her. The trellis groaned again, and she heard it crack.

Below her the ground was only feet away. And with a whispered prayer, she released the trellis. Seconds later she crashed into the ground, pain shooting through her hip as she landed.

Taking precious seconds to assess the damage, she realized she was essentially unhurt and jumped to her feet, already looking upward for Antonio.

She could see him silhouetted against the light from the open doors. One minute he was standing there and the next he was falling, arms and legs waving in the air like a cartoon she'd seen once as a child.

Frozen, she watched as he slammed into the concrete. Blood trickled from his mouth and ears, his legs bent at impossible angles.

She knelt beside him, aware that there were more figures on the balcony now.

"Go." The word was barely a whisper, Antonio's eyelids fluttering with the effort to speak. "Go, *carita*. Go." Life fled from his body as if ordered by his words, and Isabella choked on her tears.

Then, jumping again to her feet, she ran.

VIRGINIA WAS uncharacteristically hot, the heat coming off the tarmac in waves as they stepped off the airplane. The landing strip wasn't much more advanced than the one in Montana, this one little more than a strip of asphalt in a field surrounded by a small forest of trees. Unlike its predecessor, however, it had no welcoming committee, and no shots were fired as they cautiously descended from the plane. Even though he hadn't really expected the gunman to find them again this quickly, Reece was relieved at the silence that greeted them, the only sound the cicadas singing in the trees.

The flight had been long and cramped. Simone hadn't said much of anything to anyone. Which he supposed beat the hell out of her singling him out for the silent treatment. Martin had slept almost the entire way. Which in and of itself was a concern. His wound seemed to be healing nicely, but his color still wasn't good. And if Reece were honest, he'd have to admit he was worried about his brother.

Still, there wasn't an option to leave him behind. The only place he could be certain he was safe was here with him. Anywhere else and he was a sitting target for whoever was hunting them. A surefire way to get Simone's attention. It was a rock and a hard place, but Reece couldn't see any way around it.

He could only hope that the arrival of Simone's Marguerite would mean that they would no longer have to handle things on their own, the additional manpower buying some time for Martin to rest.

Tate walked beside him, scanning the tree line. Like Reece, he had his gun ready. But except for a few birds adding their melody to the insect chorus, the clearing was quiet. Albert, the pilot, was staying with the plane. He'd wait until they were safely away, then move to another airport for refueling and the flight back to Montana.

According to Tate, the man was a consultant of sorts, flying for the CIA when requested, operating a commuter service the rest of the time. Tate swore he was trustworthy, but Reece wasn't completely convinced.

"Does Albert know why we're here?"

"No." Tate shook his head, his eyes still on the forest surrounding them. "I only told him we needed a ride."

"But he's bound to have questions. If nothing else, someone shot up his plane."

"It's not like it's the first time." Tate smiled, the humor not quite reaching his eyes.

"So he's not going to tell anyone?" He was being repetitive, but he wasn't even certain that he trusted Tate, let alone a complete stranger.

"He'll hold his tongue. Memories are long in this business. And traitors don't survive."

"Unless they're very good at what they do."

Tate shot him a sideways look, his expression inscrutable.

"If Tate says we can trust Albert, we can." Simone walked up beside them. "Besides we're a bit past the point of worrying about it, don't you think?" It was clear that she was talking about more than simply the pilot, but he let it pass, instead concentrating on his brother, who was just behind them.

"You okay?" He slowed his pace, allowing Martin to catch up. Thoughts of Simone swirled in his head, threatening to overwhelm him. It was all so damn complicated.

"I'm fine," Martin answered. "You're the one who looks like the walking dead."

He forced a smile. "Being chased by a killer tends to do that to a guy. But you're the one who got shot."

"Really, it's okay," Martin said, touching his chest to demonstrate. "It's even starting to itch and Simone says that's a good sign."

His blind faith in Simone was either really stupid or really admirable.

Probably both.

He sighed, letting his anger go. It wasn't going to help their present situation if he was off his game. "There's a car pulling into the clearing."

Simone produced the Sig, and all four of them slowed their progress. "There's no reason to believe it's anyone but Marguerite. She'd said it would be a green sedan. A Cadillac."

"The CIA certainly pays well." The words were out before he could stop them, Simone and Tate both shooting him a look. "Sorry."

"Why don't you and Martin stay here." Tate's gaze met Simone's and she nodded. "Use those bushes for shelter. We'll signal when we're sure it's clear."

He started to argue, having just wrestled Simone into a plane because he'd let her take the lead, but closed his mouth. She'd made it, after all.

"We'll split up. You go left, I'll go right."

She nodded, already sprinting toward the tree line to the right.

Reece watched as they inched their way forward, cutting his eyes from side to side and then back to the green Cadillac. A figure had emerged from the car. The driver's side.

So far no reinforcements.

At least that he could see.

The figure waved. And Reece could see Simone break away from the trees, heading for the person by the car—presumably Marguerite.

The woman crossed the clearing toward Simone, and when they met they embraced briefly before Simone turned to signal all clear.

Martin and Reece emerged from behind the bushes, following Tate as they made their way over to Simone and Marguerite. He should have felt relief. There'd been no ambush. But instead he felt nothing, only a strange sense that they'd stepped off the edge of a very tall cliff—the euphoria only a precursor to hitting the ground.

"This is Marguerite." Simone motioned to the older woman standing beside her.

"And you must be Reece." Her smile was charming, the lilt in her accent decidedly French. "Simone has told me much about you."

Obviously not everything, or the woman wouldn't be smiling.

"This is my brother-in-law, Martin," Simone said. "And you know Tate."

It might have been his imagination, but he thought Marguerite's smile cooled a bit as she turned to face him.

"Tate." She took his hand. "It's been a long time."

"Too long, Marguerite." Tate's words were genuine and the older woman smiled. Perhaps Reece had only telegraphed his own distrust onto the woman. "And I certainly wouldn't have picked this as the reason for our reunion."

"You're sure that they're all dead?" Marguerite asked.

"Yes," Simone said, her eyes full of pain. "I was there with Ed. And there was a picture in Mather's obituary."

"And Bea?"

"We don't have physical verification," Martin answered. Unlike Reece, his brother clearly had no problem feeling like a part of the team. "But we believe she was killed in Montana."

"And you think it's all related to Maurice's death?" Marguerite asked, the five of them walking toward the car.

"It seems logical." Reece joined the conversation, realizing that he was a part of things whether he was comfortable with the fact or not. "The time line alone seems to support it."

Marguerite looked up at him quizzically.

"Maurice was murdered first, followed by Mather and then Bea. At that point there was an attempt on Simone."

"Several attempts, actually," Martin said, rubbing his shoulder with a grimace.

"And then he attacked us at the rendezvous, killing Ed," Reece concluded on a sigh.

"So Maurice's postcard worked against you." Marguerite's eyes narrowed.

"It wasn't his fault." Simone ran a hand through her hair as they stopped next to the Cadillac. "I'm the one who led the killer to the rendezvous."

"You didn't have a choice." Tate's words were meant to comfort, and for a moment Reece found himself almost liking the guy.

"No." Simone sighed. "I didn't. But I don't have to like it."

"Have you arranged for us to get into Langley?"

It was Marguerite's turn to sigh. "I couldn't do anything officially. As you can imagine there's a lot of disquiet over Maurice's death."

"Suits scrambling to cover their asses," Tate said.

"Well, there is that." Marguerite smiled, her face lighting with the gesture. She had clearly once been a beautiful woman, and she wore the remnants well. "But this is something more. Something coming from outside the Company. I'm not sure what."

"So we're screwed?" Martin asked, his tone mirroring their combined disappointment.

"Never count an old dog out, my boy." Marguerite's smile turned to a grin.

"Especially one as wily as you." Simone reached out to squeeze the older woman's shoulder.

"What have you got?" Tate asked, cutting through the banter.

"I have arranged a way for you to access Maurice's office. Unfortunately it will have to be in disguise, and you'll only have a small window. I wish I could have done more."

"I'm sure it'll be enough," Simone assured her friend.

Reece could only pray that she was right.

CHAPTER EIGHTEEN

"HOW THE MIGHTY have fallen."

Simone glanced over at Tate, suppressing a smile. He was pushing a housekeeping cart as they walked down the hallway toward Maurice's office. "Hey, we've done worse."

"Yeah, but my old man was a janitor, and I swore I'd never follow in his footsteps."

In all the years she'd known him, it was the first time he'd mentioned anything at all about his past. As if he'd followed her train of thought, his face closed, all traces of humor disappearing.

"His office is still at the end of the hall, right?" she asked, working to change the subject. She, more than most, understood the need to keep the past buried.

"Yes. On the left."

So far Marguerite's prep had worked flawlessly. Their van and IDs had gotten them past security at both the front gates and the entrance to the building. Their uniforms were perfect down to the smallest details. Even her shoes were accurate, the white leather squeaking slightly as she moved forward.

A denture plate and glasses had altered her face, the hairnet and dirty-blond wig turning her into a woman who made her living cleaning up after others. Tate looked similarly changed in blue coveralls and baseball cap, the insignia the same as the company that held the cleaning contract for the building. His new nose marred his classic looks—that and the scruffy beard.

She smiled, thinking of all the different personas they had used and discarded over the years. There was something comfortingly familiar in the process, if not the actual appearance.

"We're almost there."

Simone stopped, pretending to dust a water fountain, her other hand on the butt of her gun. Tate moved forward as she watched the hallway behind them. As soon as she was convinced it was clear, she followed him, checking once again before she stepped into the office. Tate closed the blinds. Simone shut the door and then clicked on the light, the two of them working in tandem as if they had not been separated by the years.

"Where do we start?" Tate asked, moving to stand in front of Maurice's desk.

"You start with the files," she said. "Watch for false bottoms, locked drawers, that kind of thing. And I'll start to work on the computer."

She sat in Maurice's chair, the familiarity of his cologne filling her senses. In the beginning she'd hated Maurice. Hated him for pulling her off the streets. Hated him for making her a part of D-9. But with time she'd changed her mind. His gruff exterior had hidden a surprisingly gentle soul and she'd grown to care about him in a very real way, recognizing that in his own way he'd cared about her, too.

He'd been a dichotomy. Keeper and father figure—rolled into one. He'd forced them all into servitude of a sort.

Playing on their weaknesses. But at the same time he'd made them better people. Saved them from themselves.

And now he was dead.

"You all right?" Tate looked up from the files he was rifling through.

"Fine. Just remembering" She shook her head, forced a smile and turned on the computer. It whirred to life, the CIA emblem filling the screen. Seconds later a box opened, a white line flashing for a passport entry.

"Fly fishing."

"What?" Simone looked up at Tate with a frown.

"Fly fishing," he repeated. "It's the password. What can I say?" He shrugged. "Maurice was looking forward to retirement."

She typed the password in and the computer buzzed a moment and then was silent, waiting for new instructions. The idea of Maurice in a lure-studded vest and waders seemed incongruous with the commanding-officer intensity that had marked his days heading D-9. "How'd you know what it was?"

"He told me."

The Maurice she knew wouldn't have told him anything.

"Look, I told you he was worried. The last time we met he gave me his password—just in case."

That actually made sense. At least a little. But she filed the thought away to examine again later. "Well, it worked. I'm in. You finding anything?"

"Nothing yet."

She opened a directory, searching the list of documents contained there. Most of them were pretty routine. None of them anything that seemed to be remotely connected to D-9 or the Ramirez junta. She clicked on a few of the documents just to be certain, scanning the contents and then closing them again.

"You were right. There's a false bottom here," Tate said, the surprise in his voice making her smile. He'd always underestimated her hunches.

"Can you open it?"

He was silent for a moment, then there was a pop. "Got it." He shot her a triumphant look and pried the metal bottom out of the drawer. "There are more files." He frowned down into the drawer. "D-9 files."

"Missions?" She stood up.

"No." Tate waved her back down, pulling the stack of files from the drawer. "Personnel."

"Us?"

Tate flipped through the files, his frown deepening. "Yup, everyone is here."

"Do the files have our new locations in them?"

He opened a file folder and scanned through the documents inside. Then did the same with two more. "Looks like pretty much everything's here. Our recruitment papers."

"Recruitment my ass, it was indentured servitude."

"Beats the hell out of a prison stint," he countered, and she nodded, giving him the point. "Anyway, it's all here. No operation details, but our psych evaluations are here." He flipped through a few more pages. "Staff notes. More evaluations from after Sangre de Cristo. There's even information about our lives after D-9. Looks like Maurice kept pretty close tabs on us. Did you know that Mather was gay?"

"What the hell does that have to do with anything?"

"Nothing. Sorry." He turned another page. "Shit."

"What?" Simone spun around to face him.

"The page with her relocation information is missing. I can see where it's been ripped off. The heading's still here."

He held it out and Simone took it, scanning the words still attached to the clip in the file. "Are the others the same?"

Tate thumbed through the other files, then nodded. "Looks like everyone's relocation information is missing. There's a little bit more of Ed's left. Part of a city name. San Be… I think."

"San Bernardino, maybe, it fits with what we know. But it doesn't matter, does it? The point is that someone's clearly been in the files."

"Someone interested in finding us." Tate scowled down at the papers in his hand.

"So you think he stole the papers when he killed Maurice?"

"Not possible," Tate answered, shaking his head. "Maurice was killed at his house. So unless it's an inside job, the killer would have to have been here first."

"Did you know that the files had been compromised?" She needed to ask the question.

Tate's face tightened in anger. "What are you asking me?"

"Nothing. I don't know." She rubbed the back of her neck. "It's all just happening so fast. And I can't help but wonder why it was Maurice called you back into the game. Why not me or Bea or even Ed?"

"I already said I think it was because I was closer. Or maybe it was because you had a new life. And I told you I didn't have anything like that."

"I'm sorry."

"It's fine. Besides, happily ever after is obviously not all it's cracked up to be."

It was meant as a throwaway comment, a way to relieve the tension between them, but instead Simone heard the truth in it. The fact that her one attempt at a normal life had ended in complete failure—last night notwithstanding.

"Let's take the files with us. Maybe there's something there that'll give us a clue as to what happened, who'd want Maurice dead."

Tate nodded and grabbed a manila envelope, sliding the files inside. "How about the computer?"

"So far nothing," she said, turning back to the computer. "But I've still got a couple of directories to look at. You finish with the file cabinets and I'll see what's here."

They went back to work, the silence between them no longer comfortable.

"Simone, did you love me?" He stared down at the papers he was going through, purposely not meeting her eyes. "I mean the way you loved Reece?" She could tell that he wasn't digging for compliments. He was trying to understand, so she honored him with the truth.

"Not like that."

"But you did love me."

"Yes. I did."

"Look, Simone." He sounded nervous now, and she kept her eyes on the computer screen, knowing he'd prefer that. "Whatever happens, I just want you to know that I care about you, too. At least as much as I can care about anyone," he qualified. "I probably shouldn't be saying stuff like this. But it's just that seeing you after all this time. It brought up things…"

"I know." She looked up then, a tiny smile playing at the corners of her mouth, the tension between them dissipating.

"Some things never change." He shrugged, going back to the file drawers, thankfully taking her cue to drop the subject.

She turned her attention back to the computer and Maurice's directories.

The second directory, like the first, came up empty, so she moved to the third one. The list of files seemed as innocuous as the others. There were budget reports and meeting memos. None of them dated over five years ago.

"This is pointless. There's nothing here that dates back to D-9."

"We're not looking for something that old. We're looking for something that happened recently. Something that will probably link back to D-9. Is there a calendar there?"

She felt stupid not to have thought of it herself. "There's one on the desk. I flipped through it, but there were no names or appointments listed that seemed out of the ordinary."

Tate closed a drawer and held out a hand. "Let me look at it. Maybe I'll see something you didn't."

She handed him the day-planner and turned back to the computer.

"Doesn't it strike you as odd that there are no appointments in here?" Tate asked. "Nothing at all except routine meetings and the occasional visit to the dentist?"

"What are you getting at?" The minute the words were out, the reality clicked into place. "He's got another calendar. This one's just a decoy."

Tate nodded. "He always was a cagey bastard. Is there anything on the computer that looks like a calendar?"

She opened his e-mail program, thinking that there might be something there. But the calendar there was also devoid of any personal appointments. She flipped the screen back to the directories, Tate moving to stand behind her shoulder.

"What about that one." He pointed to a file buried inside of two others. The label read *daze*. "Seems sort of simple—but..."

"Hiding in plain sight is sometimes the most obvious choice."

She clicked to open the file, and another password box popped up.

"Looking kind of like we found it."

"Except we're locked out again. I don't suppose Maurice happened to give you another password."

"No such luck, I'm afraid." He frowned.

"Well, I'm betting it'll be something personal. Like fly fishing. Only problem being that I haven't a clue what he's been up to the past ten years. You met with him. Any idea what might have been important?"

"I got the feeling he was still living in the past. D-9 marked the zenith of his career. He kept his job after Sangre de Cristo, but he was never part of the inner circle again."

"All right then, so maybe it's something to do with D-9." Just for the hell of it she typed in Sangre de Cristo. Nothing happened.

"Maybe it's one of our names? We're the closest thing to family the old man ever had."

Simone typed in Tate's name. First, then last. Then both. Again nothing. She was typing in her own when the essence of Tate's words hit home. "Family."

"What?" he asked, his brows drawn together.

"Maurice considered us family." She typed the word in

and the little computer sang, the password box disappearing to bring up another list of files. The first was a series of memos Maurice had written to himself. There weren't many, but just skimming them, Simone knew they were worth pursuing. She hit Print, and moved on to a second file.

This one yielded the calendar. Divided into days, there were meeting notations on almost all of the pages. Some of them a mirror of the public one, others showing meetings with upper-level Company personnel as well as several high-ranking diplomats.

There was even the notation of his meeting with Tate. Much later than Tate had led them to believe.

"I thought you said your last meeting with Maurice was weeks ago. This is dated right before his death." She pointed to the calendar entry.

"I don't know how to explain it. But I wasn't there. Maybe he was going to call and set it up?"

Simone stared down at the computer screen, considering the idea. "You're thinking he was killed before he could contact you?"

"It's possible. Scroll back and see if there's not a listing that corresponds with the earlier date."

She obediently scrolled back and sure enough, Maurice had a notation of a meeting the week Tate had originally indicated. In addition, unlike the first entry there was a secondary note indicating that Tate had agreed to help. "Looks like maybe you're right."

She moved on to several other entries, and like Tate's, most of them had secondary comments, as if Maurice was using the calendar as a diary as well as a way to record appointments.

"What about right before the last notation," Tate said, reading over her shoulder. "Say the previous two days. Maybe that's what we're looking for. The meeting Maurice was talking about."

She moved the cursor forward, scanning the notations, stopping cold when she reached one, two days prior to the entry about Tate. "Oh, my God."

The entry read: *Isabella Ramirez.* And after that, with a different time stamp, Maurice had entered one word.

Trouble.

CHAPTER NINETEEN

"COME AND SIT. They'll be back when they're finished and not before." Marguerite materialized at Reece's elbow, her voice full of concern.

"I can't help myself. I just keep thinking if I stand here long enough, their car lights will show up in the drive." Reece turned to face the older woman, knowing his expression was sheepish.

Marguerite lived out in the country, in an old stone farmhouse more suited for the hills of Provence than the urban sprawl of Virginia. Yet somehow, she'd managed to find her little piece of heaven in the wake of the expanding D.C. metropolitan area.

"It's just over those hills," she said, following his train of thought. "You can sort of see the lights." Indeed, the sky appeared brighter along the upper line of the hills, but not enough to obliterate the stars. "So come with me and have something to eat. There's no telling when you'll have the time again."

They were all agreed that this was just a break in the storm, that Carlos, or whoever was chasing them, would find them again—and failing that, *they'd* find him, one way or the other eliciting a showdown.

Reece allowed Marguerite to guide him back to the

table. Martin was already there, tucking into a simple meal of stew and French bread, the wine that accompanied it a superior vintage. French to her core, Marguerite was not the type to suffer bad wine, not even out here in the boonies.

"Tell us about Simone," Martin said, as usual oblivious to the undercurrents. "What was she like when you knew her?"

"You forget." Marguerite's smile was gentle. "I know her now." Her gaze met Reece's and he felt as if there were a message. One he was choosing to ignore.

"I know that." Martin's voice held a note of exasperation. "But I want to know what she was like in D-9."

"She was quiet. Always turned inward, that one. I'm certain that's why Maurice chose her."

"What do you mean 'chose her'?" Reece asked, curious despite himself.

"Maurice picked the members of D-9 very carefully. Always people who had nothing to lose. No family or friends. No connections, or perhaps unfavorable ones they would just as soon leave behind."

"And Simone fit the mold," Reece prompted, almost afraid to hear the answer.

"She must have. Otherwise I can't believe Maurice would have recruited her. But she never talked about her past, if that's what you're asking. I think maybe she confided in Bea. The two of them were close. But I'm not even certain of that, really."

"So there's nothing you can share." He sounded desperate and hated the fact.

"I'm afraid the answers you seek can only come from Simone."

Reece nodded, knowing that she was right. "You said that Maurice looked for outsiders. But surely there had to be more to it than that."

"There was." She paused, her expression thoughtful. "He also looked for certain talents. Natural tendencies he could fashion into useful tools for the division."

"And Simone's silence was one?" Martin asked, clearly not understanding.

"Perhaps not the silence itself. But what it said about her as a person. Simone feels things very deeply. Her childhood taught her to hide this, but never completely. She is sensitive to the world around her. And that makes her invaluable when it comes to infiltration."

"Infiltration?" They both asked, almost in unison.

"Yes. Simone was better than anyone I've ever seen at getting into and out of places that are seemingly inaccessible. She has an innate ability to read the environment and find clues that no one else could possibly see. She could access anything."

"And once she was inside?" Reece prompted.

"I am not sure you want the answer to that." Marguerite reached out to cover his hand.

"It's like hearing about a stranger. Someone I don't know at all."

"Perhaps so." Marguerite shrugged. "We all are different people at different moments in our lives. But inside. Here." She touched her heart. "We are always the same. It is our ability to love that keeps us human."

"Maybe. Or maybe it's the ability to keep some part of us sequestered away from everything around us. To keep a bit of our soul isolated from the disappointments of the world."

"Are you talking of Simone, or yourself?" Marguerite's eyebrows disappeared into her snow-white hair, her blue eyes knowing.

"Both, I suppose," he said, laughing at himself. "I'm not sure I know which way is up at the moment. Everything I thought I knew has been turned on its side."

"Or maybe you were looking at the world the wrong way to begin with, and now…" Again the Gallic shrug. "Now you are seeing it as it really is."

"Which leaves me where?"

"That is for you to decide. You and Simone."

Martin cleared his throat. "Uh, guys, before you dig any deeper into Reece's psyche, maybe I could have a little more stew?"

"There's more on the stove, *chéri*." Marguerite waved Martin in the direction of the kitchen, her eyes never leaving Reece's face.

Reece watched as his brother pushed away from the table, heading for the stew pot in the kitchen. "I'm not sure where to go from here. Some things, once broken, can never be repaired."

"Yes—" she nodded "—but the remnants can often be built into something entirely new."

It was the same thought he'd had last night. Although by the light of the day he hadn't been as certain of it. Simone, despite the intimacy of the night, seemed only to have pulled further away.

Martin stepped back into the dining room, the fragrance of beef and onions filling the air.

"But I am an old woman," Marguerite said, her eyes wrinkling as she smiled. "What do I know of such things?" She got up and went into the kitchen, and Reece spooned a bite of stew.

"She's right, you know." Apparently Martin was not as oblivious as he'd seemed.

"About what?"

"Starting over. Building something from what's left. It's obvious to me that you still care about Simone. You've never really stopped. And just because you have a few bumps in the road, it doesn't mean you should just hang up your driving gloves and call it a day."

"There's a message in all that, I take it? Something beyond the Indy 500 analogy?"

Martin laughed. "So I'm not as good with the turn of the phrase as Marguerite. But I am your brother. Which means I know you. And you still want Simone. It's as simple as that."

"Nothing is ever that simple, Martin. Especially in a marriage."

"Only because both of you are so determined to make it complex. The way I see it, it's pretty damn straightforward. You love her. She loves you. And life is too damn short to piss that kind of thing away. How's that for to the point?"

Reece sighed, wondering when his little brother had become a man. Clearly, he'd spent too many hours trying to right the wrongs of the world and not enough time seeing his wife and brother for who they really were.

"You're a great attorney, Reece," Martin continued. "So you, more than most, know that the answer is sometimes right there in plain sight. At least think about it. All right?"

"Yeah." He nodded, his thoughts on Simone. "I will. As soon as we're done with all this."

"No. Think about it now. Before there is no more *this*."

He looked up to meet his brother's somber gaze, and then broke off to look out the window again. Maybe they were right. Maybe it was as simple as recognizing what was in front of him and grabbing on to it.

But the truth was, it wasn't up to him. At least not entirely.

Simone had to want it, too.

"SO YOU HAVE a reference to Isabella Ramirez, and missing parts of D-9's personnel files. Anything else?" They were all sitting in the dining room, the old oak table having been witness to many such conversations.

Simone sat by Reece. Martin sat on her left, next to Tate, with Marguerite sitting between Tate and Reece. They looked for all the world like any other dinner party, except that this one was about life and death.

"We brought home copies of a few more files. A couple that appear to be Maurice's take on events happening around him. But I don't believe they contain anything of real importance." Simone met Tate's gaze across the table and he nodded his agreement.

"But at least we know now that Isabella is behind what's happening," Tate added.

"You don't know that," Marguerite said. "You only know that Maurice saw the woman. And that something worried him enough to send the postcards."

"But surely if you connect the dots. With Carlos in the country and Isabella meeting with Maurice..." Martin said.

"No." Reece nodded toward the older woman. "Marguerite is correct. There is logic certainly that would make it seem likely that Isabella is involved. Maybe even pulling the strings. But there isn't enough evidence to give us any degree of certainty."

"Well, this isn't a court of law, Reece, and I'm not sure we have the luxury of waiting for absolutes." Tate crossed his arms, glaring at them all. "I, for one, don't much like the idea of sitting around here waiting for definitive answers while that bastard out there closes the noose."

"So what are you proposing we do?" Simone asked, more inclined to action than waiting.

"I think we need to go to the source."

"Nicaragua?" Simone asked, following his train of thought from force of habit.

"Yeah. Isabella. I say we confront her with what we know." He paused, looking at each of them in turn. "And then we put an end to it."

"But wouldn't it make more sense to try to find Carlos? After all, if we're right, he's the one who has been hunting us," Reece said.

"If we go to Nicaragua, I guarantee you, Carlos will follow." Tate crossed his arms, his gaze encompassing them all.

"That actually makes sense. I mean, if he's tracking us, why not lead him where we want him to go?" Simone said.

"But you don't even know where Isabella is," Reece protested.

"Actually, I have a little information," Martin said. "I was doing some surfing earlier. And I came across a news story. Apparently there was a minor uproar in Managua last night. The news is sketchy, but basically they're saying there was an attempted coup. The Ramirez junta is being blamed, specifically Isabella."

"Is she still in Managua?" Tate asked.

"I don't know." Martin shook his head.

"What else do we know?"

"Just that Antonio Montoya is counted among the dead. He was one of Hector's henchmen, right?"

"Yeah." Tate frowned. "But none of this feels right. If Isabella was going to stage a coup, my guess is it wouldn't be in Managua. She'd know that Ortega and his supporters are strongest on their home territory."

"You're saying that if she was going to try and overthrow the government, she'd wait to do it from her own position of strength," Simone said.

"Exactly. So that means something else is going on here."

"Maybe the Nicaraguan government got wind of her interaction with Maurice." Simone considered the idea, realizing that it had validity.

"Aren't we really saying she murdered him?" Martin asked.

"We're saying it's possible," Marguerite conceded. "But we still have no proof."

"Doesn't matter if she did or didn't do it," Reece speculated, once again sounding every inch the prosecutor. "If the Americans know she was here, they'll be putting pressure on Ortega's government for answers. Even a hint that the president's mistress was involved would be enough to threaten the current trade negotiations. And when you factor in who said mistress is, I can see that there would be great pressure on Ortega to do something about it."

"So, what?" Simone asked, filtering through his thoughts for an answer. "The supposed coup is a cover-up?"

"I think it's possible. A way to save face. Mark her clearly as an enemy."

"But that could mean that Isabella is dead," Tate said.

"Not necessarily." Reece sat back, steepling his hands, considering the facts. "If she were dead, he'd have no reason not to report it. There'd be some repercussion from her followers, but not enough to threaten the government. And news of her death would leave him free to blame her for any misunderstanding with the Americans."

"You would have fit right into D-9, Reece," Marguerite said with approval. "But even if we assume that Isabella killed Maurice, what of the other murders? She is clearly no longer in the States."

"Carlos." Tate spat the name out. "Who better to do Isabella's dirty work than her brother? Maybe Isabella didn't kill Maurice at all. Maybe she was only here to get information to feed to her brother. And once that was accomplished, Maurice became a liability."

"And so Carlos killed him." Marguerite said the words out loud, trying them on for size.

"And then, using the locations Isabella stole, began hunting."

"Well, I can certainly buy that Isabella and Carlos would want revenge. But why now?" Marguerite reached for her wineglass and took a sip.

"I don't know," Tate said. "Maybe because Isabella finally had access to Maurice? Or maybe she only just now found out about D-9. Either way the point is that it would have taken time to gather enough information to be in a position to take action."

"So we're saying that Isabella finessed a meeting with Maurice. Which obviously worried him—" Simone shot a look at Tate "—since he called you about it. Then, after the fact, he discovered the missing information, and sent the postcards. Apparently also planning to call you in for another personal meeting." She frowned, wondering again why Maurice had called Tate at all. He'd never been a favorite, as far as she could tell. Maybe under the circumstances proximity had been the mitigating factor.

"I'm not following," Reece said, interrupting her thoughts.

"Sorry. There was a notation in Maurice's diary about a meeting with Tate after he met with Isabella."

"But there wasn't a meeting." Reece looked from Tate to Simone, his eyes narrowed in speculation.

"No. He never contacted me," Tate said, his gaze full of regret. "We think maybe he was killed before he could."

"Apparently, Maurice used his calendar as a sort of diary—recording impressions of a meeting after the fact. There's nothing recorded after his notation to meet with Tate. So it follows that he never actually set the meeting up, just planned to."

"But he *did* send the postcards." This from Marguerite.

"Yes, only he never made it to the rendezvous because Carlos got to him first." Reece summed it all up with one sentence, and for a moment nobody said anything.

"So I'm right. We need to head for Nicaragua," Tate said. "End this once and for all. We owe it to Maurice."

"And the others," Simone said, gripping the edge of the table in anger.

"So how do we find her?" Marguerite asked.

"I think that's fairly easy," Tate said. "If Reece is right, and the coup is only a cover, then I'm betting she's retreated to the safety of mountains."

"To *El Ojo de la Tormenta,*" Martin said to no one in particular.

"So we head for Nicaragua." Simone looked to Tate, her mind made up. She owed it to her friends.

"Not so fast." Reece held up his hand. "We aren't even certain she's at the compound. And even if we were sure, she'll have security out the wazoo."

"It won't be the first time we've taken on the odds. And I'll tell you this," Tate said, staring daggers at Reece, "I haven't made it this far sitting on my ass and waiting for something to happen. Sometimes you have to go to the source. Stop the puppeteer and you take care of the puppets at the same time."

"Meaning Carlos and Isabella. Two for the price of one?"

"There's logic in what he's saying, Reece," Simone said.

"I can't say that I agree. But I'll defer to your experience." It was as close as she was going to get to his acquiescing. "However, considering that the alleged coup is all over the news, I still don't see how the hell you're going to get into the country, let alone the compound, without raising alarms throughout Central America?"

Tate shot a look at Simone, who hesitated and then shrugged. "It's possible. I still have contacts. And I suspect—" she held Tate's gaze "—that you do as well."

He nodded.

"So how soon do we go?" Simone asked.

"Yesterday would have been best," Tate said, "but I'll settle for tomorrow."

"Then we have much work to do." Marguerite stood up, gesturing for Tate to follow.

He hesitated, looking from Reece to Simone and then back at Reece again. "It will be best if you stay here."

Reece opened his mouth to argue, but Tate didn't wait for an answer, following Marguerite into the kitchen.

"He's right." Simone laid a hand on Reece's arm, feeling him tense beneath her touch. "You and Martin need to stay here. You're not trained for this kind of thing."

"And you haven't been active in almost ten years."

"Except for the last few days." Her tone was placating, but his frown didn't lessen. "Look, I know it's hard for you to let someone else be in charge. But we do know what we're doing. And Martin is in no shape to travel to Central America. If he stays, someone needs to stay with him."

"Marguerite can—" he started, but she interrupted.

"I'd rather it be you. I'd trust Marguerite with my life, but she's not exactly in prime condition. She's got to be nearing seventy, and I'd feel better if you were here, too. Besides, we can't ignore the fact that Carlos, or very likely someone working for him, is still out there. And although I think Tate is right, and our departure will draw him away from you and Martin, I can't be certain."

"I don't like any of it." His tone was stubborn now, but she knew she'd won the round.

"For what it's worth, I don't like it either. But it's the best we've got." She started to reach up to touch his face, but instead, she turned and walked away. The time for a normal life had passed. This was a time for war. Something had been started all those years ago in Sangre de Cristo.

And now the time had come to bring it to an end.

CHAPTER TWENTY

REECE LAY AWAKE, staring up into the eaves of Marguerite's attic. The room obviously served as a retreat for the older woman when it was not occupied by last-minute guests on the run. A half-finished watercolor sat on an easel near the gabled window, and another dozen or so canvases lay scattered about the room. Somehow the idea of Marguerite as a painter fit his view of her far more than the image of Marguerite as an elite CIA operative. But then what the hell did he know?

And of course it had been many years since Marguerite had worked black ops. There was certainly a commonality between her and Simone. She had the same stillness, as if she was focused internally as much as externally. Watching without watching.

He rolled over on a sigh. So much had changed, and yet surprisingly so much was the same. Simone had revealed an entire side to her life that Reece had never known, but he still felt like there were secrets. An invisible wall that separated them.

Only he had no idea why it was there. Just that Simone was still refusing to let him in.

Oh, maybe she'd cracked the door a little. Told him what she'd been forced to tell. But nothing more—nothing voluntary.

It shouldn't matter. But it did.

A few days ago all he'd been worried about was nailing Zabara and getting Simone to sign the papers. And now, he was lying here, papers signed and Zabara convicted, wondering how he could convince her to work with him to try to figure out what the hell it was that still stretched between them.

He could still feel her body moving under his. Smell the soft sweet scent that was some impossible combination of soap and shampoo and Simone.

God, he had it bad.

He swung out of the bed and walked over to the window, leaning against the overhang to peer out into the night. The window was open, and a cool breeze washed across his exposed skin, leaving a trail of gooseflesh behind.

His grandmother had always said that goose bumps meant someone was walking over your grave. But Reece didn't think she'd meant it quite as literally as their current situation. Tomorrow, if everything played out as planned, Simone would walk away, taking the danger with her.

It made sense. She and Tate were certainly more prepared to deal with what lay ahead in Central America than either he or Martin, but some part of him, some chauvinistic part no doubt, hated the idea of letting her go on her own. He ought to be there with her. He'd begun the journey and somehow it seemed important that he finish it.

Again with the philosophical bullshit. Playing CIA agent evidently had that effect on people. His laugh was harsh, breaking the silence of the night.

"Something funny?"

He turned to see his wife standing in a pool of moonlight. "How long have you been standing there?"

"Long enough to admire the view." She let her gaze travel the length of him, a small smile turning the corner of her lips.

"I'm glad someone is having a good night."

She sobered immediately. "I…I shouldn't have come."

"Then why did you?"

She shook her head, her face in shadow. "I'm not sure really. I guess it sounds lame to say I couldn't stay away. But I'm leaving tomorrow and I—"

"Needed a little goodbye send-off?" He instantly wanted to take the words back, but it was too late.

Her face hardened. "No. Obviously it was a stupid idea." She whirled around to go but he was faster, crossing the room and grabbing her by the arm.

"I didn't mean it the way it sounded. I'm just confused, Simone."

"Join the club."

He loosened his hold, but she didn't leave. They stood for a moment, the only sound in the room the whisper of the curtains moving in the breeze. "Why do we do this to each other?"

"Because we don't know how to love each other anymore." She looked so sad.

"It used to be so damn easy."

"Or maybe we just never noticed the effort. Either way, it's different now."

"But not over." He held his breath, waiting for her to answer.

"You said that this morning. And for a moment I admit I wanted it to be true. But I've been over it and over it, and I don't see how it can be any other way. Surely you can see that. I mean, look at us. We're standing in a strange house in the middle of the night just hours before I head out on a mission with God knows what kind of results. What kind of life is that?"

"It's *our* life, Simone. The one we were given. You've got to admit the alternative's not so great." His attempt to joke fell flat; her dark eyes filled with pain.

"So what? We start over?"

"Is it such a bad idea? We love each other." She opened her mouth to argue but he stopped her. "Don't bother denying it."

"I wasn't going to." She tipped back her head, moonlight silvering her face and neck. "I was going to say that it's not enough to build on. We need more."

"What? A shared past? We have that."

"One built on lies."

"Not all of it." He slid his hands to her shoulders, needing the physical connection. "Stop fighting me."

"I don't want to." Her eyes were full of confusion now. "But there's still so much you don't understand. I'm not the woman you think I am."

"But I do know who you are. You're the woman I married. For better or worse and all that that implies. Look, sweetheart, nothing is guaranteed in this life. Nothing. So we have to make do with what we have. Maybe moments, maybe days, maybe a lifetime. I don't know either. I just know that I can't walk away. I can't."

"Me either." She whispered the last on a shudder, and he bent to kiss her, wanting only to take away the pain in her voice.

The contact was like sticking a match to kerosene, the instant inferno threatening to envelop them both. He pulled her closer, relieved when her arms threaded around his neck, her body pressed tightly against his.

It was as if they'd never come together before. As if they were discovering every part of each other for the first time. The tender place on her neck that made her shiver when he kissed her there, the soft, smooth velvet of the skin across her breasts, the growling sound she made low in her throat as she ground against him.

She was his world. Had been since the first moment he'd met her. And at the moment, nothing else mattered. He reached for the hem of the T-shirt she was sleeping in, sliding it up and over her head, tossing it to the floor, his hands aching for the feel of her.

Running his palms over her shoulders, he let them slide along the curve of her back, across her buttocks and up again until he cupped both breasts, his heart threatening to burst from his chest.

He circled each nipple with the pad of his thumb, delighting in the fact that she responded to him so quickly. With a little cry she flung herself against him and they kissed, tongues tangling together, moving as if desire had choreographed the motions. Thrust and parry, accepting, repelling, drinking each other in as if they were parched.

The kiss deepened and he traced the line of her lips with his tongue, nipping the corners of her mouth before trailing kisses along her cheek to the soft lobe of her ear. He bit it gently, feeling her respond beneath his touch. They knew each other so well, and yet they didn't know each other at all.

There was something exciting in the idea. And frightening. He'd been right when he'd accused her of hiding behind her secrets. But he'd been hiding, too. Hiding from intimacy. From the idea of depending upon another person so deeply that to exist without them seemed all but impossible.

She reached down to cup his balls and it was his turn to writhe against her. There was so much he wanted to do to this woman. With a groan he swung her into his arms and carried her to the bed. Bathed in moonlight, it seemed an almost magical place. A safe place.

He looked down at her for a moment, allowing himself to drink in her beauty, and then she lifted her arms, beckoning him, and he was lost. Bracing himself over her, he rubbed a knee against the moist juncture between her thighs, and then bent his head to savor her breasts. Kissing first one, then the other. Teasing her with his tongue before finally taking her into his mouth and biting her nipple, her responsive cry almost his undoing.

He tasted the other nipple and then trailed kisses along her stomach, tracing the soft skin between her thighs, finally allowing himself the pleasure of tasting her, his tongue thrusting where he longed to follow, sucking and pulling, nipping and teasing until he felt her rise off the bed in her release.

He slid upward again, lying with his head against her chest, cradled there between her breasts, listening to her heart beat, as she slid down from the rapture he'd given her. Then suddenly she moved, and they flipped over so that she was straddling him. Her fingers circled him, moving up and down, the sensations washing through him on a wave of pure pleasure.

She teased him with her hands until he couldn't stand another minute, and in one deft move he lifted her, sliding inside as he impaled her with his penis, the wet, hot moisture surrounding him like a velvet glove. Grasping her hips, he moved her up and down, setting the rhythm. Bracing her hands on his shoulders, she took up the dance, pulling upward so that they were almost disengaged and then slamming home again with a force that threatened to send him spiraling out of control.

But he wasn't ready to surrender, and bending his legs, he pulled up to a sitting position, cradling her against him, rocking slightly so that he moved inside her, the motion sending her squirming against him, craving release.

He smiled, kissing her cheeks and her eyelids, his hands cupping her breasts, his thumbs circling her nipples, each movement designed to drive her higher, to drive him higher. Their very stillness causing tremors of passion to ripple through them.

Then he kissed her. And with a cry she pushed him back again, pumping hard against him, the exquisite pain building inside him until he was meeting each and every thrust with one of his own, the two of them driving together, reaching out for that moment of bliss.

And then it was there. Just within grasp, and taking her hand, they found it together, the intensity threatening to shatter him into tiny pieces. But he held on—holding her, loving her, knowing that even if he never had this moment again—he would treasure it always.

THE MOONLIGHT SPILLED across the bed like a silvery blanket, and Simone stretched with contentment and snuggled deeper into Reece's warmth. There was something so wonderful about waking in the middle of the night and not being alone.

She'd fought the impulse to come to him. Figured it was better not to complicate things more than they already were. But then she'd realized that maybe there wouldn't be another chance, and if she'd learned anything in life, it was that one had to seize the moment.

None of their problems had been solved. Hell, they'd scarcely been discussed, and yet somehow here in the moonlight she could almost believe him when he said they had a chance to start again.

"You're awake." His voice rumbled through his chest and her contentment spread.

"I was thinking about what all you said. About us. About starting over."

"And…"

"And I don't know," she said, lifting up on one elbow.

His face darkened as he frowned.

"No. Wait," she said, putting a finger over his lips. "I didn't mean that I don't want to. It's more that I don't know how. We've started patterns that aren't easily broken, you know? I mean, technically we're divorced."

"Actually, the papers are still sitting on the table, unless the local PD decided to start delivering mail."

His words made her think of Laura and she fought a wave of grief.

"I'm sorry about Laura. She didn't deserve any of this." His deep voice was comforting, and she lay again across his chest.

"I just wish I could change things, you know? Fix it so that you and Laura and Martin would never have been involved in my problems."

"But life's not like that, Simone. It can't be orchestrated. Whatever's going to happen is going to happen."

"So you're saying we have no control over it?"

"We have some, but I think too often we make the mistake of thinking we're omniscient. That we can order our lives any way that we want. And in the end I think that's what hurts the most. Realizing that we never really had that kind of control in the first place."

"You're not talking about me anymore, are you?"

"No. I guess not. Or maybe I'm talking about us both. You wanted a fantasy life, and I wanted everything kept in its designated place. Not really all that different. I had a picture of who I thought you were and I didn't want that to change. Which, when you think about it, isn't all that realistic." He stroked her hair, his fingers soothing and exciting all at the same time.

"Maybe. But it doesn't mean you needed to have all this dropped on you out of the blue."

His laughter rumbled beneath her ear. "I can think of better ways to have found out. But the truth is, a part of me was trying to keep your secret even as I pushed to uncover it. A part of me didn't want to know, Simone. I was as afraid as you were of what it would do to our relationship."

"But you still pushed."

"I've built my entire adult life around finding and defending the truth. It's part of who I am."

"I know that. It's part of why I fell in love with you." But it was also the reason she was so afraid to be totally honest. Tate had told her to come clean with Reece. To be true to her past. But looking at him now, in the moonlight, she just couldn't. Couldn't admit to him that underneath all the polish and pretense, she was no better than the people he prosecuted every day.

"Something's wrong." He frowned down at her, his eyes probing.

"It's nothing really. It's just all of it, I guess. So much is happening and it's all happening too fast." Her stomach clenched with regret. He'd given her the opportunity, handed it to her on a silver platter, and still she couldn't take it.

He tipped her chin so that she was looking into his eyes. "I honestly don't know where we go from here, Simone. I won't pretend that sleeping together has solved everything. But maybe it's a beginning."

He leaned in to kiss her, his touch this time gentle, cherishing. There was a covenant in the connection. One she could not ignore. A part of her brain urged her to run, but her heart was stronger, and so she stayed.

She ran her hands along the sharp planes of his face, the friction of his beard stubble against her palms as erotic as if he were kissing her there. For the moment at least there was nothing standing between them. Not her past. Not their mistakes. Not their fear. Nothing. Here in the dark of Marguerite's house they were safe from everything that threatened to tear them apart.

She deepened the kiss, her hands exploring his shoulders and back, memorizing every inch of him. Knowing that later her memories might be all she had. He flipped her onto her back, his weight on top of her welcome. She inhaled the hot male smell of him, letting it drift through her body, filling her senses.

His hands found her breasts, his tender stroking sending sparks of joy skittering through her. This was where she wanted to be. This was where she belonged. Reece was home in a way that defied all she had done to subvert it. He was her safe place. And she'd be a fool to throw that away.

"I'm here," he whispered, as if reading her mind. And then he was there. Deep inside her, living, breathing, a part of her.

They moved in tandem, slowly at first and then faster, languid exploration giving way to deeper, darker needs. In and out, deeper and faster. Now. She wanted him now.

And he was there, hands joined with hers as the world broke again into raindrops of glittering silver, and she laughed as he held her close and they spiraled away toward the moon.

Later, much later, she awoke again. This time to complete darkness. The dark before dawn. As a little girl she'd always hated the hours before sunrise. She'd lain awake in the dark, shaking with fear. In a vague memory she recalled a woman, not her mother, trying to comfort her, telling her that soon it would be morning and everything would be all right.

But the woman had never understood—it wasn't the dark she was afraid of.

It was the light.

Morning always meant the death of her dreams.

CHAPTER TWENTY-ONE

ISABELLA STOOD on the lanai staring out at the garden, the flowers originally planted by her mother. She'd been home for almost twenty-four hours, but she still could not dispel the horror of Managua. Again her family had been threatened. And again there had been great loss, Isabella escaping only by the sheer determination of the men who served her.

From the street outside the palace, she'd made her way to the river, and Ramón. As Antonio had promised he'd been there with a boat, ferrying her away from the city. From there she'd been driven in three different cars, all of them traveling at breakneck speeds to assure that she was whisked safely into the mountains.

To *El Ojo de la Tormenta.*

But the valley gave her no peace of mind. Not this time. The cost had been too high. Antonio was dead, along with others. And to make matters worse, Manuel was claiming that it had been a coup attempt. The man had tried to kill her, and when he failed he had still tried to spin the night's events in his favor.

There had been no word from her brother, and she was beginning to worry. If something happened to him, none of this would be worth it. Not her survival, not her friends' deaths—none of it.

"There is no further word." Ramón walked out of the house, clicking his cell phone closed in the process.

"Nothing from Ortiz?" She turned to face the older man, her thoughts still back in Managua. The last she had seen of Ortiz, he had been standing in her bedroom, trying to prevent Manuel's killers from taking her out, his body thrown in front of the door as if he personally could stop the assault.

"There is no word. But we have no one left on the inside." There was the faintest hint of rebuke in his voice. Ramón was and always would be her father's man. And though technically the old man worked for her now, in many ways he still considered her a child. "I think we can presume him dead."

Isabella dipped her head. Ortiz would be missed. "We must compensate his family. Make sure that they want for nothing." She waved a hand toward the outbuildings of the compound. Somewhere beyond the main gate, Ortiz's wife, children and grandchildren were suffering.

Suffering because of her.

Her only comfort was that the men who had died had known they were sacrificing for her father's sake, and had gone willingly. Her father had commanded incredible loyalty. The kind that had been prevalent in her country a century ago but had begun to die out with the coming of politicians and their treaties aimed at destroying the old way of life.

"It's already been taken care of." Ramón nodded but did not leave. Evidently he had more to say.

"What is it?" Isabella snapped, regretting the sharpness of her words immediately, but she was so tired.

"I think we need to talk about repercussions."

"From Manuel or the Americans?" There was no question that Manuel wanted her dead, but if the Americans thought she'd had something to do with Maurice Baxter's murder, she had no doubt that they too would want her to pay.

"I don't think that the government will do anything further. We are not seen as a threat directly. We both know the stories they are releasing are only a cover. Ortega is upset about the Americans and the pressure they are placing on the government to admit to being involved with the CIA man's death."

"But Manuel had nothing to do with it. Surely just denying it would serve his purpose."

"You were his lover, *carita*. The Americans will never believe you acted on your own."

"Even knowing about Sangre de Cristo?"

"They cannot afford to take a chance. They'll want Manuel to pay."

"Which is why he isn't openly blaming me."

"Exactly. He knows he'd be dealt a death blow in the backlash. Better to try and divert attention."

"Then I'm not sure I see how there is danger of repercussion—"

"You are a child in so many ways." Ramón cut her off, his voice sorrowful but not condemning. "If Manuel found out about the meeting, you can be certain the Americans know as well."

"But then why haven't they admitted as much?" She rubbed her temples, trying to stop the pounding in her head.

"Because they prefer to do a political dance on the surface while taking action well out of the public eye."

"Just like before." She spat the words out, anger making her speak her mind. "Perhaps they will send my father's killers. I would love nothing better than to face them."

"You have no proof that it was the Americans."

"It was definitely a gringo. I have eyes."

Ramón sighed. "And you cannot let it go."

"My father died in Sangre de Cristo because someone he trusted killed him. I remember this, I carry it here—" she pounded her heart "—always."

"I know it hurts, but there are more important things than vengeance."

"You and Antonio, you sound the same." She pushed back her hair. "I'm sorry. I meant nothing against Antonio. You know that I loved him. If I could change things…"

Ramón reached out to touch her shoulder. "Antonio did what he had to do to keep you safe. Had it been me, I'd have done the same."

Again she felt the swelling of tears, but she swallowed them whole. There was no room now for emotion. The time had passed for regrets. She must instead concentrate on the present.

"Have you heard from Carlos?" The question was cautious. As if Ramón were trying to gauge how truthful she would be with him.

"I have heard nothing since I left Managua." And the silence was killing her, her fears blossoming more with each passing hour.

"Your brother is a cat, he will land on his feet." It was the closest Ramón had come to comforting her and Isabella appreciated the gesture.

"He is all I have, Ramón. My blood." She touched the crucifix. "My heart."

"I know, *carita*."

But she wondered how he could possibly understand.

Turning back to the garden, she gripped the railing, the

metal cutting into her skin. In a matter of hours her web had not only tangled but broken, and now all she could do was wait to see where the strands would fall.

"WHERE'S SIMONE?" Reece asked as he walked into the living room, rubbing a towel through his hair.

"She's gone," Martin said, looking up from the computer with a frown. "I figured you knew that."

He swallowed frustration, hot and bitter, as it rose in his throat. There hadn't been a chance to talk about last night. And now it was too late. He sorted through images of the night before, his mind settling on the morning. She'd stayed with him, waking in his arms. And then they'd made love one last time.

One last time.

The words echoed in his head.

God, there was so much he still wanted to say.

"She thought it would be easier for you." Marguerite came up behind him, holding two plates of scrambled eggs. She held one out to Martin, who grabbed it like he hadn't eaten in a week.

Reece, on the other hand, couldn't even stomach the idea of eating, and he waved Marguerite away. "Easier for her, you mean." He hated the way he sounded, but he couldn't believe she'd walked out on him—again.

"You don't mean that." Marguerite's wrinkled face drew into a frown.

"No, I don't." He sighed. "I just hate that she left without a word." The truth was, they'd exchanged more than words upstairs. Maybe she'd thought that was all they'd needed.

Maybe she was right.

But just at the moment he wanted nothing more than to tear out of the house after her.

"They'll be fine." Again Marguerite's voice was purposefully calming. "She and Tate share a difficult past. But they work well together. He won't let anything happen to her."

"You know as well as I do that she doesn't need anyone to take care of her, Marguerite. Not Tate—not me." He wasn't proud of the way he sounded, but it hurt that she didn't need him.

"You're wrong." Marguerite had rescued the plate of eggs and was offering it to him again. "She does have needs. And you, my friend, are the only man she believes can fill them. Just because she has gone today, does not mean she has no intention of coming back. The most important gift you can give her is to be here waiting when she does."

He took the plate, still not wanting to eat but realizing she'd keep offering until he took it. Moving over to the table, he dropped down into a chair and stirred the eggs under the pretense of eating them. "On some level I know that you're right. It's just that I'm not used to sitting on the bench, you know?"

"So now we get to the real problem." Marguerite smiled, walking over to the window. "You are not comfortable with the shift of power. Until now it has been all about you, no?"

He started to deny it, but deep inside he knew that she was right. It hadn't been his intention certainly, but he'd been the one to leave the house every day, expecting that she'd be there when he came home. He hadn't exactly been Archie Bunker, but still, he hadn't really given a lot of thought to what her life was like.

"But she always seemed happy." He said it aloud, as if Marguerite had been listening to his internal conversation.

"And I'm sure she was," Marguerite said. "But there is more to a relationship than contentment. There is the excitement and adventure of discovering each other. And to have that fulfillment you must be partners in every sense of the word."

"Maybe Simone left you behind so that you could learn a thing or two from Marguerite," Martin laughed.

Reece chucked the towel at him, and for a moment he thought he'd hit something, the sound of breaking glass filling the air. Then he saw Marguerite whirl around and dive away from the window.

A second report left no question as to what they were hearing. "Get down," Marguerite yelled, crawling toward Martin, who was frozen in his chair. She yanked his arm, and without comment he dropped to the floor, eyes wide.

Reece followed suit, just as the plate of eggs he'd left on the table shattered into pieces, a bullet meant, no doubt, for him slamming into the table.

"There's a panic room in the basement." Marguerite motioned toward the kitchen. "The door's in there. If we can make it, we'll be safe." She crawled forward, then stopped as the gunman, seemingly aware of their intent, peppered the doorway with bullets.

"And you thought Simone was going to have all the excitement." Martin, apparently, was finally with the program, his fear dissipating in a rush of adrenaline.

"What we need is a diversion."

Marguerite nodded her agreement, reaching for a floor lamp. Lifting carefully, she slid the lamp across the floor until it was just at the edge of the window. "When I move it in front of the window, you go."

There was no room for argument.

Marguerite lifted the lamp higher, its shade wavering in front of the window. Reece motioned for Martin to move and he scuttled crablike into the hallway and on into the kitchen. The metal lamp clanged as the shooter targeted it, the shade spinning off to fly across the room. Marguerite dropped the base and bent double, running across the room.

Reece moved into the hallway and was turning to follow Martin when he heard something fall. Spinning back around, he saw Marguerite on the floor clutching her stomach, and in seconds he was back, his arms around her, pulling her across the floor.

"Let me go," she said. "You need to get to the panic room. Simone will never forgive me if something happens to you."

"Well, she won't forgive me if something happens to you, either. So we go together. All right?"

Realizing he wasn't going to give in, Marguerite nodded, and they moved forward, inching their way along the hallway. Marguerite held one fist against the wound in her stomach in a seemingly futile attempt to stanch the blood. Her shirt was soaked with it, leaving Reece afraid to think about what that might mean.

Moving closer to the kitchen and the now-open doorway to the basement, Reece could see his brother already moving down the stairs. "We're almost there, " he whispered, sliding his hands under her arms and knees, preparing to pick her up for the final dash across to the basement. But before he could stand up, all hell broke loose in the kitchen.

The door splintered from the impact of gunfire, this time the volley clearly caused by a machine gun. Whoever this guy was, he meant business. There was no question of running now. They'd have to crawl.

But first they needed another distraction. The towel he'd thrown at his brother lay at the edge of the hallway, still partly in the living room. Reece reached forward and grabbed it, moving quickly back into the hallway.

Armed with the towel, he motioned Marguerite to join him at the entrance to the kitchen. Martin was back now, standing in the doorway to the basement, waving for them to come on. Reece tossed the towel toward Martin, a bullet catching it neatly as it arced its way across the room.

"Damn." Martin's voice mirrored the frustration Reece was feeling.

Marguerite was leaning against the wall now, her breathing labored. It was clear that she was losing too much blood.

"Go on," she whispered. "I'm not sure I'd make it anyway."

"Nonsense. We'll get you to the safe room. You'll be fine."

"I think maybe I'm past that." She lifted her hand, revealing pulsing blood. "So go."

"I told you, I'm not going to leave you." He took her arm and draped it over his shoulder. "We'll do it together."

"Fine." She nodded, accepting his determination. "We'll go together. But I can make it on my own." In testament to her words, she summoned her strength, working herself to a kneeling position.

"Are you sure?" Reece asked, trying to ascertain if she was really up to the task.

"Absolutely. Remember I'm a CIA operative." She smiled, albeit weakly, and the kitchen exploded again with gunfire, this time from closer range. "It's now or never."

Reece counted to three and they launched themselves out into the kitchen. It was only as he reached the doorway and turned to help Marguerite that he realized she was no longer with him. Instead, she was acting as a decoy, standing up near the sink, bullets making her seem to dance.

He lurched forward, intent on reaching her, but Martin got to him first. "It's too late," his brother said. "Don't let her have done it for nothing."

Martin pulled him back, and they scrambled down the stairs just as the kitchen door slammed open, a final shot echoing through the kitchen.

Footsteps sounded above them as Martin pushed Reece through a metal door at the rear of the cellar. "In here. Hurry."

Reece made his way into the tiny room as Martin turned to slam the door against a hail of bullets. For the moment at least they were safe. But outside the killer was waiting.

And upstairs, their friend lay dying.

CHAPTER TWENTY-TWO

"ALL RIGHT, so let's go over it one more time," Tate said, glancing at her from the passenger side of their newest car, a silver Jeep Cherokee.

"We've been over it three times already, Tate." Simone sucked in a breath and tightened her hands on the steering wheel. "We change cars a couple of times to be sure no one is following us, then snag a ride on a courier plane heading for Honduras. From there we meet up with a local operative and make our way into Nicaragua, find Isabella and take her out. It's not like I haven't done this before."

"Sleep on the wrong side of the bed, sunshine?" Tate teased.

"I slept fine, thank you. I just want to get this over and done with."

"So what, you can go back to your old life? I thought that was history?"

"It is...was... I don't know." Which pretty much summed up the problem. "I shouldn't have walked out without saying something. He'll think I don't care."

"No. He'll think you had your mind on business. Come on, Simone, I've met the guy, he's one focused dude. If he were the one heading out, like to a really important trial or something, would he be whining about forgetting to say goodbye?"

"That's not a fair comparison and you know it. He's not going to get killed while he's trying a case. We, on the other hand..." She trailed off, staring out at the road ahead of her.

"Hey, I was just trying to help." He held up his hands. "You're the testy one."

"I'm not testy. I just wish I'd said goodbye." She pictured Reece lying in bed, the rumpled sheets highlighting his nakedness.

"Honestly, Simone, you really have gone soft." His tone was light, but there was a note of rebuke there she couldn't ignore.

"Loving someone doesn't make you soft."

"Like hell. Just the idea of love can make a person lose his edge. And it's not worth it. Believe me."

"Sounds to me like you have firsthand knowledge of the subject."

"No. I don't." His denial was a little too glib to be totally ignored, but she didn't want to press it. "Anyway, we weren't talking about my love life, or lack thereof, we were talking about yours."

"Actually, *we* weren't talking about it."

"Come on, Simone. If he's really worth it, he'll be there when we get back." Tate sounded almost angry, and she glanced over at him in surprise. "I'm sorry. It's just that we've got dead friends, and a killer on our ass, and all you can think about is your ex-husband. I'm a little worried about your priorities."

He was right. She'd almost lost sight of what was important. "What time do we have to be at the first rendezvous?"

Tate looked at his watch. "We've got about an hour."

"And we're about twenty miles away?"

"Something like that," he said, trying to follow the train

of her thoughts. Which wasn't an easy thing to do, considering she wasn't sure exactly what she was thinking. All she knew was that she needed to see Reece. Needed to be sure things were right between them before she left. Or at least that he knew she'd be coming back.

She yanked the wheel, the Jeep screeching at the mistreatment.

"What the hell are you doing?" Tate bellowed.

"I'm prioritizing," she said, turning the car back the way they'd come. "And right now, my marriage is my first priority."

"Great. Just what I needed, a partner with relationship issues." His frown was genuine, but she could tell from his tone that he'd accepted the fact that she was going back regardless of what he thought.

Fortunately, they hadn't gone very far, so there wasn't much ground to cover. They pulled through the stone gate marking Marguerite's property and onto the gravel road that led to the house.

The fields outside seemed strangely quiet. So much so that Simone slowed the car and rolled down the window.

"What is it?" Tate asked, following suit with his own window.

"Not sure." Simone shook her head, silencing him. Marguerite's house stood just ahead, mica in the slate roof glittering in the sunshine. Nothing seemed out of place, and except for the slow crunch of gravel, there was no extraneous sound. But her senses were on alert. Carefully she steered the Jeep into the bushes by the side of the drive, killing the engine.

Moving as quietly as possible, she and Tate slid out of the car, Tate stopping to retrieve a rifle to supplement the handguns they already carried. Nodding toward the house, Simone motioned Tate to the left as she dashed across the gravel and into the bushes on the right side.

Together they made their way along what was left of the driveway and then split up as they reached the house, Tate taking the front and Simone moving toward the back. The sides of the house were shaded by birch and poplar trees, the accompanying shrubbery making access from this angle nearly impossible.

She moved as close to the house as she dared, the skin on her neck prickling at the sight of a shattered window. Unfortunately her perceptions had been dead-on. She swallowed a wave of fear, knowing that the only chance Martin and Reece had now was if she kept her wits about her. Sending a small prayer heavenward, she inched toward the back of the house, hoping that Tate had read the signs as well.

It was tempting to go back and be certain, but time was clearly not on their side, and until she knew if the killer was still on site she couldn't take the chance of wasting valuable seconds. The backyard was really no more than a small circle of cropped meadow grass surrounded by more trees.

The back door sat squarely in the center of the house, surrounded by a small covered porch. The screen door had been ripped off its hinges, the door itself hanging drunkenly from one hinge.

Not a good sign.

Keeping her back to the wall and her gun drawn, Simone slid against the stone siding until she reached the step leading up to the battered door. Giving herself a silent count of three, she swung out, leading with the Sig.

Nothing moved.

Carefully she stepped up onto the porch and, after a fraction of a second, moved into the kitchen, back to the door, sweeping from left to right in a large circle. At first glance the room seemed to be empty, but then she looked down.

Marguerite's body sprawled across the floor, one hand thrown out as if she'd been waving. Simone choked on bile and swung back again, this time taking in every nook and cranny over the barrel of her gun. Certain that for the moment at least she was alone, she knelt beside her friend, feeling for a pulse.

But the effort was wasted.

Marguerite was dead.

"WHAT CAN YOU SEE?" Martin asked, pushing Reece to the side so that he had a better view of the monitor.

The panic roomed was well equipped. Guns, provisions, all the latest gadgets, including a monitor that switched between views of the various rooms in Marguerite's house, as well as a couple of outside shots. So far they'd yielded nothing. But Reece was pretty damn certain the killer was still present. It was just a matter of finding him.

"Still nothing," he said, glancing over at his brother. "I'm going to switch to the outside view again. Maybe he's given up."

"No way," Martin said, agreeing with Reece's assessment. "He's out there."

Reece switched the camera view to the front of the house, panning first across the yard and then widening the shot to include most the drive. He scanned the video, rejected it for showing him nothing and was about to move to the next camera when Martin's hand shot out, touching the screen in the upper left corner.

"There. You see that?"

Reece moved closer to the monitor, shaking his head. "What do you see?"

"That sparkle, there. See?" He pointed again. "That's sun against metal. Can you move closer?"

Reece examined the control panel and then slid a lever upward. The camera zoomed in closer, the grainy detail revealing the right bumper of a car, as well as a part of the grill. The rest was obscured by the scrub that lined the driveway.

"It's a car." Martin frowned at the screen. "You think it's the killer's?"

Reece pushed the lever all the way up, the picture blurring for a moment and then coming clear. The word *Jeep*, was unmistakable. "Damn it."

"What?" Martin grabbed Reece's arm, searching his face.

"Tate and Simone were driving a silver Jeep."

The words hung between them for several long minutes, then, galvanized into action, Reece switched the camera view again. The front of the house filled the screen, the angle indicating the camera was somewhere in the eaves. Below, he could see the front porch. Movement to the left prompted him to zoom in.

Tate.

The man was moving cautiously, keeping to a group of fruit trees that edged the front yard. He was watching the house, carefully making his way closer.

"Where's Simone?" Martin asked, his voice filled with anxiety. "Do you see her?"

"She's not with Tate," Reece said, switching the camera again. The living room came into view. Empty. And then the upstairs bedrooms, one by one. Again all empty.

Reece pressed another button and a view of the kitchen sprang to the monitor. At first it seemed to be empty, and then Simone's back popped into the picture.

"She must have been kneeling beside Marguerite." Martin moved closer to the monitor as if maybe by doing so she'd see him. "Do you think…"

Reece shook his head. He'd seen Marguerite. There was no way she'd survived.

"Is there some kind of sound system? Can you tell her we're here?"

"No. I looked. There's a wireless system on the wall over there. But it won't work unless there's someone on the outside wearing the headphones."

"So then we'll just go out there. She's probably worried sick." Martin had already turned for the door.

"Wait." Reece held up his hand, and his brother returned to the console. "Look at that." He pointed to what looked like a shadow in the doorway. Flipping the cameras again, he pulled up the dining room. The shadow took shape.

The back of a man. A man holding a gun.

He clearly hadn't seen Simone yet, but he was on guard, which meant he was probably aware of her presence. It wouldn't be long before he found her.

"I've got to get up there." Reece reached out for one of the guns on the wall, checking the magazine to be certain it was loaded.

"Take the headset," Martin said, flipping it to his brother. "Can you hear me?"

Reece held the earpiece to his ear and nodded. "Unlock the door. And then the minute I'm outside you shut it again. You understand? As long as you stay in here, you'll be safe."

Martin looked like he wanted to argue, but instead he nodded, his eyes telegraphing his concern. "Be careful, Reece."

"Always."

The door slid open and Reece slipped through, satisfied to hear it closing again behind him. Taking the stairs two at a time, he made himself stop when he reached the top, back against the wall.

From this vantage point he could just see Simone's shoulder and arm as she ducked down once more, possibly to check on Marguerite. "Can you see her? What's she doing?" He whispered into the headset.

Immediately it crackled with life. "She's back down by Marguerite. I can't really see anything."

"What about the intruder? He still in the dining room?"

"Yes," Martin answered, his voice sounding tinny. "He's coming your way."

Reece debated the wisdom of trying to reach Simone before the killer. And decided, considering trajectory, he was better off staying put. With a little luck, he'd be able to intercept the guy before he got to Simone.

A voice in his head reminded him that she was probably far better prepared to take the guy on than he was. All of which meant that maintaining position was the best way to go. Simone straightened up, her back still to him as she reached over to the counter to pick up a bullet frag.

A sound from the dining room had her spinning around, and she took a step forward, her gun trained on the door.

The killer drew back, and Reece fought against the impulse to call out a warning. Better to keep his position unannounced.

Simone waited, and then hearing nothing else, relaxed her stance slightly, moving toward the hallway leading to the living room. Probably looking for Tate.

"You see Tate?" Reece whispered into the microphone.

"Not yet. He's left the front. Maybe he's in the entry hall. There's not a camera there."

Reinforcements on the way. Reece released a breath he hadn't realized he'd been holding.

Simone stepped into the hallway just as a shot rang out. Their assailant stepped into the kitchen, crouching to avoid Simone's return fire as she pivoted back toward the dining room. Not waiting for any further invitation, Reece burst into the room, his gun pointed at the killer.

"Take one more step and I'll blow your head off."

The man froze but didn't drop his gun. Simone, however, had no such reaction. In one swift move she rolled off the floor and hit the killer's gun hand, sending his gun spinning across the kitchen floor. Then, moving back, she pointed her gun at the man, as well, shooting a quick triumphant glance in Reece's direction.

"Who the hell are you?" Her tone was cool, bordering on icy, her eyes narrowed as she studied the man.

He was clearly of Latin origin, and prepared for battle. A second gun peeked out between his back and his jacket.

"He's got another gun," Reece warned.

"Throw it over here." Simone's gaze never wavered. "Now."

The man hesitated a moment, eyed both of their guns and then with a look of pure hatred, threw the gun at

Reece's feet. He bent and picked it up, careful to keep his own weapon trained on the killer.

"I'll ask again," Simone said. "Who are you?"

"Your enemy," the man swore, his English heavily accented.

"Look, we can do this the easy way. Or I can make it a hell of a lot harder, but either way you're going to tell me what I want to know." Simone lowered her gun, pointing at the man's knee.

"I'll take the hard way," the man said, his tone taunting.

Simone squeezed off a round. The man screamed and then fell back clutching his leg, his enmity now a palpable thing. "Tell me who you are," she said again, pointing at the other knee.

Reece's gut roiled as he stared at Simone, and then he remembered Marguerite.

"My name is Carlos Ramirez. I think you knew my father." If hatred could kill, Simone would be past tense.

Reece had seen a lot of loathing in his day, but this was beyond anything he'd experienced. The man's face literally contorted with fury.

Simone opened her mouth to respond, but before she could say anything, there was a noise in the hallway. Simone jerked in response, and Carlos, seeing the opportunity, dove for the gun on the floor.

Reece aimed but before he could fire, another shot emanated from the hallway, the bullet's impact knocking Carlos back to the floor. Tate stepped into the room. "Miss me?"

Simone swung on him, her eyes shooting sparks. "What the hell did you do that for? Now he's useless to us."

"He was going to kill you."

"Only if he got to his gun. Which meant he had to get past me. And believe me, that wasn't going to happen."

"All right," Tate said, holding up his hands. "Next time I'll let you get shot."

Ignoring their bickering, Reece crossed to where Carlos had fallen, one hand thrown across Marguerite's leg. Somehow, his touching her seemed profane, and so Reece bent over to move the offending limb. As he lifted the arm, Carlos's fingers closed around his, the man's fading eyes flickering open.

"Cruci..." he whispered. And Reece leaned closer, trying to understand the words. The man let go of his wrist, reaching for something around his neck. Reece lifted his gun, but all Carlos did was rip something from his neck and then hold out his hand. "For Isabella..." he whispered, trying to say something more, but before he could speak again, he exhaled, his body going slack.

Reece reached over to pick up the object in Carlos's now-lax hand. The tiny gold crucifix glittered against his palm.

"He dead?" Tate asked, pushing the man's leg with the pointed toe of his boot.

"Very," Reese said, dropping the cross into his pocket.

"Everyone okay?" Martin said, rushing into the room. "I saw it all on the monitor. You were awesome." His words seemed to be meant for everyone, but Reece didn't feel particularly awesome. It had been Tate who'd managed to stop the threat. And the idea of it didn't sit well at all.

Still, everyone was safe. At least for the moment.

"We've got to get out of here." Tate was walking around the kitchen, wiping things off and rearranging this and that.

"What are you doing?" Reece frowned.

"Sanitizing." Simone said, coming to stand beside him. "We don't have time to explain things, and so it's best if we clear out any evidence of our ever having been here. When someone discovers the bodies, they'll think they took each other out."

"We're just going to leave Marguerite here?" Martin's voice echoed Reece's bewilderment.

"We have to." Tate's voice brooked no argument, but Reece didn't give a damn.

"But it's over. Surely now we can come forward and explain everything."

"It's not over by a long shot. Carlos wasn't in this by himself," Tate said. "You heard him say Isabella's name."

"Yes, but it was just a dying man's last thoughts." Reece's hand closed around the crucifix.

"We can't be sure of that." Simone's hand on his arm was soothing. "Until we take this to the source, we'll never know for certain it's over."

"So we're going to South America." It was his turn to speak in absolutes.

"Like hell…" Tate started, but Simone cut him off.

"There's no way I'm leaving them here. Not now. We have no idea how many people Isabella has on our tails. It could just be Carlos, or there could be an army. And I'm not taking a chance with my family."

Reece nodded, his gaze meeting Simone's, not really sure if he'd won or lost, but delighted that she'd referred to them as a family. It was a start.

"So what made you come back?" he asked, reaching out to wipe a smear of dust from her cheek.

The corner of her mouth twitched with the hint of a smile. "I forgot to say goodbye."

CHAPTER TWENTY-THREE

"POR FAVOR, estimado Dios, no Carlos."

The cry echoed through the private courtyard then died, punctuated by the softly falling water of the fountain. Isabella dropped the phone, her empty hand clenching, her nails digging into her palm, drawing blood.

Not Carlos.

Please, no.

But there was no denying the message.

Her brother was dead.

"Isabella. What is it? Is someone here?" Ramón ran into the courtyard, his gun drawn.

"No. There is no one here."

No one at all. She was alone. The gringos had taken everyone from her. Her mother, her father, Amon, and now Carlos. She was the last Ramirez.

"What is it, then?" Ramón holstered his weapon and knelt by her side, his warm hands kneading her cold ones.

She stared up at Ramón, not wanting to say the words, as if by speaking them, she was making them true, making them irreversible. But even as she had the thought, she knew how ridiculous it was. Carlos was gone—semantics wouldn't change the fact.

She lifted her face to her father's friend, not bothering to hide her tears. "Carlos is dead. He was ambushed in Virginia."

"How can you know that?"

"I had a phone call. A man I know in the States. One of the men who moves our product. He heard of it, and thought I should know. The killer was CIA."

"This source of yours, he is certain?" Ramón rocked back on his heels, his expression skeptical.

"Positive. He says there is intelligence to back it up. A woman was found at the house. She's a confirmed operative."

"This woman, she's alive?"

Isabella shook her head. "No. They killed each other. At least that is what the CIA believes. But my source believes there were others involved."

"He has proof of this?" Ramón frowned.

"No hard evidence, but he says that there are others who claim the woman was used as a cover-up. A way to hide the identity of the real killer."

"Any idea who it might be?" He released her hands, moving over by the fountain.

"I believe it is the person who killed my father."

"So Carlos found the truth." It was a statement, not a question.

"I don't know." Isabella shook her head, even in her grief working to find the right way to spin the truth.

"Perhaps as painful as it is, this is all for the best." Ramón turned to face her, his expression impassive.

Isabella jerked to her feet, the phone falling from her lap to clatter against the tile floor. "How can you say such a thing?"

"You know I would never wish you pain. But your

brother, he was dangerous. Always thinking with his heart and not his head. His actions threatened us all."

"He was my father's son. And as such he deserves your respect." She drew herself up to her full height, anger momentarily overcoming her grief.

"*You* are your father's daughter, Isabella. You carry his legacy. And you know as well as I do that your father would never have tolerated the man your brother had become."

"If my father had not been murdered, perhaps Carlos would have been free to grow into a better man. Everything, it seems, comes back to that day in Sangre de Cristo." She reached down to pick one of the orchids trailing along the edge of the fountain.

"Despite the fact that you have had no contact with your brother—" Ramón paused as if waiting for her to contradict him.

She waited, careful to keep her thoughts from her face.

"Even though you had nothing to do with what happened in America," he continued finally, "I think we have to consider the possibility that it will be assumed that you were in on his plans. You were in America. And apparently that meeting was not as private as you had thought. Coupled with the events in Managua, it seems quite plausible to conclude that you were working with Carlos."

"Let them think what they want. What do I care?"

"You know as well as I do that we cannot withstand that kind of scrutiny. Since your father died, we have managed to create a lucrative business with the drug trade."

"But it is only a means to an end, no? We transport cocaine in an effort to raise money to support my father's cause. For the betterment of our people."

"You are living a dream, Isabella. This is a war we can never win."

"Not as long as the Americans continue to side with the government."

"The Americans will always side with the winners." He spat into the fountain in disgust. "They want only what makes their country stronger."

"All the more reason we should fight to drive them from our country."

"I applaud your idealism, Isabella. But me, I am a practical man. And the cocaine, it makes us rich."

"Money isn't everything, Ramón."

"No, but it is a good start." He shrugged, tossing a small pebble into the fountain. "And you'd do well to remember that none of this—" he waved a hand around the luxurious courtyard "—would be possible without it."

"You have turned into a cynic, my friend."

"No." He shook his head. "A realist. And as such, I think we need to consider increasing security even more."

"But I feel already as if I am living in a gilded cage."

"It is the price of power." He shrugged. "And I think it is wise. I do not fear Ortega's people, but the CIA is another matter entirely."

"No." She clenched her fist, thinking of the Americans responsible for the destruction of her family. Let them come. They would find that she was a far more dangerous adversary than her brother had been. "If we noticeably fortify we will invite the very attention you fear. Put our people on alert. And maintain the extra patrols. But beyond that, do nothing."

"I still think..."

"I am in charge here. Do not forget that." She opened

her hand, her heart shriveling like the ruined orchid petals in her palm. She would wait. And if they did not come—then she would become the hunter.

One way or another the Americans would pay.

"HOW MUCH LONGER?" Reece asked no one in particular. Martin and Tate were immediately in front of him. Simone directly behind him. Tate's man, Derek, was leading the way. Derek was CIA, working undercover in Honduras. He'd been in place long enough to be familiar with the terrain, and it was his job to get them safely across the border to a safe house near *El Ojo de la Tormenta.*

"Maybe an hour more." Tate called over his shoulder.

The cloud-forests of Nicaragua were named because high in the Isabella Mountains heavy moisture combined with the mountain air to cover the peaks with mist and wisps of cloud. It made for an eerie beauty heightened by the majesty of the towering oaks and pines. Ferns littered the forest floor, a carpet of green decorated with a delicate lace of wild orchids.

They'd been walking already for almost half a day. The only signs of life, the birds in the trees, and the occasional sound of an animal rustling in the undergrowth. The cargo plane they'd caught in Virginia had dropped them near Danli in Honduras, just miles from the border into Nicaragua.

Despite the fact that the civil war was long over, there was still unrest among the inhabitants of the mountains. Tourists avoided the place, leaving it to drug dealers and revolutionaries. The best Reece could tell, in actuality it had changed little from the powder keg that had led to the massacre at Sangre de Cristo.

Isabella Ramirez's stronghold was located in a small

valley nestled among the foothills of Cerro Mogoton, one of the tallest peaks in the area. According to Tate's intel, the family compound masqueraded as a coffee plantation, but in reality, it was the center of the organization's drug-smuggling operations.

"You holding up okay?" Simone moved up beside him, adjusting the backpack she wore. Like Tate, she was dressed in camouflage pants and a mud-colored tank. Even considering the humidity and unforgiving terrain, she seemed right at home, the suburban housewife disappearing into someone almost unrecognizable.

"I'm fine." He studied her face as they walked.

And then she smiled, and suddenly he saw the woman he loved. It didn't matter what kind of clothes she wore, or even what kind of life she lived—or had lived. She was Simone. It was as simple as that. "You handled yourself really well back there."

His thoughts turned to Virginia and Marguerite. "I couldn't save her."

"I know. And she knew it, too, believe me. We all know that sooner or later in this business there's going to be a bullet with our name on it. It's just a part of the game. I know that sounds cold, but it's the only way you can deal with the fallout."

"But it doesn't make it hurt any less to lose people you love."

"No." She shook her head, swatting at a mosquito. "Nothing takes that kind of pain away. But you learn to push it down. To lock it away somewhere. I think it's like surgeons. Every day they take people's lives into their hands. And if they let the losses matter, if they let them alter their confidence in themselves, they'd never operate again. And that would be a loss for everyone. So they shut it all out, and in the process they shut out other emotion as well. I think the divorce rate among surgeons is one of the highest in the world."

"Except the CIA?" He'd meant it as a quip, a way to lighten the moment, but she took him seriously.

"We don't get divorced, because we don't get married. It's just not in the cards."

"But you did—to me." He couldn't help himself.

"Yes, but I thought D-9 was finished. That I was free. A foolish notion, it turns out. But I wanted it so badly."

"Wanted what, Simone?" He stepped over a fallen log, wondering what a therapist would think about them facing their problems while trekking through the Nicaraguan mountains. "Marriage? A relationship. What did you want?"

"I wanted you." She shrugged. "And I didn't stop to think about what the long-term repercussions might be. I just reached out and took what you were offering."

They walked in silence for a moment, the sound of Martin's laughter filtering back from up the trail.

"I'm glad you did." And he found that he meant it. Really meant it.

"Even with all this?" She waved at the mountain framed by a canopy of trees.

"Yeah." He slowed, adjusting his backpack. "It's given me the chance to see you—to see us—in a different way. And I think maybe that's a good thing."

She nodded but didn't comment.

"I'm thinking we should stop here and rest," Tate called to them, before Reece had a chance to say anything more.

He fought a surge of irritation and then reminded himself that his marital problems weren't Tate's fault.

He'd made his own bed. The only question now being whether or not he'd be sleeping in it alone.

SIMONE STOOD at the edge of the precipice, looking down at the jagged rock below. At the bottom of the ravine, she could see the silver ribbon of a creek winding its way through the trees.

Tate, Reece and Derek were studying the map Derek had brought, consulting a compass from time to time. Simone had no doubt that they were on target. Derek was too much of a professional for anything else to be true, but it was always better to double check. Make sure that everything was proceeding as expected.

The thought made her want to laugh. Nothing about her life was turning out as expected. Just a week ago, she'd been worrying about what to fix Martin for dinner and whether or not she should sign her divorce papers, and then with a single gunshot her entire reality had shifted, sending her plunging into a nightmare that should have been a journey she made on her own.

Yet here she was, standing on the side of a mountain, her husband and brother-in-law just behind her. She wondered suddenly if she'd been wrong to try and keep her past a secret. If maybe Reece could have accepted her, warts and all. There was no way to know. And maybe that was for the best.

Maybe Reece was right and they could build a new future. But to do that she had to come clean. She had to tell him everything. The idea appealed, but she still wasn't sure she was up to taking the risk. It was certainly ironic as hell that she was more afraid of emotional commitment than she was of walking into an armed compound of Nicaraguan guerrillas.

"You seem quiet. Worried about what's ahead of us?"

She'd been so lost in thought, she hadn't even noticed Martin coming to stand beside her. "A little. I'd be a fool if I wasn't concerned."

"But you've done this kind of thing before, right?" Martin sounded nervous. And she felt a wash of guilt for dragging him into this.

"Yeah. A lot of times." She said the words to comfort him, but she hadn't lied. She and Tate and the other members of D-9 had been in situations Martin couldn't even conceptualize. Assassination of prominent officials, bombings that were blamed on terrorists, insurgent operations to free dissidents the U.S. government openly chastised. Their job had been to clear the way for U.S. policy when normal channels of action simply wouldn't do.

And they'd gone into every operation knowing they were expendable. That if anything went wrong, there would be no rescue mission. No public acknowledgment that they'd even ever existed.

After Sangre de Cristo the remaining members of D-9 had survived on their wits, avoiding roaming bands of guerrillas as well as government-backed mercenaries.

They'd had no papers, and no chance of rescue.

But they'd come out of it alive.

To hell with the government.

"It must have been hard."

She surfaced from her memories, trying for a moment to make sense of his words. "We didn't know any different. D-9 beat the hell out of the lives we all came from. We weren't exactly cream of the crop, you know?"

"I don't believe that," Martin said, his loyalty unswerving. "People don't change that much, Simone. And from where I'm standing you're pretty much top of the line."

She wondered if she'd ever viewed the world with such idealism. Maybe when she was two. The image of her mother coaxing her to steal from a beggar presented itself front and center.

Then again—maybe not.

"Things aren't always that cut-and-dried, Martin. But thanks for the support." She smiled and turned back toward the rest of the group.

She looked down at the map and the X that marked Isabella's compound, pushing away all thoughts of her personal life. "How far from the safe house is the compound?"

"About an hour by road. But since you'll be hiking in, you'll have to take a more circuitous route. I figure it'll take you maybe three hours."

"You're not going?" She frowned.

"No." Derek shook his head. "I'll stay with Martin and Reece. Can't risk blowing my cover. I'm taking a big enough risk just escorting you in."

"We appreciate your help," Tate said. According to Tate, the two men had worked together on a previous D-9 operation, Derek providing intel and backup support. Simone had never met him, but that wasn't all that unusual, considering sometimes an operation called for team members to work from different locations. So far she'd been impressed with the man. On very short notice he'd provided not only his expertise but also the supplies they needed to make the trek and infiltrate the compound.

Derek shrugged. "Just glad I was available."

"You've been in Central America for a while, right?" Reece asked.

"A couple of years." He folded the map and stowed it in his pack.

"So have you had dealings with the Ramirez organization?"

"Not directly. My work has primarily been in Honduras. But any work with drug trafficking in this area is going to mean at least indirect contact with the Ramirezes. They keep things pretty close to the vest. None of the over-the-top spending or posturing for territory you see with some of the other cartels."

"So they don't work with any of the others?"

"No. Not if they can help it. They have their own network, and for the most part their own contacts for transportation and sales. We've tried to infiltrate the organization several times, but with no success. You've got to understand that this family in particular has ground support from the locals that you don't see anywhere else."

"Because of Sangre de Cristo."

"Yes. And because of Hector Ramirez. Whatever else he was, he was a man of the people. He believed Nicaraguans deserved more than they were getting from the government of the time. And for all I can see, he was right."

"But if they're so careful, and if they have the kind of support you're alluding to, isn't it going to be close to impossible for Tate and Simone to get inside?"

"If it was anyone else, I'd say there wasn't a prayer."

Simone ran a hand through her hair, exchanging a long look with her husband. Once upon a time she'd believed D-9 invincible. But she'd been wrong.

Dead wrong.

CHAPTER TWENTY-FOUR

THE SAFE HOUSE was more of a euphemism than anything. In reality, it consisted of two rooms carved into the rock of the mountain. A stand of pine obscured it from all but the most scrutinizing view. It reminded Reece of a cave he'd seen in Scotland once. It was reputed to have been the hideout for clansmen during the uprising. He'd thought at the time that it would have been a hellish existence. And now it looked like he was about to find out.

However, after spending most of the day hiking the mountains it was a relief just to sit down. He wasn't in bad shape for a city boy, swimming, workouts and a weekly basketball game staving off the beer belly and atrophying muscles of some of his colleagues. But there was no way he was in the same league as Tate and his buddy.

And Simone's daily insistence on running and working out took on new meaning in light of their current predicament. He'd thought her obsessed. She was in fact simply staying prepared. Even Martin seemed to be taking it all in stride, the simple resilience of youth allowing him to bounce back from his gunshot wound almost as if nothing had happened.

Derek was lighting a fire in the hollowed-out cavity that served as a cook stove and heater. A natural chimney wound its way up and out of the mountain, keeping the room free of smoke.

"Is this ours?" Simone asked, clearly referring to the CIA. She was unloading food from her pack.

"No." Derek shook his head. "It's been here longer than we've been in the country. It was probably discovered by a herdsman or hunter, and then modified for use as a shelter. The mountains are littered with places like this. The guerrillas used them during the civil war. And now the drug kings use them to stash product if there's some kind of threat."

"So aren't we worried that someone knows this place is here? Like maybe the Ramirezes?" Martin asked, emerging from the second room, which was really no more than a second cavern divided from the first with a tattered old blanket.

"There's been no activity here in years," Derek said, kicking at a pile of animal droppings to underscore the thought. "I only knew it was here because a colleague who worked the area a few years back told me about it. And when I heard about your situation, I figured this would be the perfect spot."

He moved to the frame that served as a makeshift door, pointing down into the valley below them. "That's *El Ojo de la Tormenta* there in the distance."

Reece could just make out the glint of red rooftop at the far end of the valley against the dark green of slopes of Cerro Mogoton.

"There's a road running just below here, along the west side of the valley." Derek pointed to a tiny rutted track below them, appearing and disappearing in the trees off to their left. "It cuts back between the mountains, connecting the valley to the main road coming from Ocotal. There's no exit from this end, except by jeep trail. And even that's limited to a track through the highland over there that ultimately loops back to the valley road."

"So you all are going in from the east?" Martin asked, shading his eyes with his hand as he looked out toward the right of the mountain. Here the land seemed undisturbed by human intervention, the undergrowth heavy beneath the trees as the mountains played out to the fertile valley floor. A small river curled lazily through the valley, the scene bucolic despite the implied danger of their mission.

"It looks so peaceful," Simone said, coming to stand beside him, zeroing in on his thoughts.

"And dangerous." Tate pointed to the glitter of a windshield on the road.

Reece grabbed a pair of field glasses, moving them along the line of the road, finally settling on a black Hummer moving slowly away from them toward the end of the valley. "Patrol?" He asked, still following the vehicle.

"I say the odds are on it." Derek had also picked up a pair of glasses. "The timing's right. I didn't have time to put together serious intel, but there've been eyes on the compound on and off for years. According to what I was able to put together, they patrol the perimeter area every six hours or so."

Simone checked her watch. "Is there a foot patrol, too?"

"Not out this far. That's why you should be able to make it to the compound without being spotted. But there'll be guards once you get there."

"More so with Isabella in residence, I'd say," Tate said, also checking his watch.

"Do we know for certain that she's there?" Reece lowered his glasses, the Hummer now gone from sight.

"Yes." This from Derek. "I got confirmation just before you arrived."

"Visual?" Simone asked.

Derek shook his head, putting down his binoculars. "Just verbal. Source-of-a-source kind of thing. But it's reliable."

"I hope so." Reece shot a glance at the assembled company, thinking that they were banking a hell of a lot on the word of one man. But Simone and Tate seemed satisfied, so he let it rest. "What time are you going?"

"Early morning." Simone moved back into the shelter, and the others followed. "Just before sunrise, right?" She looked over to Tate for confirmation.

The man nodded, his face harsh in the shadows of the cave. "I figure it'll take us at least a couple of hours to make our way to the compound and then another hour or so to make it inside."

"What's the plan once you're inside?" Reece asked, not completely sure he wanted an answer.

"Find the target and neutralize." Tate was quick to answer.

"What he means," Simone said, shooting Tate a reproving look, "is that we're going to locate Isabella, and try and see what can be done to end the violence. We didn't kill her father. Maybe we can make her understand that."

"Yeah, and I just won the Clearing House Sweepstakes," Derek said with a laugh.

"We're going to at least try." Simone's tone allowed no room for argument, but Reece saw Derek and Tate exchange glances.

"Is there something going on here we need to be aware of?" Reece asked, centering his attention on Tate.

"No." He shook his head. "I guess I just want to be sure somebody pays for what happened to my friends."

"I feel the same way, Tate," Simone said. "You know that. But if we take out Isabella Ramirez and we're wrong, there will be hell to pay and you know it."

"Not if they don't know we did it." His roguish smile, intended to cajole, didn't seem to faze her at all.

"The minute we got Derek involved, we put it on the radar. We need to exhaust all possibility of settling this without starting an international incident. You know I'm right."

"And if we can't settle it?" His eyes had narrowed as he considered her words.

"Then we'll have to deal with it the old-fashioned way." She shrugged, her face hardening into an icy mask of indifference. Only Reece could see her eyes, and he knew she wasn't going to take that route easily.

But she would take it. Of that he was certain. Too damn much had been lost.

"All right then," Derek said, moving a pot of coffee off the fire. "I suggest we all get something to eat, and then a little shut-eye. It'll be showtime before we know it."

Tate held out a cup for Derek to fill, while Simone poured a can of beans into another pan and placed it on the fire. The smell of ham and tomato filled the air, and the rumble of conversation punctuated with laughter filled the tiny cavern.

And Reece was reminded of his days in the Rangers. The camaraderie of the men just before a mission. Except that this time he had family involved. His brother and his wife. And he knew damn well that their jocular conversation was false bravery. A way to buoy up courage in the face of uncertainty.

The situation wasn't exactly the same. But one fact was identical. Like every mission he remembered during Desert Storm, there was a hell of a good chance that someone wouldn't make it back alive.

SIMONE SAT on a rock and looked down into the silent valley. The moon was bright. Almost three-quarters. But it had risen early and would set soon, which meant what was beautiful now would not be a detriment later, the ensuing dark cloaking their approach to the compound. She and Tate had gone over their plans and checked and rechecked their gear. Everyone was inside now, sleeping. She'd tried, but restlessness had won out, and finally she'd given up and come out here to try and relax.

The moonlight obliterated most of the stars, but on the very edges of the horizon next to the black of the mountains she could see one or two sparkling. She'd read a story once about a princess who'd jumped into the sky. She couldn't remember exactly why, but Simone had loved the story and, as a child, had often wished she could escape the same way.

It seemed so wonderfully free up there.

"I woke up and you were gone." Reece's voice was warm against the chill of the night. He settled next to her on the rock, his presence comforting.

"I couldn't sleep." She pulled her knees up, wrapping her arms around herself. "So I came out here. It's so beautiful. Times like this I always think about how oblivious most of the world is to the ugliness that exists out there."

"Maybe that's why you do what you do?"

"I wish it were that noble." She reached over to twine her fingers through his, grateful that he didn't pull away. "I joined D-9 because I didn't have a choice." He waited in silence as she worked to gather her thoughts. He'd given her an opening, and this time she was going to tell him the truth—all of it. "My mother was a prostitute. Actually, that's giving her too much credit. My mother was a drug addict who used her body to support her habit. I grew up in a series of crack houses in L.A. The perfect childhood."

His fingers tightened on hers.

"I stayed until I was around eleven. I blossomed early. And suddenly my mom saw me as a commodity. And I knew I either had to fend for myself or she'd drag me further into her nightmare. So I ran away. Hitched all the way to Chicago. Not exactly a panhandler's paradise, Chicago. But I got the lay of the land soon enough." She closed her eyes, trying to keep the memories at arm's length. "Hooked up with a guy named Booker. He played fast and loose with the rules, but usually managed to come out on top. We grifted together for a couple of years, then one night he just disappeared. Along with most of my worldly possessions.

"So I was on my own again. I tried grifting by myself, but I wasn't making a living. Hell, I wasn't making enough to eat. So when a man I knew offered to deal me in to his drug network, I said okay.

"You'd think as much as I hated the stuff, I wouldn't have wanted to be involved in any way. But when you're hungry and dirty, and craving anywhere with a roof, you loosen your morals a bit."

Simone looked down at their joined hands, marveling

that he still hadn't pulled away. "It worked okay for a couple of months. I was only a runner so I wasn't taking much of a risk. But before I could celebrate my newfound wealth, I got caught in a sting. Looking back on it, I realize it must have been in the works for months. Surveillance, undercover work, the whole bit. But at the time, I just knew I was in trouble. I was holding about thirty kilos of product when it went down. One hell of a lot of money.

"I'm sure everyone involved thought I was trying to make off with the payload. But I just wanted to get the hell out of there. So I ran. And over the years, I'd developed a knack for it, disappearing in crowds, using parts of the city that no one else even knew existed. I evaded capture for almost a month. Hid from the Feds, the locals, and some pretty serious thugs who worked for the organization."

"Why didn't you dump the drugs?"

"I knew they were the only thing keeping me alive. The authorities needed them for proof. And the guys I was working for just needed them period. As long as I kept them in my possession, I figured I was safe." She sucked in a breath, then slowly released it. It was over. All of it dead and buried.

"Anyway, it was Maurice who finally ran me to ground. He was a hell of a tracker in those days. Caught me in my own double back. Pretty damn amazing, really. I thought I was screwed. And maybe in hindsight, I was. But it turned out he was putting together D-9. And he thought my particular skills, such as they were, would be a great asset to my country. In return, he handled the drugs, the Feds, the bad guys, and the couple dozen police departments with my picture on the bulletin board."

"Doesn't sound like you had much of a choice."

"I didn't. But then again it was more ambiguous than that. Maurice was tough. Hell, he was capable of a lot of things, strong-arming not the least of it. But in his own way, even in the beginning, he cared about me. He saw something in me that I didn't even know existed—he saw hope. So despite the fact that I didn't have a choice, in a very real way Maurice saved my life. He saved me from the streets, and he saved me from myself."

"So you joined D-9?"

"Well, actually, I went through a testosterone-induced, hell-inspired training program first. That's where I first met Tate and Bea. From there we joined the rest of the team. And you pretty much know the rest."

The night got suddenly quiet, even the wind in the trees dying down. Simone fought against a wave of panic, staring out into the night.

"I'm so sorry," he said finally.

"For what? Giving me the first home I ever had? Having the singular honor of being the only person in the world who ever told me they loved me? No, Reece, believe me, you have nothing to be sorry for."

"Neither do you," he whispered, pulling her close, wrapping her in his arms, the beating of his heart against her ear comforting beyond words. He stroked her hair, then tilted her chin to look into her eyes. "I love you, Simone. I always have. And I suspect that I always will. Whatever you were or weren't in your past is irrelevant. What matters is now. That's it. Just that we're here together now."

"But there's so much between us."

"Garbage. All of it. How many people are lucky enough to find the kind of love we have? And we were willing to throw it all away just because the going got a little rough?

We're going to make it out of this alive. And we're going to go home. We're going to start over, and build a life together. One step at a time."

"You make it sound so simple." She reached up to trace the line of his cheek, to memorize the feel of his skin.

"Maybe it is. Maybe it's just about believing in ourselves. And trusting that what we feel for each other is enough to get us through whatever gets thrown at us. You're not a little girl on the streets anymore, Simone. You're a grown woman with an amazing heart and a family who loves you. That's not a bad place to be. All you have to do is reach out and take what we're offering, Martin and I."

She looked up at him, the moonlight turning his hair silver, and she knew suddenly that nothing would ever be the same without him in her life. And that no matter the risk, no matter if all they had was one more day, she wanted it. Wanted it with every fiber of her being.

"I love you, Reece," she said, cupping his face in her hands. "I can't promise you the perfect life. But I can promise to be there with you, whatever life may bring."

"That's all any of us can ask for, Simone." And he bent his head to press his lips against hers, the kiss a covenant, more binding than any piece of paper ever could be.

He held her close again, and together they watched as the moon set, the stars popping out of the now-darkened sky like little diamonds against a swath of midnight-colored velvet. Maybe the princess had been wrong to jump into the sky. Maybe there had been happiness waiting for her right here on earth.

She'd only needed to open her eyes and recognize what it was she had.

CHAPTER TWENTY-FIVE

IT DIDN'T FEEL like morning. It was still dark outside, and Reece had really only gotten a few hours of sleep. Simone was standing over him, the look on her face telling.

"It's time?" He rolled to a sitting position, stretching sore muscles.

She nodded "You don't have to get up, I just wanted to let you know I was going."

There was a world of meaning in her words, but he didn't want to dwell on any of it. Right now he had to let her concentrate on what it was she needed to do. It was the only thing he could contribute toward her safety.

Tate was shrugging into his pack. And now that he was standing, Reece realized Simone was already carrying her gear as well.

Derek handed Simone and Tate their guns along with extra ammo. "I cleaned and loaded them both. You should be good to go."

"You still have ammo, right?" Tate asked. "Just because you're staying here, doesn't mean you're out of danger."

"We're fine," Derek said, his eyes cutting to the gear by the fire.

"All right then," Tate said, giving a last tug at the backpack.

Simone nodded, then turned to Reece. "You understand

why I've got to do this?" It was a concession that she asked.

"I do. I don't like it. But I definitely understand." What he really wanted was to beg her to let him go with her. But he knew that in doing that he was sending the wrong message.

"Okay." She leaned up to give him a brief kiss, then turned to Tate. "Let's do it."

"Simone." Martin stood, bleary-eyed, blinking owlishly in the firelight.

She walked over and gave him a hug, whispering something that made Martin laugh.

"If you're finished with the long goodbyes?" Tate prompted.

She nodded, hugged Martin again and then they were off. Reece stood and watched until they'd disappeared into the undergrowth, resisting the urge to grab the field glasses to follow her descent.

"You all right here?" Derek asked. "I thought I'd do a quick check to make sure we're still alone up here." He patted the Beretta in his waistband.

"Yeah. We're fine. Be careful out there."

The other man nodded and set out in the opposite direction Tate and Simone had gone, heading instead toward the road.

The first rays of sunlight were just peeking over the mountain, lines of pink and orange streaking over the mountaintops. Reece had never felt so helpless and, weirdly enough, at the same time hopeful. It was an odd combination to be sure.

"I guess this is it," Martin said, coming up to stand beside him. "Feels funny to just be standing around waiting."

"Well, we're not exactly in our element." It was an understatement really.

"I think we've held up pretty well actually, all things considered. I mean, there's a lot to be said for training and all that, but a little brainpower still goes a long way."

"So what did Simone say to you?" he asked his brother. "I heard you laughing."

"She told me she loved me." He ducked his head, clearly embarrassed. "And she asked me to take care of you."

"And that's funny?"

"Well, you're not really the kind of guy who lets people take care of him, you know?"

"Maybe it's about time I gave it a shot." He wrapped an arm around Martin. "How about you fix us some breakfast."

"You realize you're taking your life in your own hands?" Martin grinned, then sobered, his words taking on a more sinister cast in light of Simone and Tate's mission. "Where's Derek?"

"He's checking the perimeter." Reece glanced down at his watch. "But he's been gone longer than he should have. I'll tell you what. You go see if you can figure out how to at least make the coffee, and I'll go see if I can round him up."

"Sounds like a plan." Martin was already heading for the stoked fire and the charred coffeepot.

With a last look in the direction Simone and Tate had disappeared, Reece headed out in search of Derek. What had passed for a trail petered out after a couple hundred feet, and Reece was reduced to pushing his way between saplings and scrub. He soldiered on another thirty yards or so and then stopped, thinking that if he didn't turn around and go back Derek would be looking for him.

He turned to go, but stopped when something glinted silver in the dappled light off to his left. His first reaction was to hit the ground, thinking that it might be the barrel of a gun. But swallowing a mouth full of leaves, and hearing the uninterrupted chatter of the birds, he pushed to his feet, turning in a slow circle to try and locate the anomaly again.

At first there was nothing, and he almost convinced himself the whole thing was a product of his slightly overstimulated imagination. Then he saw it again. A brief sparkle as the breaking sunrise filtered through a gap in the trees.

He reached for his gun, surprised almost as much by the fact that he automatically went for it as by the fact that it wasn't there. He frowned, then remembered it was lying beside his pack. He'd put it there last night when he and Simone had finally settled down to sleep.

It was tempting to go back for it. But there was nothing indicating a real threat, and in the time it would take him to go back, it was totally possible whatever it was out there would disappear.

Moving as quietly as possible, he edged toward where he'd seen the glint of silver. Suddenly the trees parted, opening into a man-made clearing. At one end Reece could see the end of a car track, the ruts similar to the ones Derek had pointed out earlier as a part of the road.

At the other end of the clearing was a battered shed, currently sheltering a dark blue Range Rover. It was the bumper Reece had seen glittering in the sunshine. He waited in the shadow of a pine tree, making certain that nothing in the clearing moved. If there was a vehicle out here, he had to assume it had an owner somewhere.

After waiting maybe five minutes, he moved around the

edge of the clearing, using trees for cover, until he was next to the shed. Again he paused, listening for signs of life. Except for the chattering of a squirrel, everything remained quiet. Stepping into the shed, Reece laid his hand on the hood of the Range Rover. It was cold. Whoever had left it here hadn't done so recently.

Just inside the shed he waited for his eyes to adjust to the shadows, surprised to see that there was a door in the back leading to another room. Keeping his back to the wall, he moved forward, stopping every two steps or so to make certain he didn't have company.

It was only when he reached the rear of the Range Rover that he heard a noise. A voice. Muffled by the door, which was only partially open, he couldn't make out what was being said. Despite an internal bell ringing out a warning, he inched closer until he was standing at the edge of the door frame, the only thing separating him from the person in the room the door itself.

"Green October, this is Blue Delta, you copy?" the person in the room asked, the voice still slightly muffled.

There was a pause followed by some static as the caller waited for someone on the other end of the radio to respond.

"Green October, this is Blue Delta, you copy?"

The voice sounded familiar, but without moving closer there was no way Reece could identify it. And he sure as hell wasn't going in there without knowing exactly what it was he'd be facing.

"You copy?" The voice asked again.

"I'm here." The voice at the other end of the radio line was hard to understand, the distance making it reverberate, sounding almost like an echo.

"Excellent. Any problems with privacy?"

"None at all. She hasn't got a clue."

Reece frowned, the feminine pronoun putting him on alert. Despite the danger he moved closer so that he could hear.

"Copy that," the man in the room said, a trace of laughter in his voice. "Everything is a go here."

"...time...as scheduled..." The other voice was breaking up, but apparently the words satisfied the caller.

"Good. I'll complete my end of things, and meet you at the rendezvous at the agreed-upon time."

"...careful..." the disembodied voice said. "Sheridan...dangerous...than he looks."

Reece grimaced, forcibly containing himself from running into the room.

The man in the room laughed. "No worries. It'll be a piece of cake. They're amateurs. Hell, they'll be dead before they realize what hit them."

Reece clenched his fists, wishing he had his gun. The radio man's intent was clear. He was supposed to kill the team members remaining at the hideout. Best to pull out now and regroup. They needed a plan.

He'd actually started his retreat when something the man had said pulled front and center. Amateurs. He'd called them amateurs.

But Derek was CIA.

Reece forced himself to move forward again, sliding an inch at a time until he was at the very edge of the open door. Sucking in a breath, he glanced into the room, his vision confirming what he'd already guessed.

The man at the radio was Derek.

They'd been betrayed.

"Blue Delta out," Derek said. "And Tate? Be careful out there. Simone Sheridan is no pushover."

"EVERYTHING ALL RIGHT?" Simone asked as Tate crawled in next to her. She was lying on her stomach in a tall stand of grass, looking down at the stone wall that ran along the perimeter of *El Ojo de la Tormenta.*

"Yeah. Derek said everything's quiet. Martin's making breakfast. Reece was just back from checking for intruders. So they're both fine."

She'd known they would be. But she couldn't help worrying just the same. In fact, it had taken every ounce of self-control she possessed not to follow Tate and insist on speaking to Reece. But she'd known it would be better if she let Tate do it alone. She needed to prove to herself that she could separate her two lives. At least long enough to take care of Isabella.

"What're you seeing?" Tate asked, picking up a pair of field glasses.

"There are two sets of guards," she whispered. "The first is about a hundred yards to the east." She lifted her own glasses as Tate shifted so that he could see them better. "Best I can tell they're stationary. Three of them. All armed. One with a rifle."

"And the second group?"

"Only two, but they're mobile. Driving what looks to be a modified golf cart. They're both carrying machine guns. I'm guessing there are more like them as they only seem to patrol about a four-hundred-yard stretch of the wall. Takes maybe fifteen minutes for the whole rotation."

"So we ought to be able to get in after they've passed by?"

"Seems like a real possibility. I'm thinking if there were security cameras, they wouldn't need the patrol."

"The intel seemed to indicate that cameras are only

used at the entrance and along the wall where there's access from the road."

Simone lowered her binoculars. "What I've observed seems to back it up. So I make it three more minutes," she said, checking her watch, "and then the patrol ought to have reached the end point and be turning back. That should give us about an eight-minute window."

As if they'd been cued, the white cart appeared for a moment between the trees that spotted the grounds beyond the stone wall.

"That's it." She scrambled to her feet, already moving down the rise. "Time to move."

She could feel rather than hear Tate behind her, amazed at how quickly the two of them had rediscovered their old rhythm. It was as if they'd never left D-9. She reached the flat just before the wall, and sprinted across the little bit of open ground, keeping low and hopefully out of sight.

She stopped at the wall, using a fallen log and a colony of ferns to hide behind. Tate slid in next to her. From this vantage point all they could see was the wall. It was about eight feet high and covered with moss, the stones wet from the humid air of the valley.

They listened for a minute and then, satisfied that the patrol had not deviated from the norm, Tate pulled out a grappling hook. After two almost lazy circles, he tossed it at the wall, its barbed fingers finding instant purchase among the slabs of rock.

Simone was up and over in less than three minutes, which left them about four. Fortunately, Tate was up in two, throwing the grappling hook to her, and then jumping. She wound the rope and stuffed the hook into her pack, then followed Tate as he sprinted toward another stand of trees.

Just as she reached the safety of the trees, she heard the whine of the golf cart's engine, and the patrol popped back into sight. "Well done," Tate whispered. "Seems we haven't lost our edge." His smile was intimate, and she swallowed a thread of discomfort. She and Tate had a history and just because she'd moved on, it didn't erase everything that had been between them.

The patrol passed by the trees and disappeared again from sight.

But all of that would have to wait.

"Follow me," Tate mouthed, indicating a rocky outcrop fronted by grass.

Simone nodded, keeping low as she raced across the open expanse, dropping down behind the rocks. They continued their forward progress, using trees, rocks and once even an overturned Jeep to keep from being seen. Finally, in what seemed like slow motion, they reached the second wall.

Unlike the stone wall, this one was meant to keep out unwanted guests. Cement blocks presented a smooth front topped with barbed wire, and up in one of the towering oaks, Simone could see a security camera as it arced back and forth, presenting a seamless view of the fence and the area just beyond where they were lying.

It was much the same up and down the wall, at least as far as they could see. Using the binoculars, Simone identified three additional security cameras. But fortunately, their intel had already indicated the presence of the cameras, and so they were prepared.

Tate produced a metal device about the size of a Band-Aid box. The cameras were digital, their continuous feed subject to interference just like cable TV or a satellite link-up. Press the button on the jammer and presto chango, the feed broke into a million pixels staggered across the screen as they cleared and regenerated.

It would only buy a couple of moments, but that was more than enough time.

The same oak that held the camera also had spawned a mutant branch that curled in on itself and then sloped downward over the fence, tangling with another tree on Simone and Tate's side of the wall.

All they had to do was climb their tree, jam the signal, and take those precious seconds to climb onto the oak branch, using it to get over the fence. Then the picture would clear with no one the wiser.

All that remained was to stay above the camera until it arced away from the ground beyond the oak, and then they could simply drop to the ground and move out of range. In theory it ought to work like clockwork. Of course, reality usually had a couple of surprises in store—that's what made their job fun.

Simone shimmied up the tree, stopping when she reached a junction between two sturdy branches. Tate followed. They waited a moment to be certain that they hadn't been seen, and then Tate pushed the button. "Go," he whispered.

She shot out along the gnarled old branch, crawling across it like a spider monkey, Tate right behind her. She vaulted over the wall and teetered for a moment as she struggled for balance on a branch just above the camera. She was so close now she could hear it whirring as it changed focus, the signal restored.

The camera turned slowly, panning the area below. She waited one beat, then another and as it reached the far end of its arc, she swung out and dropped to the ground, then sprinted forward until she knew she was out of range of the camera.

Stopping behind the comparative safety of an old shed, she was relieved to find Tate just seconds behind her. They crouched low behind the building, waiting for alarms or some other sign that either they'd been seen or that the interruption of the signal had caused concern.

The compound was quiet.

"We did it." Simone breathed out a sigh.

"Did you have doubts?" Tate looked honestly surprised, and despite the gravity of the situation, Simone almost laughed, relief making her giddy.

"So what now?" she asked, risking a quick look from behind the shed. Derek's intel had included aerial shots, so she had an idea how the compound was laid out, but it all looked different from the ground.

"We wait." Tate checked his watch. "The internal patrol ought to be by in about ten minutes. Once they've passed we'll have another window. Maybe fifteen minutes to gain access into the hacienda."

Isabella's bedroom was at the far end of the building, separated from the main rooms by a private courtyard. According to the plans, there was a tiny door in the back wall of the courtyard used to transport heavy gardening supplies like dirt and fertilizer.

Assuming it was still there, they planned to use it to gain access to the courtyard and Isabella. It was still very early, and the odds were she'd be in her room. And if she wasn't, then sooner or later she was bound to come back.

And when she did, they'd be ready.

CHAPTER TWENTY-SIX

"HEY," MARTIN SAID, poking at the flames of a small fire, "I think I've finally got the hang of this."

Reece held up his hand and shook his head.

"What?" Martin whispered, dropping the stick with a frown.

"We've been had." Reece crossed the little cave to where he'd been sleeping. "Derek and Tate are up to something. I don't know what, but I overheard Derek telling Tate he was going to take care of us."

"As in..." Martin drew a finger across his neck, his eyes going wide.

"Exactly." Reece grimaced as he rummaged around in the blankets he and Simone had shared last night. "We don't have much time. Have you seen my gun?"

"Not since yesterday." Martin knelt by his own blankets and patted them down. "Shit."

"It's okay." Reece reached into his pack, digging around until his fingers closed on the butt of a gun. "I took Carlos's. I don't think anyone knew I had it."

"Good thinking," Martin said, eyeing the entrance to the cave with trepidation. "So what do we do now?"

"We get the hell out of here. I don't want to get cornered. Derek should be just behind me."

They moved quickly out the entrance to the shelter and around a fall of rock, the boulders effectively hiding them. "You said Tate, too? Does that mean that Simone…" He trailed off, looking guilty for having the thought.

"No." Reece shook his head, his stomach knotting with dread. "Simone is in danger, too. Last thing Derek did was tell Tate to watch his back."

"But I don't understand—"

Reece waved his brother silent as Derek emerged out of the woods on the path. He stopped for a moment, pulling out Carlos's gun and checking the magazine, then after a quick look around, he stepped into the cave.

It was tempting to try and take him out while he was inside, but the lighting was dim and presumably Derek was good with a gun. Reece wasn't bad, but he wasn't an expert, either. Better to wait for the man to come back out.

Seconds ticked by, and then Derek stepped out of the cave, his scowl indication of his displeasure. "Reece?" he called. "Martin?"

Silence filled the clearing.

Reece waited as the man walked first to the edge of the trees and then back toward the entrance, pausing about a foot from where they were hiding. Moving slowly, his weapon ready, Derek turned in a circle, his gaze raking the trees and the pathway for signs of movement.

Reece signaled Martin to get down, and then shifted so that he was crouched at the edge of the pile of rock. Exhaling slowly, he tightened his hand on Carlos's gun. More than anything he wanted to fire. To take the son of a bitch out. But he needed to talk to him. To find out what Tate had planned for Simone.

It was risky. He knew it, but if he could incapacitate the

man, so much the better. He'd save the killing for later. He flipped the gun around until he was holding the barrel. Then when Derek pivoted so that his back was turned, Reece pushed away from the rocks, slamming the gun against the side of the man's head.

The bigger man fell to one knee, but was far from out. Pulling to his feet, he rushed Reece, his shoulder hitting with the accuracy of a linebacker. Reece was thrown to the ground, the gun sliding out of his hand, toward the pile of rocks.

As the two men fought, Derek worked to turn his gun toward Reece. He shot once, but missed, the bullet strafing the packed clay ground instead. Reece managed to get in a solid right, connecting with the man's jaw, his gun arm flailing as he tried to regain his balance.

Reece dove for Derek's middle, knocking the other man back toward the rocks, but just before he connected, Derek rolled right, and Reece slammed headfirst into the boulders. Fighting pain and a wave of dizziness, he tried to roll to his feet, but only managed a crouch, Derek's face swimming in and out of focus as the man leveled his gun.

Instinct said to try to move, but his body wasn't having any of it. And he blew out a breath, not even flinching when the weapon fired.

A minute passed and then another, Reece's mind clearing with his vision. Derek was down, Martin standing at the edge of the rocks holding Carlos's gun.

"You all right?" Martin asked, his gaze still on Derek.

"Thanks to you." Reece reached over to feel for a pulse.

"Is he dead?" There was a finality to the question that told Reece that Martin was already fairly sure of the answer.

"Yeah." Reece stood up, searching his brother's anguished face. "It was him or me, Martin. You didn't have a choice."

"I know. I just never thought I'd..." He held out the gun, and Reece stuck it into the waistband of his pants.

"So why the hell did he want us dead?" Martin asked, still staring down at the body.

"No idea. Only thing I can figure is that somehow Tate's been a part of this from the beginning. Maybe he's working with the Ramirezes. I honestly have no idea. I only know we've got to get to Simone before something really bad happens."

"You think he's going to kill her?"

"I don't know for certain. But I sure as hell think it's a possibility."

"So what do we do? Hike down there and try to sneak in the back door?"

"It's appealing, but we're neither of us trained for that kind of operation." Reece slid his hand in his pocket, his fingers closing around the little gold crucifix. "No, I think we're going to go for a more straightforward approach."

Martin raised his eyebrows in question.

"There's a Range Rover over there in a shed. We'll take it down the mountain to *El Ojo de la Tormenta.*"

"And then what?" Martin frowned. "We just walk up to the front door?"

Reece smiled, knowing full well the expression lacked all semblance of humor. "Exactly."

GETTING TO THE BACK WALL of Isabella's courtyard was proving to be a bit more difficult than anticipated. Perhaps in light of the threat from Managua, the compound had more than the reported number of guards. And while they seemed to be totally unaware that there were intruders on the grounds, it had slowed progress considerably.

Simone crouched behind an enormous oak tree, surrounded improbably by three sago palms, their massive fanned branches providing excellent protection. Tate knelt a couple of feet away at the foot of the oak.

"Isabella's got a fucking army up here," Tate said, his gaze following three men armed with Uzis walking the back perimeter of the hacienda. Isabella's home was part retreat, part fortress, the white walls unadorned except for the bright red geraniums spilling from windows flanked by deep blue shutters.

Two stories in most places, the hacienda was roughly rectangular in shape, built around a central courtyard. At the back, a second structure was linked to the first with a walled garden. This second building housed Isabella's private quarters, her own walled courtyard located just to the east.

The oak and palm tree cluster sat about fifty yards from the back wall of the courtyard. Unlike the rest of the house, it was overgrown with ivy and some kind of flowering creeper. It gave the enclosure a lush, exotic feel, and also managed to obscure all signs of the little door.

"Maybe the damn thing doesn't exist," Simone said, frustration mounting.

"It's there," Tate said, his eyes still on the passing group of guards. "We've just got to figure out how the hell to get over there without being noticed."

"Easier said than done." Simone watched as the group disappeared, only to be replaced by another one. It seemed there were guards everywhere.

"What we need is a distraction." Tate shrugged off his pack and began rummaging through it, pulling out a hand grenade.

Simone shook her head. "Overkill." Literally. If something exploded—it might buy them precious minutes, but ultimately it would send the entire compound crashing down on their heads.

"I wasn't going to blow anything up." He nodded toward another group of palm trees, the tree in the center brown and withered. The palms sat next to a small pond full of ducks. "I was thinking more along the lines of a fire."

Simone looked at the dead palm fronds littering the ground at her feet. They were match dry. Perfect tinder. Tate already had the grenade open, pouring the powder into his hand. "It won't take much," she said.

Tate nodded, handed her his pack, and before she could comment further, dashed across to the edge of the pond. He disappeared into the foliage, and Simone held her breath, waiting.

Four minutes passed, then seven, then ten. Two sets of guards made their way along the outside of the hacienda, separated by exactly five minutes. Isabella obviously believed in punctuality.

Before the next group appeared, Tate dashed back across, sliding to a stop next to the oak. "Done."

"I don't see anything," Simone said, peering out at the ground by the palms.

"Give it a little time," Tate said, using his binoculars for a better look. "I can see the flames. It's just going to take it a minute to catch."

They waited, Simone holding her breath. At first she thought he'd failed. That the ground cover wasn't dry enough to ignite. But then suddenly the ducks flew off the pond, squawking noisily, and a plume of smoke broke free of the palms. Ten seconds later, the dead palm burst into flames and all hell broke loose.

The guards rounding the building broke into a run, and

the three men at the corner of the hacienda also sprinted toward the fire.

Without waiting to see what would happen next, Tate dashed out of cover and across the now-empty yard to the wall, Simone following on his heels. Tearing at the shrubbery, he pushed the ivy aside and motioned for Simone to crawl behind it. She slipped between the wall and a huge vine of wisteria, the smell of damp earth surrounding her in the quiet shadows. Tate crawled in behind her, dropping the heavy ivy back into place just as another group of guards rounded the corner, heading for the burning palm.

"Nice move," Simone smiled, already turning to look for the little door into the courtyard.

"Spent a lot of time as a kid hiding in the shrubbery," Tate said with a shrug. "Some things never change."

Simone crawled forward on her hands and knees, feeling along the moss-slick wall of the garden. She'd gone about a hundred feet, and was just about to turn to complain to Tate that they were on a wild-goose chase, when her hand hit metal.

"I think I've got it," she whispered back to him, her hands exploring what she couldn't see.

"The door?" Tate pushed through the ivy, stopping next to her.

"It's more of a hole really. Maybe three feet square." She pulled a couple of strands of ivy off the wall, revealing one side of the so-called door. The metal was rusted. Clearly whatever it was, it hadn't been used in a long time.

"Can you open it?" He was feeling with his hands, too, ripping ivy from both sides of it now.

"No." She tugged at the handle she'd uncovered to demonstrate. "It's either locked or rusted shut. Either way, it's not budging."

Together they worked to clear away more of the vines that clung to the metal, finally clearing the entire structure. Just above the handle was a jagged, rusty hole, probably the remains of a lock or keyhole. Now, however, even without the original mechanism, it still served its purpose well, sporting a chain and padlock.

"Shit." Simone's whispered expletive seemed really loud in the enclosed space between wall and vegetation. Outside, beyond the ivy and wisteria, she could still hear muffled yelling from the palm trees.

Tate pulled off his pack, rummaging around in it again, this time producing a pair of bolt cutters.

"Well, aren't you the little Boy Scout," Simone said with a frown. "What the hell else do you have in there?"

"Just a few odds and ends I thought might be handy. I saw these at the shelter and figured they might be of some use."

"Pretty damn handy." She shifted so that he could reach the chain, and watched as he worked to cut through one of the links. She couldn't really put her finger on it, but something about this whole operation felt too easy. Almost as if it had all been choreographed somehow.

The idea was ridiculous, and yet, she couldn't shake it once it had sprouted. Even as Tate broke the link and yanked the chain free, she tried to replay everything that had happened, working to put a name to the niggling worry that was teasing her brain.

"We're in." Tate dropped the cutters and pried open the door, the metal screeching in protest. The sound seemed abnormally loud to Simone, but in actuality she doubted anyone would have noticed it unless they were standing right beside the door.

Simone reached out to stop Tate, to try to put a voice to

her concern, but her hand met empty air; he'd already crawled through the doorway into the garden. With a sigh, she followed him, the bushes on the inside of the garden just as concealing as the vines had been on the outside.

Tate pushed back the fronds of a waist-high fern and peered out into the courtyard. "It's empty."

Simone moved closer, her eyes confirming his pronouncement. Drawing her gun, she stepped into the empty enclosure. Water splashed out of a lily-clad fountain surrounded by myriad orchids, their delicate blossoms gently scenting the air.

To the left a doorway led into what was presumably Isabella's bedroom. To the right a small table and chaise were arranged for an optimal view of the little garden. An ornate breakfast tray sat on the end of the chaise, the remnants of a croissant and some orange juice signaling that someone had been here—recently.

Simone realized she was smelling coffee along with the heady scent of the flowers.

"She was just here," Tate said, his voice tight with frustration.

"Maybe she's in the bedroom." Simone gestured toward the door with her gun.

Tate raised his hand to signal quiet as footsteps crunched in the gravel immediately outside the wall. Moving silently, he closed the distance between them, his lips by her ear. "You go on inside. I'll wait here and make sure we haven't got visitors."

She hesitated, hating the idea of splitting up. Something still didn't feel right.

"I'll be right behind you," he whispered in assurance, obviously seeing the doubt on her face. "It's time to put an end to this once and for all."

CHAPTER TWENTY-SEVEN

"I STILL DON'T understand what you think this is going to accomplish," Martin said, looking over at Reece.

"Hopefully it's going to get us inside the compound. Which will be that much closer to Simone. After that we're on our own." Reece downshifted as they took a hill at top speed, the right wheels of the Range Rover momentarily lifting off the ground.

"I don't know if you've noticed, but we're already pretty much on our own." Martin's glib comment was meant to ease the tension but somehow it only seemed to add to it. "I still don't see what Tate has to gain by having us killed."

"He eliminates witnesses. If he's really been behind all of this, then I'm guessing he's the one who killed Bea and Mather. Maurice, too."

"But what about Carlos? He's very real. And very dead."

"I don't know. It doesn't all fit together, I'll admit. But maybe Tate used him. Lured him into all of this so he'd kill us."

"But it didn't work."

"No. So Derek got the job."

"Well, I suppose that's two for the good guys." Martin

smiled, then sobered, obviously thinking of Marguerite. "So why go to all this trouble. Why not take Simone out early on and avoid the fallout?"

"Again, I'm just speculating—" the engine whined as they took another curve without slowing "—but I'm thinking he needed Simone to kill Isabella. So he orchestrated things in a way that would make Simone believe Isabella was responsible for the deaths of her friends and, conceivably, *us*. Make her angry enough to kill the woman. Then once she'd done his dirty work, I'm guessing Tate planned to take her out of the equation, too."

"Only we're talking about more than speculation here. And if you're right, then we've all played right into Tate's hands."

"Except that we're still alive."

"So you think Tate's the one who framed you? Seems like he'd want you out of the way, not in the middle of it all."

"Nah, he knew Simone would worry about us. Maybe even abandon the quest. So he figured out a way to give her even more incentive. Find Isabella and clear my name, give us back our life."

"But he can't have known she'd do that. You're divorced."

"But Simone is loyal."

"No shit," Martin sighed. "The twenty-thousand-dollar question, though, is why? Why the hell after all this time would Tate suddenly decide he wanted to eliminate the members of D-9?"

"I agree that's the big question. But it's got something to do with Isabella Ramirez and whatever the hell really happened in Sangre de Cristo all those years ago. And I'm betting Isabella's visit to Maurice is what set this whole chain of events in motion." He slowed the car as they approached the compound, the main gates looming up ahead.

Martin tugged nervously at his collar. “You’re sure we can pull this off?”

“It’s not exactly a stretch.” Reece sighed, pulling the car to a halt in front of the gate. “I am an attorney. Just not in private practice. But they don’t know that.”

“You’d better hope not.” Martin blew out a breath. “So I’m what, your associate?”

“Hardly,” Reece stepped out of the Range Rover and pocketed the keys, pushing Derek’s sunglasses up on his nose. “You’re an intern. First-year law student. Believe me, you look the part.”

“And once we’re inside, what do we do then?”

“I haven’t got a clue. But we’ll improvise.” He met his brother’s eyes over the top of the car. “We don’t have a choice. If I’m right about all of this, Simone’s life depends on it.”

Reece walked up to the gate, wishing there were some way to smuggle in the gun. But he knew damn well that they’d be searched. And besides, there was no reason for Carlos Ramirez’s attorney to arrive packing a piece.

Fingering the little crucifix, Reece said a silent prayer and knocked. A little window slid open, the occupant on the other side obscured by shadow.

“I’m here to see Isabella Ramirez,” Reece said, using his most arrogant courthouse voice.

“And you would be?” the man spoke in accented English.

“Reece Sheridan. I’m an attorney.” He passed the business card Tim had given him through the window. It seemed like eons ago that he’d had a drink with his friend to discuss the possibility of opening a practice together. "I'm here on behalf of Isabella's brother, Carlos."

The man took the card, and moments passed while he presumably examined it. "Carlos is dead."

"I know. That's why I've come. He requested I bring something to his sister."

"Give it me," he said. "I will see that she gets it."

"No." Reece shook his head. "I promised I'd give it to her myself."

He heard the man say something softly in Spanish. There was silence and then the man spoke again. He was clearly talking on a radio or phone. Reece heard his name, and Carlos's, then another silence, followed by the creaking of the door slowly opening.

Four men stood on the other side. All of them heavily armed. The gatekeeper stood to one side, an automatic machine gun held in plain sight, his expression giving nothing away. "Come in."

Martin shot him a look of trepidation, but Reece ignored it, instead stepping through the doorway, motioning his brother to follow.

"No." The gateman shook his head, waving the machine gun. "Just you."

"I'm sorry," Reece said, ignoring the gun, acting as if they were having a perfectly normal interchange. "This is an associate of mine. And I'd prefer he stay with me."

The man hesitated, shot a look at a cordless phone lying on a table, then at his compadres and shrugged. "In here." He directed them into a small courtyard leading to a guarded archway and presumably beyond that to the main house. Behind them, Reece could hear the gate being shut and locked.

Two more men came out of what appeared to be an office of some kind, both also carrying weapons. That made seven. Not exactly great odds. But Simone was inside somewhere, and he wasn't about to give up without a fight.

"Turn around," the gatekeeper said, handing his gun to one of his associates. "We need to check for weapons."

Reece held out his arms, nodding at Martin to do the same. The man was anything but gentle, his sneer indicating that he'd probably like to do a whole hell of a lot more than just search them. But it was over almost before it had begun, and the gatekeeper was nodding toward one of the other men. "Go with Jaime. He'll take you to Ramón."

"But we're here to see Isabella," Reece said, feigning irritation. "I have no time for underlings." It was a bit of a risk, but he'd learned long ago that punks responded to authority.

"No one sees Señorita Ramirez without seeing Ramón first. *Comprende?*" The man's eyes narrowed as he dared Reece to look away. But Reece had been playing this same game with every loser that had come into the courtroom. Playing and winning. The gatekeeper held his stare for one beat, two…and then, with a frown, he dropped his gaze.

Maybe Reece's world and Simone's weren't that far apart after all.

Without giving the man a second look, Reece moved to follow Jaime. Martin fell in step beside him. "That was ballsy," Martin whispered.

"No." Reece shook his head. "Calculated. But I don't have too many more tricks up my sleeve, so this had better work."

They walked through the elaborately carved archway, the gravel path changing to saltillo tile as they entered yet another courtyard, this one featuring a beautiful lanai. Wicker furniture was arranged artfully in groupings designed to take advantage of the breeze, crystal vases and lamps glittering in the sunlight.

If it weren't for the cadre of armed men flanking the edges, the place would have seemed idyllic.

"It isn't often we have American visitors at *El Ojo de la Tormenta.*" An older man in an immaculate linen suit stood in yet another archway, his bearing patrician, his expression purposefully neutral. An adversary surely, but one to be admired, not rejected. "You worked for Carlos, I'm told?"

"I represented him, yes." Reece, too, kept his tone noncommittal, the two men sizing each other up. "And I'm here at his behest."

"To see Isabella." Despite his facade, Reece could hear a trace of skepticism in the old man's voice.

"To give her something. Carlos was specific that if anything should happen to him, I was to get this to Isabella." Like a magician producing a dove, Reece opened his hand, the little crucifix glittering in the light.

"*Mi Dios.*" The old man started to reach for the cross and then stopped himself, his eyes going cold. "Where did you get that?"

"Carlos gave it to me. He knew that he was in danger. And he wanted to be certain that the crucifix was given to his sister should anything happen to him."

"And now he is dead," the old man spat. All attempt at neutrality forgotten in his grief. "How am I to know that you are not the one who pulled the trigger?"

"Because I tell you I am not." Reece closed his hand on the cross. "But if you would prefer that I take it with me, then so be it." He turned to go, trying to ignore the gunmen standing in the other archway.

"Wait." Ramón held up a hand, and Reece turned back to him. Martin watched the two of them, his expression carefully masked. "Isabella would not wish for me to be inhospitable to a friend of her brother's." It was clear by the way he used the word that he hadn't decided whether he believed Reece or not. But at least for the moment he was giving him the benefit of the doubt.

Ramón moved out onto the lanai, motioning for Martin and Reece to take a seat. Martin glanced at his brother, his eyes full of questions, but Reece simply nodded and took a seat in the chair opposite the old man's.

A woman appeared in the archway, carrying a tray with a pitcher and glasses. She set it on the table next to Ramón. He nodded, and she carefully filled three glasses, giving one to Reece, one to Martin and the last to Ramón. Without a word, she turned and left, the old man sitting in silence until she had withdrawn. Then he lifted his glass. "We drink to Carlos."

Silently, Reece raised his glass, with Martin following suit. They all drank, Reece fighting his frustration. Simone was somewhere inside the compound, quite possibly in trouble. And he was stuck sitting here drinking sangria.

"Do you know the history of the crucifix?"

Reece considered bluffing, and then decided against it. "No. Carlos only told me that it was important for me to get it to Isabella." He opened his hand again, the cross bright against his palm.

"It was a gift from their father. Carlos got it on the day he was confirmed. Isabella has one exactly like it. After Sangre de Cristo." He paused, frowning. "You know of this, yes?"

Reece nodded.

"After Hector's death," he continued, "there was only Isabella and Carlos. Everyone wanted them dead. The government feared that if even one Ramirez was left alive, the dream of rebellion would not die. So we had to hide them. Carlos in America. Isabella here in the mountains."

"But surely after the furor died down, your government lost interest?" Reece was caught up in the tale despite himself.

"After years had passed and the government was more secure, interest diminished but never went away. And we all believed that it was better to keep the two of them apart. That way it would be more difficult to eliminate them. But there was a price to pay. Isabella had lost everything, and now she could not even be with her brother."

Ramón stopped to take a sip of his sangria, studying Reece for a moment before continuing. "So Carlos told her that any time she felt alone, all she had to do was touch her crucifix, and he'd be there, if not in body, then in spirit. For many years, that promise sustained Isabella. Sometimes I think it is that cross that kept her alive."

"And now?"

"Now she is a grown woman. The head of her family. She mourns the loss of her brother, and I know she will be grateful that you have brought her the crucifix."

"Will you let me give it to her?" Reece asked, certain already of what the answer would be.

The old man shook his hand. "I'm afraid that I cannot allow that. I have nothing but this card—" he flipped it so that it was lying in the flat of his palm "—to prove that you are who you say you are."

"And I have nothing else to offer except my word that I mean her no harm."

Again Ramón studied his face, and again Reece knew that he was found wanting.

They sat for a moment, each of them assessing the other, then the older man nodded to the men still standing in the archway. Gatekeeper and one of his compadres came forward, guns in hand, motioning Reece and Martin to stand.

"If you really worked for Carlos, then you will understand the delicacy of the situation, and you will give the cross to me." Ramón held out his hand.

The crucifix was Reece's only ace. If he gave it away, the hand was played. And yet, he knew that sometimes the only way to get what you wanted was to sacrifice it all. He thought of Simone, of what Tate might be doing to her, and slowly opened his fingers, reaching out to drop the cross into the old man's hand.

Keeping his gaze steady, he turned to go, ignoring Martin's flash of confusion.

Please God, let him have played it right.

He took a step toward the gatekeeper and then another, his whole body rigid with tension.

"Mr. Sheridan?"

Reece stopped, heart pounding, and turned around.

"Carlos did not have an attorney." Ramón's expression was shadowed. "Perhaps now you will tell me how you came to have his crucifix. And why it is that you want to see Isabella."

THE HALLWAY WAS DARK after the bright light of the garden and Simone stopped for a moment to let her eyes adjust.

Three doors opened off the hall. According to the plans she'd studied, the one on her immediate left led to the rest of the hacienda.

The door directly across from her was open, the corner of a claw-foot bathtub in view. Which left the door at the end of the hall. If their intel was right, this was Isabella's bedroom. And since she'd clearly just been in the courtyard, there was a chance she'd still be inside.

Simone tried to summon her anger. For Marguerite, for her friends. But instead she only felt sadness. So much lost and nothing gained. Killing D-9 wouldn't bring back the people who died in Sangre de Cristo. Nothing could do that.

Still, she had to see it through. Until things were settled with Isabella, there could be no new beginning with Reece. Hell, there could be no beginning at all. She looked back over her shoulder for Tate, but he'd moved from her direct line of sight.

They'd opted out of radio contact for fear that they would be overheard, so for the moment at least she was on her own. But it was easier knowing that Tate had her back.

She moved down the hallway, not certain what to expect. She'd seen a picture of Isabella, but it was a surveillance photo, so it was hard to discern anything about her beyond her basic features.

As she reached the end of the hall, Simone realized that the door was slightly ajar. Tightening her hand on the Sig, she waited a beat then pushed it open. The room was quiet, and she exhaled, not certain if she was relieved or disappointed.

"I have been waiting for you."

Startled, Simone spun around to see a small woman standing in the corner holding a gun. The shadows in the room kept her from clearly seeing the face, but she knew without a doubt that this was Isabella Ramirez. She was tiny, but there was no denying the power that emanated from the woman.

"You don't know me," Simone said. "How could you possibly have known I was coming?"

"You killed my brother," the woman said. "It was not unrealistic to believe that you would come for me as well."

"I did not kill your brother," Simone said in all honesty. "Although, I can't say that the thought didn't cross my mind. He killed my friends."

"D-9," Isabella spat, moving into the light. She was barely more than a child, but grief had etched lines on her face. Marks that should only have been present in a much older woman. "If not for you, my father would be alive."

"You've got it all wrong." Simone said, sidling to the right, trying to gain the advantage. "We were there to save your father. Not to kill him. Our mission was to get him out of Sangre de Cristo, alive."

"Even now, after all these years, you lie. After everything that has happened, surely there can be truth between us?"

"I am telling the truth," Simone said, moving again, but this time Isabella moved as well, almost as if they were dancing. "We were there to rescue Hector."

"Rescue him? Why would the Americans do that?" she asked. "My father hated everything American."

"When it suited him, maybe." Simone shifted, keeping the distance between them. "But your father benefited from his allegiance with the CIA."

"You are telling lies again."

"I am telling the truth. Your father made a deal. He traded information on drug trafficking in exchange for guns and ammo. It was a deal that benefited both parties. And when the government targeted the junta, we were sent in to make certain that your father escaped with his life."

"But that would make him no better than a traitor." Disbelief colored her voice.

"No. It made him a pragmatist. Nothing is achieved in a vacuum, Isabella. Your father was a great man. But to accomplish what he needed he had to compromise along the way. Trafficking in drugs brought money—selling the dealer out brought much-needed military support for his junta. Both decisions that had to made."

"Even if I accept that—and I'm not saying I do—I know for a fact that one of you killed him."

"How can you possibly know that?"

"Because I saw my father's killer, and it was a gringo. Like you."

"You saw your father murdered?" She moved again, Isabella mirroring her steps.

"*Sí.* I was there, hiding behind his desk. I saw my father plead for his life. Saw the gun pointed at his heart, and watched as his blood stained the tiles of the floor."

"Did the killer see you?" Simone frowned, an odd thought flitting through her head.

She nodded, her face contorted with the pain of memory. "I screamed. I tried not to but I couldn't help myself. I'd already seen so many die. But to watch my father lose his life in such a way. I could not keep quiet."

"And the assassin found you."

"I thought he would kill me, too. He laughed and raised the gun. But then a mortar exploded the wall behind me.

And I ran, only stopping when I reached the square. I have never forgotten that day, or that man."

"You said a gringo, that doesn't mean he's American."

"I heard his voice. Definitely American. Arrogant bastard." Her anger was edged in pain. "And the only Americans in the village were your D-9."

"You can't know that for sure."

"I am certain. I have had many years to verify the fact."

Talking was getting them nowhere, and Simone knew she needed to gain the upper hand, as much for Isabella's sake as for her own. If Tate walked into this scenario, he'd shoot first and ask questions later.

Hoping for an element of surprise, Simone dropped to the floor and rolled to the left. But just as she was righting herself, a cloud outside shifted, light from the window spilling across the room, momentarily blinding her. Acting on instinct alone, she jumped back to her feet, ducking out of the light, simultaneously lifting her arm, ready to return fire, but Isabella wasn't shooting. Instead, she was staring, her dark brows drawn together.

"I know you," she whispered. "In the plaza, by the fountain."

And suddenly instead of her enemy, Simone saw a little girl, the one she'd carried to safety all those years ago. It seemed that fate had a wicked sense of humor.

CHAPTER TWENTY-EIGHT

ALLEGIANCES SEEMED to shift like shadows in the moonlight here in Nicaragua. The men Reece had thought were on his side had betrayed him, and the people he'd believed to be his enemies had the potential to be reluctant allies.

Ramón had listened patiently to Reece's story, interrupting only now and then with questions. And so far they were still alive. There had been a moment when he'd reached the part about Carlos's death. All of the men standing guard had lifted their guns, anger marring their faces, but Ramón had waved them down, his own anger carefully banked.

In telling it, Reece realized that even then, Tate had been orchestrating every move, shooting Carlos not because he was a threat to Simone, but because he could have blown Tate's cover.

"So you believe your wife and this man are here at *El Ojo de la Tormenta.*" There was a note of disbelief, Ramon's gaze shooting to the armed men standing on the lanai.

"Don't make the mistake of underestimating D-9. Don't forget that they infiltrated Sangre de Cristo. And even more important, they managed to get out of the country in the middle of a full-scale civil war."

"But that was years ago."

"People don't change that much. And believe me, my wife is as capable now as she ever was." He quashed the image of Simone, her eyes flashing as they made love. He needed to stay focused on the negotiations.

"How do I know that you haven't fabricated this entire story to gain access to Isabella? You already lied to me about Carlos and the crucifix."

Reece clenched a fist, restraining the urge to slam it onto the table. "But I gave it to you as well. As a sign of good faith. Which you accepted, or I would not be standing here."

"True, but you could also be, how do you say, playing me?"

"Are you willing to risk Isabella's life on that?"

Ramón spread his hands. "It is a dilemma. One that I must consider carefully."

Reece swallowed irritation. Time was passing and he was accomplishing nothing. But nothing would be gained by allowing his emotions the upper hand. "Look, every minute we stand here talking, our chances of helping Simone and Isabella fade. I love my wife and I want to help her. I think you feel the same way about Isabella."

"She is like a daughter to me. Her father was my closest friend."

"Then help me protect her."

"But you said that your wife is here to kill Isabella."

"No. Simone is here to confront her. To try and end the hostility between them. She believes, wrongly, that Isabella is behind the death of her friends, and the attempts on our lives." He waved a hand to include his brother. "It's Tate who wants them both dead."

"But you do not know why."

"Does it matter?"

Ramón studied Reece for a moment as if judging his sincerity, and then he nodded at his men. "You will go to Isabella. Be cautious. If these people are present, they are very dangerous."

Reece stood up, but Ramón motioned him to stay. "We will handle this our way, *señor*."

"My wife has no idea what's going on. And I sure as hell didn't come all this way just to see her get caught in the cross fire."

Again there was silence, and again the old man nodded. "Take him with you."

Martin started to follow, but Reece waved him still. Ramón tilted his head, acknowledging the unspoken. If things went south, at least Reece could be certain that his brother would be out of the line of fire. Martin opened his mouth to protest, then closed it again, accepting that there was no room for argument.

"I'll need a gun." It was a brash request, but he wasn't going to go into battle unarmed if he could help it.

The man beside him shook his head in protest, his expression making it clear just how little he trusted Reece. Reece ignored him, focusing instead on Ramón, waiting, his silence both commanding and respectful.

The older man held his gaze, the two of them locked in a duel of wills, and then with a sigh, Ramón reached into the breast pocket of his coat, producing a small pistol. He held it out to Reece, his expression grim. "Remember, *señor*, you will be surrounded by my men at all times. If you harm so much as one hair on Isabella's head, I will personally see to it that you and your family are destroyed. Am I making myself clear?"

"Absolutely," Reece said, taking the gun, his tone deceptively genial. "And if your men hurt Simone, I'll send you straight to hell."

"THE EVENTS OF Sangre de Cristo seem to haunt us both." Isabella had moved to stand by the bed, one hand resting on the rosewood post of her bed, the other by her side, still holding her gun.

"Some things are hard to forget." Simone, too, relaxed her stance, shooting a look at the doorway, wondering where the hell Tate was.

"If you had not pulled me away from the fountain, I would be dead. It seems I owe you a great deal."

"You owe me nothing." Simone said, trying to reorder her thoughts, make sense of what was happening. She still had the sense that something was wrong, reality twisted to serve a purpose she had yet to recognize. And now, looking at her adversary, she found it hard to believe that it was Isabella pulling the strings. Not because she wasn't capable, but because she looked as confused as Simone felt.

"I see you ladies are getting reacquainted."

They both turned as Tate stepped into the room, his gun drawn, his smile revealing what she should have seen from the beginning.

"*You.*" Isabella whispered, her hand rising to her throat as if she wished the word back. Her gun clattered to the floor, forgotten in her horror. Her eyes locked on Tate, her hatred reflected there. "You killed my father."

Everything fell into place, and Simone raised her gun, pointing not at Isabella but at Tate. "It was you?"

Tate shrugged, his face impassive. "I had no choice. The man knew who I was."

"That you were in D-9? What the hell did that matter?" Simone asked, still trying to make sense of it all.

"He knew that I was using my contacts through D-9 to traffic drugs."

"You knew my father, and still you killed him?" Isabella asked the question as if she couldn't fathom the idea that anyone could possibly have known Hector Ramirez and still wanted him dead.

"He wasn't a threat until D-9 was ordered to bring him in. I knew he'd be so fucking grateful he'd give the CIA anything they wanted. And what could be better than a rogue agent?"

"He wouldn't have sold you out." Isabella was insistent.

"If you believe that, you're still as naive now as you were all those years ago when you hid behind the desk."

Anger ripped across Isabella's face, breaking through her immobility. She reached for her gun, but Tate was faster, shooting at the space between her fingers and the revolver.

"Move away from the gun."

Isabella shot Simone a look, and she sighted her gun. "*You* drop your gun, Tate."

"I would," he shrugged, "but then nobody would be armed." He slid over to retrieve Isabella's gun.

"I'm not kidding, Tate. Drop it."

"Nice threat, Simone." He pocketed Isabella's gun and backed up so that he could see them both. "But you're not going to shoot me."

"Don't test me."

"It's not up to you, actually." His smile was terse. "The gun doesn't work."

She shifted it to the left of Tate, and fired.

Nothing.

"I'm afraid Derek did a little more than reload it. Figured it would help me keep the upper hand."

"So you could kill Isabella? I don't understand."

"I think I do," Isabella said, her voice still full of loathing. "He was afraid of me. Of my conversation with Maurice Baxter. I was opening up something you thought long buried, no?"

"Apparently you're a quicker study than I gave you credit for. I thought when your father died my secrets were safe. Especially with D-9 dismantled."

"You never stopped trafficking, did you?" Simone asked, her fingers clenching around the useless Sig.

"Abso-fucking-lutely not. I lost a little ground without the inside info I got from D-9, but I still had a lot of friends in the right places. Over the years I've built quite a little empire."

"And my meddling in the affairs of Sangre de Cristo threatened that." Isabella sounded calmer now, but Simone suspected her tone was deceptive.

"It was all dead and buried along with your father. But you and that idiot brother of yours couldn't let it go."

Isabella grabbed a vase, throwing it at him with a curse that Simone couldn't translate. Tate ducked, and Simone took the opportunity to launch herself at him, but he got off a shot first, the bullet knocking her to the ground as it tore into her hip.

"Temper, temper, ladies."

"You killed my father. And now you have killed my brother, too," Isabella said, holding herself perfectly still.

"He killed himself. Meddling where he wasn't wanted. When I saw him in Missoula I knew he'd have to be stopped. But first I figured he might be of some use to me."

"You were there? In Missoula?" Simone fought a wave of pain and nausea, not certain whether it was her wound or Tate's words that were making her sick. "You saw Bea killed?"

"*I* killed her." He said it as if it meant nothing—as if Bea had meant nothing.

"But you said…"

"Carlos couldn't shoot a caged bear."

Isabella cursed again in Spanish as Simone tried to comprehend all that Tate was telling her. "What about Mather and Maurice? Did you kill them, too?"

He nodded once. "The old man was easy. Mather put up more of a fight. She always did seem to have the devil's luck when it came to survival. But in the end, suffice it to say that I won the day."

Tears blurred her eyes, and she dug her nails into her palm, the added pain helping to clear her head. "And Ed?"

"Stupid bastard. He walked right into it."

"But they were your friends, Tate. Your family."

"I tried to tell you before, Simone. Family is highly overrated."

"You shot Martin, didn't you?"

"Not on purpose. At least not the first time. I was just trying to get the lay of the land, but he saw me. The mail lady, too. Thought I'd killed them both, but evidently I'm losing my touch."

"You bastard." Simone tried to get to her feet but failed, her leg refusing to support her.

"It's just business, Simone. You know that."

She struggled for breath, the pain taking on a life of its own, threatening to rob her of all coherent thought. "So was it you who followed us in Port Aransas, or was that Carlos?"

"It was me. And me in Raton, as well. You always were quick on your feet." His smile was fleeting and never reached his eyes. "Carlos was never on your trail. At least not until we got to Missoula. It never occurred to me that he'd still be there."

"So it was him at the airport?"

"Yeah. And he damn near fucked everything up," Tate said, his expression dismissive.

"But what about the rendezvous?" Simone asked, still struggling to put the pieces together. "*Someone* was shooting at us."

"That was Derek."

Ice-cold dread washed through her. Reece and Martin were with Derek. "He's not CIA?" She already knew the answer, but some perverse part of her prayed that she was wrong.

"Should have been." Tate shook his head. "He has a knack for it. But no. He's never worked for the Company. Only for me."

"All right, so it was Derek at the rendezvous and Carlos at the airport, but how did Carlos find us at Marguerite's? No one knew we were there." She fought to maintain her composure, knowing that she couldn't do anyone any good if she allowed her fear to take control.

"I had Derek arrange that. It was a simple matter to

follow Carlos and manipulate things so that he got the necessary information to put him back on the trail. The bastard played right into my hands. I needed to tie up loose ends."

"Martin and Reece," she whispered, her mind reeling.

"Exactly." Tate's smile was hollow.

"You set my brother up." Isabella's hands were clenched, her face flushed with anger.

"I only gave him the in he'd been looking for. It served my purposes, sure, but Carlos condemned himself with his hatred. Besides, it was Simone's fault we went back. Who knows—if it hadn't been for her desire to set things right with her husband, Carlos might still be alive."

"You'd have killed him anyway," Simone said. "Or had him eliminated."

"Standard operating procedure. You haven't lost your edge, Simone. Too bad you lost your nerve."

She couldn't bring herself to ask about Reece and Martin. Not yet. "I still don't understand why you didn't just kill me like the others. Why the elaborate charade?"

"I needed to keep you motivated."

"Motivated for what? To help you find Isabella? You did that on your own."

"I needed help getting into the compound. But more importantly, I needed cover. If I took Isabella out, there would always be a chance that I'd be discovered. But with you along for the ride, all I have to do is twist the evidence a bit and it'll be like I was never even here."

"So all of your talk about old times. Our relationship. That was all bullshit?" In light of the situation, it was a ridiculous question, but his betrayal cut deep and she needed to understand.

"No." His voice was somber, his eyes darkening with something akin to remorse. "You're the one thing I really do regret about all of this. I meant what I said, Simone. I care about you."

"But not as much as you care about yourself."

Again he shrugged. "Got it in one."

"So what now?" Simone asked, watching Isabella inch toward her bedside table. Maybe she had another gun.

"Now, sadly, the two of you are going to kill each other. Isabella in a rage over the death of her brother."

"And me?"

"You have many reasons to kill her. She killed your friends, and now sadly she's killed your husband and brother-in-law."

White-hot fury replaced the pain, and Simone stumbled to her feet, lunging at Tate. He hit her in the head with the side of the gun, sending her spinning back to the floor.

Simone felt sick, mentally and physically. And stupid, too. She'd sensed something was off, but she'd failed to put it all together. Tate had always been in the right place at the right time. Had the right contacts, the right information. It had been right in front of her all the time.

"What have you done to Reece and Martin?"

"I haven't done anything." He glanced down at his watch. "But if things are on schedule, Derek should have finished them off by now."

His words cut through her with the efficiency of a knife. They'd believed in her, trusted her, and she'd led them to slaughter.

But even as the idea occurred to her, she quashed it. There was nothing to be gained in giving in to grief. It wouldn't help anyone. Maybe Reece had managed to escape. Either way, she owed it to him to try and find a way out.

Isabella was watching her, too, her dark eyes solemn as she slid in front of the bedside table.

Simone blinked, clearing her head to concentrate on the man in front of her.

"So you used us all. Reece, Martin, Marguerite, even Carlos."

Isabella reached behind her, sliding out the drawer.

"What about the missing information in the files?" Simone asked, struggling for something to keep his attention away from Isabella. "You arranged that, too, didn't you?"

"It was easy enough to set up. Maurice trusted me. It never occurred to him that I was a threat. And the missing files were incentive for you to believe that Carlos and Isabella were in fact up to their necks in all of this."

"And you sent the postcard." She dared a look in Isabella's direction. The woman nodded slightly, her hands still behind her.

"Nice touch, don't you think?" Tate sounded thoroughly pleased with himself now. "Allowed me to kill two birds with one stone…so to speak. Additional incentive for revenge. I even added the bit about the code on my card, so that you'd be able to find the others. I was afraid you'd see through that one, but fortunately you were distracted."

Her heart twisted as she thought again of Reece and Martin, her chest tightening as the grief mixed with her pain. "If I could walk, I'd…"

"Do what? Thank me? Jesus, Simone, what were you thinking? You're hardly the soccer-mom type."

The drawer squeaked as Isabella yanked it open, fumbling to right the little pistol in her hands. The gun went off, but the shot went wild, and Tate leveled his own gun on her with deadly calm. "Do it again and I'll kill you."

"You're going to kill me anyway."

"Yes." He nodded, the two of them squaring off with their guns. "But I can make it very painful. You decide."

Isabella shifted her weight, and Tate, recognizing the movement for what it was, fired, the impact of his bullet knocking the gun from her fingers. Isabella stood frozen, staring at her now empty hand.

"You're lucky I'm such a good shot," Tate said, bending to scoop up the little pistol. "So what do you say? Shall we put an end to this? Once and for all?"

The words were an eerie reflection of what he'd said to her before. If only Simone had stopped to think about it, maybe it wouldn't be too late.

She scanned the room, looking for a way out, but saw nothing. Just when she had everything to live for—her luck had run out.

REECE WALKED into the hallway just as someone screamed. Panicked, he rushed forward, only to be stopped by one of Ramón's men, shaking his head, motioning quiet. Pulling his emotions into check, he crept forward, back to the wall, straining to hear something more.

Through the crack in the door, he could see Tate's back, and Simone lying on the floor, her leg stained with blood. Isabella wasn't visible, but he deduced from the way Tate kept swinging his gun back and forth that she must be somewhere on the far side of the big canopied bed.

It was clear from his stance what Tate intended to do, and Reece knew they had to act fast or he'd lose Simone forever.

Gatekeeper, whose name was really Escobar, flanked the door on the other side, three more men standing across the hall. If they rushed the room they'd be able to kill Tate, but there was no guarantee that they would be able to save Simone and Isabella in the process.

Better to try and throw off Tate's aim, and then take him out.

Reece signaled to Escobar that he was going to try and tackle Tate. It seemed conceivable, since the man's back was to him. However, he wanted to be certain that someone was behind him with a gun, ready to help if he succeeded, or to take the bastard out if he failed.

Escobar nodded his understanding, and Reece silently counted to three and then launched himself through the door, aiming for Tate's knees. He hit the other man hard, the two of them falling to the floor. The gun went off as Tate threw out his arms to catch himself, but the bullet lodged safely in the floor.

Shifting almost before he hit the ground, Tate knocked Reece back, sending him crashing against the wall. Using the same momentum, Tate pivoted toward Simone, leveling the gun, his intent deadly.

But Escobar was first, the rifle crack echoing through the room, everything suddenly going still.

For one minute, Reece thought that the man had missed, but then Tate dropped to his knees, clutching his chest, almost in surprise. A blossom of blood spurted from just below his solar plexus, the gun clattering to the floor as Tate's fingers jerked open in a macabre dance with death.

One minute he was staring up at Reece, and the next he was gone.

"Reece," Simone's whisper reached him as if she'd screamed, and he clambered over Tate's body to reach her side. "I thought you were dead."

Seeing her smile was worth every bit of hell they'd been through, the love reflected there enough to carry him forward the rest of his days.

"You're hurt." He slid his arms around her, helping her to sit up.

"It's not bad. Just tore up my hip a bit."

Judging from the blood, it was a little more than that, but he was satisfied that the injury wasn't life-threatening. She reached up to run her hand along his cheek, needing to touch him, to reassure herself that he was indeed alive. "I was so afraid."

"Me, too, sweetheart. Me, too. But everything is okay now. We're going to be fine." For the first time he remembered Isabella, and he looked up to find her standing at the end of the bed unharmed.

Escobar stood at her side, his rifle pointing at Simone and Reece now. The other men had crowded into the room as well, their weapons also at the ready. Maybe he'd been too quick to assume they were out of danger.

Simone's hand tightened on his as her eyes raised to meet Isabella's. Seconds passed as the two women contemplated each other, and then Isabella signaled her men to lower their weapons. "It is over." Her gaze dropped to Tate's body, and then back to Simone. "What happened here will stay here, *sí?*"

"I'll find a way."

And Reece knew that he'd help her do it. Isabella had

been as much a victim as any of them, and at the moment, that was all that really mattered.

"You saved my life once, a long time ago." Isabella waved her hands at the gunmen filling the room. "And now I have saved yours. There is nothing more between us. Go."

Reece pushed to his feet, reaching down to help Simone stand. Wrapping an arm around her waist, he helped her hobble past the guards, through the hacienda and out onto the lanai.

Ramón Diego stood by the same table where Reece had left him, almost as if he hadn't dared to move. Reece nodded at the question in the old man's eyes.

Martin jumped up at the sight of them, his face full of joy. "You're all right."

He rushed to Simone's side, offering another shoulder to lean on, and together the three Sheridans walked out of *El Ojo de la Tormenta* into the sunny brilliance of the Nicaraguan day.

EPILOGUE

"YOU LOOK incredibly domestic," Reece said, grabbing his briefcase before slamming the car door.

"Well, if you'd been here twenty minutes ago, you'd have gotten a completely different picture." Simone put down her trowel and smiled up at her husband. "Ten budding martial artists in the basement is not exactly the Donna Reed model of homemaking."

With Reece's connections, it had been easy enough to find a way to combine her unique talents with her need to give something back to the community. It was her tribute to Maurice, Bea, Marguerite and the others. A way to make their deaths count for something. And a way to keep other kids from taking the wrong path. Between the martial arts classes and a couple of board appointments, her days were busy, and she felt fulfilled in a way she'd never thought possible.

"Any news from Laura?" Reece had crossed to the mailbox and was sorting through the mail, the mundane act taking on new meaning in light of all they'd been through.

"She's supposed to be released sometime next week. The doctors are still amazed at how quickly she's recovered. I don't think they really understand the power of family." She stood up, wiping dirt from her hands.

"And friends," Reece said, tucking the mail under his arm. "There's a card from Martin." He held out a postcard and despite herself, Simone shivered, remembering the one Tate had sent.

Forcing herself to relax, she took the card from Reece, laughing when she saw it. Beer steins of every imaginable description covered the front, a breasty woman in the center extending a frothy mug. The caption read, *So Many Beers, So Little Time*.

The note on the back was equally pithy. *Life is good. Send money*.

Simone smiled. "Looks like he's settling back in just fine."

"More than fine, I'd say," Reece laughed. "Considering everything that happened, Martin must be a regular celebrity. At least in the eyes of the ladies. I predict he'll be trading on that scar for a long time to come."

The scar, like the rest of the fallout from Tate's betrayal, would no doubt have residual effects. But they'd come a long way in the weeks following their return from Nicaragua. Her hip was recovering nicely. Not even a limp. And the time in the hospital had given her and Reece a chance to talk. To get to know each other again—as real people this time.

Of course there'd been briefings, but the CIA's primary interest was in closing the files on D-9. Which meant there hadn't been much of a probe. And as she'd promised, they'd downplayed Isabella's role in the affair. She'd already paid enough.

It was time to bury the dead and leave them be. The future beckoned, promising, if nothing else, to keep them on their toes.

"Did you file?"

Reece nodded and produced a sheaf of papers. "As of three o'clock this afternoon I'm officially a candidate in the race for District Attorney."

She hugged him, delighted to see the spark of excitement in his eyes. "It'll be a landslide. After all, over half the voters in Nueces County are women. All you have to do is smile and they'll be putty in your hands."

"The only woman I want to feel sliding against my fingers is standing right in front of me." He dropped the papers, briefcase and mail on the porch, then closed the distance between them.

"Oh yeah? Right here in the front yard? What will the neighbors think?"

"That I'm a really lucky guy." He cupped her face with his hands, his smile crooked. "I paid a little visit to Judge Adams today, too."

"Is he in charge of one of your cases?" She contained a smile, pretending not to understand.

"Very funny, Mrs. Sheridan. I think you're more than aware that he's the judge handling our divorce."

"Or lack thereof." She covered his hands with hers. "So what did he say?"

"He dismissed the case. No grounds, apparently."

"Apparently." She reached up to kiss him. "It's just as well, really," she whispered against his lips, "because I ran out of mulch, and had to make do with the materials at hand."

Laughing, Reece swung her into his arms, the warm ocean breeze rippling across the bed of bright red zinnias, each plant carefully banked in the shredded remains of what had once been a divorce decree.